Aim

MASTER OF DEATH

First published in Great Britain in 2024

Copyright © Aimee Girdham
The moral right of the author has been asserted.
All rights reserved.

All characters and events in this publication, other than those clearly in the public domain, are fictitious and any resemblance to real persons, living or dead, is purely coincidental.

No part of this publication may be reproduced, stored in a retrieval system, or transmitted, in any form or by any means, without the prior permission in writing of the publisher, nor be otherwise circulated in any form of binding or cover other than that in which it is published and without a similar condition including this condition being imposed on the subsequent purchaser.

Editing, Design, typesetting and publishing by UK Book Publishing.
www.ukbookpublishing.com

ISBN: 978-1-917329-11-8

'A reader lives a thousand lives before he dies. The man who never reads lives only one.'
                                                  George R.R. Martin

'There is no friend as loyal as a book.'
                                                  Ernest Hemingway

For Gramps

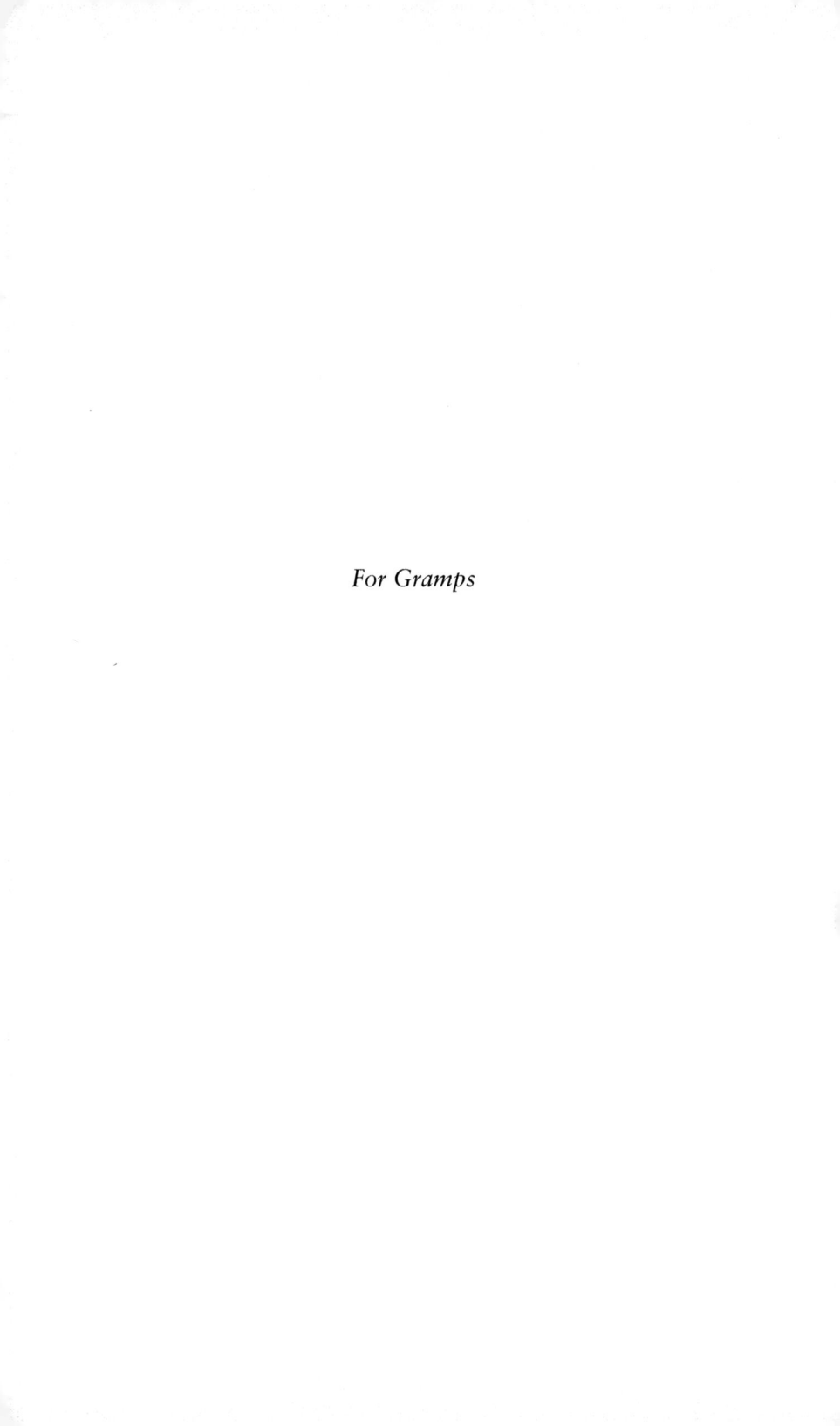

Darkness.
It was all she could see.
The chair.
It was all she could feel.
Fear.
Her own, was all she could smell.
Silence.
It was all she could hear. Aside from her pounding heartbeat and her erratic breathing. The darkness heightened all her senses as she tried to figure out where she was. Her head frantically moved left and right, and her eyes darted all around the room. She tried to work out any outlines of people or objects in the room, which would give a clue as to where she was, but to no avail.
All she could see was the darkness.
Her head pounded like a band of drums were playing inside her head.
She did not know how she got there, or how long she had been there already.
She did not know what time or what day it was.
She did the only thing she could think of doing in that moment.
Scream.
Her lungs burned in conflict as the noise bounced off the four walls in the room.
She did not know what to do next.
But one thing she did know was that she would put up one hell of a fight to get out of there, even if it killed her.
She heard the unlocking of a door and momentarily a stream a light entered the room, bathing it in one big spotlight. It was blinding and she had to squint to allow her

eyes to adjust to the brightness as she looked around the room before the light was gone.

She was sited in the centre of the room with several torturesome instruments placed on a metal tray a few yards away from her and she could make out an electric saw, a chainsaw, a hammer, and several knives positioned against it. She was dressed in a baggy plain black t-shirt and grey tracksuit bottoms that smelled musty and clearly did not belong to her.

Out of the corner of her eye, she spotted a large dog cage with a padlock fixed to the opening with an old and worn thin duvet screwed up in the corner and an empty plastic food tray.

In that moment she realised she was a prisoner.

And she was in prison.

The door slammed shut and again she was submerged into darkness.

She heard the steady rhythmic thud of footsteps approaching nearer as the man descended the stairs.

She was breathless in fear and anticipation.

CHAPTER 1

"Come on, Josh!" Lavinia Newbourne bellowed. Friday night was Speedway night and she had gone to watch her local Speedway team, Scunthorpe Scorpions, race against Poole Pirates.

Speedway is a motorsport, usually where two teams race against each other over a series of fifteen heats (races). Each team consists of seven riders, two riders from each team ride in each heat. Each heat consists of four anticlockwise laps around the oval shaped track. The rider who came first, received three points, second place got two points, third place got one point and for last place, no points were awarded.

The bikes had 500cc engines that ran on methanol fuel and reached a speed of 60mph, no brakes, and no gears. They could also accelerate faster than a Formula One car and reach the first bend from the tapes in under three seconds.

Lavinia had been following Speedway for fourteen years, since she was six years old. It had been her father Alastair's passion ever since he had joined the police force at eighteen years old, after he had learnt that his colleague's father had been a Speedway rider. Alastair tagged along with a group from work one evening and the rest was history.

Alastair, Lavinia and her older sister, Mindi, had been as far north as Edinburgh and as far south as Plymouth and to most tracks in between, including Peterborough and Stoke, supporting their team. It served as a great weekend break and family outing where Lavinia had many great memories from visiting home and away tracks.

The two-minute timer sounded from the referee box, situated above the stands, overlooking the start/finish line.

Before the two minutes were exceeded, all four riders were present at the tapes.

The start marshal signalled the riders to line up, and they revved their bikes using the throttle as they waited for the red light to signal green. On green, the two riders in gates one and two looked left at the tapes, while the riders in gates three and four looked to the right at the tapes. Two short seconds later, the tapes went up and the riders let their clutch out in reaction and sped off to the first bend.

It was a tense race.

And this was the theme throughout the meeting, with the progressive scores 46-44 by the end of heat 15.

The Eddie Wright Raceway, home of the Scunthorpe Scorpions, roared into noise, as supporters cheered, clapped and sounded air horns. The Scorpions' 'Catch Me If You Can' blared out from the speaker as the riders came around for a lap of honour due to the win.

CHAPTER 2

Beginning of summer meant sun, sweat and sweltering heat, which was why Lavinia woke early as her room felt hot and stuffy, even with her window open letting in a sporadic breeze.

Sunlight creeped through the gaps in the curtains, forming a warm spotlight on the carpet.

Lavinia glanced at her digital alarm clock displayed on her bedside table which read 7:26am. She lay in bed for a few moments, thinking of nothing, before getting up and donning on sports gear for a morning run. She wore a pair of black sports shorts and a navy tank top with a mesh back. Lavinia had always been a sporty person, being great at rounders and athletics in secondary school, playing netball in college and now she had found a new passion for lacrosse at university. She had never minded running when she played sports, but she had never been able to get into running as a sport itself. However, to get fitter for lacrosse, she had recently taken it up and had surprised herself. She often went running with Alastair but this morning she went alone. As she tied her hair up in a half up half down do, with a bun, her eyes landed on a series of photographs blu-tacked onto her wardrobe door before she left.

As she prepared her upbeat running playlist to play through her wireless Beats headphones, she thought about the photographs in her room and about life.

A couple of them were of Lavinia as a baby on her first birthday with a cake in the shape of a one, and her mum, Maire, who had passed away from breast cancer when Lavinia was just six years old. Since then, Lavinia had gone through primary school, secondary school where she completed her GCSEs and then onto college, learnt to drive, bought her first car, and had now completed her second year of studying Forensic Investigation at Staffordshire University. All the milestones in life that Maire would not be there to celebrate.

However, her father, Alastair, was, and she was thankful to him for everything he had done. She had always been a daddy's girl growing up, they had been each other's best friend, and she would follow in his footsteps. He was a Detective Inspector with the Lincolnshire Major Crime Team (MIT) in Scunthorpe and had been for twenty-eight years. He had entered the police force when he left college at eighteen years of age. He flew up the ranks, aced all his exams, and became one of the best and youngest officers to be made detective in record time. After all, his mind worked differently to others as he was able to read in between the lines, think differently and faster than most, and find possible clues and answers within the impossible. After Maire had passed away, Alastair unhealthily threw himself into his work as a distraction. It had only worked for so long, until his earlier case had dominated both his work and personal life and had almost got him killed. He had been ordered to take four weeks' annual leave, taking time out from work and spending more time with his family, before his DCI, Walter Wilson, allowed him to return to work.

Another photograph was of her and her elder sister, Mindi. It was taken when Mindi was seven years old, and Lavinia four years old. They were stood side by side in a park, Mindi wearing a dress and sunglasses in the shape of pink hearts and Lavinia eating an ice cream with her hair in pigtails. Now Mindi was a Family Law Paralegal with a Solicitors Firm in Doncaster. She had graduated with a First Class degree with Honours in Law from Chester University and had gone on to do her Legal Practice Course straight after in Manchester. Aside from Alastair, Mindi was one of the most hard-working people Lavinia had ever known and

CHAPTER 2

always had an excellent work ethic. She was good at what she did and was very knowledgeable about her specialism. She had also very quickly gained a good relationship with her clients, and Lavinia had already seen a more confident person in that short time. She was working towards her training contract which she was due to receive next year.

Mindi and Lavinia both had the same face shape and sharp features, often getting mistaken for twins. They were both the same height and had the same length hair. Whilst Mindi's hair was a dark chocolate brown, Lavinia's was a lighter shade of brown with bleached blonde balayage.

On her run, she let the music take over and her legs carried her to the beat. She spotted several stunning butterflies flying around in the warming summer air, and honeybees pollinating lavender plants, which gave off strong fragrances. She passed other runners and several dog walkers who had the same idea to exercise while the air was slightly cooler than it would be later.

Thirty-five minutes and three miles later, she returned, and showered before opening her wardrobe to scan for clothes to wear. She opted for khaki cotton shorts, a white Cami top and flip flops, completed with striking red sunglasses.

She made her way down the stairs, along the wooden hallway and into the living room. It was a modern room, with a light grey carpet, a glass dining table with six white leather chairs placed around it, a glass and white wooden cabinet with ornaments and keepsakes proudly displayed in it. Two black leather sofas were placed around the wine-coloured rug in front of an electric fireplace which was hung on the brick wall, and a TV stood to the right of the fireplace. The patio doors led out into the garden where the rest of her family were sat on two wooden benches that faced each other with a matching wooden table in between, under a gazebo, tucking into breakfast.

The garden was small and rectangular but held many features. A triple oak barrel water feature was placed in the corner of the patio, the sound of the streaming water giving off a calming atmosphere and was topped by a black cast iron pump. The peach and cream patio tiles went around the perimeter of the garden with the recently mowed emerald green grass in the centre. Coral, pearl white, blush pink, sunflower yellow and cherry red rose bushes lined the entire west wall and emitted wonderful fragrance and vibrant colours. The rose garden was dedicated to Maire as roses were her favourite flower and she had dreamed of doing something very similar in the garden, but she never got around to completing it.

Their black, white and brown tri-coloured German Pointer named Star, greeted Lavinia with her tail wagging but soon reverted her attention back to the table that was laden with various foods. She was stood eagerly by Alastair's side, her eyes wide with wonder, who fed her a slice of bacon and looked up when he heard Lavinia approach. The food ranged from toast and pastries to fruit salad, yoghurt, eggs and bacon. A vintage teapot with ruby red poppies delicately painted onto it was filled with loose leaf English Breakfast tea along with a cafetiere filled with strong ground coffee.

Alastair and Mindi were sat with her grandparents, Maire's mum and dad, Jen and Geoff, all in conversation whilst eating. Geoff was flicking through the morning's newspaper.

Jen and Geoff had been married for fifty-five years, and lived in Telford, Shropshire. Every time Mindi and Lavinia visited them, they would wake up early and sit on their grandparents' bed all morning with a cup of tea whilst they were told stories of their life back in the day. When they were courting, they would often go to watch a film, but due to curfew they would always see the ending of the film before the beginning, and to Lavinia, it always sounded like something from a Nicholas Sparks novel.

Her grandparents were visiting for the week. With Alastair's ever unpredictable work pattern, Mindi working

CHAPTER 2

full-time and commuting every day to Doncaster, and Lavinia at university, it was difficult to make regular visits. However, since Alastair was forced to take annual leave and Lavinia was currently on her summer break from university, Mindi took a few days' annual leave as well to spend time with family.

Alastair, Mindi and Lavinia lived in a large tranquil village 7.6 miles outside of Scunthorpe in North Lincolnshire. Scotter was home to a parish church named after St Peter, overlooking a well-groomed graveyard. It also had a primary school, a village hall, a barber, two hairdressers, a beauty salon, a Methodist Chapel, a Co-Op with a Post Office, three pubs and a restaurant/hotel. A strip of takeaways from Indian, Fish and Chips, Thai and Chinese were accessed from the main road. A family butchers was extremely popular with the locals. The picturesque riverside was a popular location for dog walkers, to have a picnic, and for children to feed the ducks, or paddle in the cool water.

After breakfast, they went for a morning stroll around the village, to the riverside, taking Star with them on their walk before it got too warm.

The riverside was scenic in all seasons. In spring, the flowers awakened with colours and scents, the air warmed up bringing gentle breezes and the ducklings fluffy and flourishing. In autumn, the days became shorter and colder, and the leaves of the trees turning from green to brown as they fell slowly to the ground. Winter brought the freezing temperatures, the snow and the frozen river; like a postcard picture, with footprints and dog prints disrupting the white blanket that covered the banks. Currently in the height of summer, with temperatures reaching mid- to high-twenties and occasionally low-thirties, the water glistened in the sunlight. At that time of day, the river was quiet, the only sound was the quacking of the ducks and the steady stream of water running.

Star sniffed eagerly at the ground, nose in the grass as she walked briskly along the bank, following the trail of scent. Lavinia closely followed as she held tightly onto the lead.

She spotted the ducks with their ducklings, whose legs swam frantically trying to keep up, all heading under the bridge in the same direction, like something had caught their attention. Like someone was feeding them from their back garden on the other side of the river.

Following her curiosity, Lavinia trailed them.

As she went over the bridge and crossed the road to the other side, her eyes landed on something large and pale.

The raft of ducks obstructed her view.

But she knew it wasn't food.

It might have been rubbish that had been thrown into the water, as it sadly happened more often than she liked to admit. She recalled that just last week, she had pulled a large grey plastic bin out of the river that somehow kept finding its way back in. Someone else had pulled it out only a few days before she did and placed it onto the sloping banks. There had also been several empty crisp packets and coke cans thrown in too. There was a rubbish bin nearby, but it seemed people were too idle to walk to it and that angered her. Too many marine animals and mammals died from digesting plastic or getting trapped in plastic.

She moved further down the grass bank to get a better look, expecting to paddle into the cool refreshing water to retrieve whatever rubbish had been left that time.

But what she saw wasn't rubbish.

It was a human body.

CHAPTER 3

Crime Scene tape was placed around the perimeter of the river, acting as an outer cordon, to keep the public, the press and unauthorised personnel out. The inner cordon was placed nearer the body, to protect and preserve the scene and any potential evidence with forensic significance.

PC Samantha Briggs manned the outer cordon, keeping a crime scene log of anyone who entered or left the scene, the time they did so, their reason for entering and what their job role was, along with an ID check and their signature.

Lincolnshire Major Incident Team had arrived on scene, along with the Forensic Pathologist and Scene of Crime Officers (SOCOs). The Crime Scene Investigation vans had had a major makeover and were now comparable to a mini office where everything had its own designated space. There was room for exhibit transportation, with a desk, complete with Wi-Fi, and space to store equipment needed for any crime scene, whether volume, serious or major.

The MIT consisted of Detective Chief Inspector Walter Wilson, Acting Detective Inspector Harris Forster, who had temporarily replaced Alastair Newbourne, Detective Sergeant Kelly Morgan, Detective Constable Harry Norton and Detective Constable Tom Watkins.

DCI Walter Wilson had a protruding beer belly, greying hair and tired eyes that showed his many years on the job. His stance and presence conveyed authority. His sleeves were rolled up to just past his elbows and his shirt was tucked into his grey suit trousers. He had mentored Alastair in his early days as detective, when they were both much younger and remained great friends throughout their careers, often playing golf together on the weekends, taking their annual fishing trip around the UK waters or having dinner together with their families. Wilson had been married to Denise for 31 years – she was the headteacher of the local primary school.

It had taken DI Harris Forster slightly longer to get to Detective Inspector, being in his mid-forties, but he still had plenty of work life left in him. He had been a slow burner, taking his time to take his detective exams and had failed many times before he got the promotion and was able to progress up the ranks. But years on the force meant experience and that was worth a lot. He believed that experience taught you everything you needed to know but, then again, he was very old school.

DS Kelly Morgan was a young woman in her early thirties working in a male-dominated job and was currently the only woman on the Major Crime team. She was constantly proving that she was as good as, or even better than any man in her role as Detective Sergeant. Her jet-black hair, arched eyebrows, full eyelashes and electric green eyes showed great intensity; she was determined, dedicated, hardworking and she would not take any shit from anyone. She wore a black midi bodycon skirt, a white cap sleeved blouse and black ballet pumps, which were more suitable out in the field than her black heel court shoes that were only worn in the office.

DC Harry Norton's chestnut brown hair styled in a sophisticated traditional side parting made him appear slightly younger than his thirty-eight years. He had always worked in public services, where firstly, he had joined the Military at seventeen years of age fresh from Army Cadets. After five gruelling years, he decided a change of career was in order and opted to become a detention officer at Humberside Police based in Hull. It was interesting work, and Norton had not considered joining the police as a detective, but the subject was approached on many occasions and when it was time to move on, that was the career choice for him. It had

CHAPTER 3

been a good move as he quickly settled and excelled in his role as Detective Constable.

DC Tom Watkins was in his mid-twenties, with an attractive and athletic frame. He had strong cheekbones and a square jawline. His sandy blond hair was styled into a side parting with a slight quiff, and the other side close shaved which highlighted his striking and sensitive sapphire blue eyes and stubble. He had taken the Police Constable Degree Entry Holder Programme route. After completing two years' probation, learning on the job and in the classroom, he was sworn in as a PC. There was a lot of scepticism within the police force about this route, especially from the older generation who had years of experience on the job that the classroom just could not teach and had had to start from the bottom and work their way up over the years via exams and promotions, which were thanks to hard work and not just handed to someone on a plate. However, this has been a fairly recently new way of entering the force that was not available years ago. Tom had been a quick learner and was respected by his team whom he had learnt so much from, but he also felt like he had to prove himself that he was just as good as the others who had served a long time. Tom had been through a lot over the years since he had joined, but that just made him more resilient and adaptable, all qualities of a great detective in the making, which is why when he took his detective exams he had passed with flying colours.

The SOCOs were like a business of flies, buzzing around the crime scene, sketching the scene, with coordinates and measurements, collecting and packaging potential evidence whilst Marcus Carver, the Specialist Forensic Photographer, moved around with precision, capturing digital documentation of the scene via videography and overview, approach and close up shots of the scene, the evidence and the body in situ.

Together, the Senior CSI and his crew had carefully dragged the body out of the water and placed it onto a blue plastic sheet that was covered by a white tent to protect and preserve the body from further contamination, from environmental factors and from the public's prying eyes.

Forensic Pathologist Dr Hayleigh Ryan was present to confirm life extinct and conduct a preliminary examination of the body in situ. This would include any obvious findings that may have contributed to the cause of death, approximate estimation of time of death based on physical and chemical changes to the body including rigor mortis, livor mortis and any other comments or suggestions based on what she visualised in that moment. The body would then get transported to the morgue for the post-mortem.

Dr Hayleigh Ryan was an attractive woman, in her early forties with high cheekbones, straightened shoulder-length silky autumn-brown hair, which was tied up in a high ponytail and whisky brown eyes that showed a certain fierceness and professionalism. She had always had a passion for science from a young age and an understanding of the human body after death and the processes it goes through. She had studied Medicine at Imperial College London for five extensive years before qualifying as a doctor, undertaking Pathology training and then specialising in Forensic Pathology. She had only been in the job for eight and a half years but was the most experienced Forensic Pathologist in Scunthorpe.

A small crowd had gathered around the outer cordon.

Another police officer, who introduced herself as PC Polly Frances, was questioning Lavinia and family.

"How often do you walk this way to the riverside?" she asked in a soft feminine voice as she scribbled in her pocket notebook.

"Most days, twice a day," Lavinia replied.

"Can you talk me through the route you usually take?"

Lavinia described the route she walks from her house to the river, down the high street and back to her house.

"And did you notice anything suspicious recently either by the riverside itself or along your usual route?"

CHAPTER 3

"No, nothing. I usually see several other dog walkers that I recognise and stop and chat to, and several residents out and about, but nothing out of the ordinary."

Once the body was secure in the tent, Hayleigh knelt in her Tyvek coveralls, donned a pair of long cuffed blue gloves before placing a purple latex pair over the top, and scanned the body from head to toe.

The victim was a young woman with long natural wavy brown hair and a slim, slender frame. Where she once wore full red lips, they were now blue, blistered and seemed shrunken. Her eyes were shut as if she was sleeping peacefully. What ruined the serenity was the atrocities that told Hayleigh the story of her last moments alive and the horror behind it, and her face showed nothing but horror.

Where once she had ten fingers, there were none left. The same occurred with her toes. Her left ear, and left eye were also missing. Ligature marks were visible around both of her wrists and ankles.

Most cases she worked on, her bodies had either died from natural causes, died of a pre-existing medical condition, or had been shot dead or received a fatal knife injury. That is how glamourous life as a Forensic Pathologist got in Scunthorpe.

But this case was unique and terrifying, and despite the spring-summer heat, she shivered.

Hayleigh had asked a SOCO who was just about to gear up in personal protective equipment, to fetch the detectives on the case. Two minutes later, he appeared with the whole mystery gang in tow, and they donned on the protective equipment before entering the tent together.

The size of the tent was small, so the increasing number of bodies made it feel claustrophobic.

"Thought you'd want to see the body in situ before it's removed," Hayleigh said as she was crouched in the centre by the body with the detectives standing on either side.

Marcus Carver weaved himself in and out of the detectives to take more photographs. He sighed deeply with annoyance at the number of alive bodies, who were making his work difficult to complete. He had already taken overview shots of the body and the scene in the water, and overview shots of the body in the tent. Each overview shot consisted of four images which would create a panorama view when stitched together. He had moved onto approach shots, which would show the relationship between the objects in the tent or the scene where the body was situated and the positioning of the body at the crime scene. Close-up shots would document the evidence with evidence number markers and scales in the picture. They would also document injuries the victim sustained, also with a scale to show the size of each wound. This process would be repeated back in the mortuary.

Hayleigh had taken the rectal temperature of the victim to test her core temperature versus the ambient temperature. Due to the body being in the water, and naked, her core temperature was low at 24.5°C from heat loss through radiation, conduction and convention. If she had been wearing clothing, her temperature would have been slightly higher as she would be more protected from the environment. The air temperature was currently at 19°C. Hayleigh calculated the average body temperature of 37°C and subtracted that from the rectal temperature just taken and divided it by the general rate of temperature fall per hour, which as a rule of thumb was 1.5°C. This meant that she had been dead for at least eight hours.

After a few minutes of silence to allow the detectives to take in the scene in front of them, Hayleigh broke it by saying, "From my initial examination, it is obvious she died from suspicious circumstances. The coagulated blood shows her wounds were ante-mortem, before death. The blood loss that occurred would not have been enough to kill her, although she would have been incapacitated, she was weak and the stress and fear of what was happening to her, may have been enough to strain her heart and ultimately lead to cardiac arrest, but I'll be able to determine more at the post-mortem. Rigor mortis has set in fully, even if the water kept her cool enough to slow down the rate, and due to her rectal temperature, I would say she has been dead for at least eight hours. I did notice purple discolouration on her back." Together Hayleigh and the Senior SOCO carefully turned her onto her side, so the detectives could see. The discolouration was a bluish-purple colour and blotchy with white areas that appeared across her back.

"This," Hayleigh started as she pointed to her back, "is livor mortis." She looked up to see blank faces staring directly at her as if waiting for an explanation. She took the silence as her cue to carry on. "Livor mortis is the gravitational settling of the blood that appears as this bluish-purple discolouration on the skin. Once a person is dead, the blood can no longer circulate so it settles. If the victim is lying on their back when he or she dies and is not moved for a while, the blood will begin to pool at once. After six hours, with applied pressure, the skin will turn white. And this, ladies and gentlemen, is what happened with our victim."

And rigor mortis is the stiffening of the muscles in the body after death and can estimate time since death based on which body parts have become stiff. After six hours, the eyelids, jaw and neck start to become stiff. After eight to twelve hours, rigor is complete.

"So, no evident cause of death?" Wilson asked.

"No, her blue blistered lips may be as a result of something she ingested, but once I open her up, I can find that out and hopefully determine a conclusive cause of death," Hayleigh stated, as competently as always.

"Did she suffer?" Morgan asked the inevitable question that everyone in the tent had thought but not dared to voice.

"I am afraid she would have been in extreme pain. She was alive when the killer tortured her."

Silence took over once again. Everyone in the tent was absorbed in the body in front of them and imagined the pain she had endured.

"I will let the SOCOs finish here and then I'll have the body transferred to the mortuary. I will do the post-mortem straight away," Hayleigh informed, slowly standing up from her crouching position.

The detectives nodded and mumbled their thanks before leaving the tent and disposing of the overalls.

Wilson walked over to Alastair where PC Frances had just finished taking their statements. "I'll take it from here," he told her. She nodded in understanding and left them to it.

"You sure you don't want to be in on this case, Alastair? I can take away your annual leave just as quick as I ordered it."

"You have got all the expertise you need. Besides, I am giving you an extra pair of hands that are more than capable. Lavinia will be conducting work experience with the team whilst she is on summer break from university."

"Then I've got a great detective in the making," he replied, knowing that Lavinia was just like Alastair. He turned to leave but hesitated and added, "If you change your mind, you know where I am."

With that, he headed back towards his BMW 3 Series iPerformance Saloon and drove back to the station, windows fully down, enjoying the breeze with Bryan Adams blasting through his speakers.

CHAPTER 4

Lincolnshire Police Station, based in Scunthorpe, was situated in the town centre. It was a long and tall brick building with five storeys in total; each storey housed a different department of policing or forensics.

The second floor belonged to the Major Incident Team. Within the MIT office, there were three separate offices, one for the DCI and DI, and the other that served as a large conference room for briefings to be held. Several desks were situated in and around the main room and were occupied with the basics of a telephone, a computer and a desk chair.

DCI Wilson was sat in his office, gathering notes and details to prepare a briefing for when his team returned. He had a pile of files on the top of his desk for him to read and check through that seemed to grow every time he walked into his office, like someone had fed the files with MiracleGro.

He took off his glasses, placed them on the desk in front of him and rubbed his eyes, with the palms of his hands, while trying to take in this morning's events. The scale of horror behind the murder was one he had never seen before. It seemed like the killer was vengeful or angry and had taken his anger out on the poor soul he'd claimed the life of.

The doors to the MIT squeaked open to reveal his team. He noticed that the door needed oiling and made a mental note to ask someone down in reception or one of his DCs to put some WD40 on it. Wilson took a deep sigh, got up from his desk, picked up his glasses which he placed into his shirt pocket, picked up the notepad he had been writing in, and walked out of his office. He then proceeded into the conference room shouting "briefing in five minutes" to his team as he went.

****

The mortuary was in the Pathology department at the Scunthorpe General Hospital, three miles from the police station.

Alastair had been there countless times, even in his sleep when cases had occupied his mind. However, this time he had the company of Lavinia, who had also been there on numerous occasions, not for the purpose of an investigation but to see Maire. She had been an Infection Control Nurse, and her office was situated along the same corridor.

From entering through the Main Entrance, they went through a set of double doors that were in front of them, climbed a flight of stairs, went through more doors, down a long corridor and up a further two flights of stairs before eventually arriving at the entrance to the department.

The reception was to their right as they entered, with a waiting room and several rooms off it; on their left was where blood tests were carried out. The lunchtime news was on with subtitles and when the machine displayed the number 21, an elderly gentleman with a walking stick slowly stood up and walked into one of the rooms, where a patient and smiling nurse was waiting to take a blood sample.

A young lady of no more than twenty-five years old sat behind the desk and looked up from her computer screen as Alastair and Lavinia approached the desk. She smiled, showing a row of perfectly glistening white teeth and her long chestnut brown hair flowed down past her shoulders, which wore a mustard yellow tie knot headband. Her glasses accentuated her high cheekbones and thin face. The name badge pinned to her uniform read Courtney.

CHAPTER 4

Courtney was the complete opposite of her colleague, who stood at the back of the room shifting through some paperwork. Her colleague, Joan, was older with sandy blonde hair tied up in a ponytail, piercing green eyes and yellow stained crooked teeth from years of smoking. She was in her late forties but looked much older.

As Alastair visited the mortuary often, he had got to know the staff on reception and always had a friendly conversation with them. But he had not recognised Courtney and guessed she was new to the job. He guessed Betty, who had been there the last time Alastair was, had already left to study Nursing at university. He had wished her well and every success in her future, not knowing when he would see her next, if ever.

"Good afternoon, how may I help?" Courtney asked in a well-rehearsed professional and polite tone.

"Hi, can you tell Dr Hayleigh Ryan that Alastair Newbourne is here to see her. She'll know who I am."

"Just one moment please." Courtney picked up the telephone and dialled an extension number to the mortuary.

After two rings the phone was picked up.

"Hello, Dr Ryan's office. This is Zoe Collins speaking." Zoe Collins was a newly graduated medical student from Malaysia. She had undertaken an eight-week internship at the mortuary being Hayleigh's assistant, helping with admin and the relentless task of paperwork and with the autopsies. She passed tools, weighed the organs, inserted them back in and stitched up the body afterwards. She was then offered a full-time position after those eight weeks as Hayleigh was extremely impressed with her work ethic and thankful for an extra pair of hands. Zoe then got a permanent work permit and moved to the UK after she graduated.

"Hi, this is Courtney from reception, I have an Alastair Newbourne here to see Dr Ryan."

"Okay, I'll be right through. Thank you."

A couple of minutes later, Zoe appeared. She was tall and slender and wore a blue knee length dress with white roses on it. She was 5'6" and had chocolate brown almond shaped eyes with short black hair that was styled with loose curls. She wore a friendly smile, and she exchanged pleasantries with Alastair, whom she knew fairly well and introduced herself to Lavinia.

"Hayleigh is currently in a meeting. She'll be ten minutes, but you can wait in her office until she returns," Zoe explained as she beckoned them to follow her and used her ID card to activate the open mechanism on the doors.

Offices occupied both sides of the corridor where the clinical smell of hospitals followed them. They walked past several blood banks that had the appearance of a standard household fridge and buzzed noisily. As they approached Infection Control, both Alastair and Lavinia could not help but turn their heads as they walked past what had been Maire's office. On the display board outside they still had memoirs written by Maire's colleagues and photographs of the team displayed. Lavinia had read them so many times, she could recite them all from memory.

"I wish I had known your mum, she seemed very well liked and respected among the staff and great at her job," Zoe offered in a soft tone as she noticed Lavinia looking at the board.

A right turn at the end of the corridor led them to another set of double doors with writing above it in block capitals that told them they had reached the mortuary.

Zoe once again used her ID card where the machine signalled green to permit entry and she pushed the doors open to reveal a white room that smelled strongly of bleach and dead bodies.

The door opened to a spacious room with three stainless steel pedestal autopsy tables all aligned in a row. Worktop units decorated the left side perimeter with three offices

CHAPTER 4

occupying the right east wall. A wall of steel fridges looked monstrous against the north wall.

The main room where post-mortems were conducted, was the largest room. Before Hayleigh obtained permission to extend the mortuary by putting in a further two rooms, there was just one large office space. That had now been divided into two offices, one for Hayleigh and the other for Zoe Collins and Marcus Carver to share, with an extra room on the end for relatives, which could be accessed by a separate side door. Hayleigh had thought it was inappropriate for relatives, who were grieved by the loss of a loved one, to be immediately met with the horrors of the steel tables where bodies lay vulnerable and exposed. She thought it would be more caring and thoughtful for relatives to have their own room with privacy to grieve, and attached to that, a small thin rectangular room with a two-way mirror for viewing. Just before the entrance into the mortuary, there was a small side room for PPE, which housed shelves of disposable aprons, masks, gloves and shoe covers, and provided a bin for waste with a very basic washroom.

Zoe took them through to Hayleigh's office, which was like any other standard office that housed an oak desk with a leather office chair sat behind it and one in front, a computer with a mouse and keyboard, a telephone and a mountain of paperwork were the only items on her desk.

A small two-seater sofa, overlooked by a tall black standard floor lamp, brought by Hayleigh herself when she first started working there, was placed in the far-right corner of her office. She found it useful and more comfortable than her desk chair, when working very late at night through into the early hours of the morning – and that happened more than she liked to admit. But, unfortunately, bodies had the habit of turning up at all hours of the day and night.

A single filing cabinet stood tall with its back against the wall behind her desk which was neatly labelled in chronological order. Alastair knew Hayleigh was a very organised person and was not surprised to find her office in immaculate condition. Zoe gestured to the vacant chairs as Alastair and Lavinia took a seat and declined the offer of tea or coffee.

"I understand this is about the body found in the river at Scotter?" Zoe queried.

"It is, yeah," Alastair clarified. "Has Hayleigh completed the autopsy yet?"

"She was going to do it as soon as it arrived, but she got called away to a meeting before she had the chance. She'll be happy that you're here to witness it," Zoe joked, knowing that Alastair usually missed them on purpose, and usually turned up to the mortuary in perfect timing, just after they had finished. It was almost like he stood and watched from the outside and knew exactly when to come in. Alastair had witnessed several autopsies conducted by Hayleigh and he enjoyed how she worked. Meticulous, thorough and scientifically. He didn't mind the smell, or the procedure anymore, and still found it fascinating to watch, but he didn't feel the need to continuously watch them taking place. After all, he just wanted the intelligence sourced from them so he could do his job.

Today, he wasn't just there to find out information that could potentially aid in the investigation, he was there for Lavinia to witness her first post-mortem before undertaking work experience with his team. She would be the eyes and ears for Alastair who would follow the case as closely as he could from afar, but he knew this experience would prove essential for Lavinia. She was just like Alastair who wanted to know the horrors behind the victim's death and get a feel for who the victim was when they were alive.

"That makes one of us."

They could hear the echo of high heeled shoes clicking down the corridor. A few seconds later, surprise showed on Hayleigh's face as she walked into her office. She leant against the door frame, a file in her hand as surprise turned

CHAPTER 4

into confusion and her brows creased together as their eyes met. "I didn't expect to see you here."

Alastair and Hayleigh had a complicated past, and one that was rarely spoken of. They had known each other most of their lives, starting back at secondary school, where they had dated for just over two and a half years. They broke up within the first month of college when Alastair had met Maire. They did not speak to each other again and went their separate ways.

It wasn't until years later, when Alastair turned up at a crime scene, fresh in uniform, a crime scene that Hayleigh also attended as the Forensic Pathologist, that their paths crossed again. At the time, Alastair was married with two young children and Hayleigh was dating, but had recently broke it off as he was being difficult about her career choices and said she was married to the job, which meant she couldn't be married to anyone else.

But when Hayleigh met Maire and her children, Mindi and Lavinia, she became a close family friend and stepped up to help Alastair look after his children when Maire passed. Since he submerged himself in work, he had missed milestones in their lives that Hayleigh had been a part of, such as Lavinia's first day at secondary school, first time they both rode a bike, she was there for every illness and when they needed help with their homework. She had been like a second mother to Mindi and Lavinia and had been a rock for Alastair while he needed time to heal and slowly get back to his normal self. Despite Hayleigh's hectic work schedule, though, she had still managed to juggle looking after Alastair's children, but it had been hard on everyone.

They had grown accustomed to each other again, comfortable in each other's company where old feelings resurfaced but were never voiced. They had great chemistry, always had and possibly always will.

"Me neither. I am only present strictly to offer my support to Lavinia during her first post-mortem – having been witness

to plenty myself, I know what it is like the first time around."
A mischievous grin was plastered all over his face.

"And it just so happens that you're here to witness the post-mortem of the murder case that you would, under normal circumstances, be a part of?"

"That is purely coincidental."

Hayleigh stared at him in a 'what the hell do you think you're doing' kind of way before sighing and her shoulders slumped in defeat before agreeing. "Fine, let me just change my shoes, my feet are aching so bad in these." She walked round to her desk, still giving Alastair the look which he returned as a sassy grin and she muttered "You owe me", before she picked up her trainers and sat down on the two-seater sofa to change her footwear. She only wore high heels for important meetings, but she felt more comfortable working in trainers. A lesson she had learnt the hard way in her early days of training.

She picked up her pristine white medical coat from the coat stand placed just inside the entrance to her office, tied her auburn hair up in a ponytail and walked into the autopsy suite with Alastair and Lavinia in tow, before all donning protective equipment, a pre-post-mortem ritual.

She walked over to the metal fridge, home to the dead. Each compartment had the capacity to store seven bodies and she opened the middle compartment door to reveal the body that was hidden inside. Hayleigh then pulled the slab she was laid on. The body was completely covered in a white sheet, and together Hayleigh and Zoe holstered the body from the slab onto one of the autopsy tables and removed the white sheet. All the medical instruments had been sterilised prior and were now lying on a wheel trolley next to the body. Marcus Carver was already snapping away. Until Zoe had got a more permanent job, Marcus had helped Hayleigh out a lot and she was thankful for everything he had done for her, but he was not trained as a mortician but as a Forensic

CHAPTER 4

Photographer, at Hayleigh's expense, so there was only certain jobs he was permitted to do.

Hayleigh had advertised for a Forensic Photographer more than a year ago to take on the responsibility of documenting the crime scene and the body in the morgue, and selecting the photographs to place into case files and for the detectives to have a copy for their investigation, as she didn't have time to do that in addition to all the post-mortems she conducted and reports she compiled. Marcus was the only one who had applied for the job, but he had had a passion for photography ever since he was young, understood the camera and the technicalities of it. Before forensics, he was always fascinated by nature, but she was willing to give him a two-week probationary period to see how he got on and he had proved more than capable. He had been the perfect candidate. Almost too good to be true.

On arrival to the mortuary, the body would have, again, been photographed by Marcus, with the date and time of arrival, the details of the people or person who transported the body to the mortuary and the details of the person who received it, all documented in the log for chain of custody and continuity purposes. The body bag would also be searched for trace evidence including hairs and fibres.

Dictaphone poised in her hand; Hayleigh was ready to set about her work.

Primarily the process entailed an X-ray of the body – which did not show anything unusual – and then an external examination which involved looking for any visible signs of injury or trauma, tattoos, scars or any distinguishing features that would help to identify the body, aka Jane Doe.

Hayleigh opened the victim's mouth to look inside. She had evidently had braces in her lifetime as her teeth were straight, and she must have regularly visited the dentist too and possibly undertaken whitening treatment. Using a magnifying glass, Hayleigh spotted a few dark fibres on the inside of her cheeks and on the corner of her mouth, suggesting she was gagged. Nothing was lodged in the back of her throat, but there were bite marks on her tongue. It would have been an involuntary action on her part when in excruciating pain and not able to scream out due to the gag forcing her to be quiet. Hayleigh took samples of the fibres inside her mouth using tweezers and placed them in a test tube which she would label later and send off to the laboratories to analyse.

The body was turned on her side to allow better access to her back. Other than what Hayleigh had already disclosed at the crime scene, there appeared to be nothing else to report. Just as the body was about to be placed down again, Lavinia spoke up.

"Hold on–" She held onto the victim's side to keep her up and moved her hair out of the way. It had been visible for a split second only, but enough to catch Lavinia's eye. Hayleigh and Alastair stood beside Lavinia and bent down to get a better and clearer view of what she saw. They then briefly stepped away from the body to allow Marcus Carver to photograph the mark.

"A tattoo possibly," Lavinia suggested. "But a botched one. It looks like it was a rushed job and not done very well as the ink has smudged slightly on the outline."

The tattoo appeared to be an outline of a symbol, with a horizontal line going across the centre with two perpendicular vertical lines coming down. The tattoo was drawn in black ink and about three inches in diameter.

"Very well observed, Lavinia. I missed that," Hayleigh praised, giving her a big smile and then turned to Alastair to say, "she has your attentive skills," to which he chuckled in response.

"Any idea what it could mean?" Alastair asked.

"I have never seen something like this before, but I have to agree with Lavinia, it doesn't look professionally done." Hayleigh traced her finger very lightly over the tattoo. "It

CHAPTER 4

appears it was done ante-mortem. It's rough and slightly swollen with coagulated blood around it as it broke the skin. It hasn't had time to heal properly so I would say it was done shortly before her death. It may be personal to the victim or personal to the killer."

"How likely is it that the killer did the tattoo, or could she have got it done of her own accord beforehand? Like at one of these pop-up stalls you see in shopping centres or even at a tattoo parlour?" Alastair suggested.

"It's certainly a possibility that she had it done of her own accord shortly before her demise. The killer could have also branded her with this mark for some perverted gesture," Hayleigh agreed. She had described the colour, the shape and the approximate size of the tattoo along with the location to her Dictaphone to type into her report later on. Marcus took a close up shot of the tattoo.

Thirdly, the internal examination.

This was a different story altogether as Jane Doe would expose her inner darkest secrets.

A 'Y' incision was made from both shoulder blades and ended at the top of the pubis region. Hayleigh then got a knife to cut the skin adhering to muscle and bone so she could be fully opened, and this revealed a thin layer of fat underneath the pale layer of skin.

The ribs were cut with shears and the breastplate removed for better access to the organs underneath. They were taken out individually by Zoe who weighed them before passing to Hayleigh to inspect, slice and take samples for further analysis including urine and blood for toxicology.

An ear-to-ear incision was made over the top of her head and the scalp was carefully peeled back which distorted the face to expose the skull. Hayleigh examined the polished white naked skull but saw no fractures or indentations that would indicate blunt force trauma. With a face shield placed over her head that covered her face and neck, the top section of the skull was removed using a Stryker saw. With power and precision, the lightweight tool effortlessly cut through bone and exposed the brain, a complex map of soft tissue, cell and vessel branches that connected to the rest of the body.

The brain was then carefully removed. Zoe passed it to Hayleigh after it was weighed, who inspected it before taking a serrated knife and slicing it like a loaf of bread. Again, no haemorrhages or haematomas were present.

After Hayleigh had finished and retrieved enough samples that were placed into labelled tubes ready to go to the laboratories, the organs were placed back into a clear plastic bag and returned to the body cavity, which was then neatly stitched up.

She was then hosed down, all the blood travelling down the steel table and disappearing down the sink, and the instruments thoroughly washed and disinfected before Jane Doe was wheeled back into the fridge and their scrubs placed into a biological waste bin.

You could tell so much about a person's lifestyle, purely from the condition of their organs. For example, a smoker's lungs become blackened and mottled in appearance, an alcoholic's liver deteriorates over time as well, starting with a fatty liver which can progress to liver fibrosis and ultimately cirrhosis.

Cancers and diseases can also alter the appearance of organs.

However, all of Jane Doe's organs were fit and healthy, she was a non-smoker and did not abuse alcohol either. There was nothing evident that had caused her death or any factors that attributed to her death, no subdural or epidural hematoma, no haemorrhages, no disease of the major organs, such as the heart, she did not have cancer and she did not suffer from a myocardial infarction. Hayleigh would hopefully find out if drugs were involved when she got the toxicology results back in a few days. She doubted the victim took drugs, due to the condition of all her other organs, but it could still be a possibility that she was drugged by her killer.

CHAPTER 4

Once they were back in Hayleigh's office, they discussed and concluded the findings for Alastair and Lavinia to take back to Wilson and the team, and compiled a small Manila folder that contained a simplified initial post-mortem statement and a selection of crime scene and morgue photographs.

****

Back at the station, the conference room was by far the most luxurious office in the department.

It had a grand oval shaped mahogany table in the centre with ten black smooth leather Cavello chairs with modern chrome legs sat around it which were now occupied by the team. A traditional whiteboard was at the front of the room with a 14" Polaroid Smart LED TV on a stand in the corner, to the right of the whiteboard. This was mainly used to review CCTV footage. A series of floor to ceiling windows on the west wall gave a panoramic view of Scunthorpe.

The Steelworks emitted smoke into the atmosphere, and several houses, shops and cars could be seen in the distance due to the clear blue skies that stretched far over the horizon.

With the blinds drawn closed and the windows open, it made the heat in the room more bearable, and they were able to concentrate better.

The whiteboard had been added to with the name Jane Doe in the centre along with preliminary findings they knew from the crime scene.

The investigation had officially begun.

There were no identification cards found with the body, such as credit or debit cards or a driver's licence or passport. They simply didn't know who she was.

Missing Persons were searching through their database for anyone that was reported missing in the last week that matched the victim's description. Hopefully they would get a result within the next couple of hours.

Wilson would do a press conference if Missing Persons did not come back with a match, to try and speed up the identification process. He wanted very little published by the media, though, as he knew what they were capable of and did not want the investigation detailed to the public.

In the meantime, they went through the intel that they knew so far and established lines of enquiry to pursue. Wilson was stood at the front of the conference room next to the whiteboard while everyone else took a seat and had their notebooks open and pens poised ready to scribble down important notes from the meeting. Wilson wrote notes, times and dates on the whiteboard as they discussed the case.

They found that they didn't have much to go on, which wasn't surprising at this stage, especially with no identification. They could not inform immediate family members of her tragic death or interview the people who last saw her or those who reported her missing or last had contact with her, because they did not know.

They did, however, know that she had been dead for at least eight hours, according to Hayleigh. She was found at 09:33 in the morning, which put the time of death around 1:30am and possibly discarded in the river between the hours of 1:30am and the time she was found. The logic would be to dispose a body before sunrise in darkness as that would be the most opportune time, but there was no evidence to suggest otherwise. No nearby residents had seen or heard anyone or anything suspicious. The investigation would be focused on narrowing down the timeframe.

"Anger springs to mind when I look at this case. The killer maybe wanted revenge for something as the victim certainly felt pain," Wilson told his team.

"Do you think he cut off her fingers and toes so we couldn't identify her via fingerprints?" Norton asked, thinking aloud.

"It's possible but if he didn't want us to identify her, he would have chopped off her head as well so we couldn't

CHAPTER 4

make visual identification," Wilson responded, making a valid point.

"That's harder to achieve, more room for error, it's subjective and less confirmative than fingerprinting," Morgan stated matter-of-factly.

"Only if you have ante-mortem records to compare or mitochondrial DNA samples from the mother," Harris bit back, with an equal matter-of-fact tone that matched Morgan's. Mitochondrial DNA was inherited solely from the mother. The father may not be the father of that specific child in question, if he or she was born from a previous marriage, for example, so it was more accurate to obtain DNA samples from the mother for comparison.

At that moment, Alastair and Lavinia walked into the conference room. Surprise lit up on Wilson's face as the others followed his stare.

"Came to drop the post-mortem results off before making a formal statement," Alastair answered the unasked question as he threw the thin Manila folder onto the table and slid it across to Wilson at the other end, all the while holding his gaze.

"You were not authorised to attend the post-mortem. Although I'm not completely surprised since you haven't stuck by the rules since day one." A thin smile formed at the corner of his lips. Alastair was Wilson's best detective and he knew that he wouldn't have got where he was today without bending the rules slightly. He was his own person, but he got results and at the end of the day that's what mattered.

Alastair just smiled and shrugged his shoulders before saying, "Well it looks like you have your hands full and are mega busy, so I simply saved you all a job. And besides, as you are aware, my daughter Lavinia is here to undertake placement while I'm off and before she goes back to university in September. I was merely accompanying her to her first post-mortem."

"Better make use of those badges of yours, I suppose, and sit down," Wilson referred to the Visitor lanyards that both Alastair and Lavinia wore around their neck.

Introductions were made and a summary of what they had discussed so far in the meeting was communicated to Alastair and Lavinia. In turn, they then uncovered what had occurred at the post-mortem.

Lavinia opened the folder and took out a photograph. She showed the photograph of the tattoo that she had spotted on the victim's neck to the team before pinning it up onto the whiteboard as she described it. "As you can see, it appears as an outline of a symbol of some sort. It looks fresh and doesn't look like the ink had time to dry as it has smudged slightly, suggesting she had it done recently. We think it's possible the killer branded her with it. Of course, there's always the possibility that she had it done of her own accord shortly before she was killed. There is a slight red marking and a minute scab that hasn't had time to heal properly where pressure was applied and broke the skin, so she was still alive when she had it done."

Silence took over the room as everyone absorbed what Lavinia had just disclosed to them.

Wilson looked at Alastair in disbelief. It seemed that Lavinia had inherited his investigative skills and analytical mind, and he knew in that moment that she would be a welcome asset to the team in Alastair's absence. She had already proved herself in that one statement.

"Any idea what the symbol might mean?" Tom asked.

"No, but it might be worth speaking to tattoo artists around Scunthorpe to see if they have seen it before or know what it means," Lavinia answered.

"Good shout," Wilson said.

"Also, a sample of the ink has been taken, so we'll see if that brings us any leads as to the ink type or needle used," Lavinia concluded.

CHAPTER 4

"There's currently eleven tattoo studios in Scunthorpe," Harris informed the team as he read from a Google search on his Apple MacBook.

"First line of enquiry: split those up between yourselves. Lavinia, you'll be partnered with Tom to question four of those eleven companies; Morgan and Norton, I want you to also interview four and Harris the remaining three. I want reports of your visits and will request another meeting upon your return to discuss findings, if there are any."

A chorus of "yes, sirs" echoed around the room.

The meeting lasted a further ten minutes before they were all dismissed to carry out their tasks.

Wilson indicated to Alastair that he wanted to speak to him in his office. They were both nursing a small measure of whisky in glass tumblers. Wilson had received the set of Dalmore 15-Year-Old Single Malt Edition with two engraved branded Stag glass tumblers last Christmas. They were both whisky connoisseurs, having the appreciation for the fine spirit with strict views on how to drink it properly.

That was with a generous measure and a single large rectangular ice cube.

However, they did not have access to ice cubes at that precise moment, so they just had it as it was, straight out of the bottle. No matter what time of day it was, Wilson's motto was that it was five o'clock somewhere and somehow that made it acceptable to have one small drink before noon!

The Dalmore 15-Year-Old Edition was a stunning amber coloured liquid that was warm, fruity, nutty and spicy all in one, with notes of classic winter spices including cinnamon and nutmeg, a rich palate of dried fruit and spices, finished with sweet dark cherry flavours.

It was like having Christmas cake in a drink.

"This whisky tastes better than I remember," Alastair said in appreciation as he held it up to the light to admire it. The liquid glowed like a fire.

"It's soft, well rounded and well balanced with great flavours of Christmas. One of the best I've ever tasted," Wilson agreed before changing the subject. "Lavinia already seems to fit extremely well into the team."

"She's a younger female version of me," he responded proudly before adding, "I'd like to say I taught her well, but I can't take all the responsibility for how she's turned out."

"That's been between you, Maire and Hayleigh. She's turned into the perfect mixture of all her influences in her life. She may not remember Maire, but I see a lot of her in Lavinia."

"Me too. Mindi has definitely taken after Maire though."

"What about Hayleigh?"

"What about her?"

"I know about your complicated past and your equally complicated present, but is the future going to be just as or less complicated between you both?"

Alastair sighed. "I haven't had enough whisky to divulge that information."

"We'll save that for another time then."

"That particular conversation, or drinking enough whisky?"

"Both. How about this weekend?"

"Sure."

****

They exited the station and immediately located Tom's voltaic blue Vauxhall Corsa parked in the staff car park, as it was the only blue car there. Many of the cars were silver, red or black.

"You won't lose your car anytime soon," Lavinia joked as she made her way to the front passenger side.

"That's the beauty of it being this colour," Tom replied, smiling wide with triumph as he looked over the roof at Lavinia, unlocked the car door and slid into the driver's side.

CHAPTER 4

Radio 1 blasted over the speakers as he turned the key in the ignition and made a dash to turn the volume down.

"So, I have one rule in my car. Passengers are always the DJ. I have a couple of CDs in the door your side or Spotify. It's over to you."

"Radio 1 is fine," Lavinia decided, but she still took the CDs out of the car door and flicked through them one at a time. He had a Drivetime album and the latest Now That's What I Call Music.

"Got them both as a present when I got this car. Only play them occasionally. CDs seem to be old school now. It's all Spotify and downloaded music nowadays."

"Now That's What I Call Power Ballads is a great album for the car, if you like a mixture of 80s and more recent music," Lavinia suggested.

"I do, I'll have to give that one a try."

"Definitely." She placed the CDs back in the car door.

"Okay, so where to first?" Tom asked as he looked at Lavinia, who in turn looked at the list in her hand that they'd complied of tattoo studios to visit.

"Tattoo Art at the top end of the High Street," she replied as Tom reversed out of the space, put the car into gear and headed to the town centre.

Scunthorpe Town Centre was a hive of activity and was busier than Lavinia had ever seen it. The latest edition to the town was a Steelworks Sculpture that featured a period lamppost and depicted a female on a bicycle and a male worker in the 1940s stood on a stone plinth. It was a monument to honour the steelworkers and recognise the town's steel heritage.

Up to half price sales were advertised in most shop windows by unmissable large red and white banners and signs to entice people to spend money.

Tom and Lavinia made their way to the top end of the High Street to begin their enquiry. On the way, Tom gave a few pointers for interviewing since it would be her first official interview since joining.

"I will take the lead, but feel free to ask a few questions of your own as long as they are not leading questions or made out like we are treating them as suspects, because they're not. We are just simply asking questions."

Tattoo Art was a small studio squeezed in between a nail bar and a Euro Exchange shop. There was a large window where the main room could be seen from the street that held a leather sofa used for waiting customers, and the reception behind a small basic desk with a till and leaflets. The door to the shop was on the side.

As Tom and Lavinia walked in, the ding of the bell attached to the door sounded and they spotted a very built, muscular man in his early 30s sat on the leather sofa with his legs apart and as wide as his grey ripped jeans would let him. His hair was tied up in a man bun at the top of his head and he displayed a full tattoo sleeve on his right arm. His ear stretcher was so big that Lavinia could clearly see straight through it and an industrial piercing on the opposite ear.

Designs were wallpapered around the room, showing off skill and talent from a variety of different tattoos from outlines of letters, numbers, names, the Greek alphabet, Chinese symbols and other symbols that they did not recognise to full-on colour of characters from comics, mystical characters and punk rock tattoos.

A man, presumably the owner, appeared from the hallway that led into two separate tattooing rooms. He was a big beefy round man with a salt and pepper goatee. He wore plain black jeans and a black t-shirt with the company name embroidered on the left breast in hot pink. He also wore tattoo sleeves on both arms and on his bald head.

"Hello, how can I help you?" He had a surprisingly pleasant deep voice, which was croaky from years of smoking.

Tom displayed his ID badge, Lavinia followed suit as she had been given a temporary one and they introduced

CHAPTER 4

themselves. The man, who introduced himself as the owner, Sid, looked surprised by their visit.

"Is it possible to ask you a few questions regarding a tattoo?"

"Um yes, we can go into my office." He gestured for them to follow him, and he led them down the hallway, past the two rooms, where he poked his head around the second one and apologised to his client, telling him that he would be back momentarily. They then rounded the corner and took the steep stairs to the first floor of the building. At the top, the owner sounded like he was having an asthma attack and a sheen layer of sweat formed on his forehead. He needed a few minutes to recover and then he led them into his office.

The office appeared the same size as the reception downstairs, immediately below this room, but it looked slightly bigger as it had less furniture and was simple in design rather than the ostentatious tattoo design wallpaper. It overlooked the busy High Street, where the window was ajar.

The oak wooden desk and ergonomic chair was situated near the window. A double wardrobe took up most of the wall, with client files, financial and business files and a safe.

"What's this about?" Sid questioned, sitting down at his desk and reclining in the chair once he had enough breath in him to speak again.

Tom and Lavinia stood in front of his desk as they spoke to him. Tom got a picture up on his mobile phone and passed it to Sid as he asked, "Can you take a look at that tattoo and tell me if you recognise it?"

"Sure."

There was a moment of silence as Sid studied the image on the screen and shook his head as he passed it back to Tom.

"I'm sorry but I don't recognise it and I have no idea what it could mean. I've never seen it before."

"Do most of your clients get tattoos that are symbolic to them, or do they just have designs that they like for no particular reason or meaning?" Lavinia asked this time, and Tom was impressed with the question.

"It varies. Some just like the design and simply want it done to add to their collection, but the majority of clients want it for a particular reason whether in memory of a loved one, for friendship, for their dead pet, for a partner. The reasons are endless."

Tom got up another image on his phone. This time it was a close-up facial image of Jane Doe, taken at the morgue once her hair and face had been washed and made up after the post-mortem. He handed the phone to Sid once more.

"Do you recognise the woman in the photo? Has she come here before, or have you seen her around at all?"

"It's hard to tell."

"I know, but anything you might know would really help us."

"Again, I'm sorry but I don't recognise her."

"Thank you for your time. If you think of anything in the future, then please don't hesitate to get in touch with us." Tom passed Sid his card with his office number on it and then they saw themselves out.

Next, they were headed to Tattoo and Body Piercing Studio further down the High Street. On their way, they discussed the interview they had just come from as they walked.

"What do you think?" Tom asked Lavinia.

"I think he is telling the truth."

"What makes you say that?"

"What makes you doubt him?" Lavinia asked back, which made Tom chuckle.

"Tattoo artists are very hesitant at giving police information. It's like a cult and they like to stick together. They work with various symbols every day and dodgy punters from all backgrounds, and I noticed pretty much every symbol ever designed on the wall in his studio, so I am surprised that he hasn't come across ours before."

CHAPTER 4

"They're artists, not actors, and he was genuinely confused when he looked at the image of the symbol, he held the right amount of eye contact, didn't do a nervous tick, he didn't change his rhythm of blinking, it was even and consistent throughout, his breathing was steady, when he got his breath back, and his voice was steady as well. All signs he was telling the truth."

"You got a psychology degree as well now?"

"No, dadave me an in-depth crash course on studying interviewees."

"That explains a lot. I'm not saying you're wrong or that I'm right, but we can't rule anything or anyone out until we know for certain, because even though Wilson is all supportive on gut feelings, he will keep saying gut feelings aren't evidence and won't stand up in court. I don't want you to be on the receiving end of that argument."

"Have you?"

"Once or twice, but your dad was always there to save the day. He is an inspiration, and he is what I aim to be. You're lucky you have a father like that."

There was a very slight sadness to Tom's voice that Lavinia noticed and she wanted to ask him what he meant, but they had arrived at their next stop before she had the chance to.

The Tattoo and Body Piercing Studio was different to the previous one they had visited as it was exceptionally bigger and opened out onto more space. This studio was a multipurpose workspace that, from the name, obviously offered tattoos and piercings but they also did haircuts.

There was a large reception desk manned by a trained receptionist just inside the entrance who directed people to the waiting room and asked clients to fill out a couple of forms while they were waiting. Lavinia spotted a group of teenagers who were all dressed similarly in ripped jeans and branded trainers with a face full of make-up that made them look older than they were, all inside the waiting room that was filled with Chesterfield sofas. A couple of them started to fill out the forms but the others were sat on their phones, showing each other messages and posts from social media.

The ground floor offered space for haircuts with three separate stations all currently occupied by clients. The noise of a hairdryer filled the room, so Tom had to speak louder to the receptionist to be heard above the noise.

"Hi, I'm Detective Constable Tom Watkins and this is Lavinia Newbourne, we're from the Lincolnshire Police Major Investigation Team. Can we speak to the tattoo artist?"

"One moment please," the receptionist said politely as she used the telephone on the desk to dial a number. She spoke with the tattoo artist, whose name was Dave and when she hung up, she directed them to the second floor where they were met by Dave.

Dave was a young man and similar looking to the guy they saw in the waiting room at Tattoo Art Studio, except that he didn't have a full sleeve, just a few on both arms and he had jet black hair instead of a man bun. He was taller and slimmer but had a kind approachable face.

"Hi, I'm Dave. It's not very often we get the police around here," he greeted them with a handshake.

"It's just routine enquiries." They followed him to his work room that held a swivel armchair and an adjustable face cradle chair in the corner with instruments and ink displayed on the worktop. There was a stereo placed on top of a set of drawers that was turned right down to almost mute, but the thumping of the beat could still be heard and felt.

"Is it just you who is in charge of tattoos?" Tom asked, aware of five rooms in total on this floor.

"There's me and my colleague, Felicity, next door. She's currently with a client."

"We will need to speak with her as well."

"What's this about?"

CHAPTER 4

Tom used the same process as he had done previously, giving Dave his phone with the image of the symbol shown on it to look at. Like with Sid, he denied recognising it or knowing what it meant, and the same thing occurred with the image of Jane Doe.

"I'm afraid I can't help you. It's not very often we deal with small symbol tattoos like that one, it's more larger designs that cover full body parts like sleeves or legs and we're big on colour."

"Have you had any clients recently wanting a small outline tattoo similar to one we've just shown you?" Lavinia questioned.

"Probably in the last month. I believe it was a wave tattoo on the wrist. Didn't take five minutes to complete but it wasn't the woman you're after."

Tom asked to speak with Felicity and Dave disappeared for a few moments while he fetched her.

"This is my colleague Felicity, and these are the police," he introduced. Felicity was different to what they both had expected. She had very thin and high cheekbones, light grey eyes and matching light grey hair that had clearly been dyed that colour, but it suited her. She wore minimal make-up and was slender even with the slight round baby bump that had started to show. She had tattoos on her chest and all up her neck that were shown off by the black vest top she wore. And apart from a tattoo sleeve on her right arm, which seemed to be consistent with tattoo artists, that was all they could see.

"Is it okay to ask you a few questions regarding our initial investigation?"

She nodded in agreement.

"I'm going to show you a picture of a tattoo and I want you to tell me if you recognise it or if you understand what it means." Tom handed over his phone once again.

"I don' believe I've seen it before, but I cer'ainly don' kno' what it means. It's a rank tattoo 'oever did it wa'nt good." She spoke with a loud but distinct Yorkshire accent.

"Do you recognise this woman. Have you seen her around at all?"

It took a moment before Felicity replied, "Aye, think that lass came with a friend t'other week."

"Can you tell me more about that?"

"What's to say? The friend wan'ed an Elephant on her thigh mandala style and this lass stayed with 'er the 'ole time."

"How long were they here for?" Lavinia piped up again.

"Three hours. Was very detailed."

"What did they talk about during the time they were here?" Lavinia again.

"Sommat an' nothin'. Nowt worth repea'ing. Asked them abou' life, the usual conversation openers. That lass didn' really give much away, the focus was on 'er friend."

"Did you get their names?"

"We'll have the client's details written down in our booking log which is with reception," Dave informed them.

"The lass's name wa' Isla. Tha's all I kno'."

"Do you have CCTV footage for the day they came in?"

"Yeah, we should do, it automatically gets overridden every two weeks. We haven't had to use it in the past for police investigations and it's on 24/7 so no one really has anything to do with it. You can take a look now if you want, I have a few minutes before my next appointment," Dave helpfully stated.

"That'll be great. Thank you, Felicity, for your help."

Felicity disappeared back into her room while Dave showed them to a small office area that displayed a computer on top of a desk. Screen 1 was divided into four square sections each with a different view of the building: the front, the back, the main room with the reception desk and the hairdressers, and the waiting room. Screen 2 was divided into five square sections of the five rooms on the second floor, two for tattooing – they recognised the room they had just come from and saw on the screen that Felicity was busy filling in the tattoo on the client's back – two for piercing, where the seven teenage girls they'd spotted in the waiting room had

CHAPTER 4

split up and piled into both rooms, and one for the office they were in now. They could see themselves on the screen.

Screen 1 and Screen 2 alternated every two minutes on the computer.

"We can change the time lapse between each screen, but two minutes seems a good amount of time."

"Isn't there anyone who keeps an eye on it in case anything happens?"

"Not solely for this but sometimes if staff aren' busy with clients, they may take a break and come up here but like I said, we haven't had anything happen since we opened up twelve years ago."

"You mentioned the booking log in reception?"

Dave gave reception a call and found out that Grace Sanderson made an appointment for Wednesday 25th May at 11:30am for a tattoo and searched for that time and date on the system. There were several options displayed on the screen to select the location. Tom told him to select the reception, but Dave set the time for 11am as the clients were advised to arrive at least fifteen minutes before the appointment. And sure, enough they walked in at 11:17am.

"Freeze it right there," Lavinia ordered as Tom placed the image on his phone of Jane Doe next to the computer screen for comparison. He had seen worse CCTV quality, and this was rather good in comparison with colour, decent viewpoints, and clear pictures.

They were all silent for a moment whilst Tom's and Lavinia's eyes darted backwards and forwards from the CCTV image and the image of Jane Doe on Tom's phone. There were similarities regarding the features on her face including the shape of the nose and the lips and her high cheekbones and pointy chin.

"It's her," Tom concluded.

"Yes," Lavinia agreed. "Can you still email a copy of this to us?" she then asked Dave.

"Yeah sure." He was handed Tom's card with his details.

"Thank you for your time. We really appreciate it."

On their way out they stopped by reception again to ask if Grace Sanderson had left a contact number. Tom made a note of it, and they exited the studio.

"Blimey, that was more successful than I thought it would be. A right proper Yorkshire lass that Felicity was," Tom said with his best impression of a Yorkshire accent. He wasn't too bad at it either, Lavinia concluded.

They visited the remaining two tattoo studios, The Ink Stop and Inked. The response from both artists was the same as Sid in Tattoo Art; however, the artist in Inked, Robert, told Tom and Lavinia that it appeared to represent the radius when using the mathematical calculation Pi to find the circumference of a circle.

"You know Pi?" Lavinia had asked, bemused.

"A little. My son is currently studying his GCSEs at school and that was the topic of his maths homework," Robert had replied. They had a brief conversation about it.

When they left Inked, Tom smirked at Lavinia, impressed about her mathematical conversation with a tattoo artist.

"What?" Lavinia questioned him.

"You know Pi?" he asked Lavinia's question right back at her.

"Yes, don't you? Pi times radius and all that?"

"Kinda left my school days behind as soon as I left. Didn't want to be taught useless things and funnily enough I have never once needed to use Pi since those days. I was just too eager to join the Police."

"I see. Were you one of those disruptive ones that thought they were cool but were actually arseholes?"

"Now that hurt." He jokingly made a show of placing his hand on his heart as if her words had wounded him. "I wasn't bad at maths or English. Hopeless at science and only really enjoyed PE. So, remind me what Pi is?"

****

CHAPTER 4

Harris made it back to the station and was in the conference room typing up his report when Tom and Lavinia walked in. They had returned before Morgan and Norton.

Tom and Lavinia had stopped by Starbucks on the way back to the car to get coffee to take back to the office.

"Where's my coffee?" Harris asked as his eyes landed on the paper cups held in their hands.

"In the coffee machine," Tom joked as he sat down, opened his laptop and logged on.

Nine minutes later, Morgan and Norton strolled into the conference room. It seemed like they had had a similar idea to Tom and Lavinia as they each had a Costa Coffee in their hand with goodies for the team in a brown paper bag.

With coffee and goodies on the go, the team settled into the meeting.

Wilson started off the meeting with a disappointing start. "So, no matches from Missing Persons."

"No matches for the symbol or the ID either," Morgan offered.

"No one seemed to recognise it or had any knowledge about it. Same with Jane Doe," Norton added.

"There was one artist at Tattooz who told me she might have seen it before but tattoos hundreds of clients a week so she couldn't be certain; but other than that, nothing from my side either," Harris concluded.

"We had the same issue, with the majority of studios we interviewed," Lavinia supplied, putting emphasis on the word majority and added a dramatic pause for Tom to continue.

"So, a Grace Sanderson made an appointment with The Tattoo and Body Piercing Studio on the High Street in the town centre on Wednesday 25th May at 11:30am–" he checked his notes as he went- "to get a mandala styled elephant tattooed on her thigh. She was accompanied by her friend who was called Isla. We don't know any more than that, but she matches the description of our Jane Doe." It was Tom's turn to take a dramatic pause.

"My God," Morgan whispered in disbelief.

"We checked the CCTV, and we believe it is her. We should get that emailed to us within the next day or so. We also have a contact number for Grace Sanderson."

"Great work. Contact her after this meeting and arrange an interview ASAP. She's the only one at the moment that can lead us to a formal ID and her parents or next of kin," Wilson instructed.

"As for the symbol, another artist at Inked thought it could be a reference to Pi," Lavinia added.

"Come again?" Harris asked, brows creased in confusion as the others stared at Lavinia with questioning faces.

"The mathematical calculation to work out the circumference of a circle," Lavinia explained like it was the most obvious thing in the world.

"Ask Grace Sanderson about this symbol when you interview her. Maybe she can confirm and give some insight into our victim and her occupation. Once your reports have been written up and an interview with Grace arranged, I've booked a meal at the pub. First round of drinks on Lavinia for it being her first day."

CHAPTER 5

Tom contacted Grace Sanderson and arranged an interview at noon the following day. He had not divulged any information to her but explained that her name had popped up in an ongoing investigation and they wished to ask her a few questions. Grace explained that she didn't think she would be of much help but agreed anyway.

The reports did not take long to complete and within a couple of hours they were sat at a round table in the pub, nursing the first round of drinks that Lavinia had bought.

"To Lavinia, for making it through the first day," Wilson announced as they toasted and clinked glasses.

"Well done for surviving," Tom whispered as he leant towards Lavinia sat next to him.

"Well, I couldn't have done it without your guidance, so thank you," she replied sincerely.

"I think you would have been just fine." And he had meant it. She was, after all, the daughter of one of the best detectives the squad had ever had.

Wilson had pre-ordered a selection of scampi, cod, and chips with mushy peas for everyone for tea, which arrived two drinks later.

"Right, Lavinia, a little tradition we do with new additions to the team. Have you ever played two truths and a lie?" Harris questioned.

Lavinia had to think of three facts about herself and the others would have to guess which one of those was the lie.

"Who hasn't?" she responded. She thought for a moment before coming up with: "I broke my right ankle when I was younger after landing awkwardly on the trampoline, I accidentally pushed my sister off her bed which broke her collarbone as a result, or I completed a tandem skydive at fifteen thousand feet for my sixteenth birthday."

Wilson knew the answer, so he stayed quiet while the others had a guess. Having a father-son relationship with Alastair and being a constant in his life, their families knew each other very well and often got together for dinners or holidays.

Tom immediately said, "Well you seem an adventurous type, so I'd say skydiving is true."

"I feel you're too nice to push anyone," Morgan added.

"I think breaking your ankle on the trampoline seems a truth, they catch you out," Norton stated, which got approving nods from the others.

"I'm thinking breaking your sister's collarbone is the lie," Harris concluded and looked around the table for support.

"Yeah, we'll go with that one as the lie," Norton agreed.

"For detectives, you're pretty good, but not that good. Wrong," Lavinia laughed, shaking her head and smiled widely in triumph and the others looked defeated.

"So, what was the lie?" Tom asked, confused that they got it so wrong.

"Breaking my ankle. I did have a trampoline, but I only sprained my ankle on it, I've never broken a bone in my body." Lavinia touched her head as if it were made of wood.

"Interesting. That was a good round."

"You did break your sister's collarbone then?" Morgan asked quizzically.

"Accidentally, yes. My mum was doing our nails and because she's the eldest, she got to have them done first, which I didn't think was fair at the time, so I pushed her. I didn't think I pushed her that hard, but she lost balance, fell off the bed and obviously landed awkwardly on the floor."

"Remind me not to get on your bad side," Tom joked.

"How old were you?" Morgan asked, gaining interest in the story.

CHAPTER 5

"I don't know exactly but young. It's certainly not a recent thing," Lavinia answered.

"I can't believe you had us fooled," Tom laughed, taking a gulp from his pint.

"I'm guessing you like playing that game because you usually can pick up on the lie."

"Usually, yes, but not this time," Morgan replied. She was fond of Lavinia; having another woman on the team was nice and it did not take her long to earn respect. Morgan knew that she had a long way to go and needed more experience, but she was in the right place for that and saw the potential. Lavinia had reminded Morgan of herself when she was that age, young, determined and driven.

Once they had devoured the food, they went their separate ways. Tom dropped Lavinia off at her house before making his own way home.

Lavinia saw the living room light lit up orange like a fire behind the curtains and knew Alastair would be waiting up for her. Her suspicions were correct when she entered the house.

"How was your first day?" he asked eagerly, placing his book down on the chair arm as he got up to greet her.

"Good. You didn't have to wait up."

"I know, but I wanted to hear all about your day."

"Isn't that just the same thing as wanting an update of the case?" Lavinia's left eyebrow arched upwards.

"Not really," Alastair whispered and then chuckled.

"We have a potential ID for the victim. She and a friend went to a tattoo parlour in the town centre so we're interviewing her tomorrow afternoon. Other than that, no luck regarding the tattoo symbol."

"So, no tattoo artist that you or anyone else interviewed saw it before or knew the meaning of it?"

"Nope. There was one suggestion that it could represent the circumference of a circle, but that seems a bit too far-fetched."

"I would bet my life savings that it does not represent the radius. Where the hell did he get that from?"

"His son is apparently studying his GCSEs and came home with Pi homework."

"The mind plays tricks on us and sees what it wants us to believe and deceives the eyes. It makes the mind fit whatever people believe or are thinking at that time. For instance, this tattooist obviously forced his mind to fit Pi because that's what he associated the symbol with. What he saw would've been just that."

"Well, that would certainly explain why he thought that."

"I am surprised by the lack of recognition. Would you like a cup of tea?"

"No, thank you, I'm just going to head up." Lavinia made a move to head up the stairs to her bedroom but when it registered what Alastair had just said, she hesitated before saying, "Why are you surprised?"

"Well, it's just that if anyone would recognise the symbol, I thought it would be tattoo artists since they work with various symbols every day, new and old, normal and unusual. I would believe at least one would have come across it during their career. The fact that no one seems to know it surprises me. Unless they are withholding the truth of course." He added the last line as an afterthought.

"You're starting to sound like Tom now." Lavinia was beginning to get annoyed and made her way up the stairs. She disappeared into her bedroom.

"He's a good guy. Very rare to find these days," he shouted after her.

CHAPTER 6

Lavinia arrived at the station early the next morning, travel mug gripped in her hand filled with tea, only to find Wilson working in his office, a cup of coffee on refill, as he studied files and read over reports. And at 7:45am, they were the only two currently in the office.

"You're early," Wilson commented without looking up. He knew exactly who it was. He called it intuition.

"So are you."

"Yes, I have to be; you don't."

"I know, I woke up early and couldn't get back to sleep so I thought I would be more useful here than wasting time twiddling my thumbs at home."

"You are your father's daughter. This is just the start of it all."

Lavinia wasn't sure if he was referring to the lack of sleep and the early morning starts or their first victim. But his statement applied to all.

"So people keep saying."

She settled into her space, getting comfortable on the office chair before logging onto the computer. She went straight to her emails and found a forwarded email from Tom. He had sent it at 03:21am with a note in capitals simply stating, 'MAN IN CAP?'. Attached to the email was a copy of the CCTV footage from Dave at the Tattoo and Body Piercing Studio, and a screenshot of the image of Grace Sanderson and Isla when they walked into the shop. She downloaded both attachments, saved them onto the case folder on her Dropbox and watched the footage once more.

As the video came to life, she recognised the faces of the receptionist, clients and objects in the room from the first time she had watched it in Dave's office. She concentrated harder at looking at the surroundings this time, whereas before, she was looking for a specific person and watched faces come and go. She noticed the parlour got a lot of custom as it always seemed to be busy, but then again, the business offered several services that appealed to a wide range of different people. The receptionist was fluent in her every action which showed she had experience of working there. She knew what she was doing. And handed every customer a piece of paper and a pen to fill in a questionnaire about their health, personal details and what they wanted doing. Lavinia was familiar with the questionnaire as she had filled out a similar one every time she had had her ears pierced. The customers then sat in the waiting room and filled it out before being called shortly afterwards.

She waited until Grace Sanderson and Isla came into view and watched them closely like a hawk stalking its prey. She logged every move and every detail about them. She could tell that Grace was excited to get her tattoo done as she was constantly smiling and laughing with Isla. They were full of life. Reality then hit Lavinia as she would later have to inform Grace of her best friend's death and knew that laughter would not escape her lips any time soon. They, too, had conducted the same routine as many before them, they were not any different, only unbeknown to her, Isla would be murdered several days later.

Lavinia heard Wilson evacuate his office as he made his way over to her desk. "Is this the CCTV footage you requested yesterday from the tattoo studio?" he immediately enquired.

"Yes, I'm just going through it properly. Grace and Isla have entered the studio and are waiting to be called." She pointed them both out in the waiting room. Shortly afterwards, a man with a cap low over his face came into view. She immediately understood what Tom had meant

CHAPTER 6

and realised he must have watched it last night and that is why he had sent it at the time he did. The man in the cap approached reception and Lavinia assumed he asked the receptionist a question as her response was to look at the computer for something. She then nodded and handed him the same form as Grace and Isla only moments before. He went into the waiting room while she used the desk phone. Lavinia switched to the waiting room camera and saw that he had his back to it, but he could clearly see Grace and Isla opposite him. He took his cap off and pretended to be busy filling out the form and momentarily looked up at them both, but they were too busy in conversation to notice. Wilson and Lavinia could only see the back of the man but what they saw wasn't thrilling. He had scruffy sandy blond hair that desperately needed a haircut as it had started to grow too long and out of place. Other than that he looked like every Tom, Dick and Harry, dressed casually in jeans and a t-shirt. Average height and average weight. Then Grace and Isla were called away a minute later and disappeared. The same thing happened to the man in the cap exactly four minutes later.

Under Wilson's instruction, she switched back to the reception camera that had a view of the front door and skipped ahead ten minutes later and then another three until the man with the cap came back into view. This time he had his cap back on, still over his face so they could not see him clearly and saw him pay in cash. He exited the studio, disappearing once more. His face never got captured by the Closed-Circuit Television.

They skipped ahead by half-hour increments until they saw Grace and Isla leave.

"So, this man in the cap is an interesting character. Do you think he could be our killer?" Lavinia thought aloud.

"It's possible he's stalking them before making his move."

"He seems too confident. They were right there in front of him when he took his cap off, but never once looked at the cameras."

"It's also possible he's been there before to check the place out. He would have noted where the cameras were so he could avoid them."

"But how would he know that Grace and Isla would go to that exact place?"

"Seen them there before? Or stalked them long enough to know Grace had an appointment there?"

"We need to know how far in advance she made that appointment and ask the staff if they have seen them there before."

"Hopefully by the time we find that out, the others will be here, and we can have a briefing."

Lavinia was on the phone to the studio's receptionist, Judy, when Tom walked through the door. He gave her a surprised look which quickly turned to confusion as he listened on. She thanked Judy for her help and hung up. She barely had time to replace the phone on the receiver when Tom had a million questions to ask. He was perched on her desk.

"How long have you been here for?" He opted for his first question.

She glanced at her watch. "About an hour and a half."

"I take it you got my email then?"

"Yes, thank you. Noticed you sent it very early this morning."

"3:21 to be precise, wasn't it?" He laughed while Lavinia glared at him.

"It's bad that you can recall the exact time you sent it."

"As Hayleigh would say, sadly bodies have a habit of not sticking to the normal nine-to-five office hours, which means we must work at odd hours of the day and night. Which I'm sure you are fully aware of."

"Only too well. The odd birthday party here or holiday there had to be either cancelled or gone ahead without Alastair."

"It's hard, but that's the reality of working in this job."

CHAPTER 6

"Have you ever missed anything important because of this job?" Lavinia wondered.

"Plenty. The worst was my Nan's 80th birthday which turned out to be her last. She passed away a few days later."

"I'm sorry. Surely, they can make allowances for people who have families and things going on in their private life? Don't you have the choice whether to work or get that time off?"

"You always have the choice but when it's a killer or a violent offender on the loose murdering innocent people, you always feel you have to put the job first. And by doing that I'm protecting my family. Isn't that why people choose to do this job, to protect the public? We can't protect people if we're not here. We all understand the pressure and the commitment of the job when we sign up. If something were to go wrong and we were sunbathing on the beach or partying, who do you think will feel responsible because we didn't do everything possible to protect life? We feel guilty either way and we all make sacrifices. It's something we learn to live with, and I know this team would rather sacrifice a suntan for someone else's life. But I do regret not attending my Nan's birthday, I wasn't to know it was her last and it's a decision I have to live with."

"What happened for you not to go?"

"It was the biggest case of my career and got me to where I am now. I was a police officer involved with a serial killer who raped several fourteen-year-old girls. He posted as a police officer at one of his own crime scenes and murdered one of my colleagues. He nearly killed me, but I managed to get to him first. I got a commendation award for bravery and promoted to Detective." There was a slight resentment and sadness to his voice as he told Lavinia.

"Your Nan would be so proud of what you've achieved and who you've become. That would have been the best birthday present you could have given her. If she's anything like my Nan, she would have wanted you to choose your job instead of a party that she wouldn't have wanted in the first place since, according to her, you don't celebrate your birthday when you get that old, apparently, and age is just a number."

"Well, she drew the line at her sixtieth and said no more parties. Didn't want to be reminded of her age. It was just another day of the year." They chuckled light-heartedly. "So, have you found anything interesting about our man in the cap?" he asked, changing the subject.

"Yes, very interesting things," Lavinia simply replied.

"You're not going to tell me until the briefing, are you?"

"Nope." Lavinia grinned.

"Thought so." He shook his head and snickered as he got up from her desk and went to his own. He only had time to respond to one email when Harris, Norton and Morgan strolled in just before 9am.

By 09:06, the team were sat in the conference room.

Wilson started by giving a brief recount of things they had all discussed previously which led nicely onto what Lavinia had to say.

"I asked Judy, the receptionist at Tattoo and Body Piercing Studio, to look at appointments from the past month to see if the man in the cap had been there before. Turns out he had an appointment on Thursday 19th May for a nipple piercing."

The team understood the relevance of the date. Only six days before Grace went for her tattoo.

"A nipple piercing?" Norton asked astonished, his face looking shocked.

"It's someplace hidden. You wouldn't know about it if you briefly met him so it's not an identifiable feature. He couldn't go into a tattoo and piercing place without having something done," Lavinia clarified.

"And you can easily take out a piercing. Not so easy to cover up a tattoo," Tom added.

"Couldn't he have just queried about getting one done without having to go through with it?" Norton asked, still getting over the shock that the nipple was an area people got pierced.

"He would have needed to see as many rooms as he could to suss out the location of the cameras," Wilson added.

"Did he use the same name for both appointments?" Harris asked.

"Yes, John Smith."

"How creative," Morgan replied sarcastically. She hated when suspicious people used generic fake names.

"And obviously an alias."

"I would have used two different names under two different disguises if that were me," Harris offered.

"I don't think he would have had time to come up with a new disguise," Lavinia stated.

"How do you mean?"

"The receptionist told me Grace Sanderson also had an appointment the same time as the man in the cap, but to get her hair done. Maybe he saw this girl and picked his target there and then and made a split decision to check out the cameras in case he found her back there. He wouldn't want his face to be on CCTV and it's the one place they have in common. He overhears her making another appointment afterwards, but for a tattoo, the one she got recently, so he follows suit and bingo. He would have had to use the same disguise and name as before."

"Either he targeted Grace from the start, or he was searching for a target," Wilson concluded.

"The studio gets plenty of custom from young adults and teenagers, which to him, might have been the perfect place to go looking for someone," Lavinia clarified.

"But it was Grace's friend who was the victim, not Grace herself." The killer's choices did not make sense to Morgan so she couldn't follow his logic.

"I think he went looking for a victim or had someone else in mind at first. He was just scanning the crowd, looking for possibilities, giving himself options. Then he saw Grace and liked what he saw so decided to stalk her a while. Then he saw Isla with Grace at the later appointment and that was it. His mind was made up and she was the one," Lavinia clarified, trying to keep up with the logic herself.

"I agree it is confusing, but if we have any chance of catching this killer, we need to think like him. We need to walk in his shoes, and we need to act like him," Wilson declared.

****

Grace Sanderson worked as an Optometrist, who performed eye and vision tests and had worked at Specsavers in Scunthorpe Town Centre for the past two and a half years.

Tom and Lavinia rarely frequented the town centre, and both had not been as many times in the past year as they had in the past week.

They arrived at Specsavers and announced their arrival to Grace Sanderson's colleague who had greeted them upon entry. She looked to be a similar age to Lavinia and wore a tight black bodycon skirt that stopped just above the knee and showed off her perfectly tanned slim legs, where her black heeled work shoes accentuated how toned her calves were. The embroidered white blouse had the top two buttons undone, showing more skin than was appropriate and was tucked into her skirt. The piercing blue eyes bore into Tom's. Tom held the door open for Lavinia so when he walked in after her, the woman stood to attention and gave him a big bright seductive smile. Her silky-smooth chocolate brown hair was curled at the bottom and hung below her breasts. Lavinia thought she would be more suited to working as something more extravagant than in an Opticians. "Good afternoon, how may I help you?" she spoke directly to Tom in a sweet and soft professional tone, not even registering Lavinia who was stood beside him.

Tom and Lavinia both showed their ID badges to the woman, who looked aghast when she learned they were detectives.

CHAPTER 6

"We have an appointment with Grace Sanderson," Lavinia stated, matching the woman's professional tone and making her presence known.

"She'll be on lunch at one, I suggest you come back then."

"She's expecting us," Tom corrected her.

"Oh, I'll let her know you're here." She strutted off, purposely swaying her hips as she walked for Tom's benefit which did not go unnoticed, but he wasn't complaining. Lavinia shot daggers his way.

"What?" He laughed at her reaction.

Another woman dressed in a short-sleeved dress carrying her Michael Kors handbag came into view, whom they immediately recognised as Grace Sanderson from the CCTV footage. She spotted the detectives waiting for her and gave them a short smile to acknowledge their presence before turning her head back to her colleague. "Thanks, Jess, taking an early lunch but I'll probably be back before the hour."

"See you later," Jess replied before turning her attention back to Tom once more. "It has been a pleasure, Detective Constable Tom Watkins."

"See you around."

"You know where to find me."

Tom, Lavinia and Grace exited Specsavers and turned left to walk down the High Street.

"Seems Jess has taken a shine to you," Lavinia commented once they were out of view and earshot.

"I wouldn't pay any mind to her. She flirts with all the customers, but it gets her a sale. She has the highest number of sales in a day than others do in a week. Our custom has nearly doubled, with new customers coming in every day," Grace explained.

"I can see why," Tom stated. "I might have to start getting my eyes tested," he joked and glanced over to Lavinia to document her reaction and was spotted doing an eye roll before she met Tom's amusing glare.

"You certainly do if you're going to fall for her attention," Grace stated, which received a laugh from Lavinia.

"I see, women sticking together. Ok, ok, well, what if it was the other way around and I was working in Specsavers, you'd have a different reaction then," Tom argued matter-of-factly.

"Don't flatter yourself, Tom," Lavinia said jokingly and laughed, and it was Tom's turn to give Lavinia an offended look. They had only been partners for a short period of time, but they had great banter and chemistry already. He knew, from experience, that you just click with some people, and that's what had happened between Lavinia and himself. It was nice to work with someone new who felt as if she had been a part of the team for a long time.

They located a Costa Coffee restaurant halfway down the High Street and decided to sit in and grab a coffee. Tom stood in the queue to be served while Lavinia and Grace found a table in the corner away from other customers. Lunchtime rush hour had started, and office workers celebrated their hour's freedom by taking a walk to and around the town centre searching for food or someplace to sit that wasn't behind their desk in a stuffy room.

"Tom's only human but it's funny winding him up about that sort of thing." They both smiled at each other.

"I didn't like Jess at first. It always seemed to me that she was selling herself rather than the glasses, but you can't argue with her statistics. I think that's why she's still around, to be perfectly honest. But she is one of my best mates and one of the nicest and funniest down-to-earth people you'll ever meet. So, apart from Jess's unorthodox ways, why do you need to speak with me?"

"I want you to look at a photograph and tell me if you recognise the people in it."

"Ok," Grace agreed sceptically.

Lavinia reached in her handbag and grabbed a light brown Manila folder which she placed on the table in front

CHAPTER 6

of her and opened it up. It was a copy of the CCTV image that showed a clear face of Grace Sanderson and Isla at the reception desk as they entered the studio. They had been frozen in time. She slid it over to Grace, who picked it up and studied the photograph as Tom arrived with a tray of coffees for the table. He had an americano, Lavinia had opted for chai tea latte and Grace had ordered a hazelnut latte.

Grace did not look up but instead answered Lavinia's question. "It's an image of my friend and I when we went to the Tattoo and Body Piercing Studio further down the High Street." She pointed in the general direction of the location of the studio they had recently attended and was confused as to the question posed to her. "I don't get what that has to do with anything. I'm of age and paid for my tattoo. Isla just came with me."

"It's ok, we're not here for anything like that," Lavinia clarified and Grace's tense and worried face relaxed slightly as Lavinia pointed to the image of Isla. "You said this is your friend Isla?"

"Yes, she wanted to come with me but wasn't interested in tattoos. She only has a couple of piercings."

"What's her full name? And how did you two meet?"

"Isla Armstrong. We've been friends since Secondary School. Why are you interested in Isla? What has she done?" Grace's tense and worried face returned.

"I'm so sorry to inform you of this, but we think she was found dead yesterday morning."

"Dead? You think?"

"Yes, we need to formally identify her, but from photographs we are certain it is her. Can you think of anyone who may have wanted to cause her harm or was there anything suspicious that you noted within the past week or so?"

"Cause her harm? She was murdered?"

"I'm afraid it appears so. I'm very sorry, Grace."

"I.. um...I didn't hear from her for a few days, but that's not necessarily suspicious. We don't always talk every day. I just assumed she was extremely busy working. Shit." Grace stared at her coffee and fiddled with a Pandora ring she wore on her left middle finger.

"What did she do for work?"

"She's a nurse on the Disney Ward." It did not go unnoticed that Grace had talked about her in the present tense.

"At Scunthorpe General Hospital?"

"Yes."

"How long had she been working there for?"

"Four, nearly five years."

"Was there anyone she worked with that she was particularly close with? Friends or otherwise?"

"There was a guy she liked; he had been her mentor when she first started."

"Do you know anything about this guy?"

"His name is Harry, he's very attractive, she told me he works out daily, great with kids. All this is what I got from Isla."

"I understand this is a big shock to you, and very hard to comprehend right now. I am extremely sorry for asking you these questions, but you have been really helpful and anything you say may aid in the investigation of finding Isla's killer."

Tears had clouded Grace's eyes and when she blinked a couple had rolled down her cheek. She quickly wiped them away and took a sip of her coffee with a shaky hand. "I want to help. I just don't know what to say."

"It's okay, take your time. Is there anything else you can tell me about Harry?"

"Like what?"

"Do you know how long he had worked at the hospital before Isla?"

"I don't know, a few years possibly, enough to become a mentor."

CHAPTER 6

"Any idea where he might live?"

"I don't know."

"Do you know Isla's parents?"

Her head snapped up at the mention of her friend's parents. Had they been informed? She wondered but her suspicious were soon confirmed. "Have they been told?" she asked quietly. Lavinia noticed Grace was not the same woman they had first met in Specsavers only twenty minutes earlier.

"They haven't, no. We've not long found out about Isla including her surname, but we will need a formal visible identification to confirm it's her."

"Will I have to do that?" Her horrid look intensified at the thought which did not go unnoticed by Lavinia, and she didn't know what to say.

Tom noticed her lack of response and jumped in. "No, we wouldn't ask that of you. We will contact her parents."

"Do you know her home address?" Lavinia asked.

"Yeah, I can write it down."

Tom handed her a pen from the inside of his jacket pocket, and she wrote the address on a napkin, still with shaky hands, before passing both the pen and the napkin to Tom.

"What happens now?"

"With the information you provided us, our priority is to contact her parents and then speak to her colleagues at the hospital. We are conducting an official investigation into her death, and I promise you we will find her killer for your closure and her parents."

"Thank you." It was barely audible, but Tom and Lavinia left soon after. They left Grace still sat down staring into space in disbelief trying to process what had just occurred.

When they left, Lavinia said with a sad voice, "I feel so sorry for her."

Tom stopped walking to face her, and Lavinia looked to him as he spoke. "I could tell. Listen, it doesn't get any easier telling people their loved ones have died, it is the most daunting thing to have to do but it just becomes a part of the job. You handled it really well and I know it's easier said than done, but you must not let it bother you, at least while at work."

"I know."

Tom embraced her for a moment. "Better?" he asked her when he let go.

"Better," she confirmed, and although she smiled and seemed like she had got it together, inside she was crying.

CHAPTER 7

That night at home, Lavinia had shed a couple of tears in front of Alastair. She had felt deflated for the rest of the day and dreaded speaking to Isla's parents after the weekend. It was waiting for Monday to arrive that was the most nerve-wracking.

The only thing working a murder case such as this one, was that keeping track of the days. You work all week without realising, rarely getting a break. But Alastair understood more than anyone the harsh demands of the job with the long working hours and kept a close eye on Lavinia to make sure she didn't fall into the same pattern he had done years previously.

"It was harder than I thought, and her reaction was difficult to watch," Lavinia admitted to him, a sodden tissue clasped in her hand as she unloaded her feelings. They were sat at the table in the kitchen, both nursing a coffee with a decent measure of brandy in it. Hayleigh had been round for tea and left not long before Lavinia couldn't hold it in any longer. It was she that detected Lavinia wasn't feeling herself and needed to talk. Before she left, she had told Alastair to give her the coffee with brandy in it and he had to admit, it was even relaxing himself. Mindi was sat the other side of Lavinia. Her support bubble.

Alastair's phone lit up with a message from Tom. He briefly glanced at it and smiled. "It seems Tom is worried about you. He's asked how you're doing."

"Tell him I'm fine."

"I'll tell him you will be." And that's exactly what he did. "I'm going to tell you the story of a man and his reaction to his first murder investigation. In 1981, the force was very much different to how it is today. At twenty-one years of age, he had been policing the streets for three years and all he got was petty crime, robberies, burglaries and keeping teenage gangs off the streets. When he made detective constable, he was able to attend murder scenes. While the thought appealed to him greatly, it wasn't exactly glamorous. His first case was of a prostitute who had been raped by a gang of seven men and beaten to a pulp beyond recognition. This man's reaction was to throw up in a nearby bush which got him a reputation. It was his one and only time but even now, after his successful career, people still mention it. The victim's friend's reaction is one the man would never forget. They had been on the streets together during their whole career, they were flatmates and great friends who always looked out for each other. And she could not stop crying. The man had to be the one to inform her of her friend's death because he was the one who threw up. At first, he couldn't find the right words to say and nothing he did say seemed to help the young lady who was completely broken. She committed suicide a couple of days later, and there was nothing the man could do to help save her. His words had been empty words as she did not trust the police. They had failed her many times and she believed they would fail her once more. Turns out they did because instead of protecting a life, they took a life."

"The point is," Alastair continued after a brief pause for Lavinia to take it all in, "no one forgets their first murder case, they just learn to deal with it properly and not let it affect them the way it once had. You have a great team behind you and that counts for a lot. And it seems you have a great friend in Tom, who cares very much. If you can get one person like that, you are lucky, but to have a whole team like that, well, it's what gets you through the tough times. Everyone has those hard days, but it's your family and friends that get you through it." He indicated to himself and Mindi as he said that.

CHAPTER 7

Lavinia knew that Alastair had been referring to himself when he talked about the man in his story and she completely understood his words and meaning, and instantly felt much better. She knew she would be able to face the Armstrongs come Monday morning and deal with whatever else came her way because she had an army of loving people who would support her through thick and thin, no matter what.

"Thanks, Dad and Mindi." She drained her cup, placed it on the worktop by the sink and gave him a long hug. He kissed the top of her head. It was times like this she was thankful for her father and her sister, who joined the hug. She was thankful for them both every day and appreciated everything Alastair did for them and their family, but he understood the rollercoaster of emotions one goes through more than anyone and he was able to talk her through it in a way that made her feel much better. She couldn't begin to think what she would do without them.

****

It had turned out that Lavinia did not have to worry about informing the Armstrongs as it was arranged that Monday morning for Tom and Lavinia to speak to Harry Nightingale, Isla Armstrong's mentor at the hospital, instead, while Morgan and Norton spoke to Isla's parents, Susan and Greg.

"Did Wilson know about me being upset yesterday after we spoke to Grace and is that why we're going to the hospital instead of the Armstrong residence?" Lavinia wondered, and asked Tom, once they were in the car on the short ride to the hospital.

"He doesn't know a thing. It was I that offered to speak with Harry. Thought it would be slightly less upsetting informing the boyfriend than the parents."

"It won't be for them, but thank you."

"I'm sure it won't but for you it might be. Have to ease you into this gently," he pointed out.

Scunthorpe General Hospital, situated off Church Lane, was the main hospital for the North Lincolnshire region and a part of the Northern Lincolnshire and Goole NHS Foundation Trust. The decades-old standard red bricked buildings with black roofing, stood tall and wide.

The visitor car parks always filled up quickly, although there were a few empty spaces still available, if lucky, and Tom managed to reverse into a space that had not long been vacated.

Just outside of the Main Entrance, were several patients in gowns and/or wheelchairs smoking who only moved out of the way of the entrance if they needed to. Tom and Lavinia entered through the double automatic doors and turned right. The sign that hung from the ceiling directed them further down the corridor and to the left.

Maire had completed countless bank shifts on the Disney Ward during her career at the hospital. She had loved working on this ward and was admired by all the staff, parents, and children alike.

Rainbows, unicorns, stars, and colourful drawings completed by the children met them as they walked through the door to the ward. Hand sanitisers were placed on the wall inside the door and it was mandatory for anyone entering or leaving the ward.

Reception was straight ahead at the desk, where the woman behind it was talking on the phone.

An attractive male nurse was saying goodbye to a cheery young boy, no older than five years old and his mother who was ecstatic to take him home. The boy had a very cute dimple in his cheek whenever he smiled, and a bandage had been wrapped around his head with a dressing over the left ear. The boy shyly gave the nurse a hug and handed him a thank you card that he had designed himself.

When they disappeared, he displayed the card on the reception desk and turned his attention to Tom and Lavinia. "Hi, is there anything I can do to help?" he said in a polite and soft male voice, noticing the receptionist was still busy on the phone and typing away on the keyboard.

"Yes, we're looking for Harry Nightingale." Tom showed his ID badge. It was standard procedure.

"At your service." He smiled a charming smile as they shook hands with each other and underwent the usual introductions.

"It seems your reputation proceeds you," Lavinia said, referring back to the young boy.

"I try."

"Is there somewhere more private we can talk?"

"Yes, the staff room. Please follow me."

The staff room was a basic room with five plastic chairs placed around a circular table in the centre of the kitchen. A seating area with dark blue cushioned seats were placed around in a living room area format with a small standard TV on the wall. Harry gestured towards the dark blue seats for Tom and Lavinia to take.

Before she could sit down, Lavinia's eyes landed on a shrine board on the wall dedicated to Maire, similar to the one in the Pathology corridor, with team photos and cards written by the staff who had the pleasure of working alongside her. Her heart was overwhelmed by the gratitude of the staff and, for a moment, she was distracted by memories flooding her mind as she scanned over the board.

This did not go unnoticed by Harry. "You're her daughter, aren't you?"

She turned her gaze from the board towards Harry and simply replied, "Yes."

"I figured with the surname, but I didn't want to say anything."

"It's okay. The team have said enough with these heart-warming words."

"It's only the truth."

"Did you work with her?"

"Plenty of times, I learnt so much from her and greatly respected her, as did everyone else. She was a natural with the children, but I guess she had plenty of practice with you and Mindi."

"You know of us?"

"She talked about you two and Alastair all the time. Her love for you all went deeper than anything I have never known."

Lavinia needed to change the subject quickly otherwise she would start crying there and then and wouldn't know when she would be able to stop. She had only been young when her mother died, so memories were few and far between and pieces of a puzzle, but she got the sense that Maire loved her job just as much as the staff loved her. She had been told by two different people just how much she was liked and respected, and wished her mother were here now.

"So, I understand you mentored Isla Armstrong when she first started on this ward four, five years ago?" she asked.

"Probably closer to five years, but yes, I did. How did you find that out?"

"Isla's friend, Grace Sanderson. We spoke to her yesterday and your name cropped up."

"For what purpose?"

"Do you know Grace?"

"I've met her a few times."

"She told us that you and Isla were close. I assume you got to know each other quite well."

"I would say that, yes."

"What was the extent of your relationship?"

"Colleagues, mainly. We would flirt with each other all the time and I believe our feelings towards each other were mutual."

"Did you ever act upon those feelings?"

"I took her out on a date."

"When was this?"

CHAPTER 7

"I'm sorry but when has my private life been any of your business?" The politeness he had shown them earlier had now been replaced with impatience.

"Ever since we found Isla had been murdered, that's when."

"What? No that can't be true," Harry denied.

"When did you go on this date?" Lavinia repeated.

"Um… it was last Friday night, the…the 3rd of June."

Lavinia quickly added up the dates and times in her head.

"That was the night she was last seen. And you were the last person to see her alive."

"And what? You think I kidnapped her and killed the woman I was fond of after our date?"

"I don't know, you tell me."

"I would never do anything like that to her, I could never do anything like that."

"Tell us what happened that night."

"I took her to Miller and Carter Steakhouse, the new one in Bottesford. I picked her up at her home address just after 6pm. We ate and I dropped her back off at home at half ten that very night. She was on the early shift the next morning and did not want a late night."

"Were you working that Sunday morning as well?"

"No, she was covering a shift for Angela."

"Did you try to contact her at all afterwards?"

"Of course I did, but she didn't answer any of my calls or texts."

"And you didn't think that was suspicious?"

"Yes, but I thought she was ignoring me, friend zoned me, that kind of thing, and I didn't want to push her so I left it, and I would have spoken to her on our next shift."

"Did anything happen on the date to make you assume she wouldn't talk to you afterwards?"

"No, we had a great time. I enjoyed every minute with her, and it just all felt so natural."

"When was her next scheduled shift after that Sunday morning?"

"Today."

"Well, she clearly did not show up for work. So, what did you do then?"

"Talked to Angela and when she hadn't heard anything, I was worried."

"Not that worried to report her missing."

Harry hung his head low as if he were ashamed that he did not react to her silence sooner and had only just realised the consequence. "I'm sorry," he whispered with a melancholy look upon his face.

"Where did you go after you dropped Isla off?"

"I went straight home."

"Can anyone verify that?"

"I live on my own, but I promise you I never did anything."

Lavinia could tell he was speaking the truth. He looked distraught and she knew he felt guilty. Not of murder but the fact that he had failed in his duty of care to report her missing. He would carry that guilt for a long time. "Do you know if there was anyone who may have wanted to hurt Isla? An ex-boyfriend for example?"

"I know she was in an abusive relationship with her ex but that ended years ago. She hasn't seen or heard from him since then."

"Do you know his name? How long they were together? What happened?"

"I don't know much, she refused to talk about it and kept saying it was in the past and that's where it should stay. I think they were only together for six months; she got some sort of order against him; he kept breaching it and got arrested a few times. I only got minute details here and there and that's what I've been able to piece together."

"When did their relationship end?"

CHAPTER 7

"Before she came to work here. So, at least five years ago. She did mention a few times that this was a new slate for her and that she wasn't happy where she had worked previously, and the boss caused her a lot of issues. I feel that was just a cover story."

"Is Angela on shift today?"

"She's on shift now."

"Great. Would you be able to bring her to us?"

"Of course." He slowly stood up as if that motion caused him great pain. "I really am sorry I can't help anymore, and no one feels more hurt or guilty about Isla than I do."

"I assure you that you have been great help. Thank you, Harry. Don't beat yourself up about it, if you're not the one who killed her, then you have nothing to worry about."

When he had left, Lavinia perched on the edge on the seat, put her elbows on her knees and rubbed her face in her hands. "Do you think it's her ex that killed her?"

"I really don't know. He's a strong suspect given his history of abuse, but the way this case is going anything could have happened to Isla and it could have been anyone who killed her."

****

The Armstrong residence could quite happily be compared to a small private mansion, with no immediate neighbours residing nearby, acres of land that stretched for miles and held space for a barn with four horses. The gravel driveway had a separate entry and exit route and the house itself loomed grandiose. Stone steps led the way to the front door, where pillars stood either side of the doorway with a majestic lion brass knocker on the door.

Morgan and Norton stared at awe at the sheer size of the place and knew then that they were a wealthy family.

"It seems even death can't escape the rich and wealthy," Morgan stated as they ascended the steps to the front door.

"It would seem so," Norton agreed and he used the brass knocker to bang on the door three times.

A few seconds passed until they were met by an elderly woman who was clearly employed as their maid, and she looked confused at the visitors. "No visitors expected today," she told them in a thick Portuguese accent. Morgan and Norton produced their ID badges and introduced themselves. The maid looked horrified. "I bring you to them." She left the door open wide for them to enter and scuttled off down the hallway, leaving Norton to shut the door behind him.

"My whole house could fit in this hallway," Morgan acknowledged, looking in all directions, taking in her surroundings. A single stairway in the centre of the hallway separated into two, one meandering up the left side and the other climbing on the right side from the landing. A family portrait surrounded by a gold frame hung imposing on the wall, where Morgan recognised Isla as she stood beside her brother and behind her mother.

The maid took them through the kitchen, which was a light and airy room. Marble worktops glistened as the sun's rays wrapped around the room. An island was situated in the centre with two stool chairs placed either side of it and Norton guessed that space was used as the breakfast bar. Every known kitchen gadget and equipment was placed around the room, and Norton noticed the impressive coffee maker and the juice maker that currently stored freshly squeezed orange juice in its container. Pasta of all varieties and rice were stored in glass jars on the worktop, along with a spice rack and a toast machine that also had capacity to make an egg at the same time. A small pantry room was located just off the kitchen and was used for storing food. Norton could only guess what other appliances they had stored in the cupboards.

The patio doors were wide open and were accessible from the kitchen. They followed the maid outside where they saw

CHAPTER 7

a man, whom they assumed was Greg Armstrong, swimming laps in the pool, while a glamourous woman, his wife Susan, was sunbathing on a sun lounger in a swimsuit, reading a book and drinking a cocktail. Her large white brim sunhat covered her hair and shielded her face from the sun.

"Ma'am, sorry to disturb but police here to speak with you."

The woman who had her back to them slowly turned around, swinging her model-like long and tanned legs around so she could view her visitors. Her large brown RayBan sunglasses nearly covered her whole face. She picked up her gin glass that was laid on the table beside her and took a sip.

"Police? To what do I owe this pleasure?" She spoke with a soft, well-rounded voice that enunciated of being well educated. Greg evacuated the pool with urgency, grabbed a towel from his sun lounger and joined his wife.

"What do the police have any business doing here?" He, too, was well spoken but was more abrupt with his words than his wife was.

"I'm sorry to have to inform you, but your daughter, Isla, was found dead yesterday morning."

The Armstrongs were submerged into silence until Susan's gin glass slipped from her fingers and shattered on the ground. It seemed a metaphor for her shattered heart. She collapsed onto the floor and was comforted by Greg, who helped her inside to the kitchen. He grabbed a bar stool for her to sit on and then walked over to the whisky cabinet, grabbed a bottle and two glasses and poured each of them a generous measure. With shaky hands, Susan drained the liquid in one.

"I'm going to have to ask you some difficult questions. When was the last time you saw your daughter?"

"Last Saturday," Greg replied quickly.

"Is it usual not to have contact with her for a few days?"

"What exactly are you insinuating? That we had something to do with her death?" Susan cried.

"Of course not, Mrs Armstrong. We want to find out what happened to Isla just as much as you do. These are routine questions, that's all."

"With our jobs, it's not unusual, no. We all come and go as we work shifts, and sometimes we work extra shifts as well so we're never really 100% sure who is around in the house," Greg explained, who seemed to be holding up much better and stronger than his wife.

"Were you aware that Isla was working an extra shift on Sunday morning?"

"Yes, we were."

"And you didn't see her after her shift that day?"

"No, it was a twelve-hour shift, so she would have left early in the morning, before we woke and then she would have worked her normal shift after that. We were both working Monday when she got back and assumed that she would be catching up on sleep."

"You didn't check up on her?"

"She messages one of us if she needs anything. If we don't hear from her, then she's either working, sleeping or out, but she always tells us where she's going. That's how it's been for years with all of us."

A young man, dressed in sports gear, draped a towel over his shoulder as he entered the kitchen. He had clearly been working out as he was sweaty and had a slight warm post-workout glow to his face.

"This is our son, Jack. Jack, this is the police. I'm sorry I forgot your names."

"That's all right. I'm Kelly Morgan and this is Harry Norton." They shook hands.

"I hope I haven't had any more speeding tickets?" Jack asked the detectives, and Morgan could not tell if he was joking or being serious. He grabbed a drinking glass from the cupboard and poured himself fresh orange juice from the machine.

CHAPTER 7

"I wish it were. It's about your sister, she was found deceased yesterday," Greg informed him, looking down at his own drink clutched in his hand.

"No, that can't be. I only spoke to her on Friday."

"In person?"

"No, I rang her on her break."

"Did she say anything to you that you thought was odd or suspicious?"

"No, we discussed Mother's birthday," Jack said quietly but Susan, once more, had already broken down in tears again realising her beloved daughter would not be there to celebrate her big birthday bash and the family had been torn apart. Nothing would ever be the same again. It would be extremely difficult on every birthday, every Christmas, and every milestone that Isla would have taken but no longer could. How could you fully comprehend the loss of a loved one, especially a child? As expected, Susan was not coping very well. "We were planning a surprise family gathering," Jack admitted.

"Might as well cancel that now," Susan managed to say in between sobs.

Morgan thought they could still go ahead with the plans but use the day as a memorial dedicated to Isla and the celebration to her life, but she did not voice her opinion, not wanting to cause friction between the family any more than they already had. At a time like this, families reacted differently. They had both seen families come together in unison, other families remained the same like nothing had happened as they wanted to get on with their life instead of wasting it grieving, whereas others were forced apart by the heartbreak and strain it brought upon each person. Morgan could see the latter eventually happening to the Armstrongs but prayed it was the former, and that they would put aside any differences and support each other to get through the hard times, that neither of them had ever had to experience before now.

"How aware were you of Isla's dating life?"

"She rarely spoke to me about it. She closed us out for a brief period but then started to open up before she closed the door on us again," Susan said with regret in her voice.

"What was the reason for her shutting you out?"

"A few years ago, she was in a relationship with an older guy she met at college. I made a mistake with him, and Isla and I fell out for a quite some time. Then she got herself in another relationship which turned out not be a healthy one and we helped her through it, that's when she started to open up. She didn't say much about Harry, probably being paranoid that I would make the same mistake all over again."

"Harry?"

"Yes, Harry Nightingale. He mentored her when she first started working at the hospital, but they had started seeing each other briefly."

"The man you say she was in an unhealthy relationship with, what happened?"

"Domestic violence. He beat her, stole from her and controlled her. She didn't have much contact with us throughout that relationship, if you could call it that."

"How did he react when she left?"

"She left when he was at work, so he didn't know until he came home. Isla moved back here, and we got a non-molestation order against him."

"Did you ever hear from him after Isla left him?"

"Of course we did. Afterall, he knew she would be here, but he never saw her. He threatened us and harassed us, but we called the police every time he showed up at the property and they arrested him, mainly for breaching his order."

"Is he still in prison now or has he been released?"

"I want to say he's still in prison, but I don't know. If he's not, we haven't heard from him. If we had, he would be six feet under by now."

****

CHAPTER 7

Tom and Lavinia sat in silence until they heard a light knock on the door. They turned their heads to look at the source of the noise and Lavinia stood up to greet their guest. A tall, slim and tanned woman with hazelnut coloured hair tied up in a bun was stood in the doorway. She had a natural make-up look lightly covering her face and comfortable flat black Hush Puppies footwear.

"You wished to speak with me?" Angela greeted politely.

"Yes, hi Angela, thank you. Please take a seat. I've noticed that your accent isn't local."

"No, it's not, I'm originally from Birmingham."

"What brought you to Scunthorpe?"

"The job. I applied for hundreds of jobs after graduating university, got a handful of interviews and only got one job offer, here in Scunthorpe. It's not the first place that springs to mind for job searching but I knew I would be stupid to turn it down. I guess it could be worse."

"And is this when you met Isla?"

"Yes, she was originally from Hull, but because her parents are medical practitioners here, they moved to be closer to the job."

"What do her parents do?" Lavinia asked, surprised by the revelation.

"Her mother is a paediatrician, and her father is a neurosurgeon."

"I understand you two were close friends?"

"Yes. We've known each other about five years now. Pretty much hit it off straight away but it's hard not to be friends with Isla."

"Did she ever confide in you about a previous abusive relationship?"

"Is that why you wanted to talk to me?"

Lavinia glanced over at Tom who returned her look; a look was all they needed to communicate as she sat down next to Angela.

"Partly," Lavinia admitted. "Isla was found dead Monday morning, and we need to know if there was anyone who might have wanted to hurt her."

"What? Oh my God, no." Her eyes filled with tears, and she did not hold them back. Lavinia got up, grabbed a box of tissues that were on the worktop and when she returned, placed them on the table in front of Angela. She reached over to grab one out of the box, blew her nose and wiped her eyes with shaky hands. "Do you think her ex did this?"

"That's what we're here to find out. It seems no one knew a great deal about their relationship."

"It started out fine, you know the honeymoon period as they call it, and then it got a bit controlling, they fought a lot and then it turned violent."

"Did she tell you this herself?"

"Eventually."

"Was she scared or frightened?"

"It was the unknown that frightened her the most. She wanted to keep her friends and family away from it all in case he came after them. That's Isla all over, caring and selfless, even when it was her who needed us the most."

"But she left him eventually?"

"Yes, I think it was Grace, another close friend of Isla's, who finally convinced her to leave along with her family. She told me that they got an order against him, so he couldn't touch her or her family."

"What's her ex's name?"

"Carl Foster."

"Do you know where we can find him?"

"Last time I knew, it was on the Westcliffe housing estate, but I couldn't care less where is now. It sounds awful but I hope he's on the street with nowhere to go and no one to turn to."

CHAPTER 8

The first kill had made him hungry for more.
The woman currently sat on the chair in the basement would be the one to feed his hunger and since he was rumbling on emptiness, he was eager to perform his killing sooner rather than later.

He must wait.

It heightened the suspense and the pain felt by the victim which was exactly the reaction he was after.

His mouth watered, knowing the sweet taste of victory was upcoming.

But until then, he watched, and he waited.

****

She startled awake, looking around confused.

She took her time searching the room, looking for a sign of recognition that would never come.

Pain soared through her like a knife was cutting into her flesh. She looked down at the source of the pain and her eyes widened in horror. A knife had not only cut into her flesh, but bone too, as her fingers were missing on her left hand. She slowly moved her head over to the other side, but all five fingers were still there on her right hand.

She gave a sigh of relief at the small mercies.

Her head felt heavy and sore, like she was hungover, but she didn't drink that much last night. Did she?

Suddenly, memories came flooding back to her in flashes of images and clips.

She remembered a man, Jack? John? No, Jake, they had met that night, and they got a McDonald's takeaway on the way back to his apartment. She remembered seeing the block of flats he lived in that looked luxurious and upmarket, and then a sudden realisation came to her.

This couldn't be his doing, could it?

Her brain was aching from thinking too hard.

She looked down at the clothes she was wearing and noticed a plain black baggy t-shirt and grey tracksuit bottoms. She did not recognise the clothes and instantly knew they were not hers.

She smelt a weak sweet scent on the neck collar of the t-shirt like whoever had worn these clothes last, had worn perfume.

She felt sick.

Who had these clothes previously belonged to?

Had there been someone else before her? Someone else who was sat in the exact spot she was currently sat in now, on the same chair, wearing the same clothes with the same confusion and fear?

What had happened to her?

She could feel the acidity of bile rising and burning at the back of her throat, and even though she managed to keep it down, it left a queer taste in her mouth.

She only then realised how thirsty she had become, but there was no sign of water, and she tried to keep her mind occupied with good thoughts and memories to help her get through this ordeal.

The clothes she currently wore had replaced her black and red gradient evening gown that she had worn to the Annual International Parker, Prescott, and Skinner Event.

Dwayne Parker, Gordon Prescott, and Marvin Skinner were very successful businessmen and barristers who had set up their own firm thirty-two years ago. They had attended Law School together and always dreamed of owning their own firm one day. That dream became a reality when Parker

CHAPTER 8

had purchased a dilapidated building that was used as a café once upon a time and made it into a two-storey red bricked office that stood out from the other local shops. The renovation made it onto the papers and local news channels. With the increase in clientele, five-star reviews and increasing publicity, they were slowly able to expand their firm. Their annual event took place so colleagues from all the branches, national and international, could meet, and law graduates could complete a job application, and attend the event to network and/or get recruited. It enabled Parker, Prescott, and Skinner to informally interview candidates they were interested in, in a unique and unorthodox way. It had worked for them for the past twelve years and it had become an extremely popular event.

This year was no different.

Madison McKinley was a recent law graduate herself and became a Criminal Law Paralegal with the Parker, Prescott, and Skinner firm in Sheffield. Madison had been recruited via the event a year before where a handful of candidates were selected to undertake a two-week probationary period with the firm and at the end only two were selected. Madison McKinley and her peer Cassie Nolan. They, too, had worked magnificently in a team and soon became colleagues and great friends.

Her mind reminisced back to that night.

A Roman silver limousine had picked up Madison, Cassie and their colleagues, outside the Sheffield office at 17:30 that evening to drive them to the venue. Other colleagues from different departments including Wills and Probate, Conveyancing and Family all clambered in as well. The venue was hosted at the Cutler's Hall in the city centre of Sheffield, a twenty-minute drive away but what better way to arrive than in style.

The limousine sat sixteen people and was magnificent with carpeted flooring, heated leather seating, LED and mood lighting, stereo system, LCD TV and the bar area for drinks and stunning glassware. Prosecco was awaiting them on arrival in crystallised flute glasses, with more Prosecco available in ice buckets.

The city was always extremely busy with traffic especially during rush hour, but it had been even more so with the event taking place and guests arriving at peak times. There was a small car park situated around the back of the building, but spaces had to be reserved beforehand. The train station was located nearby with either a twelve-minute walk or a six-minute bus ride, and hotels had been booked all around the city centre, making it easier for guests to attend and find their way to the venue. A steady stream of people exited taxis or limousines as they dropped them off outside the main entrance.

The Cutler's Hall was a Grade II listed building that had been built in 1832 and with grand architecture, excellent transport links and historic and majestic rooms, it served as a perfect venue for a large event such as this one.

Once the limousine pulled up outside, an official dressed in a smart pristine white and gold suit with white cotton gloves and a red banner displayed diagonally across their body with '*Parker, Prescott and Skinner*' advertised on it, opened the door for guests to exit.

A red carpet had been laid down with more officials standing either side of it, acting as a Guard of Honour as guests slowly made their way to the entrance. The press were constantly snapping away, afraid of missing a single moment. The pictures would make the morning's paper.

Madison McKinley's black and red gradient one shoulder chiffon dress matched her brown and red gradient hairstyle. Her long hair flowed down past her shoulders and was curled at the posterior. The dress flowed down to just above the ground with a beaded crystal waistline decoration. The same decoration adorned the neckline. She finished the outfit with pointed toe faux pearl ankle strap heels.

CHAPTER 8

Cassie Nolan chose a sparkly silver side slit dress. The spaghetti straps criss-crossed over her bare back with a front side slit that opened just above her knee and side pockets. Her outfit was accompanied by silver stilettos.

Together, they walked along the red-carpet side by side, cameras clicking from all directions while reporters talked over one another as they broadcasted the arrival of guests. They climbed a series of stone steps before stepping over the threshold into the entrance where they were met by Security.

There was a small queue of guests waiting to walk under the metal detector or have their bags searched. Madison noticed that Security was thorough with their examinations, but she could not blame them. A year and a half ago, at a massive, televised event in London, similar to this one, Security had been negligent in checking bags properly, which resulted in a suicide bomb exploding inside the building, injuring as many as it killed. Since then, they had upped Security and police cruised in the nearby area. The Cutler's Hall had had a metal detector installed a couple of months after the terrorist attack in London, should they try to move their ideological, religious and political views further north.

It did not take Madison and Cassie long to get through Security and afterwards they were directed to the Main Hall. Stood in the foyer were two more officials, balancing a tray of several flutes filled with champagne by the palm of their hand. Madison and Cassie gladly accepted the offer upon entering.

The Main Hall was the largest function room in the building, holding up to 1,500 guests. Parker, Prescott and Skinner had hired the whole building for the night so if required, more space could be opened up to accommodate guests.

Three magnificently lavish baroque crystal chandeliers hung from the ceiling across the room, like spectral-jewelled corpses of a giant spider. The sun's rays burned through the windows where it collided with the chandelier to emit a radiant sparkle that reflected shadows upon the walls.

The patio doors that led out into the impressive botanical gardens were open, letting in a gentle breeze of the night air. Even though the night was young, the patio was already filled with guests who had gone outside for a smoke or simply for fresh air and a walk around the gardens.

Officials weaved around the guests laden with trays of nibbles ranging from lobster canapés and tomato and basil bruschetta to smoked salmon and cream cheese or prosciutto and caramelised onion chutney crackers. Other choices offered carrot, cucumber and celery sticks in a tall glass with either a cream cheese and chive or a hummus dip at the bottom. Sweet and savoury pastry bites, tartlets and rolls were also available, including dark chocolate and salted caramel bites, mini lemon meringues, macarons and fruit tarts.

The live orchestra had taken their seats on the stage and had begun to play a classical melody, tickling the strings to bring their violin to life and engulf the Hall in an instrumental hug. It was peaceful, soothing and atmospheric.

The hall was a constant buzz of noise as guests chatted to old and new colleagues, friends and other familiar faces or were introduced to new people who had only one thing in common. They worked for Parker, Prescott and Skinner.

Time seemed to go by slowly as Madison and Cassie stayed within their known group, chatting away absentmindedly, drinking champagne and endlessly eating hors d'oeuvres.

When the time came for the welcome speech presented by Parker, Prescott and Skinner themselves, the guests had gathered before the stage, like a crowd gathered to watch The Killers at Glastonbury Festival.

The room automatically turned down the volume level, eagerly awaiting to hear what would be said. Their presence enough to silence a room. A microphone was placed in the

CHAPTER 8

centre of the stage, a few feet in front of the orchestra as Parker stood directly behind it, with Prescott and Skinner on either side of him.

"I would like to start off by saying Good Evening, Ladies and Gentlemen, old and new colleagues and friends, it is our pleasure to host you this evening," Parker began, "and to celebrate not only the company's success over the past year, but your own individual successes. Many have been promoted, recruited and transferred, so congratulations. This firm would not be what it is today or where it is today without any of you. Your hard work, dedication, determination and drive is what makes Parker, Prescott and Skinner the number one law firm of the year, providing excellence in international legal services, for the seventh year running. We have been recognised for our commitment, excellence and communication in providing exceptional client service, this annual event has led us to have excellence in business development by creating an innovative way to secure new business and deliver legal services across the world. It also allows communication and relations between staff from different firms in the UK and around Europe. Finally, access to justice is a fundamental right for all and we can celebrate this outstanding achievement in providing fair and equal access across all of our firms. These achievements are due to the work you do every single day. Thank you, have a great evening and keep it up! Without further ado, I have the pleasure of introducing a very good partner and friend of mine, Gordon Prescott."

There was a chorus of claps and cheers until Prescott was ready to deliver his part of the speech. "How can I top that speech? Welcome, guests and graduates. For our employees, it is time to have one night off work and eat and drink all you can. For graduates, tonight is the night that is all about you. Your time to show us who you really are. Your knowledge, experience and expertise all play a key role in ensuring a place at one of our firms. Why are you different to other candidates that are here this evening? What skills can you bring to the company that we haven't already got? But the key question is why you? Why should we hire you and not the person standing next to you? You have made it through four tough years of non-stop hard work, and you should be proud of your achievements. Make tonight count. Thank you."

Another chorus of applause and then it was over to Skinner to wrap it up and whose speech was even shorter than the previous two. "Parker and Prescott have pretty much expressed all that needs to be said, so I will make my speech as short as Parker. One final thing I would like to mention is that we have recently opened a new firm down under in Melbourne, Australia thanks to Jake Wright, who is our Special Guest this evening and is the manager of that firm. It is people like him that we are grateful for and look forward to what this next year holds for everyone."

A final cheer and round of applause filled the hall before they disappeared from the stage to socialise with their guests, and the orchestra danced into life once more.

"Well, that speech lasted so long that I finished my drink," Cassie said in a sarcastic tone to Madison as she looked down at her empty glass. They both laughed.

"The bar?" Madison asked.

"You read my mind." They walked off in the direction of the bar that had become crowded since the speech ended. It seemed that other people had the same idea as they patiently waited in line to be served.

Madison noticed a tall, dark and handsome young man with black cropped hair, matching eyebrows and an attractive masculine face stood nearby, and as she looked his way, he caught her eye and she swiftly turned away. His suit hugged his biceps so she could tell that he was physically fit, and he wore a Rolex watch on his right wrist. He took one more look at the queue of people waiting for the bar in front of

CHAPTER 8

him and instead of waiting, he slowly made his way towards Madison and Cassie.

"Excuse me, can I buy you two fine young ladies a drink?" he asked politely in a husky voice that was deep, hoarse and attractive. When he smiled, he showed a row of perfectly aligned white teeth. Looking at his expensive suit and designer watch, Madison guessed he was either a very rich student or a very wealthy barrister.

"Does that compliment actually ever work?" Madison challenged.

"I don't know, you tell me."

"If you can get through any time soon, sure, a drink would be great, and I'll let you know." Madison indicated the crowd of people before her.

He accepted the challenge and barged his way through, much to the annoyance of the others. Although they didn't seem to mind too much and let him past with ease. If that had been Madison or Cassie, the men would only let them past after they had a fumble of whatever they could put their hands on. He came back a short while later, with three drinks in his hands.

Madison smiled, impressed at his work. "Nice one. Thank you."

"Two Gin and Tonics for the ladies and one pint of lager for the men," he simply stated.

"How did you get past everyone so easy?"

"Simple really, I know the barman."

"Ah, that'll get you anywhere."

"So, I have not had the pleasure of being blessed with your names. Let me introduce myself, I am Jake Higgins."

"I'm Madison and this is Cassie." They all firmly shook hands as they exchanged further pleasantries. Jake's hand was surprisingly warm and soft so she held onto it longer than she should have done but he didn't seem to mind.

"Graduates or employees?"

"Employees," Cassie answered this time. "We got recruited at this event a year ago."

"Wow, impressive. Happy one year Anniversary. And you two work for the same firm?"

"Yes, not far from here actually, but we both started at the same time. What about you?" Cassie had started to get more involved in the conversation, but she knew Madison had taken a liking to him and vice versa. She was just trying to keep the conversation going so they had plenty to talk about.

"Graduate."

They continued to talk most of the night, and they found out that Jake took a break from education after he graduated two years ago but thought he should seriously start thinking about his career choices, hence why he was there that night.

"I think all students dream of working for Parker, Prescott and Skinner after they graduate. They're a noteworthy firm and looks remarkable on your CV if you work for people so established in the legal system. It's the highlight of your career with endless possibilities afterwards," Jake told them, not praising the firm enough but sounding like he was being interviewed by those very people.

A few drinks later, Jake and Madison were dancing on the dancefloor, along with several other guests. Cassie watched from afar, talking with her other colleagues, not really listening much to what they said as she kept a close eye on Madison all night.

In her peripheral vision, she noticed Madison approaching her, alone.

"I'm leaving with Jake if you want to come along, we're going to Maccies," she beamed at the thought of greasy fast food.

"You've not long ate."

"Fancy canapes and nibbles, nothing substantial for the amount of alcohol I have consumed this evening..." Madison had started to slur her words.

CHAPTER 8

"Okay. I'll stay, call me when you can. Stay safe."

"Yes, Mom. I'll call you later." She teased and saluted before hugging Cassie and giving her a kiss on the cheek. Jake came back from the men's room and made his way over to them.

"Nice to meet you, Jake. Take care of her."

He smiled and nodded as they made their way to the exit. Cassie couldn't help but think she should have gone with them, but she did not want to intrude. Madison could look after herself, she knew that, but not as well when she was borderline drunk. They had only met Jake that night and even though he seemed a gentleman and great company, it did not stop her from worrying so much.

As they left the premises, Jake used Google Maps on his phone to locate the nearest McDonald's, which only happened to be a two-minute walk away via Church Street and High Street. They turned right and walked straight until they arrived at the recognisable luminous yellow sign, which shone bright like a star in the sky against the dark night.

They ordered food at the till, taking it away with them to Jake's flat, as they ordered an Uber to St Paul's City Apartments, a ten-minute drive away. The apartment was located in the tallest building in Sheffield, offering luxury flats with great links to the city centre. The train station was five minutes away with access to a great number of local restaurants, the Sheffield Museum and Gallery, theatres and a cinema. All flats were fully equipped with kitchen equipment and utensils, a Nespresso coffee machine and capsules, toiletries, weekly housekeeping and all bills included. All residents had access to the complimentary gym, swimming pool and spa.

Uber stopped outside the front door, and as Jake bid farewell to the driver, Madison admired the beauty of the apartment exterior. It loomed out of the ground like a giant beanstalk, and the glass darkened with the night as residents temporarily shut out the world until morning. The front door opened via a key card, and they silently took the lift to the fourth floor, where Jake lived.

The doors opened to reveal a long-carpeted corridor with ceiling lights to guide them. Light brown oak doors were placed on either side, and it reminded Madison of a Hilton Hotel and she realised she would not like to live in a place like this, no matter how lavish it was. It would not feel like a home but temporary accommodation.

They walked down the corridor and took a left turn until they reached door number 426.

Jake once again used the key card to gain access to his room, which was in pitch black when he opened it up for Madison to go inside.

Jake followed and closed the door behind him.

CHAPTER 9

Both Tom and Lavinia had switched their mobile phones to silent during their visit to the hospital since they weren't allowed to answer them inside the premises anyway.

So, when they left the hospital, Lavinia checked her phone, only to find seven missed calls from Wilson, three missed calls from Morgan and a missed call from Harris, along with voicemails from each of them and several text messages, where the one from Wilson screamed, 'CALL ME NOW, IT'S URGENT' in block capitals.

"Shit, Wilson was trying to get hold of us, along with Morgan and Harris," Lavinia informed Tom, with a worrying tone. She wondered what had occurred to make it so urgent, but she knew it was never good news. Tom took his phone out of his pocket and the same thing happened on his mobile phone with the missed calls, voicemails and urgent messages.

"What's happening?"

"I don't know, but whatever it is, it's clearly urgent. I'm going to call Wilson back now." She dialled his number as they made their way back to the car and he picked it up before the second ring.

"We've got another body." There was no greeting from Wilson, no questions as to why neither of them had answered their phones, he just got straight to the point. Tom read Lavinia's shocked look and instantly knew what was wrong. He gave her the details before hanging up. Tom was stood by the driver's door and opened it but hesitated before getting in as he peered over the car roof waiting for Lavinia to unload the details.

"A body has been found on Scotton Beck. I know it well."

****

Even if Lavinia had not known the area where the body was located, it would not have been hard to find, with two police cars flashing blue, police tape cordoning off several nearby areas, prohibiting public access and the festival of cars parked nearby.

Tom drove through Scotter, entered Scotton Village and parked up behind Hayleigh's silver Nissan Qashqai, after showing the officer guarding the cordon their credentials.

The road leading into Scotton had been completely blocked off, only allowing authorised access for Scenes of Crime in their Forensic Investigation vans, police, detectives, mortuary staff to transport the body and the forensic pathologist. Diversion signs were temporarily put in place.

Tom and Lavinia headed towards the scene, where they were informed by the officer stood by the outer cordon, that the body was a short walk away, around the corner and by a clearing. Lavinia knew exactly where he meant.

They passed a small farm with a couple of brown and black horses eating grass and Lavinia wondered if they had been privy to the events of last night. Did they see the body being moved? Did they see the killer? If only horses could talk, they would make excellent witnesses, Lavinia voiced in her head. They rounded the corner, where they had drawn near to the inner cordon. Yellow crime scene tape was tied to two trees on either side of the path, and they ducked underneath it.

When Wilson spotted them, he strode over to meet them. "About time, I've been being trying to reach you both all morning. At least you're here now. I wanted you both to see the body in situ and the crime scene before too much

CHAPTER 9

disturbance. The SOCOs are already underway, and Hayleigh is currently looking at the body. You better follow me."

In silence, they all made their way over to the commotion, where the rest of the team were stood looking down at the body propped up against the tree. SOCOs were looking around the area, searching for any disposed evidence, Hayleigh was crouched beside the body taking in all minutiae detail she could at the scene, while Marcus Carver documented everything on camera.

All eyes were on Wilson as he returned with Tom and Lavinia in tow.

"Bonnie and Clyde have finally joined," Morgan joked, referring to the famous American criminal couple who, during the Great Depression, committed numerous murders and several burglaries and robberies of gas stations and grocery stores. They were shot to death by police officers in an ambush in Louisiana, where more than 100 bullets were fired at their stolen Ford v8 car. What is now known as their "death car" is on display at a casino in Nevada.

"Now, we have a young woman, in her early to mid-twenties, propped up against the tree as you can see. Same MO as our previous victim, she has no fingers or toes, her left eye has been carved out and her left ear has been chopped off, time since death is also the same, approximately eight hours with rigor mortis fully set. I'm sure Hayleigh can tell you the science but what is interesting, is the neck tattoo." He hesitated, capturing Tom and Lavinia's reaction.

"There's another one? Is it the same?" Lavinia asked with excitement.

"It's not the same but take a closer look." He indicated towards the body.

As they moved closer, Lavinia took in her features – she was tall and slim, with long brown to red ombre hair that reached just above her waist and was curled at the ends. She looked pretty and it showed that she took good care of herself. Her mascara had run, leaving black trails down her cheeks and her silver and grey blended eyeshadow glowed in the light. Had she got dressed up to meet her killer?

The victim's hands were covered with a brown paper evidence bag and tied at the wrist to preserve any possible evidence, such as skin or fibres at the incision points.

Hayleigh moved her hair out of the way as her head slumped forward, but delicately held her head in her hands as Tom and Lavinia took a long look at the tattoo.

It had been as inadequately done as the first one, but that's where the similarities ended. This one was completely different, which only added to the confusion. The outer circle was still there, but this time, there was a triangle at the bottom, with a circle on top of the point and with lines attached from the inside of the outer circle to the centre.

"Is it worth asking what it means?" Lavinia asked Hayleigh after a few moments of silence as they took in the scene.

"It's always worth asking, but I'm afraid I can't tell you the answer."

"I'm assuming this will mean something different to the first one?" Tom asked this time.

"Same killer, same MO, but yes, I believe the tattoo means something different."

"Great."

Wilson walked up to them and asked if they knew where the track concluded at the other end.

"It brings you out onto Scotter Common on Gainsborough Road," Lavinia stated. They didn't know if their killer or the victim, or even both, had entered the woods from Scotton or via Gainsborough Road.

"But Gainsborough Road is a busy main road but then you have residents surrounding the entrance in Scotton. Neither seems like a route I would take to dispose of a body or to kill," Tom added with valid points.

"Wouldn't be busy very late at night or very early in the morning, perhaps somewhere between 1.30am and 6am. This is the period that we assumed the killer disposed of the bodies

CHAPTER 9

which correlates with the time since death. Who found the body?"

"An elderly couple walking their dog. We interviewed them briefly, but an officer took them back to their house."

"Local then?"

"Very, they live up Crapple Lane, which is just across the road. They're always up and out early in the morning and usually walk this route."

"And unfortunately for them, they stumble across a body."

"Did they say anything of interest?"

"The usual, did not hear or see anything et cetera, but we'll discuss it more at the office. For now, we'll let everyone finish up here and hopefully they will have some evidence for us."

They left the mortuary supervisors to transport the body back to the morgue and for the SOCOs to finish searching and gathering evidence and followed Wilson back onto the road, where he gathered and faced his team. "Police have helped conduct house-to-house enquiries in the nearby area. We won't know what's been said until they get the reports back to us, or they call with urgent news, but I want Tom and Lavinia to speak to the residents living next to the woods and Morgan and Harris to speak to those directly opposite to see if we can get anything now. I will drive back to the office with Norton and get prepared for today's briefing now that we have another body to contend with."

Wilson and Norton swiftly left, leaving the others to get on with their designated jobs.

Tom and Lavinia started at the bungalow, situated next to the Beck. If they were to get any intelligence, they suspected it would most likely be the resident immediately next to the crime scene, and that was a good place as any to start.

The small square front garden was neatly trimmed, with various flowers flourishing in the summer heat. The stone driveway led them to the front door where two hanging baskets, in full bloom, were placed on either side of the door and an elderly woman in her early 80s was already stood in the hallway, door open to peer at the commotion outside her home.

Her short light grey hair had recently been permed, and she wore a blue and yellow floral vintage dress with sandals. A gold necklace with a matching gold cross pendant hung around her neck, and her gold wedding band and a silver engagement ring with black spinel fitted snugly around her arthritic finger.

As she spotted Tom and Lavinia heading down the driveway to meet her, her interest piqued up as she spoke first: "Hello dears, what can I do for you?" Her smile greeted them like they were her grandchildren who had come to visit for the day.

"We would like to ask you a few questions, if we may? It shouldn't take long."

"I spoke to a police officer earlier."

"They were conducting routine house-to-house enquiries, that's all. For us, it's the real detective work."

The elderly woman grinned at Lavinia's comment, as if she agreed the real detective work was more exciting.

"Of course, dears. I've just made a pot of tea for my husband and I. We would love you to join us."

"That's not necessary but thank you."

"And freshly homemade Victoria Sponge cake."

"You got us there. We would love to join you both. Thank you for the invitation," Lavinia gladly accepted.

The elderly woman scuttled off to the kitchen to prepare tea and cake for their guests, while she left the door open for them to come in. She shouted through from the kitchen to take a seat in the living room. Tom obeyed; however, Lavinia walked to the kitchen to offer help. The kitchen was small but big enough for the two of them. The worktop space was filled with a slow cooker, a book stand, with a cookbook currently open on a recipe, a bread bin, a bread maker and a fruit bowl,

CHAPTER 9

along with the usual kitchen appliances. A calendar hung up on the wall, showing a scenic picture somewhere in the UK Countryside, and was filled with various appointments and scheduled visits. A tea towel hung over the radiator and an apron on the back of the door that belonged to the elderly woman. Lavinia guessed this kitchen was constantly filled with the smell and sound of home cooking and she felt a sense of comfort.

"No help needed, dear." The vintage teapot and matching bone china teacups, side plates and saucers were stunning, delicate and intricate. It was a Royal Doulton Paisley pattern with pale green flowers and peach centres with a gold trim.

"I do apologise, but I never introduced myself. I'm Lavinia, and my partner is Tom," Lavinia said politely.

"Ethel. It's great to see the younger generation committing themselves to such jobs rather than expecting us to hand them everything on a plate," she said with conviction, as she stirred the tea before replacing the lid back on the teapot. She then sliced four equal servings of cake and placed them onto a side plate.

"I'm only actually working with the team for the summer on work experience before going back to university in September."

"Oh. That is a shame, dear, it seemed like you were one of them."

"Only temporarily."

"That's disappointing. I would stick around if I got to work with that handsome partner of yours. What is next for you?"

Lavinia laughed and enjoyed Ethel's sense of humour. "Still got two more years of university before I graduate and then I don't really know."

"There's still time to figure out what you want to do, dear. There are so many working years in one's life, it's hard to know exactly at a young age. At this rate, you'll be dying on the job if they keep moving retirement age. But for us, our life was set out before we were born. I wouldn't change it for the world, but just make the right choices and follow your heart."

"Inspiring words, Ethel. Truly."

"Could you help me carry the cake into the living room, dear?"

"I'll get the tray; you get the cake. How does that sound?"

"Like a plan."

Lavinia followed Ethel into the living room that was old fashioned but would have been very trendy and stylish back in the day. Ethel's husband, John, was sat in his armchair, exchanging conversation with Tom, who took his place on the two-seater sofa.

Ethel introduced Lavinia to John as she poured the tea and Lavinia handed him a plate with the cake on it. He gladly accepted with graciousness.

"John's been informing me of his days on the farm," Tom informed Lavinia and Ethel, as they sat down. Ethel on the armchair opposite John and Lavinia beside Tom.

"Long and tiring days they were," Ethel reminisced.

"Is that where the two of you met?" Lavinia asked, intrigued.

"John's grandfather had originally owned the land, and when he died, it was passed down to John's father. That's where he met his wife some years later. John grew up there, worked on the farm and eventually took it over when his parents were too old to look after it properly. History seemed to repeat itself as that's where John and I met and married a year later."

"That's a beautiful story," Lavinia responded.

"What's happened to the farm now?" Tom asked.

"It's still used as a farm, our kids have long grown up, started their own families and made their own life. When we got to a certain age, we had to sell because there was no one else to take over it. All the workers were family, some friends

CHAPTER 9

who have since moved on themselves and other employees stayed on under the new management," John explained.

"And I've heard that history has since repeated itself on that farm. One of the farmers who stayed was only a young chap and the new owners had a daughter of a similar age. They are now engaged. How charming," Ethel said with great delight.

"Who knew that such a farm could be a match maker," Lavinia laughed.

"It certainly has its reputation," John stated.

"Now what was it you wanted to ask us, dears?" Ethel took a fork to the cake, but it did not reach her mouth as she intensely listened to Lavinia instead.

"Obviously you've heard about the body found in the woods this morning, just behind your property. We just wondered if you saw or heard anything suspicious before you went to bed?"

"I wish we had, then maybe we could help you more. But I'm afraid not."

"Did you see anyone last night hanging around, looking suspicious?"

"Not a soul."

"What time did you both go to bed?"

"It would have been just after ten-thirty. We watched the evening news as we had missed it during the day then we headed up."

"And did you go straight to sleep?"

"John finished the crossword in yesterday's newspaper, and I read for a little while. Must've been close to half-eleven."

"I'm sorry to keep asking about your sleeping habits, but did either of you get up during the night for whatever reason?"

"I slept through until 5.45," John replied.

"I got up a couple of times to use the bathroom."

"What times were these?"

"I have no idea, possibly about two-thirty and the other about five."

"Did you hear or see anything or anyone about at the time you woke up?"

"I did notice a light somewhere in the distance, it kept moving like someone was out there walking with a torch, but it could have been anything. Next door checking on the horses as they do get a bit restless at times, it could have even been a sensor light that comes on at the stables, from a horse passing by, or one of the owners, or a streetlight. Didn't think much of it at the time."

"What time was this?"

"Around two-thirty. It was the first time I got up and I looked out of the window."

"Did you look out of the window because you saw the light?"

"No, dear, I just wanted to look out into the night. Call it being nosey if you will."

Tom and Lavinia looked at each other, both thinking the same thing. Unbeknown to Ethel, the light in the distance could have belonged to the killer as he was disposing of the victim. It would have been too dark to walk through the woods without some form of light. They did not mention their thought to Ethel and John.

They chatted some more, with further questions about the investigation that did not prove to be any more useful but mainly focused on Ethel and John's time at the farm, while they finished their tea and cake, before leaving the premises.

"It was lovely to meet you both, thank you for the tea and cake, both were wonderful. Take care," Lavinia politely said on her way out.

"It was great to hear your story of the farm. Thank you for sharing," Tom added.

"My pleasure, dear. It was lovely to meet you both too. You are welcome anytime; I'm making Cannoli next week,"

CHAPTER 9

she hinted and gave them one last smile before she closed the door.

The family next door consisted of a middle-aged couple with their teenage daughter, who the horses belonged to. They were usually up early to feed and groom them, but never heard or saw anyone around late at night or early in the morning. The horses did not need attending to during the night, so the light Ethel saw around 2.30am had not been from this family. And they could not see the wooded area where the body was found from the stables.

Morgan and Harris went to the large white house across the road, with a direct view over the woods on the second floor. The house was surrounded by a matching white fence, with a garden that grew apple and pear trees and had been freshly mowed as the lines were still visible. A *'Beware of the Dog'* sign was in the window of the porch, and the subject of that sign greeted them with deep, echoing barks as they approached the house. The Rottweiler was off the lead to roam about the garden and guard the house, and the dog continued barking, which made the owner come out and see what was occurring.

"Dave, be quiet!" shouted the owner from the porch, and looked surprised at the visitors, who had now entered the Rottweiler's territory. "He's loud and barks at anyone passing by but he's friendly." When his owner stroked him, the dog quieted, realising that the intruders weren't threatening and went about his business, sniffing the grass and marking his territory, as if he hadn't already done that.

Morgan introduced herself and her partner, Harris, and in return, the owner identified himself as Noel, and his wife, Sophy, who was inside making dinner for later.

They entered his home and went straight into the kitchen where the offer of refreshments was proffered.

"Smells lovely," Harris commented as the aromas filled the kitchen and he took a seat at the table. The kitchen was large and characteristic, with features seen in country cottages. Nothing like Harris was expecting from the outside, as he thought of modern décor but instead got a characteristic property.

"Homemade prawn jambalaya soup," Sophy informed the detectives, as she greeted them. "Is this about the body found in the woods over there?" She nodded her head in the general direction.

Jambalaya is a popular West African, French and Spanish dish consisting of meat, usually sausage, and vegetables mixed with rice. Sophy's soup used juicy prawns, colourful peppers, hot chillies, meaty sausages, fragrant garlic and ginger, smoky paprika powder, chicken stock, home grown ripe tomatoes with aromatic spices, fresh parsley, thyme, bay leaf, and cooked long grain rice.

"I'm afraid it is. I understand you already spoke to a police officer, but we would like to ask you a few more questions, if you don't mind," Morgan said.

"Not at all. I'm just making pitta breads to go with the soup, but they need proving so I will be with you soon," Sophy said; averting her attention back to the dough she kneaded with the palm of her hand. She put the dough in a mixing bowl, covered the top with clingfilm and placed it into a drawer under the warm oven.

She then joined her husband and the detectives at the table, sipping English Breakfast tea.

"Do you have a view over the woods from the front upstairs window?"

"Yes, that's the master bedroom. We can see the edge of the trail, until it's completely hidden by trees about halfway up, and then obviously the field next to it and partially the track across the road."

"So, if I was to walk into the woods from this end, you would only be able to see me until I disappeared around the corner and then again on the straight track until I was sheltered by trees?"

"Yes, that's correct."

"Have you seen anyone recently walking the track?"

CHAPTER 9

"Plenty of people opt to walk the circular route, we do it often with Dave, so it's not unusual to see people."

"Has there been anyone else who might have had access to your room other than the two of you?"

"No, only us. No one else goes into the room apart from us, and we don't have children."

"No one recently, or in the past?" Morgan encouraged.

"It doesn't have to be friends or relatives. Could be workmen?" Harris pushed trying to get them to think out of the box instead of laterally.

"There was a plumber who came to fix the radiators in our room and the adjoining bathroom, but that's it."

"When did this plumber come to your house?"

"I've got it written on the calendar. Hang on." Sophy got up from the chair and went over to the wall by the kitchen door. She looked at the current month and found the entry she was searching for. "Tenth of June, ten-thirty am."

"What was the company name, can you remember?"

"It was just a plumbing and heating services company."

"No name or initials attached to it?"

"MD, I believe, could be wrong."

"Do you know the name of the plumber?"

"Matt or Mike, something like that."

"Do you usually use this company for plumbing and heating issues?"

"No, we don't get many issues, so we tend to just use different ones. Whoever we can get hold of first or turns up to do the job."

They asked a few more questions before getting up from the table to leave. Sophy had gone back to her pitta breads, removing them from the oven and rolling out the dough to cut into large circles and fry.

"Is jambalaya soup easy to make?" Harris asked, going back to the soup, not having a clue what it was or how to make it but could not get over how aromatic it was. He paused in the kitchen doorway.

"Very. Just cook the onions, garlic, and chillies in a pan. Add the spices and herbs, the stock and the tomatoes. Fry the sausages and add them, with the prawns and peppers. Finally, add the cooked rice and season. Viola!"

"I'm going to have to remember that one."

They reconvened back on the road, near their cars. By now, most people had departed, leaving three other police cars and a police van in place.

"Anything?" Morgan asked Tom and Lavinia as they approached.

"Only that an elderly woman in the property nearest the crime scene saw a light in the distance about two-thirty this morning, but apart from that, nothing. They were all in bed at the specified time, so they heard and saw nothing. I guess that would be the same for most people around here."

"You think that light belonged to the killer?"

"It's certainly a possibility, we can't be certain, but it does fit with the pattern of time since death and the time frame he disposes the bodies," Lavinia concluded.

". What about you?" Tom added.

"The couple living in the white house opposite the wooded area can see some of the track from their bedroom window and they see many people walking up and down the path with their dogs and families every day, so it might be that the killer came this way to check out the area before he decided to dump the body here," Morgan offered.

"There's something else. At the beginning of the month, they called for a plumber to fix their radiators from a company they believe is called MD Plumbing and Heating Services. We will have to check that out and make sure it's legitimate, but he had access to the room and the window that overlooks the woods." Harris was getting excited at the potential lead.

"Possibly to work out the route he would take on the night and if there were any risks like the public living in the immediate area seeing him. We think that's his thing,

CHAPTER 9

surveying the area and possibly even the victims beforehand," Tom guessed.

"Exactly, he did that at the tattoo studio and now this. Maybe they entered the other side from Gainsborough Road, the killer drove there and parked up. The route is more hidden with no chance of the residents in Scotton seeing them as he doesn't come into view. It's all woods and track leading up to the area we found the body."

"And there's nothing en-route?"

"There is a nursing home but even that's hidden and off a beaten track," Lavinia provided.

"I'm thinking maybe he used a headtorch? Doubt he would've managed to carry a handheld torch as well as dead weight. Pardon the pun."

"How would you transport a dead body all that way? Did he carry or drag her? Or was it by some other means?"

"I'm going to walk this route from Gainsborough Road. It's a long shot but we may find something, footwear marks, drag marks, tread or tyre marks, anything, that will hopefully give an indication as to how he transported the body, or any other evidence. I think it's worth a shot and I want to walk the route that the killer possibly took," Lavinia told the rest of them.

They agreed that Tom would accompany her in case there was evidence to be found, while Morgan and Harris headed back to the station to update the others.

Harris dropped them off at the other entrance and when they started the walk into Laughton Woods from Gainsborough Road, Tom asked, intrigued, "So, how is it you know this area well? Or is that an obvious answer since it's literally around the corner from where you live?"

"I come here to pick elderberries to make elderflower cordial, and rosehips and hawthorns to make gin and jam with Alastair and Mindi every year, usually to give away as Christmas presents. Sometimes we just come this way to walk the dog."

"Sounds very exotic."

"It was actually Maire who started wild picking and her idea to make cordial, gin and jam with them, but it's still a tradition we do now."

"I've occasionally picked blackberries but never elderberries, rosehips and hawthorns."

"I used to do that with my Nan and Gramps."

"Great pastimes."

They continued to follow the path through the woods, slow and steady, constantly looking around, where Lavinia was able to show Tom the elderberries, rosehips and hawthorns in situ. Rosehip and hawthorn berries looked very similar in appearance and colour, both being a vibrant red small berry; however, hawthorns were slightly smaller and rounder than rosehips. They came across a field of horses on their right, where one striking dapple-grey horse trotted over to the fence and peered over it, gazing at Tom and Lavinia as they approached. Lavinia went up to it and stroked it.

"Hello you," she said to the horse, in a slightly high-pitched voice, like you want to speak to a dog.

"Seems like you have an admirer," Lavinia heard Tom say, who stood watching them with humour on the track.

"He's beautiful and adorable." She had one hand under the horse's chin while the other hand stroked his face. Unbeknown to her, Tom had taken a picture of the scene in front of him. The sun shone high and bright in the sky, rays seeping through the gaps in the trees, illuminating both Lavinia and the horse. Lavinia was smiling with content, and for a second, both of them forgot the reason why they were there in the first place, until Lavinia had finished stroking the horse, who watched them go and then trotted back.

They continued walking, making small talk on their route.

That was until Lavinia had spotted something in the soil. She halted and bent lower to take a closer look at it.

"Tom, I think we have a footwear mark."

CHAPTER 9

Tom crouched lower to meet Lavinia's height and studied the area she indicated. "Yep, that's definitely a mark all right."

Lavinia took several photographs of it, experimenting with filters and flash, trying to fill the frame and get as maximum detail as possible for Clive at the lab to analyse. Tom even used the torch on his phone to shine light at different oblique angles to expose the sole pattern. They could not take casts of the footwear mark in question because they did not have any equipment on them, other than a camera and a few evidence bags.

"No one else has been down this way since us now. The witnesses came Scotton Beck end and never made it further than the body so it can't be them and unless somebody has been this way between midnight and about five minutes ago but even then, both entrances are blocked off. This has got to have come from the killer," Tom thought aloud.

"That's exactly what I was thinking."

CHAPTER 10

Cassie Nolan was on her usual commute to work. She took the 07:08 train from Scunthorpe Station direct to Sheffield, taking just over one hour. At the other end, there was a ten-minute walk to the office, but on a pleasant day like today, she did not mind.

Madison and Cassie usually took the train together, since they both lived in Scunthorpe and worked at the same office, but today it had just been Cassie, which was very unusual.

Madison had never called like she said she would, and in fact hadn't called all weekend. Cassie forgave her for not ringing on Saturday as she thought she would either be too hungover or too busy with Jake. Then Sunday came and went, and still no word, so Cassie had rung several times and each time, left a voicemail. She had even messaged her on various social media platforms hoping Madison would pick up at least one of the messages. But still no reply. Not even this morning.

So, Cassie decided to take the usual commute to work on her own, hoping there had just been a misunderstanding and Madison would arrive at the office with a million reasons, or rather excuses, as to why she went radio silent.

But Cassie could not shake the feeling that something was wrong.

The possibility had briefly occurred to Cassie, that if she did not show up to work, then she would report Madison missing, but hoped with everything she had, that it would not come to that.

She cursed the early morning commute, pushing all the bad thoughts out of her mind. Being alone made the journey

CHAPTER 10

feel twice as long and gave way for more time to think, which was the last thing she wanted to do. And more time for playing out all the bad scenarios. Gazing out of the window at the blurry world whizzing past, she thought to herself that she would just have to see what the day brought.

The automatic announcement interrupted her thoughts: "the train will shortly be arriving at Sheffield. If you are leaving the train, please make sure you take all your personal belongings with you and mind the gap between the train and the platform".

Cassie realised that she had travelled on too many trains during the past year, being able to recite the announcement word by word, as she gathered her rucksack and laptop bag from the seat next to her, vacated her seat and stood by the doors ready to make an exit. This stop was always extremely busy.

As the train began to come to a halt, she saw a mass of people who stood eagerly waiting on the platform to board the train, hoping to spot a vacant and unreserved seat. Cassie knew that they would be either going on to Stockport or Manchester Piccadilly. She saw students with an MMU lanyard around their neck and one young woman, in her early 20s, loaded with thick literature and history textbooks, along with other people in work attire or casual clothing, either travelling for work, like Cassie, or going to spend the day out in Manchester. She loved to people watch and guess their story. It was a game she and Madison frequently played in order to pass the time on the train.

The doors opened and Cassie exited the train onto the platform, mindful of the impatient passengers on the platform inching their way forward to dash onto the train when it was clear. She then followed the exit signs out of the station, and through the stone façade.

When she reached Sheaf Square, an impressive entrance into the city centre, just outside of the station, she stood still for a moment and took a deep breath. It was unsurprisingly the busiest station in South Yorkshire, and at that moment she was overwhelmed by the amount of people entering and exiting the station. It was something she had never noticed properly before.

The Square was large, with an impressive cutting-edge stainless-steel sculpture and waterfall, which stretched 300-foot-long like a steel wall and celebrated the history of Sheffield City's steel resources. It gleamed in the sunlight and was popular with the tourists.

Another feature included the multi-level waterfall, where water flowed down a set of terraces. At night, the feature became an enchanting glow. It also represented and celebrated the importance of waterpower that had helped to develop Sheffield's industries.

After composing herself, she walked on, and up the stone steps to cross the road onto Howard Street. A black and white Tudor style pub was on the right, already filling up with locals munching on breakfast and sat outside enjoying the British Summer. A red bricked building on her left belonged to Sheffield Hallam University. The path led her down the centre of the buildings and continued until she made a slight left onto Arundel Gate. Her law firm was situated halfway down Norfolk Street, on the right, via Charles Street.

Cassie and Madison were usually the first ones to arrive at the office, and today was no different, apart from Madison's absence. She let herself into the office, turning off the burglar alarm as she did so, and made her way upstairs to the office on the second floor.

The office was split into three further office spaces. The first office labelled *'Paralegals'* was Cassie and Madison's, and they shared it with their colleague, Isaac Connors. The other office was home to Olivia Fletcher, Harvey Drummond and David Bryson, the Associates. And the third office belonged to the Barrister, Gordon Derek Freeman, who had the largest and best equipped office in the Criminal Law department.

CHAPTER 10

During the winter, the office was freezing, and the portable radiators were turned up on high throughout the day, whereas the complete opposite occurred during the summer, and the office was sweltering. Cassie had to open a window before she did anything else, to let the air circulate around the room.

Cassie did not know what to do next, so she boiled the kettle in the kitchen area, which again had its own private room, retrieved a mug and a tea bag from the cupboard and sat waiting.

She felt alone and the silence unnerved her.

She returned to her office, logged onto the computer, and went straight onto her emails, where she found herself staring at forty-three new correspondences, which would be shared between the Paralegals. There was usually a demand over the weekend and Monday morning was hectic for emails. Once again, today was no different. She wished she would stop thinking that because today was very different.

It wouldn't be this way if she knew where Madison was and that she was safe, but she did not know, and it was the uncertainty that scared her. It was out of character and unlike her to behave in such a way, and that was the problem.

CHAPTER 11

When Tom and Lavinia finally showed up to the station, the team were in deep discussion about the case, with files, reports and photographs spread out and littered over the table, the whiteboard filling up as more information was uncovered, and new investigative leads began to surface, and a space for another Jane Doe was given.

"So, going back to the interview with the Armstrongs...." Wilson started to say but was cut short by the arrival of Tom and Lavinia, who looked thrilled with themselves after their morning's findings.

"We found something," Lavinia announced as she walked in and got everyone's undivided attention. She took out the camera's SD card and inserted it into the computer which was connected to the big screen. She opened up File Explorer on the desktop and selected the external hard drive folder, where a list of images was visible. She double clicked onto the first image, which appeared on the screen and clicked the right arrow to advance onto the next image. Image after image flashed by until she found the one that she wanted.

"This is a footwear mark found in the soil in Laughton Woods about a quarter of a mile from where the body was found," Tom explained. "You can just make out the outline of the sole pattern. I'm not sure what this means as I'm not an expert, but Clive will be able to tell us more. We think this came from the killer. It looks fresh. Both entrances have been blocked off and guarded since the body was found early this morning and no one has had authorized access apart from the usual teams, but even they have not travelled further than the body. The witnesses walked from Scotton until they saw

CHAPTER 11

the body, so we know it was not from them. This was closer to the Gainsborough Road entrance. The killer is the only explanation."

"Fantastic work. Morgan has told me you all think the killer walked the route before he chose it as his disposal destination, so it may well belong to him. Send that straight to Clive and put an urgent request in."

"Of course." Lavinia nodded.

"Right, the Armstrongs." Wilson went back to the subject and directed his gaze to Morgan and Norton.

"To me, they appear a family of hidden secrets and problems. I know not every family is perfect, but they just put on a show to appear like that to everyone else and behind closed doors, their perfect persona perishes, and all hell breaks loose," Morgan analysed.

"How very poetic," Harris joked.

"You don't think they could have had a hand in their daughter's murder?"

"No, I don't think they could have. Their reaction seemed genuine."

"Psychopaths lack emotion; therefore, they respond differently and can hide it if they have to and appear innocent if they need to," Daniel Hargreaves stated. Daniel was a criminal profiler who had studied Criminology at Teesside University and became a lecturer in that very discipline at the same university. He had studied serial killers in depth as part of his PhD and was able to interview many. He had published several papers on his research and findings. He focused on why people became killers, as he believed they weren't born but made, and the events that influenced their behaviours. He believed that they had experienced abuse in their early childhood years, whether physical, psychological, emotional, or sexual, which then influenced their behaviour in later life, and through it all learnt to channel all emotion to appear unaffected by it, it was how they dealt with it. All this explained why they became so disruptive, revengeful and lonely, unable to form proper relationships. He studied the emotions, or lack of, of a killer and what their murders symbolise. He travelled around Europe and the USA, speaking about his research at conferences and various universities as a guest lecturer. A highlight of his career was being a guest speaker at the FBI Academy in Quantico, Virginia. He was middle aged, tall, and well-built with short grey hair and blue eyes.

"Are you suggesting that Greg and Susan Armstrong are psychopaths?"

"You would be surprised at how many parents kidnap and kill their own offspring and play the innocent party for attention and sympathy. They can appear like the perfect family, always giving up their time to help others in the community, painting themselves as saints so no one suspects them."

"Innocent until proven guilty."

"Of course, but you have to be open minded about these sorts of things. Can't always trust what people tell you."

"We know that all too well," Wilson stated.

"I have studied this case in detail, and I thank you for your update this morning, Walter. It might be too early to say but because we currently have two female victims, and there is a slight pattern already forming, it is clear he dislikes women. The reason for this, may be a woman figure in his early life did something unforgivable so he channels his anger onto women maybe of a similar age and appearance, for revenge. He imagines it's her when he kills. He hides his victims when he disposes of them, being the time of day and visibility, but he wants people to find the bodies. He is still controlling the victim and the scene even when he leaves as he is meticulous in his chosen position and disposal ground for his victims. He knows they will be found but knows he won't be spotted. He wants recognition for his work, that's why he doesn't hide them too well. He is confident, maybe walking these streets and speaking to the very people he kills beforehand. Seems an

CHAPTER 11

ordinary and hard-working person in society, someone with extensive forensic knowledge, and no family, or certainly no immediate family in the area. But he is moving extremely fast. He is angry, upset, hurt, revengeful. All things that make him extremely dangerous and can make him out of control, but he is very much in control at the moment."

"Religious?"

"Certainly, these symbols could represent a religious meaning, as many symbols do, but because we don't know much about the killer's background or the meaning of the symbols themselves, it's hard to say with any certainty."

"What makes you think he has no immediate family?" Norton asked, picking up on a point that Daniel had mentioned earlier.

"He spends time analysing his victims and murdering them, not missing out any detail. You would only find that time if you didn't have a family because his victims have become his personal life."

"When you say he has extensive forensic knowledge, are you suggesting he could work in this field?"

"Again, it's certainly a strong possibility. That would explain how he knows about such things, and prevents evidence being left at the scene, but anyone can google it. That, or he is a fan of such shows, like CSI and NCIS. He's not bothered about evidence recovery, because there's nothing to recover to begin with. He just needs to know how to prevent evidence being left behind."

"We did find the footwear mark in soil not far from the body that we suspect belongs to the killer," Lavinia pointed out.

"Did you find any other footwear marks? Or evidence?"

"No, nothing else, that was the only one."

"Do you think the killer left it there accidentally?" Morgan asked, thinking aloud.

Looking back at the image on the screen of the footwear mark Tom and Lavinia had found earlier, he surmised, "Well we can easily see the details of the pattern of the sole so it may be that the killer is heavy footed, but I believe there was some pressure behind it. If you're walking through mud normally, I would expect to see a faint pattern as you transition from the heel to the ball of your feet as contact is made, but because the contact is short, only a small amount of detail would be visible. With this pattern, it's the complete opposite, clear and detailed, so it looks like the killer pressed down on the mud and kept that contact to get as much of the sole pattern embedded into the mud as he could. To prove he is clever, in control and means business. He was probably wearing a very common shoe with an equally common sole pattern so it would not be distinguishable. He is also probably the most common shoe size for his gender, weight, and height. Again, not making it identifiable. And that's why he wanted to leave it behind for us. He's playing a game."

"What do you say about the murders themselves? He knows how to chop off fingers and toes with a clean cut."

"And it's possible he has had experience with that. Could be a surgeon since he knows what to do and where to cut. Or a butcher. Or from YouTube."

"You seem to know a lot about this killer's behaviour and history."

"I've studied serial killers and their behaviours and worked on a lot of cases. There are always common components. What do the Armstrongs do for a living?"

"They all work at the Scunthorpe General Hospital. Greg is a neurosurgeon and Susan is a paediatrician. Obviously, Isla worked as a nurse on the Disney Ward and Jack is currently studying Medicine. It runs in the family."

The room turned into an eery silence as the possibility of the killer being an Armstrong crossed their minds.

"We may have a suspect," Lavinia cut in, as she was thinking the same thing as everyone else.

"Go on."

CHAPTER 11

"We talked to Angela, Isla Armstrong's colleague and friend. She told us of a domestic violence relationship between Isla and her ex that ended five years ago. He has spent time in prison."

"Susan and Greg also mentioned that relationship to Norton and I. Isla left when Carl, her ex, was at work. He was obviously angry and tried to contact Isla, but her family managed to sort that out and they didn't speak again."

"Might have stayed hidden for a while to make it seem he had given up and when Isla's parents loosened the reins, so to speak, he was able to pounce."

"That fits with Isla, but unless he knew the second victim, that theory might not fit."

"Run a background check on this Carl person and access previous police records, sounds like it won't be too hard to find dirt on him. Our priority is to locate him. If he was not in prison at the time Isla was murdered, he is our prime suspect, and we need to find him ASAP," Wilson ordered.

"I'll get on that now," Harris offered.

"In the meantime, what about house to house?"

"A plumber went to fix the radiators in the master bedroom and adjoining bathroom on the tenth of June of the white house directly opposite the woods. He would have a good view of the woods from the window. It is worth checking MD Plumbing to confirm."

"Good work. I'll leave the checking to you and Norton. What about the bungalows?"

"The elderly woman residing at the bungalow nearest the crime scene has her bedroom at the back of the house with the window overlooking the woods. She got up to use the bathroom around two-thirty and looked out of the window. She saw a light in the distance, and because it fits with the time, we're thinking that light belonged to the killer when he was disposing of his victim."

"Any evidence to suggest it was indeed the killer?"

"None so far, but if we can get any intelligence from the footwear mark, we can place him in the woods around that time."

"Let's hope Clive can find something then. If not, we'll have to continue believing that was the killer." Wilson had been fully updated with all the information gathered from interviews and early enquiries. He turned back to the white board that was growing with the second victim. Scene images had been placed onto the board with the minimal information they had so far.

"So far the positioning of the bodies, the time since death, the MO, and the neck tattoo are the similarities between Isla and the second victim," Harris summed up.

"So, we can conclude it's the same killer."

"It's the neck tattoo that bothers me the most," Morgan admitted.

"Yeah, if we could find out what it meant, maybe we would have a whole different aspect of this crime," Tom agreed.

"Check missing persons and see if anyone matching the second victim's description has been reported missing within the last month," Wilson ordered once again.

"What are you thinking, Daniel?" Lavinia asked, noticing he had gone quiet, trying to process the new information and come up with another valid explanation that would help the detectives understand who the killer was and why he committed such crimes.

"Neither victim was sexually abused so there's no passion element to it. Purely aggression. He's angry about something or someone. I feel he's leading up to something, I don't know what, but he's certainly not done yet."

The room became silent. The prospect of more murders filled everyone with dread.

"More? We've already got two victims and are as close to solving them as the killer is to giving himself up."

"Ok, let's just focus on what we can do now. Harris, you run a background check on Carl. Morgan and Norton, check

CHAPTER 11

on MD Plumbing and interview the worker who fixed the plumbing. I want Tom and Lavinia to head to the morgue and see what Hayleigh has for us. Great work, team. Keep it up and keep going. We're not of the woods just yet."

****

Carl Foster had a record. That much Harris knew already. He spoke to Bill Somerfield, who had been the detective in charge of his case who told him that Carl was very accepting of his actions and did not try to blame Isla for anything but himself, which was unusual. Bill had interviewed many people, both men and women, responsible for domestic violence, and they always blamed their partner for their actions and spoke of them like they meant nothing. Carl, however, did care about Isla and that was shown throughout the interview as he admitted to everything he did from controlling her life by stopping contact with her friends and family to emotional abuse.

"Some may say he did that on purpose to get sympathy from the Judge to lower his sentence, but I saw it in his eyes, the feelings were real," Bill Somerfield told Harris during their conversation.

Carl had got out of prison a month ago and was currently living with his parents in Birmingham. Harris had spoken to them and learnt that Carl had got himself a permanent full-time job as a factory packer for a biscuit company. His parents had let Carl live with them since he got out as he had nowhere to go, but he didn't leave the house for months, applying for jobs anywhere and everywhere. His mother, Beatrice, admitted Carl has a bit of a temper on him at times but never became malicious.

"He's trying to get life back in order and on track. It's hard for him and he gets frustrated. He works so goddamn hard, six days a week, long hours. He goes to work, comes home and that's it. Doesn't have any friends to socialise with at work. Keeps himself to himself," Beatrice had told Harris. He could hear the sorrow in her voice.

Harris then spoke to the manager of the biscuit company, Sally Rawkins. She was fully aware of Carl's prison time.

"We're in need of workers, and if he's willing to work and doesn't cause trouble then it doesn't matter to me. Because of his record, he was on a two-week trial period which he passed so he became employed full-time. I have to say he does work hard and as far as I understand, he has no family other than parents. Hasn't taken any time off apart from the one day he doesn't work but even then, he tries to get extra shifts if possible. I can see the determination in him, he wants to make a difference to his life and I'm happy to help him make a step in the right direction," Sally informed Harris.

So, it seemed that Carl was a changed man who had repented his actions and was on the road to redemption.

Not the review that Harris had hoped to hear.

****

Morgan and Norton researched MD Plumbing and Heating Services Company, in depth. They Googled the company, searched on social media and sure enough posts from as early as 2002 were displayed on their Instagram, Twitter and Facebook pages, along with recommendations, reviews and comments from happy customers. Their website also gave four to five-star reviews. The website was professional looking and seemed to be constantly monitored and updated. The website itself was easy to navigate and the black background with orange writing was the colour scheme of the website and matched the uniform and company vans. It was effective.

"Don't you find it strange how a plumbing and heating company has so much social media coverage? Fair enough for a website, but even the company I go with aren't on social media."

CHAPTER 11

"Competitive market, they want to get noticed and the more reviews and recommendations they receive and advertise, the more recognition they'll get and as a result, more jobs."

"When you put it that way it makes sense, but I still think they're trying just a bit too hard."

Morgan rang the telephone number listed under the contact details section on the website. After three rings, it was answered.

"MD Plumbing and Heating. Matt speaking."

"Hello, I understand you fixed a couple of radiators for my neighbours in Scotton, the white house opposite Scotton Beck at number four, at the beginning of June. I have a similar issue with my radiators and was recommended your company." There was a pause and the sound of pages flicking, as if looking back in his diary for confirmation.

"Yes, it was I that completed that job for Noel. The master bedroom and adjoining bathroom."

"Yes, that's the one."

"Yes, no problem. I'm just doing a job at the moment, but if you leave me a telephone number, I'll call you back as soon as I can, and we can sort a time and a date that suits you."

"Brilliant, thank you." Morgan left her mobile number with him and hung up. She saved his number in her phone so she knew who the caller ID would be when he rang back. She turned to Norton and told him he'd confirmed the job in June at the house.

* * * *

It had been three hours since the body had been found.

So, when Tom and Lavinia arrived at the morgue, they did not expect to see the victim still splayed open on the steel gurney, with her liver on the weighing scale for Zoe to check and write on the whiteboard. Hayleigh was, once again, slicing the victim's brain like a loaf of bread, scrubs covered in blood.

Marcus was in his office sorting through the scene and morgue photographs from the latest victim, to create a portfolio.

Tom and Lavinia went to the PPE station, and put on an apron, gloves and shoe covers, before entering the autopsy room. Lavinia got close to the body, aware of, but not put off by the acrid smell, while Tom stayed back, pinching his nose with his fingers.

The victim looked more vulnerable now than she had been when they found her, with every inch of her body being examined inside and out. Her body sliced open, ribs cut, scalp peeled back, and organs extracted. She had become a shadow of her former self, thin and bare, lifeless and cold.

Tom watched Lavinia, marvelled at how close she got as she slowly circled around the body, concentration painted on her face. She was hovering over the body and looked deep into what can only be described as a crater that had once held living organs. She looked around for the organs and found they were in a plastic bag, waiting to go back into the body before being stitched up. As Zoe carried the liver from the gurney into the bag, it looked slimy to touch but appeared healthy with the normal reddish-brown colouration.

"Same story as last time?" Lavinia asked Hayleigh, who was studying the victim's brain, looking for any signs of haemorrhage.

"It's looking that way. All organs appear healthy, no sign of drug or alcohol abuse, or excessive smoking, no blood clots, no mutations, no haemorrhages, or anything, just like the first one."

Hayleigh had taken tissue samples from each organ to analyse under a microscope and placed into their relevant labelled test tube. Once she had inserted the minute segment of brain into the test tube, Hayleigh handed Zoe the rest of the brain to place into the bag and moved onto the stomach,

CHAPTER 11

emptying the contents into a deep metal bowl. The stomach had looked fairly empty, save for the pale pink liquid that spurted out. Again, she took a sample of the liquid to send to toxicology to test for drugs and poisons, to establish if the victim had taken anything ante-mortem or peri-mortem, before or during death.

As she did that, Tom turned a ghostly pale colour and looked like he might faint or throw up any minute, or both.

"This also looks the same as the first. Whatever they ate or drank, both the first victim and this one had the same thing."

"How common is it to see victims of the same killer digest the same thing before they died?"

"Very common, especially if they were held captive for some time."

"Any idea what it could be?" Tom asked, still standing a short distance away.

"Looks to be some sort of fruit drink. Due to the colour and probably one of the most common flavours, I'd say a strawberry smoothie, something like that." Hayleigh brought the bowl to her nose and sniffed. "Certainly, smells fruity," she commented as Tom screwed up his face in disgust.

"Did you really have to smell that?" Tom whined.

"The nose helps to detect. Any luck with the tattoos?"

"Not yet."

"By the way, your father is attempting to make Sushi tonight, so be warned. He keeps sending me updates and it's actually looking pretty impressive at the moment."

"I swear he's turned into a different man."

"I know, a few days off and he's turned into Jamie Oliver."

"Thanks for the warning although I'm sure he could serve you yesterday's cold beef and you'd still be impressed."

Hayleigh laughed. "I'll take a look at these samples and send this off to toxicology right away. I'll follow up on the first toxicology testing and get those back ASAP."

"Thanks, Hayleigh. Appreciated as always. I guess I'll see you later then."

"You certainly will."

* * * *

Cassie Nolan had not heard a word from Madison all day. She had partly expected it, but it was not any easier to accept. Their colleagues had asked after her, and Cassie being the friend she was, lied to them all and simply said she was ill. Whether they had noticed her demeanour as she told them was a different story, but they did not push it and for that, Cassie was glad.

Madison's parents did not even know the situation and Cassie dreaded telling them. She had contemplated ringing them to see if Madison was indeed at home, safe and sound, but she could not face the questions and the possibilities if she was not there.

She therefore decided that she would take matters into her own hands and had told Gordon Freeman that she had a doctor's appointment at quarter past four and was therefore excused for the afternoon. This allowed her to get an earlier train home to Scunthorpe before stopping off at the police station on her way home. The sooner she was able to report Madison missing, the better, before she changed her mind.

Cassie was not used to leaving work so early and was surprised by the small number of people waiting on the platform for a train. The station itself had been busy, but the 15:11 train to Cleethorpes was not.

She would get into Scunthorpe station just after four o'clock and the police station was just around the corner. Her heart was hammering in her chest, realising it had now become a reality. She was going to report Madison McKinley missing. She felt sick and unsteady on her feet and had to take a seat on the bench as she waited. Her whole body was shaking.

CHAPTER 11

Cassie had read newspapers and watched the news on the TV, where she had read and heard of murders and families torn apart by the loss of a loved one. It usually started out as a missing persons case. She just thought she would never be the one to report someone else missing, or even contemplate the worst of a close friend.

The tannoy announced that the train would shortly be arriving at platform 1B. A few minutes passed on the digital clock on the board until the train slowed as it approached the platform and screeched to a stop in front of Cassie.

The doors opened and a young man exited the train with luggage bags, placed them down onto the platform, turned around and helped his wife with the pushchair and then they walked towards the exit. Cassie's gaze followed them as they walked away, and she thought how simple their life seemed in comparison. At least in this very moment.

Once on the train, she located an unreserved seat in the middle of Coach B and sat down near the window, gazing out onto the platform. She had completed this journey many times in the past year after a long day at the office but had never felt so apprehensive about returning to Scunthorpe as she did in that moment.

The whistle blew, the doors closed, and the train glided away, gathering speed as it left Sheffield station.

The journey was a bit of a haze for Cassie, and she almost missed her stop. She hastily gathered herself and her belongings and exited the train, just in the nick of time. She left her car parked in the space at the station as she continued to walk out of the station car park and crossed the road to follow the street down to the police station.

The Scunthorpe Police Station sign loomed nearer as she advanced toward the entrance.

The automatic doors opened up into the reception area. The desk was occupied by two receptionists, one who was currently talking on the phone, the other who was typing away on the keyboard. She looked up and over her glasses as Cassie approached the desk.

Cassie did not reciprocate the warm smile that was worn by the receptionist, but instead got straight to the point. "I'd like to report someone missing."

The receptionist, named Dorsi, immediately picked up the phone and dialled Missing Persons, two of whom promptly arrived in reception to take Cassie to the conference room in their office department on the second floor, across the hallway from the Major Incident Team.

They introduced themselves as Richard Hemmingway and Kathryne Baye once they had settled around the table with a cup of coffee each in front of them. Richard was a tall man looming at 6ft. He had short silver hair and wore glasses with his brown suit. Kathryne had medium length light brown hair that was styled in a pinned-back wave hairstyle, which could be comparable to a half up, half down hairstyle. The front strands were pulled back and secured with bobby pins and gelled to smooth down loose strands. The ends were slightly wavy. Simple but elegant.

Kathryne was the first to speak: "I understand you wanted to report someone missing?"

"Y.. yes," Cassie stuttered, unsure if she could go through with it. She was more nervous now than she had been before, as she wrapped her hands around the cup to stop them from shaking.

"What relation is this missing person to you? A relative? A partner? A friend?"

"A friend."

Kathryne knew to ask simple but direct questions to get as much information about the missing person as possible. They had to establish how old the missing person was, how long they had been missing for, any history of mental illness or current illnesses, any medication they needed to take that they didn't have with them, and if they had been missing before. All this information was vital to determine the risk

CHAPTER 11

level required to prioritise the response activity and direct resources appropriately and effectively.

"What's your friend's name?"

"Madison. Madison McKinley." At the mention of her name, Cassie welled up and tears flowed down her cheeks. Richard handed Cassie a box of tissues which she gladly accepted.

"And how old is Madison?"

"Twenty-three."

"Has she been missing before?"

"No, never. She wouldn't do anything like this, it's out of character for her. That's why I'm so worried."

"I know it's hard, but you have done the right thing. When did you come to realise that your friend was missing?"

"There was an event last Friday, she was meant to stay at mine all weekend and then we would travel to work together on the Monday. She left with some guy, and I never heard from her."

"Have you tried to contact Madison?"

"Yes, text, email, Instagram, Facebook, you name it."

"And no response at all?"

"Nothing."

"Has she opened or seen any of your messages on social media."

"No."

"Any history of mental illness, or current illnesses we should know about? Or any medication Madison needs to take that she may or may not have with her?"

"No. She's missing, not insane," Cassie retorted before she could think about what she was about to say, and immediately regretted it. She hung her head low.

"This guy you spoke of, do you know him?"

"Not really, Maddy and I met him that night at the event."

"What event was it?"

"Parker, Prescott and Skinner annual event."

"We're familiar with that one."

"Do you know anything about him such as his name, occupation, home address?" Richard spoke up.

"I know his name is Jake Higgins. He attended the event as a graduate. He wasn't a recent graduate, think he said he graduated two years ago, but he took a break from education and then started to think seriously about his career."

"Do you know where he went to university? I assume he studied Law?"

"Yes, he studied Law, but I don't know whereabouts. I didn't ask."

"That's okay. Does Madison have either parents or guardians?"

"Parents, I haven't contacted them. Should I have done?"

"No, that's all right. We can do that, if you have a telephone number we can call."

"Of course." Cassie reached into her bag for her mobile phone, opened up the contacts application and scrolled down to 'Maddy Home' and wrote the number of a piece of paper that Kathryne had handed to her. She gave it back to them.

"Do you have a recent picture of Madison that we can use?"

"I have plenty on my phone." Cassie picked up her phone once again, and this time opened the gallery. She scrolled through several pictures taken from that night and instantly felt her heart break. Madison had looked so happy and carefree. They were both smiling from ear to ear, enjoying the food and the drink. Damn you, thought Cassie. Her eyes watered again, and she finally picked an image that was taken a couple of days before the event.

Cassie showed it to Richard and Kathryne. Once they had seen it, Cassie noticed something change in their eyes as they looked at one another.

"If you could wait here for one moment, that would be great. We just need to pop out for a brief second. Is it all right to take your phone, so we can get a copy of that picture?"

CHAPTER 11

Cassie was unsure what was happening but agreed and handed them her phone. They abruptly left, leaving Cassie alone in the conference room as they closed the door behind them and disappeared out of the office.

****

They reappeared ten minutes later, with an enlarged printed copy of Madison's photo and two other people in tow, whom Cassie did not recognise.

"Cassie, I would like you to meet Detective Chief Inspector Wilson and his colleague Lavinia, with Major Crime. If it's okay with you, they would like to ask you a few questions?" Kathryne softly explained.

Cassie's eyes wandered between the four people stood in front of her, before nodding her head in agreement. She was too paralysed to say anything, afraid of why Major Crime were involved. Did they think Madison was in more trouble than Cassie realised? Had Madison committed a crime? Had they already found her? Thoughts were running wild in her mind.

They all sat down; this time Wilson and Lavinia took the two seats in front of Cassie while Robert and Kathryne chose to sit in the corner of the room, to the right of Cassie, still in her eyesight but not directly in front of her, not wanting to intimidate her.

"Hi Cassie, we have been briefed by Robert and Kathryne and wondered if you could tell us more about Jake."

"I'm not sure what else I can tell you. I've told Robert and Kathryne everything I know."

"I'm sorry to do this, but we would appreciate it if you could repeat everything you told them."

And so, Cassie did just that, and explained what little she knew about him. She wished she had taken more of an interest in Jake, finding out more about him. Maybe then she wouldn't have let Madison leave with him. Ever since that night, Cassie had played various scenarios out in her mind at night. Nightmares haunted her sleep, and in her mind, she replayed the scene where they had both left together, stayed in bed all day Saturday nursing a hangover, reminiscing and eating takeaway food and then went to work as usual Monday morning. The nightmares felt so real that when she woke, she forgot what had actually happened.

"Can you describe his appearance?" Lavinia asked.

"Your average good-looking bloke. Tall, dark and handsome. He was of similar age to Maddy and I. Had black cropped hair, and he wore a Rolex watch on his right wrist. He was very attractive. You don't think he has something to do with Madison going missing, do you?"

"We're looking into it."

"We can't rule anything out yet. Can you take a look at a photograph and tell us if you recognise the person in the picture?"

"Sure." Wilson slid a picture across to Cassie who picked it up off the table and stared long and hard at it. It was a mugshot of Carl Foster when he had first been sent to prison. He looked rough, bags under his eyes, his blond hair dirty and unkempt, sticking up in all directions, his posture was slumped, and his dark eyes bore into Cassie's. She was unnerved. "I don't recognise him. Who is he?"

"Does the name Carl Foster mean anything to you."

"Should it?"

"You tell us."

"I've never known anyone who goes by that name. What does this have to do with Madison?"

"We have found Madison," Lavinia informed Cassie.

Cassie sat upright in her chair, eyes wide and flicking wildly between Wilson and Lavinia. "Found? Is she okay? Where is she?"

"She was found dead in Scotton Beck this morning. I'm sorry," Wilson said directly.

CHAPTER 11

"No, you must be mistaken. She never knew a Carl Foster. You've got her mixed up with someone else."

Wilson, Richard and Kathryne were very aware of the denial stage. When close friends and family did not believe that their loved one had gone, they simply wouldn't believe or accept it and that was one of the hardest things to deal with in the job. Neither Wilson, Richard or Kathryne wanted it to be true themselves, and seeing the heartbreak only made it harder. However, prevailing to find justice made it worthwhile and even though catching the killer did not make up for the loss of life or the hole in the heart felt by relatives, it made it easier to live with, knowing he wouldn't hurt another soul again. That's what kept them all going in times like this.

"I'm afraid we haven't. I wish we were, believe me, but the picture from your phone matches that of the body we found," Lavinia said.

Cassie's tears then left her body, she was shaking all over and Lavinia went and sat next to her holding her hand and body, letting the tears fall.

"S.. s...sorry," Cassie stammered, as she wiped her eyes and blew her nose on a tissue.

"You have nothing to be sorry for."

"Did this Carl kill her?" she whispered.

"Again, we don't know but we are investigating that possibility. He has form and he had close relations with another victim. We have no reason to believe there is a personal link between Madison and the first victim, or Madison and Carl for that matter, but we have to investigate," Lavinia explained as carefully as she could.

"There have been others?"

"One other, yes. Do you recognise the name Isla Armstrong?"

"No, was she the first victim?"

"Unfortunately, yes she was."

****

Lavinia walked Cassie out of the police station and all the way to her car, which was still parked in the train station car park. Lavinia wanted to make sure Cassie was all right to drive home as she was still in shock. And she could barely walk to her car without support from Lavinia. Her whole body was still shaking, and she felt weak from the shock. Lavinia opened the car door for Cassie.

"I'll be fine to drive. It'll help to clear my head. Thank you though."

"Let me know when you get home. And if you need anything or think of anything else that might help us, just give me a ring. It doesn't matter what time."

"Thank you. You've been so kind and understanding."

"If it was my friend, I would have reacted the same way."

"Does it get any easier?"

"I think it will once you find closure. But it'll take time, and they say time is a great healer. Just take care of yourself and Madison's parents. You'll both need each other now more than ever." Cassie hugged Lavinia and said goodbye before she got into her car and started the engine. Lavinia watched her drive off before making her way back to the station.

Lavinia entered the conference room of the Missing Persons department, where they had interviewed Cassie and a debriefing was taking place.

"Cassie all right?" Kathryne asked Lavinia as she walked into the room and sat down.

"She will be, just still a bit shocked by it all."

"At least it's another missing person found and not another unknown. In some ways, they are worse."

"It still feels unknown, since we haven't found her killer yet and we still don't really have that much to go on."

They then reflected and discussed what Cassie had told them.

"Harris is following up on Carl Foster, we will be checking the CCTV from The Cutler's Hall and locating this

CHAPTER 11

Jake guy. Thank you for your help," Wilson said, getting up from his seat and shaking their hands. Lavinia followed suit.

They walked back to their own department, where they held a meeting to inform the others what had occurred, and then Lavinia wrote up her report. It had just gone five-thirty, when she logged off and realised Tom was waiting for her.

They packed up and walked to the car park together. "What a day," Lavinia sighed as they descended the stairs.

"Heard you handled Cassie Nolan and the situation really well," Tom beamed, proud of his partner. He knew how much telling Grace Sanderson about Isla had affected her, but it seemed she was making progress.

"Thank you. It was still hard; Cassie was so broken. I couldn't just sit back and wallow in my own self-pity. You fancy homemade Sushi?" Lavinia asked as they exited through the station doors.

"I would love to, but I already have plans. Thanks for the invite though."

"No problem, anytime. Doing anything nice?"

"Just going to Colosseo, on a date." He spoke of an Italian restaurant in the town centre. He hesitated to say it was a date, unsure of what Lavinia's reaction would be, especially if she knew who it was with. They had reached their cars. Tom was beside the driver's side of his car, whilst Lavinia was by her own car, looking over the roof of Tom's car to speak to him.

"Italian, nice. I didn't know you were speaking to someone."

"I haven't for long. It's Jess, Grace Sanderson's colleague from Specsavers."

"What? No way."

"You sound shocked."

"You make a great detective, Tom, because that's exactly what I am. I just didn't expect you to go for someone like that."

"She's not what people expect. They judge her before they get to know her and she's smart, funny, down to earth, and attractive. So maybe she's a bit forward with herself, but she is just naturally flirtatious, it doesn't mean she's a bad person. It's her personality that sells glasses, not her looks," Tom defended.

"I'm sorry. It seems you really like her and that's great, I've heard she's a great person. I'm really happy for you, of course I am. I hope you both have an amazing time," Lavinia genuinely said. She really cared about Tom and wanted to see him happy, he deserved to be happy, and if Jess was that person, then so be it. She opened her car door.

"It's okay, I know you're just looking out for me, but thank you. Enjoy the Sushi, you'll have to let me know how it is."

"Of course. Enjoy the date, but make sure you undo the top two buttons of your shirt for a more relaxed look and don't wear a tie, it's too formal. Polish your shoes and don't tuck your shirt in..."

"See you tomorrow," he spoke loudly over her and laughed at what she was trying to do. He did find it cute and appreciated the advice, but he did know how to dress for a date. At least he thought he did and probably would have made himself look too formal had Lavinia not mentioned it. He got into the driver's seat and started his engine. Lavinia did the same. Out of courtesy, he gave way to Lavinia who had left first, waving to her as she departed the space, then he drove off, with a smile on his face as he looked forward to the evening ahead.

CHAPTER 12

Alastair had purchased a sushi-making kit which included a rolling mat, bamboo chopsticks, sushi rice and Nori seaweed sheets, rice vinegar seasoning, wasabi paste, soy sauce, pickled ginger, and sesame seeds to garnish. The pack also came with a 'Sushi Cookbook Guide for Beginners' and that was what Alastair had used to help him. It was all new to him, but he enjoyed the challenge and appreciated that he had the time to learn new cooking skills.

Firstly, he cooked the rice. That was the most time-consuming part as it had to be watched very carefully and was cooked properly, otherwise, he would find himself rolling the sushi in crunchy rice. Once boiled, he lowered the heat and left it to simmer for twenty minutes, stirring about every five. After ten minutes of leaving the rice to stand, he seasoned it with rice vinegar, sugar and salt and fluffed it up with a fork.

He then sliced the salmon and cucumber into thin vertical strips. Using the rolling mat, he spread a thin layer of rice onto the nori and placed the salmon and cucumber in the centre, very close to each other and rolled. Once rolled, he cut into bite-sized pieces. He repeated this method with the crunchy seaweed salad sushi and tuna, wasabi and pickled ginger maki. He sprinkled with sesame seeds. He also made smoked salmon nigri, crabstick nigri and cracked black pepper mackerel uramaki. He placed each maki, nigri and uramaki in a black plastic sushi box, covered it with a plastic lid and placed them into the fridge to serve later. He would serve them on black and red porcelain Japanese sushi plates he had purchased for this very occasion.

He had also julienned red pepper, carrots and avocado to serve in a salad with spring onion, cucumber and soy sauce to accompany the sushi.

He was ecstatic at his efforts and hoped the sushi tasted as good as they looked.

The rolls weren't perfect, but that was the beauty of home cooking, they didn't have to be. He had actually found that not using the rolling mat made the rolls more circular, which did not make any sense.

Lavinia was the first one home, followed by Mindi half an hour later and then Hayleigh.

The meal was served with Roku Japanese gin, flavoured with hibiscus tonic water and garnished with peeled cucumber ribbon and fresh raspberries. There was also a jug of refreshing peach iced tea for the non-alcoholic beverage option.

They were all sat around the dining room table, marvelling at Alastair's creations. It had turned out a success as all the sushi had been eaten and there were empty plates all around.

"So, what's next on the menu?" Mindi asked, topping up her glass with peach iced tea.

"I was thinking of making fresh pasta, possibly spaghetti and then maybe sweet ravioli for dessert."

"And here I was thinking that the only reason Alastair made detective was because he would not make it as a chef," Hayleigh teased.

Mindi and Lavinia laughed, and Alastair pretended to look offended.

"I excel in other areas of life to make up for my lack of kitchen skills." Alastair winked in her direction as he put a hand on her knee under the table. She placed her hand over his and rubbed a thumb over his knuckles.

"Well now you can add cooking to that list of yours."

"Yes, ma'am."

CHAPTER 12

"I'm glad you're using your time wisely to do something different," Lavinia said. "I was worried that you would become restless and not know what to do with yourself." She understood what the job meant to him and knew it was hard for him to adapt to the leisure life.

"I did at first, but it took me a while to realise that throwing myself into work was not healthy and I embraced the time to do the things that I never did before, like slaving away in the kitchen. And it also means you get a chance at having that exquisite culinary experience. How's your day been?"

"Another body turned up, we have a couple of new suspects and no idea about anything else. I feel we have a lot of information that doesn't lead anywhere or add anything to the investigation. We do have some leads to follow up on tomorrow."

"That's a start. All that information will add something, even if you don't know it yet. It all counts and makes sense when you have the bigger picture. Right now, you have loads of small pieces."

"Until it doesn't," Hayleigh pointed out. "Should hopefully have the tox results for you tomorrow morning. That might tell us more. There's been a backlog of tests since apparently the systems have been down which I wasn't informed of and Simon was off sick the other day, but I've chased them up and put out an urgent response."

"What are you thinking will come back?" Lavinia asked.

"The identification of the drink or any drugs ingested. The cutting off of the body parts is not enough to kill them and since there are no visible internal signs of trauma, I'm thinking drugs have to be involved in one way or another."

"Any specific kind of drug?" Alastair asked.

"Possibly one that would render the victims' bodies to eventually shut down."

"Like a muscle blocking drug?" Alastair asked.

"Like a muscle blocking drug," Hayleigh confirmed. "Can be fatal if taken in large doses."

"Any that spring to mind?"

"Well, unfortunately there's quite a few. Dantrolene, Quinine, Diazepam, Succinylcholine, Vecuronium, Pancuronium. Just to name a few."

"Never heard of them apart from diazepam."

"They're all muscle relaxants used for various medical reasons. Anaesthetics, for example. Pancuronium Bromide is used as one of the lethal injections in the US."

"What you've just said has thrown another spanner into the works," Lavinia said.

"I know, but it's a possibility you have to consider."

****

To put everyone's mind at ease about the possibility that a neuromuscular blocking drug was used in the execution of two female victims, they put on an easy watching film on Netflix, which served as an enjoyable distraction.

Alastair and Hayleigh were cuddled up on the sofa with Star, and Mindi and Lavinia in each of the armchairs. After the film, Mindi and Lavinia headed straight to bed. Alastair and Hayleigh shortly followed.

Lavinia was sat up in bed, the bedside lamp glowing beside her, and she checked her Instagram and saw Tom had uploaded several pictures from his date. Later there was a picture of their main meal with the location and name of the restaurant labelled underneath. It looked like he had had a great time and Lavinia was glad. Lavinia noticed he had taken notice of her advice, as he did not wear a tie and had the first two buttons of his shirt undone. He wore a white linen shirt and a brown jacket that looked very handsome on him. Jess was wearing scarlet red high waisted trousers with a white lace embroidered bodysuit. Her hair was wavy

CHAPTER 12

and her face full of natural make-up aside from the matching scarlet red lipstick. They looked a good couple.

She stalked Jess's Instagram for a while and she seemed to have a large group of wild friends, as previous posts were of them at various festivals throughout the summer last year, including Leeds, Parklife and Glastonbury. There were posts, pictures and videos from house parties, dinners, lunches, day sessions, birthday and Christmas celebrations. Going back a year and a half ago, Jess and her boyfriend at the time had gone on holiday to Corfu and her posts were of the picturesque scenery, white town houses and beautiful beaches. Them going out to dinner and drinking cocktails. Some were of Jess in a skimpy bikini, showing off her gorgeous, toned figure. There was no doubt that she was a stunning woman and Lavinia could see why Tom found her attractive.

Her mind then went back to the case and found that it was not easy to switch off. She wondered what lengths the killer had gone to, to stalk his victims beforehand, going back to what Daniel Hargreaves had said about him, that he is confident and possibly spoke to his victims in advance. How would he know where they were? Or who they were? Did the killer live nearby, or did he prowl social media to find a suitable candidate and then tailed them until he killed them? What was it about Scotter and Scunthorpe that made him pick his killing ground here? Did he pick them because of their beauty, was he attracted to them and that's why he went after those specific people? Scotter had a Facebook group called Scotter News Forum, where people would post about events happening in the village or if residents had items to sell. Lavinia was a member of the group but if someone wanted to join, they would have to simply click on the join group button and wait for someone to approve the request. Once in, you would be able to see other people's profiles in the group. Maybe that was the selection process he had gone through.

There were so many possibilities.

CHAPTER 13

Harris had been in the office since seven-thirty. He had received a call from the receptionist as early as seven and drove straight to the station, getting a bacon, sausage, egg and hash brown breakfast bap from the canteen along with a strong cup of coffee before he set to work.

Yesterday, he had requested CCTV footage from The Cutler's Hall for the night of the Parker, Prescott and Skinner event and with some persuasion, they granted him access to it. They gave him a copy of the CCTV footage on a CD which was hand delivered to the police station first thing that morning.

After a couple of bites from his bap and a few sips of his coffee, whilst waiting for his computer to load up, he had inserted the disk into the desktop hard drive and waited for it to pop up as DVD RW Drive (E:) under 'This PC' in File Explorer. He doubled clicked on it and Windows Player immediately opened up. Harris pressed play.

The blue loading circle appeared against the plain black background of Windows Player, showing that the video was loading. It took a few seconds before the screen changed and a menu popped up asking Harris to select the footage he required from the various different angles. From outside, through Security, in the hallways, in the Main Hall where the event took place and in the gardens.

Harris selected the outside camera and noted the time and the date on the bottom right-hand corner on the screen.

07:13 23/06/2022.

The day before.

CHAPTER 13

From speaking with the owners of the hall yesterday, every camera got refreshed before any major event, in case of accident override of footage. They wanted to be able to record the whole event in case of any wrongdoing at any time during the event. It put the owners at ease knowing that the cameras would record everything, and that worked in Harris's favour as he would be able to watch the whole event and hopefully catch Madison McKinley, Cassie Nolan and more importantly their suspect, Jake Higgins.

Harris fast forwarded the CCTV from the day before, watching people as they came and went to help set things up, from caterers to electricians to event organisers.

He quickly skimmed through the first 24 hours before he got to the day of the event.

09:16 24/06/2022

Again, he selected the outside camera and a similar thing happened throughout the morning and into the early afternoon, as last-minute preparations got underway. This time, they had rolled out the red carpet and the officials in uniform were rehearsing what they needed to do and where they were required to go. The buffet food and drinks were freshly delivered and stored in massive trolleys, making it easy to wheel into the kitchen area for storage until later. Signs were placed around the vicinity notifying drivers and guests where to head for the entrance or to get dropped off. Those who had reserved parking were directed around the back of the building, where a large sign at the entrance to the car park stated, 'Reserved Parking Only'.

To Harris, it all seemed like organised chaos.

He fast forwarded most of the early afternoon, until he approached 16:32, then he slowed the footage down.

The same street and road view were visible from the camera angle on the front of the building, and it was still daylight, which made it easier to search the crowd for recognisable faces. He knew that as the night wore on, it would become harder to see the faces of those who left and to help aid in the identification, he also noted the dresses and suits that the guests wore.

Guests started to arrive just before five in dribs and drabs, and then the mad rush came between five-thirty and six.

Taxis, Rolls-Royce cars, limousines and even a horse and cart arrived at the drop-off point at the front of the building. They had a separate way in and way-out system to ease congestion and when the four cars at the front had disappeared, the next few cars were urged to fill the spaces in order to let multiple cars drop off at any one time. It was like a vehicle carousel.

Four officials had been placed at the multiple drop-off points as they opened the door for the guests. They stood straight and upright like they had a metal rod for a spine but wore a friendly smile as they greeted guests.

Harris thought the whole thing was ostentatious, but then again, he didn't expect any different from the world's most successful and recognisable Law entrepreneurs. They wanted to make a statement and that they did.

He noticed, what seemed like the hundredth silver limousine that had pulled up outside, behind a taxi, but it was the second and third person who evacuated the vehicle who got his attention. He was able to see their faces clearly from the camera angle as it was pointed directly at them and recognised Madison's black and red gradient hair from the crime scene with her matching dress, and Cassie's silver dress with the side slit from the description Cassie had given Wilson and Lavinia.

He paused the footage, squinted his eyes and moved closer to look at the screen before confirming his suspicions and noting his observations.

17:56: Madison McKinley (MM) and Cassie Nolan (CN) arrive – silver limo.

CHAPTER 13

They were followed out of the vehicle by several others, who Harris assumed, were colleagues.

It wasn't until the limousine pulled away from the drop-off point that Harris could see the number plate. It was personalised and he wrote it down in his notebook.

LM0 SNE

Not very inventive, Harris thought.

Wilson, Morgan, Norton, Tom and Lavinia arrived at staggered times, all surprised to see Harris already making a start on the CCTV. They quickly greeted him, letting him concentrate on the footage. At times, he felt his colleagues stand behind him or beside his desk, watching the CCTV. He vaguely registered a conversation between Tom and Lavinia. Lavinia asked about Tom's date and Morgan and Norton piqued in teasing him about it. Tom blushed and changed the subject to ask Lavinia how the sushi went down. She couldn't praise Alastair enough.

Back to the CCTV, and the group made their way up the red carpet and soon disappeared through the entrance.

He decided to let the footage play on for a few more minutes before moving on.

Harris pressed the back button at the top left-hand corner of the screen which brought him back to the menu. He selected 'Security' and once more fast forwarded the footage until he got to five-thirty on the night of the event and picked up where he left off.

He played the footage and waited for about twenty-five minutes until Madison and Cassie came into view.

He thought how the killer might have chosen his victim because neither Madison nor Cassie stood out from the crowd. He only spotted them because he was specifically looking out for them, but he wouldn't have picked them out. He would remember those who arrived in a horse and cart, he would remember those dressed in trouser suits or jumpsuits because they were dressed differently to the majority of women. He would remember those being stopped by Security because his interest piqued up. Madison and Cassie had arrived in a limousine but then again, the majority of guests did. Only a handful had chosen another means of transport. They were in dresses, they arrived in a group, and they went through Security with no issues. They were just another face in the crowd.

Was that why the killer had chosen Madison because no one would realise she had disappeared?

But then Madison and Cassie seemed joined at the hip. How did Jake know that he could get Madison alone? That wasn't guaranteed. Unless he thought he was confident and liked the challenge. That would fit with the profile given by Daniel Hargreaves.

He switched the footage again to the Main Hall and played it from 18:30. He watched for ten minutes and when Madison and Cassie did not come into view, he rewound the footage back five minutes and saw them pick up a glass of bubbly from the serving tray before entering the Main Hall.

18:22: MM & CN enter Main Hall

Harris saw that the Main Hall was a massive room with a stage at the front and a symphony orchestra playing classical music. Waitresses came around with serving trays of canapes and the guests helped themselves to nibbles and drink. A small crowd had gathered by the bar area. But as Harris watched the scene in front of him, he was in awe of the three crystal chandeliers hanging from the ceiling and lighting up the room like a ballroom.

He scanned the crowd and found the two people he was looking for. Again, he thought they didn't look any different to the other guests.

Madison and Cassie were stood in the group they arrived with, chatting away, eating canapes and grabbed another

CHAPTER 13

glass of champagne from the serving tray as it approached their group.

Time seemed to slow down as Harris watched the evening unfold in front of him.

The speeches from Parker, Prescott and Skinner came and went and throughout the speech, Harris saw a guy matching Jake Higgins's description looking in Madison and Cassie's direction. Did he choose his victim there and then, or had he known beforehand and that was the first moment he spotted them all evening? Harris did not even know if Jake was the killer, they had no evidence to suggest he did it, but he was their suspect after all, after disappearing with the victim, so far making him the last person to see her alive, and that was enough for Harris to investigate.

> 19:00: Speeches – guy matching JH occasionally looks over at MM+CN. Knew who they were? Chose victim at that moment? Speech lasts 15 mins.
>
> 19:17: MM+CN leave group & head for bar. Spots JH also in queue for bar, JH walks over and engages in conversation with MM+CN.
>
> 19:21: JH buys drink for MM+CN, all talking.
>
> 20:04: JH + MM dance. CN stood watching alone.
>
> 20:11: CN finds colleagues.
>
> 20:32: JH departs dancefloor & disappears from hall – Where did he go? MM locates CN. Both go to dance.
>
> 20:42: JH returns. Finds MM+CN on dancefloor. Speaks to MM. MM speaks to CN. Hug and MM + JH leave hall. CN goes back to group.

Harris watched on for a bit longer to see what Cassie did next. He didn't have to wait long until he noticed she was hugging the group, saying her goodbyes and left. That was at 21:01. She was alone.

Harris switched back to the outside camera but was able to fast forward to 20:35 and waited until he saw the back of them. They stood on the street in front of the entrance steps. Jake got out his mobile phone, the screen illuminated his face, as he typed away on it. He pointed right in the general direction of the street, and they walked off, and out of view.

Harris could not make out what was on Jake's mobile phone screen and rewound the footage back to pause it when he saw the lit-up screen. He tried to zoom in, but the image became blurry. Too blurry to make out any shapes or writing. So, he called the tech guys on the floor above and sent a copy of the image to them.

In the meantime, he continued to play the footage, noting that at 21:03, Cassie had exited the building, and three minutes later an Uber stopped right by her, and she got in. The car drove away.

The tech team were able to enhance the image using specialist software, and Harris could view exactly what was on Jake's screen, as clear as day.

It was a view from Google Maps from their current location to the nearest McDonald's, which was, conveniently, a one-minute walk away via Church Street and High Street to the right. So, that's why they left the event and that's where they had disappeared to.

Harris then contacted the manager of that McDonald's branch, Felix Miller, to speak to the employees on shift that night and ask if they recognised a description of Madison and Jake and if they knew where they headed afterwards.

Felix passed on the details of his staff working that night to Harris. Sheelagh O'Donnell who was on tills and served the couple, Marshall Evans was also on tills, but he wasn't serving anyone at the time. Craig Ward prepared the order,

CHAPTER 13

Kayleigh Hughes was on drive thru, which also wasn't busy at the time, so she was chatting to colleagues. And Becky Taylor was on her break but worked at the back on food with Craig. Harris interviewed them all separately, but they all commented on the couple's attire. They were all aware of the Parker, Prescott and Skinner event happening that night, so it was not a complete surprise to find them 'dressed for Prom', as Sheelagh had described. Marshall Evans thought they had just met or had not known each other long due to their conversation. They were asking questions about each other, like it was a first date. But were laughing and Sheelagh processed their order, Jake paid via Apple Pay on his phone and they ordered an Uber so took their food to go, but it was too dark to see the driver, or the colour, make and model of the car.

To confirm the pickup and drop-off point, Harris contacted Uber, to see if he could locate the car and the driver that had picked up Madison and Jake. Details of journeys were kept on record in case of any dispute about payment or the journey itself.

The customer service team member on the other end of the line was very helpful in tracing back the journey. As expected, Uber drivers had been extremely busy on that night chaperoning guests to the venue and picking them up again afterwards. Harris asked if any had made the journey from the McDonald's on the High Street.

He came back with twelve different journeys, all varied times throughout the day. Harris was able to narrow it down to just two, that were within fifteen minutes of each other. One at 20:56, and the other at 21:11. From speaking to the staff at McDonald's, he knew another group came in shortly after Madison and Jake had left. Therefore, Madison and Jake had to have gone in the earlier Uber at 20:56, so Harris had asked for those trip details. The car was a Jaguar XF, and the journey was from the McDonald's on High Street to St Paul's Loft Apartments. The driver, Abdul Jayaraman.

It seemed an endless cycle of telephone conversations. But at last, he was able to trace where they had gone after leaving the event, and now knew where Jake lived.

Abdul Jayaraman was a middle-aged man who had been driving with Uber for five years. He had a good record with endless five-star reviews given by his clients. His extended family had moved from India to Sheffield for his children's education. They strived to be doctors and engineers, and the UK had many top universities for those programmes. He confirmed that he had responded to the request sent from Jake's phone and picked up a couple, matching Madison and Jake's description, from McDonald's on the High Street and dropped them off outside St Paul's Loft Apartments. They exchanged greetings with the driver when they entered the car, and he confirmed their drop-off point, and made small talk throughout the journey, which took a total of seven minutes with limited traffic on the road. He saw them enter the building and then he drove off.

****

At just after nine-thirty, Lavinia went straight up to the Footwear, Tyre and Tool Impressions Laboratory on the fourth floor to locate Clive.

Clive was an experienced Forensic Scientist, who was nearing retirement age, but was still extremely agile, and had grey wisps of hair around his head that was balding at the top. His glasses were perched on the end of his nose and were on a chain around his neck. Lavinia thought he looked more like a history professor.

She found him at his workbench, dressed in his white lab coat, studying various footwear impressions on long strips of paper. He hadn't heard her approach and Lavinia had to clear her throat to get his attention. "Morning, Clive."

"Ah, Lavinia, Good Morning. Sorry I was miles away."

"You look busy."

CHAPTER 13

"That's the understatement of the year. Didn't get to finish it last night so thought I'd come in early this morning."

"What are you looking at?"

"I am analysing the tread pattern and wear on a series of suspect samples to see if any match that found at a crime scene."

"Sounds interesting. Have you had a chance to look at the unknown footwear mark I submitted to you Monday afternoon?"

"Yes, that was my penultimate task last night. One moment," he explained, disappearing into the evidence storeroom and signed out the relevant evidence noting the date, time, description of the item and his signature in the logbook for continuity purposes. "There's nothing significant, I'm afraid," he said as he emerged from the storeroom.

"What did you find?"

"It's a generic mark, male size 11, common trainer sole." He had somehow managed to take a 3D cast from the picture that Lavinia had sent him, which made it easier to look at the fine detail. Also in the evidence box, held the original picture taken by Lavinia and his report.

"What about the tread pattern and wear?"

"There's nothing identifiable. The sole appears to be new as there's no individual tread patterns or wear, no over or under pronation or wear and tear on the sole, which you would expect to see once the individual has worn in the shoes and it moulds to their way of walking, or have worn the shoes for a while and over different terrains."

"So, to summarise, nothing."

"I've even put a copy on the database to see if we can identify it but without a known sample from a suspect for comparison, and the fact there's no unique or identifying features, it doesn't have any evidential value, I'm afraid."

***

Wilson was sat in his office, trying to piece together the scattered puzzle that was currently the investigation.

The Press were hot on him, wanting to publish the next story on the progress of the investigation and to print any new revelations. Wilson despised the media and only liked them when they could sincerely help him, and not put his career on the line by twisting false information, or printing speculation.

That morning, he had already had two in-depth conversations with two different journalists who pushed him for information. He was not ready to work with the media just yet.

Wilson's office phone rang again, and he reluctantly picked it up, bracing himself for another repeated conversation with another journalist.

"Detective Chief Inspector Wilson, Major Crime."

"It's Dorsi down in reception. I may be overthinking here, and it could be nothing but yesterday I was filling out the crossword in the paper and it struck me as odd. It woke me up at dawn thinking about it."

"What's odd about a crossword puzzle?" Wilson massaged his temples, hoping to God that she wasn't wasting his time. He had enough on his plate as it was, without investigating dead ends.

"The crossword in the paper the day that the first victim was discovered was ironically about the topic of death. I thought it odd back then, but just thought it as a coincidence. Then yesterday's newspaper also had the same topic of death for the crossword. And that was the day the second victim was found."

"Do you still have a copy of these crosswords?"

"Yes, I have four. Two copies with the completed crosswords and two left blank, just in case you wanted to see them."

"Could you bring all copies up to my office please?"

"Certainly."

CHAPTER 13

Wilson hung up and replaced the phone on the receiver. He sat thinking for a moment and had to admit that he agreed with Dorsi. The topic of the crossword puzzles were extremely well timed. He couldn't pinpoint any relevance of the crosswords to the investigation until he had studied them properly. And didn't she say they were published the same day the victims were found? Were they just a coincidence though? Or did they have a bigger meaning?

Was this about to be another spanner thrown into the works?

Dorsi promptly arrived at Wilson's office. She gave three sharp knocks on the door and entered. "They're not set out like a normal crossword, and with only seven clues, so that sent alarm bells ringing inside my head. Plus, it's sent by someone named Anonymous," Dorsi explained as she placed the four pieces of folded paper into Wilson's outstretched hand. They had clearly been ripped out of the newspaper. He glanced through them as she stood at the front of his desk, waiting to be asked questions or dismissed.

The question came first.

"Have you spoken to anyone else about these crosswords?"

"Not a soul."

"Good, let's keep it that way for now, aside from my team of course. Can you contact the newspaper and reach whoever is in charge of publishing quizzes? And check my schedule to arrange a meeting with them for some time tomorrow morning. You did the right thing by bringing it to my attention." He looked up at Dorsi to gauge her reaction and she nodded enthusiastically to show that she was willing to help and keep quiet. He thanked her again and she left.

Morgan barely waited until Dorsi had left when she entered Wilson's office, without so much as a knock. "What did Dorsi want? She looked like she saw a ghost."

"All will be revealed in good time. Can you tell the others briefing in five minutes?"

"Sure." Morgan left the office to pass on the message to the team.

They hastily gathered in the conference room, uncertain of what to expect. Harris momentarily stopped watching the CCTV footage to join the meeting.

Wilson stormed in, and the room instantly quietened. He placed the incomplete copy of the first crossword on the board and passed photocopies to his team.

"I have received new information that may or may not be relevant to the investigation but seems there could be a connection worth investigating. I have given each of you copies of a crossword, titled 'Life Extinct'. This was published in the newspaper the same morning that Isla was found." He passed around a copy of the second incomplete crossword. "Now this, is another crossword, also titled 'Life Extinct' published in the newspaper on the morning that Madison was found."

"Coincidence or related?"

"If you solve it, the answers, together with the clues, may help to decide that predicament. I also have a copy of the answers, but I want you guys to work together to try and solve it. It's not a hard one."

"There are only seven clues. Do you think that number is significant?"

"I wish I knew." Wilson threw his hands up. Why did he have to deal with this now? What was the killer up to?

"Okay, does anyone have a Bible handy for 2 Down? Matthew verse 5.38, line 42," Norton said.

"Number of letters 3,3,2,3," Tom read out. The answer went down the middle of the crossword with clues 1,3,5 and 7 Across going through it.

"We could try filling in 3,5 and 7 Across and see what letters we get for it," Lavinia advised.

"Good idea, I know 1 Across is See. See No Evil, Hear No Evil and Speak No Evil," Morgan said.

CHAPTER 13

They filled in the letters. The answer to Matthew (5.38-42) started with the letter E. Harris knew that the answer to 5 Across, Inflict Severe Pain, for seven letters, was Torture.

"People Watching a Performance for 8 letters surely is Audience," Lavinia stated, and the others agreed.

They struggled with the Man in Charge, 6 letters, clue for a few moments, until Harris suggested Master, as Boss did not fit, which they agreed upon. After inserting these clues into the crossword, they had E_E_O_ _ N_ _ _ for Matthew (5.38-42).

The other two clues left were 4 Down, Opening Act in a Play (3) and 6 Down, Immoral Act (3). Morgan offered Sin for the latter clue which worked, and Norton gave One for the former clue.

"Think of the Christianity phrase that means retaliation, which is also a body part missing on both of our victims," Wilson encouraged.

"An Eye for an Eye," Tom grasped. They filled in the blanks to the last clue and looked at their complete crossword.

"What does all of this mean?"

"Master, Torture, Sin, Audience, See No Evil, Hear No Evil, Speak No Evil, An Eye for an Eye," Harris summed up.

"Someone is obsessed with religion and biblical teachings."

"One big clue as to the behaviours behind the killings?"

"I'll arrange a meeting with Daniel Hargreaves, see if we can get any more insight from his perspective," Wilson informed.

Heads nodded in agreement around the room.

"Well, he seems to torture his victims by chopping their ear off and carving their eye out. Hear and see no evil. Maybe they committed a sin and that's why he kills them, retaliating to their crimes."

"That makes sense."

"Was there a name that came with this crossword?" Lavinia asked, although she doubted that if the killer did send the crossword to the newspaper, that he would have supplied them with a name, even if it was a false name, an alias.

"Anonymous," Wilson replied.

"Of course," Morgan responded.

"What about this other one?" Lavinia asked, picking up the incomplete copy she had of the second crossword.

"Let's try it," Tom agreed.

"This one seemed a little easier to fill in," Wilson admitted.

Across:
 3. 1 for Bad Luck (6)
 4. The End of Life (5)
 5. Son of _ _ _ (3)
 6. Slaughtered Meat (4)

Down:
 1. No one can hear you _ _ _ _ _ _ (6)
 2. Skin Inking (6)
 5. Hunted Wildlife (4)

Magpie, Death, God, Lamb, Scream, Tattoo, Game.

"Forget crossword, seems like a word association game to me," Norton verbalised.

"It all seems to associate specifically with these current murders in some way," Morgan stated as a matter of fact.

After discussing the relevance of the two crosswords, they concluded that since there were enough relationships between the crossword and the murders themselves, such as the tattoo and the reference to specific body parts that were missing from the bodies, they were prepared to accept that they were most likely sent by the killer.

It seemed he had only just started playing his game.

****

CHAPTER 13

The lack of intelligence from the footwear mark did not sit well with the team as they felt exasperated. But if it hadn't been for the recent discovery of the crossword, the team would have been completely disheartened, dejected, and dispirited.

They needed to speak to the McKinleys and inform them of the news of their daughter. It was better to tell them in person than find out from someone else. They would also be required to conduct a formal identification of Madison's body, even though they were sure it was her, they needed confirmation from a close relative. Even asking about any tattoos, scars or birthmarks would suffice, just so long as they had evidence to prove identification.

Tom volunteered to speak to the McKinleys and dragged Lavinia in tow so she could get experience at dealing with this situation.

"Does it get any easier to tell parents that their son or daughter is dead, or a sibling, or a friend, girlfriend, husband or wife?" Lavinia asked Tom as they drove towards Newland Avenue, near the hospital.

"Never. I think it's worse telling a parent," Tom admitted.

"How come?"

"It's every parent's nightmare, isn't it? Their son or daughter goes missing, ends up dead, goes down a path in life that they tried so hard not to walk down. All any parent wants for their child is to see them succeed in life and watch them grow and experience all the milestones they did. Promotions, weddings, children. They are supposed to die after the parents, carry on the family traditions, pass down family heirlooms, tell stories of the time they were young. But all that is gone in a flash when we turn up and tell the news they've dreaded hearing their whole life. Now, which number did Wilson say it was?" Tom asked as he turned right onto Church Lane.

"Twenty-seven." Lavinia looked down at the note written on her phone of the McKinleys' address for confirmation.

Tom took a left turn onto Newland Avenue and slowed down so he could see the house numbers. The road meandered around the corner and Tom spotted the house on the right. He parked on the path just outside.

They both exited the car and Lavinia walked ahead of Tom, up the driveway where a black Ford Fiesta was parked and rang the doorbell.

The door was opened seconds later to reveal a woman in an apron. She was drying her hands on a tea towel and Tom and Lavinia had obviously interrupted Mrs McKinley cleaning or cooking.

"Mrs McKinley?" Tom asked as he and Lavinia showed their identification cards.

"Please call me Bridget. What's this about?" She tried to hide her worry and confusion with a smile.

"Sorry to intrude. I'm Detective Constable Tom Watkins and this is Lavinia Newbourne with the Major Incident Team. Please could we come in?"

Mrs McKinley did not respond, she just moved aside to let them in and waited until they were stood in the hallway before she closed the door. She then pointed out the living room which was the first room to their left.

When Lavinia entered, she was greeted by Mr McKinley who was sat on the sofa watching daytime television. He was wrapped in a blanket with the seat reclined and looked pale.

"Excuse my husband, he's not been well. I was just making him my famous soup. I put in a lot of herbal remedies and spices which works wonders. I'd make Maddy it every time she was ill and the next day, she would be better. She's our daughter. I took the day off work to look after Rick, but Maddy is at work at the moment. Take a seat."

At the mention of Madison's name, Lavinia's heart did somersaults in her chest, feeling the anticipation of informing Bridget and Rick of the devastating and life changing news.

Lavinia went to sit on the edge of the corner sofa which looked out into the front garden, and she could see Tom's car

CHAPTER 13

parked on the path. Tom sat next to her while Bridget went to sit next to her husband, on the other side that faced the TV and the fireplace. She pressed mute on the remote control to silence the TV. This was Tom's cue.

"We have some very upsetting news about your daughter Madison, and I am very sorry to tell you this, but she was found dead this morning."

Silence hung in the air like thick fog and Bridget turned as pale as her husband.

"What? No, you must have the wrong person. Maddy is at work right now. She'll be with Cassie. I will ring her right now." Bridget made a move to get up off the sofa.

"Bridget. Cassie reported her missing to us after she failed to turn up to work," Lavinia informed her.

"But you can't be sure it's her."

"We will need you to formally identify the body but from a recent photograph given to us by Cassie, we are sure it's her. I am so sorry." Lavinia saw the devastation of both their faces.

Bridget welled up. Rick just sat there stunned.

"She attended the Parker, Prescott, and Skinner event on Friday evening and stayed at Cassie's all weekend. She was due to be back this evening," Rick said weakly, and Bridget collapsed onto the floor as she stood up, her legs too weak to hold her up any longer. Lavinia rushed to her side to help her sit back onto the sofa and held her as she grieved.

"My baby!" Bridget cried. "My Maddy!"

Tom disappeared into the kitchen to go and make her a cup of tea with sugar to help with the shock. Rick slowly got up from the sofa, checking if he would be all right to stand and walk without collapsing himself, and followed Tom out of the living room into the kitchen.

"Just making Bridget a cup of tea for the shock. Is there anything I can get you, Mr McKinley?" Tom asked when he saw Rick entering the kitchen out of the corner of his eye as he filled the kettle with water from the tap, clicked it onto the stand and turned it on.

"Glass of water would be great. Thank you." He sat down at the small wooden kitchen table as Tom opened several cupboards in search of a glass. When he found one, he filled it up and passed it to Rick. He took a sip with shaky hands. They could hear Bridget wailing in the next room. "Our lives will never be the same again."

"I truly am sorry for your loss. This part of the job is never easy."

"I don't know how you do it."

"Sometimes neither do I."

"Do you have children?"

"No, I don't."

"You spend your whole life trying to protect them and wanting the best for them. Maddy did us so proud. Here I was sleeping or watching TV on the sofa while Maddy was out there alone." His tone had turned bitter.

"You did everything you could."

"It wasn't enough." He drained the rest of the water from the glass and slammed it back down on the table. The kettle had finished boiling and Tom was pouring the water into a cup when Lavinia walked in.

"Bridget has given us the go ahead to look in Madison's room," Lavinia informed Tom as he poured in the milk and stirred in three heaped teaspoons of sugar. He passed the tea to Lavinia to take through to the living room.

They both made their way up the stairs.

"It's the room at the front of the house," Lavinia pointed out. Before they headed left into the bedroom, they had a quick look around. The master bedroom was in front of them, the bathroom immediately to their right. A second bedroom with a small en-suite was next to the master bedroom and Madison's room was the only one left.

They slowly opened the bedroom door to reveal a small orderly room that clearly belonged to Madison. She had made a collage on the wall of photos of her friends and family, of her younger days at school, days out, and from

CHAPTER 13

university. She beamed in each of them, loving life in that exact moment, freezing the memory in time for ever.

"She was popular," Lavinia observed. "And so carefree." There was an image of her scuba diving on holiday with friends, and she and one of her female friends holding hands as they jumped off a cliff into the water below, presumably on the same holiday. She had also completed a skydive.

The double bed was placed by the wall, with the wardrobe at the foot of the bed and the desk to the side. Smaller storage boxes were placed on the top of her wardrobe that held hats, scarves and gloves, toiletries, and stationery. Larger boxes were under the bed. These held spare bedding sets, and towels, bags, and shoes.

Tom and Lavinia searched in the drawers but found nothing of any interest. Her Apple Macbook was laid on the desk, the lid closed, and so Lavinia took out a pair of latex gloves from her pocket, placed them over her hands and lifted the screen to open it up. The laptop came to life.

It was password protected.

They would have to bag it up and take it to digital forensics to see if they could access the files, search through her browser history to locate any websites or searches, and search through her social media platforms.

With nothing else of interest, Lavinia took the laptop and glanced around the room once more before vacating. They re-entered the living room where Bridget and Rick were sat in the exact same places as before, this time they leaned into each other as if holding one another up by their own support.

"I'm sorry to interrupt but would it be okay to take Madison's laptop for digital forensic examination? You will get it back as soon as we've finished with it." Bridget nodded but remained silent. "I need to ask you a few more routine questions," Lavinia added.

"If you must," Rick replied.

"We can leave it for another day when you're feeling better," Tom offered.

"Better? I will never feel better again. I've just learned my daughter is dead. How can I feel better after that?" Denial had turned to guilt and guilt had turned to anger. All signs Tom recognised. It happened to every person they told when a loved one had died.

"He meant when you have rid of the flu," Lavinia tried to clarify.

"Suppose you'd better get it out of the way now so you can leave us."

"She met a man named Jake Higgins at the event. Does that name mean anything to either of you?" Lavinia started once she and Tom were sat down.

"Never heard of him before. Do you think he was the one who..." Rick could not finish that thought.

"We're looking into a few possibilities."

"Was she in a relationship or did she have any previous boyfriends that you were aware of?" Lavinia asked.

"No current or past. She was always so career minded. Takes after the both of us."

"Did you have contact with Madison at all over the weekend?"

"No, but I wished I had. To say that I loved her." Bridget had started crying again, tears were streaming down her face, and they wouldn't stop. Despite Rick's eyes watering too, he was the one comforting her. He gave Tom and Lavinia a look to signal the interview was over. They took the hint.

"We will assign you a Family Liaison Officer but if you think of anything else in the meantime that may be of interest then please get in touch." Tom left his card on the sofa as he got up and they let themselves out.

*****

After speaking to Carl Foster's mother, Sybil, Harris wanted to speak to Carl himself to verify a few details and ask

CHAPTER 13

him more questions about his past relationship with Isla Armstrong and his current work and home situation.

Even with Jake Higgins in the picture for the murder of Madison McKinley, they still had to clear up any information or rule out Carl Foster for the murder of Isla Armstrong. Carl had a connection to Isla, whereas Jake had a connection to Madison, but neither had a connection to both victims so it was difficult to justify one suspect.

After a few rings, it was picked up by a young male.

"Am I speaking to Carl Foster?"

"Yes, this is him. Who is speaking?"

"Hi, this is Detective Inspector Harris Forster from the Major Crime Team in Scunthorpe. I recently spoke with your mother, but you were at work. Is now a good time to talk?"

"As good as any I suppose." He had heard of Isla's death and knew the police would want to speak with him regarding his relationship with Isla. Especially since it was an abusive relationship, he knew he would be high on their list of suspects. So, when Harris called, Carl was not completely surprised.

"Are you not working today then?"

"Day off today."

"I understand you try to get as much overtime as you can, even on your days off?"

"Yes, last time I checked working was not a crime."

"No but killing someone is." There was a pause at the other end of the line.

"I didn't kill no one. I get what it looks like with my record but that was a mistake that I am paying for it now. I loved Isla; I wouldn't kill her."

"But you did abuse her. Physically and emotionally."

"I am ashamed of who I was, but now I have a steady job. The pay may not be great but it's a job nonetheless and I am starting to build myself a life again. I'm saving up to get my own place. And I'm certainly not the same man I was last year," Carl said with pride.

"You had been out of prison a few weeks before Isla was found dead."

"Then someone is trying to stitch me up for her murder. My parents picked me up at the prison when I was released and I have been here since. I can't drive and don't have access to a car."

"What about the bus? Have you taken that recently?"

"Only to and from work. If I'm on early or late, then I get a lift from my parents because the buses aren't running at that time. You can check my bus tickets; you can check the messages on my phone when I text Mum or Dad to let them know I'm on my way back and you can check with the bus driver as well. All will corroborate with me telling the truth. Ever since I've been released, I've got my head down and stayed out of trouble. I am really sorry about Isla, and I am sorry what I did to her, but I did not kill her."

All copies of recent bus tickets were forwarded to Harris, and they all checked out. Harris even checked with the bus driver, who for some reason, seemed to remember Carl Foster. Probably because he always had a friendly chat with the driver, or he became a regular commuter on the bus. And screenshots of the text messages from Carl to either his mum or dad checked out. The content of the messages were about the time Carl had finished work and had got on the bus home. The journey home took approximately thirty-five minutes and Carl had always arrived home when expected, apart from the one time when the bus broke down. Even on that occasion, Carl had contacted his parents to inform them that he would be late home. If that wasn't enough, Carl had been working between Friday 3rd June, when Isla was last seen, and Monday 6th June when her body was found. He had picked up an extra shift and there were witnesses who could corroborate his story and could, with conviction, say that Carl was at work during the time in

CHAPTER 13

question. So, he was nowhere near Isla and was nowhere near the crime scene.

He was then officially ruled out as a suspect.

* * * *

Jake Higgins was now the prime suspect.

The team still did not know of the connection between Jake and Isla, but with a strong connection to Madison, and Carl Foster now ruled out as a suspect, he was their priority.

After getting the answering machine on his home telephone and voicemail on his mobile phone, Harris tried to ring his work number and got the receptionist at the other end of the line. Eventually he managed to locate Jake at his workplace which happened to be called Higgins and Co. His father owned the company. The receptionist informed Harris that once Jake had graduated from university, his father had got him a job at his firm, but Jake didn't want to follow in his father's footsteps and take over the business when it was time.

Harris was put through to Jake and they arranged a meeting for just after 2pm, as he was busy meeting with clients all morning. But that suited Harris as it gave him plenty of time to make the journey to Doncaster.

It was just approaching 2pm when Jake and Harris sat down in a meeting room, opposite each other.

"Thank you for seeing me, I just need to ask you a few questions."

"As long as it doesn't take long, I'm very busy," Jake bluntly replied.

"Shouldn't do." Harris gave Jake a smile in his direction which was met by Jake's cold eyes and straight face that lacked emotion.

A big beefy man stormed into the room, his salt and pepper moustache enhanced his red blushed face. Harris could already guess who the man was, as he wore the same emotionless face and the same cold eyes bore into him as Jake's. He spoke in a deep voice, one that had laboured many cigarettes in his time. "What do you want with my son?" he demanded.

"Just to ask him a few questions about his night at the Parker, Prescott and Skinner event. A woman who also attended the event has since been found dead and we are treating her death as suspicious."

"My son had nothing to do with that."

"That's what I'm here to ask him. He was seen on CCTV talking to the woman and even left with her later on. It seems your son was the last man to see her alive. So please could you leave us in peace so I can do my job?" Harris sternly told him.

The man then turned to his son and said, "If you need a lawyer, just call for me personally." And he left slamming the door shut on his way out to let Harris know of his frustration.

"Your father seems a nice bloke," Harris sarcastically said to Jake.

"He's just doing what any father would do in this situation."

"Right. So, I heard you got this paralegal job right after university?"

"Yes."

"I also understand that it was your father who got you the job?"

"Yes. He is partner of the firm."

"Seems like you don't want to take after him, which is fair enough. But killing someone would get rid of his persistent shadow over your life and make you free of him. Even if it would be disappointing for him to tell people you're spending the rest of your life in prison for murder."

"Woah! I did not kill a soul. My father thinks he has my life all planned out for me, but I want to do my own thing in my own way in my own time. It was great to get a job

CHAPTER 13

straight after university because I know how competitive the law market is. I've heard from friends how many applications and interviews they have before they land themselves a job. It's more about the experience than the actual degree. Candidates need the experience, but companies don't want to recruit to give them that experience. That's why I accepted a job here so I wouldn't have to go through all that. But I am determined to make my own life. I wouldn't kill someone to give all that up."

"Nice speech. Talking of speeches, you seemed to keep glancing over at Madison and Cassie while Parker, Prescott and Skinner were conducting their speeches. Why was that? Did you decide right at that moment who your victim was going to be?"

"What? You've got this all wrong."

"We have you on CCTV as clear as day." Harris produced a copy of numerous photographs of CCTV footage stills taken on that night. Jake clearly in all the pictures, stood looking over at Madison when the speeches were made, by the bar, dancing with Madison and then leaving the event. "That is you, is it not?"

"Yes, it's me."

"Now you seemed eager to get Madison alone. Directing your attention mainly at her, getting her to dance, and then leaving with her sometime later? Why was that?"

"Cassie was, is, a great and attractive woman, but it was Madison I was drawn to. We had better banter, bounced off each other and we had that connection. We felt comfortable in each other's company."

"You left the hall for ten minutes between 20:32 and 20:42. What were you doing in that time?"

"I went to the men's room. It seemed I had gone at rush hour because there was quite a queue and then I popped outside for a few minutes for some fresh air. But I went straight back to the hall afterwards."

"And when you came back?"

"Madison and I left."

"Did you force her to leave with you, or did she go of her own accord?"

"She left with me because she wanted to. I was surprised that she left Cassie since they had been together all night, but I was delighted to spend more time with her."

"When you left, where did you go?"

"We were both craving a McDonald's and so I looked up on Google Maps where the nearest one was and that turned out to be further up the road."

"So, you walk up to McDonald's, order your food and then what?"

"Ordered an Uber."

"Where did you direct the Uber to drop you off?"

"At my apartment."

"That would be St Paul's Loft Apartments?"

"That's right."

"Then what happened?"

"We took the elevator up to my floor, ate the McDonald's in my room, watched some shit on TV, and then we slept together."

"How romantic. Did Madison leave straight after?"

"She must have. I didn't register she had gone until I woke up properly the next morning."

"Did she say where she was going and how she was getting there? Did you hear her order a taxi or see her order an Uber?"

"No, but she left a note."

"What did the note say?"

"Um... thanking me for a great night, she left her number and hoped to see me soon."

"Did you contact her again after?"

"Yes of course, well I tried to, on multiple occasions, but she never picked up or responded."

"And you didn't see her again after that night?"

"No, sadly I did not."

CHAPTER 13

Piecing together the timeline, Harris thought that she may have been abducted by whoever picked her up from the apartment. He thought it was most likely a taxi. It could have been a legitimate taxi company, or it could have easily been someone posing as a taxi driver to pick her up and abduct her without being suspicious. She was not seen after she left the apartment in Sheffield until her body had been found in Scunthorpe. She clearly did not make it back home, as no one saw her, so whatever happened to her had to be on the journey home.

CHAPTER 14

Anna Shaw was fairly new to the Scunthorpe area after making the move from Bristol. She had made the decision when she got her dream job as an Estate Agent. The money, the housing prices, the location, and the opportunity to progress further in her job suited Anna better in Scunthorpe than it did back home. She used to travel over an hour every morning and evening to get to and from work, whereas in Scunthorpe, it took her less than ten.

She felt it was the right move, as she was able to make a fresh start and become more independent living on her own. She would try to see family when she could, and they had arranged a visit in the near future. As much as she loved her parents and her sisters, Christine-Maria and Georgina-May, she did not want to live at home for the majority of her adult life.

She adored her job, and had settled into it extremely quickly, gaining a reputable relationship with clients and formed an impressive record selling houses. She was a natural at being able to see the potential in properties and selling her vision to her clients. That was why she had loved the job.

And right now, she was viewing a new modern build apartment with a young gentleman. He seemed nervous as it was his first buy. But she was glad to accompany him on his journey to finding his first home.

"The beauty of this house is the space. Not everyone likes open plan, but it maximises every available space. And I know the constant white wall colour scheme is also not to everyone's taste and feels bland, but think of it as a blank canvas to put your own personal touch to the property."

CHAPTER 14

She beamed at the prospect and became really enthusiastic about this place.

"It is a great property, you sell it really well, and I'm glad to have viewed it in person, but I just feel it's not me."

"No problem. This is why we encourage buyers to view as many properties as they can. So, they can pinpoint exactly what they want, what they don't want and have many points to compare. You'd be surprised at how many people think that they know exactly what they want and when they view a property, it turns out, it's not what they wanted after all."

"I would still like to view the other property we scheduled a view for."

"Yes, 27 Waggoners Close in Scotter. Tomorrow morning at 10am," she read from her schedule on her phone.

****

That property was a semi-detached house, the furthest in the row of four. They were all tall and slim, over three floors with a bright red front door and a small brass knocker.

The young gentleman, who introduced himself to Anna when they first corresponded as Dean Hadley, was waiting inside his car which was parked on the path outside the property. When Anna arrived, she parked on the driveway and met Dean by his car.

"Now, this family want to move out ASAP, they already have another property lined up and have already started moving out of it, so they want this property gone. That situation might be in our favour, as the guide price is £160,000."

"Right okay."

"Let's take a look at this property and take it from there. Once we've seen the house, I will ask you if you want to put an offer in. If you do, I will contact the homeowners immediately to discuss. That sound good?"

"Perfect."

"Let's go then." Anna walked down the driveway, followed by Dean, and unlocked the door with the key in her hand. Once she opened the door, they were greeted by a small hallway that ended with the living room and then onto the square garden. The first room that Anna showed Dean was the small rectangular cloakroom with a toilet and a sink that was just inside the doorway to the right. The stairs leading up to the second floor were in between that and the living room.

The kitchen was also on the ground floor, opposite the stairs on the left-hand side. Again, it was a small room but was practical for one person as it had plenty of cupboard storage space and the fridge tucked in the corner behind the door.

Dean took his time looking around each room before making his way upstairs. The second floor had the master bedroom at the back of the property, with a second bedroom at the front of the property overlooking the street, and the bathroom situated in the middle, with another toilet and sink but also with a bath and shower.

The third room had currently been turned into another bedroom. Anna knew Dean wanted space for a library, however big or small, a room where he could place a sofa, a few bookcases and have it designated as his reading/study room. She saw the space, which already had two bookcases in, and explained her vision to Dean.

"This room already has a small bookcase here under the window and the tall bookcase against the wall, so that gives you some idea of the fit and how many books you can accommodate. You could also place another small bookcase where the chest of drawers currently are. The sofa will easily fit into the space that is now filled with the bed. Even leaves some room for a nice cosy rug."

"Yeah, I can see that."

"You seem more positive and upbeat about this property than the previous one."

CHAPTER 14

"Yeah, even though it currently has a small family living in here now, it's big enough for me and has everything I need without it being too much or too big. I can already see the potential of each room, like turning this one into a library. It seems more appealing that it's hidden away on the third floor."

"That's fantastic. Well, that's the whole property. You can view it as many times as you like, I'll wait for you in the kitchen and catch up with you in a little while."

She left Dean to go around the property once more, just to double check that he was happy with it before advancing on to the next stage. He joined her in the kitchen a few minutes later, his smile widened when he told her he wanted to weigh up his options but was very much optimistic in that he might just put in an offer.

It would be Dean's first property that he was able to purchase himself after renting for the past few years. He realised that renting was too much money, and it would be a cheaper and more sustainable option to buy a house instead. It was the sense of achievement at being able to purchase his first property that kept him going.

Once he got home, he started the search again. Just for Plan B, to see if there were any properties that may compete with the one he had just seen. He was feeling positive that he could find a property similar to the one he had just viewed.

During the process, it really opened his eyes at what he was able to get with his money. It had been a massive learning curve and he thought it wasn't easy for new people to get a step on the property ladder.

He was about to give up searching as he hadn't found anything comparable and he was starting to get a headache but found himself delving deeper into the abyss of property hunting. Just one more page, he kept saying to himself, but it never was.

Several pages and properties later, though, he found one which looked even more perfect.

He then contacted Anna, attaching the listing to her. A short time later, Anna rang back and stated that the owners were more than happy to oblige a viewing, but they could not be present.

They agreed to meet at the property at 11am the following morning, after Anna's office review meeting.

***

The townhouse property was the third on the right of the cul-de-sac. Again, they were all modern builds and stunning homes with pale brown brickwork and a cream and brown exterior.

It was similar to the previous property viewed on Waggoner's Close in that there were three bedrooms across three floors. And on the first floor was the modern kitchen, open plan living and dining area as well as a downstairs toilet. On the second floor was the family bathroom, and two single bedrooms. And finally, the third floor held the master bedroom with an en-suite. Each room was spacious.

The property was in a central location, just two miles from the Scunthorpe Town Centre, with local bus routes close by, allowing easy access around the town. Nearby towns, including Brigg and Gainsborough, were a short drive away.

When both Anna and Dean first laid eyes on the property they were about to view, they were in awe.

"No wonder you wanted to view this property, Dean," Anna admitted, studying the exterior.

They stepped over the threshold and walked down the hallway, where the whole of the ground floor felt light and airy from the various windows that overlooked a spacious garden. The place smelled like coffee and the source of that smell came from the kitchen. The owner had left two mugs out in front of a coffee machine and with a note to help

CHAPTER 14

themselves. He filled them both with coffee, adding in milk for them both and two sugars for Anna.

Anna was looking out into the back garden and turned around to accept the steaming mug of coffee from Dean. They took a comfortable seat, Anna on the Chesterfield and Dean on the corner sofa.

Anna continually talked about how amazing the house was, and the things she would alter like the plain white and grey colour scheme, while Dean sat there unable to say anything, but nodded in agreement with her every once in a while.

He noticed that her speech had started to slur, and her eyes began to droop.

Her whole body went limp as her mug smashed to the floor and her world went dark.

CHAPTER 15

Hayleigh phoned Alastair asking him to meet her at Costa in the town centre for lunch. He knew she needed to discuss something as he had noticed her tense tone over the phone. He was apprehensive about their upcoming conversation and various scenarios played out in his head as he drove to Scunthorpe town centre. He parked up in Carlton Street, a car park across the road and opposite the bus station and walked up to Costa.

It was the same Costa Alastair usually frequented on his lunch break, if he got the chance to get away from the office for at least an hour. It always seemed he was in mid-sandwich when his assistance and presence were required. However, today he was in no rush.

The Baristas recognised his face and remembered his order, so when he arrived, he had a brief conversation with them before he chose his regular seat on the sofa by the window. He ordered for himself and Hayleigh, knowing what she would have, and his order swiftly arrived, moments before Hayleigh did.

There was a queue forming by the till when Hayleigh entered, since it was the lunch rush hour and she had to scan the tables before her eyes landed on Alastair. She smiled at the sight of him and immediately her demeanour relaxed.

She sat opposite him on the sofa and took a few sips of her americano before she got out a brown manila folder from her handbag and placed it on the table between them. Alastair arched his right eyebrow up in question at the folder.

CHAPTER 15

"I received the toxicology results earlier," Hayleigh started to explain, noticing his expression.

"What seems to be the problem?" He knew her and knew she would not call him just to inform him that the results were back. There was something more to their meeting other than a social call.

"They came back positive for Succinylcholine," she stated.

"What? It's one of the drugs that you mentioned last night, isn't it?" Alastair asked.

"Yes, it is a neuromuscular blocking drug that paralyses all of the muscles in the body including those used for breathing, and without ventilation support, the person dies of asphyxiation," Hayleigh explained further.

"Won't signs of asphyxiation show up in the post-mortem?"

"Depends on the type of asphyxia."

"I don't follow."

"If the victim died from hanging, strangulation or choking, then yes there would be visible signs such as ligature marks on the neck, crushed trachea and oesophagus et cetera, but with paralytic drugs, there will be little, if any, physical evidence. This is the case with Succinylcholine."

"But with toxicology tests it shows?"

"It can do." Hayleigh took the pause as her cue to carry on explaining. "Once the drug has been injected it begins to work within seconds. The enzymes in the body begin to break it down almost immediately. When we come to do the testing, there's nothing left in the body to show, but if we test for breakdown products, sometimes, we get lucky. Plus, due to the time of death, the victims would not have been able to digest it all, so we find minute traces of the breakdown products."

"Seems like we got lucky this time then."

"We did indeed. That's not all, though. I found no needle marks where the drug could have been injected during the examination of the body, so the question is how did the killer administer the drug?"

"Via a drink?" Alastair took an educational guess.

"Correct. We also found traces of anthocyanins, a water-soluble pigment responsible for red colouration, and traces of glucose and fructose sugars. Plus, lactic acid. It would also explain the pale pink liquid from the stomach contents."

"Red colouration? Sugars? Lactic acid? What are you talking about?" Alastair was more confused than ever.

"Strawberries. And milk. More precisely strawberry milkshake. The tests picked up the proteins, sugars and by products from fresh strawberries and milk. Blended together and they make a milkshake. I'm guessing that's how he administered the drug," she tapped her finger on the file as she said it with conviction.

"Bloody hell." Alastair took a look at the papers inside the file which were printouts of several peaks, known as chromatographs, which identified the separate elements in the liquid. "How does someone get their hands on a drug such as this one?"

"As I said last night, Succinylcholine is used in surgical procedures as anaesthesia, so it wouldn't be impossible to get supplies of it."

"Well Isla and her family all work in a hospital. Could they have had access to it?"

"Certainly. It would be easier for anyone working in a hospital to have access to it than someone from the outside."

"Jesus. Why Succinylcholine?"

"Well, you only need a small dose for it to start its effect, it's easy to administer, easy to obtain, it has a definitive endgame if given in large doses with no ventilation support and is difficult for forensic detention."

"Seems like the perfect murder weapon. Does Lavinia know?"

"No, none of the others do. I rang you as soon as I had the results back."

CHAPTER 15

"I'm privileged." He put a hand over his heart and smiled. "Even though we are breaking a dozen rules here since I'm not on the case."

"You're always breaking rules so don't go sensible on me now. This case is just getting worse by the minute. Sure, we've had difficult cases in the past and I don't know why I'm letting this one get to me as much as it is, but I think it's because I don't even know what's going on."

"Do you remember the "Cereal" Killer?" Alastair smiled and Hayleigh laughed at the memory.

"How can anyone forget that one?" The killer's MO was to murder families at breakfast time. As his signature, he would always wash up his bowl and spoon and leave them on the draining board to let the detectives know that he had been there. Obviously washing away any trace of fingerprints or DNA he may have left behind. That was how he managed to escape for a long time without substantial evidence, until he left his spoon and bowl unwashed in a rush. "It was his saliva and fingerprints on that spoon that nailed him in the end. That one careless mistake had cost him," Hayleigh recalled.

"It was a tough call, though, because none of his DNA were at the other crime scenes so he couldn't be linked to the crimes that way. Luckily it was his signature that linked him."

"Classic psychopath."

"Seems like this one is too."

"Aren't they all?"

"The point is, that he made one vital mistake, and it was that mistake that enabled him to be caught. This one will too," Alastair reassured her.

Hayleigh still looked tense and stressed, but her face relaxed slightly, and Alastair was glad he could help her. They finished their coffees and sandwich.

"As much as I love you and our lunch dates, I am going to have to go back to work. But thank you for this."

"Anytime, you know that. And you need to go and tell the others about the results."

They cleared their trays, walked hand in hand back to their cars, kissed goodbye and went their separate ways.

****

Daniel Hargreaves made his way into the station after being summoned once again by Wilson. The team were still sat in the conference room, with case files, paperwork and photographs scattered across the table once again, to help try and make sense of the case.

"Ah Daniel, thank you for coming in at such short notice." Once Wilson had spotted him making his way to the conference room, he had greeted him with a handshake and patted him on the back.

"Anytime. Happy to help."

After pouring Daniel a freshly brewed coffee, they got straight to work and gave him a detailed account of the crosswords, the clues, and the answers, along with the significance that they may have to the killer, the victim and to the case.

"What a cunning sonofabitch!" Daniel exclaimed after being bewildered by the crosswords. "He thinks he isn't going to get caught any time soon so he's bragging about his crimes, to the only people who can catch him. You guys. But he is being clever because he's not playing directly into your hands. He is putting you to the test by publishing these crosswords in the paper for everyone to see. He wants to see if you'll notice his message."

"Seems like we didn't the first couple of times."

"He moves fast and is probably stalking his next victim as we speak. The more he kills, the thirstier he gets."

"So, he wants to kill them quickly to get it over with and then move on?"

CHAPTER 15

"Yes and no. Yes because the more he can get away with, the more he wants to try. But also, from the stalking and torture he does want to spend time with his victims to maximise pain and fear. And that way it becomes more personal."

"If he wants time with his victims, are you saying he cares for them?"

"The killings suggest otherwise, but it's probably because he wants to cause them as much fear and pain as possible before making the final blow."

"Charming."

"He thrives on his victims' fear, which is why he does what he can to maximise it."

"I agree with Daniel's rather accurate statement there," Hayleigh said as she walked through the door to the conference room, startling the team. Daniel was stood in front of the doorway, so no one saw or heard Hayleigh approaching, but he moved out of the way at the sound of her voice. They had worked together on several previous cases so were well acquainted and greeted each other like old friends.

"Why do you say that?" Daniel asked.

Hayleigh pulled out the folder from her bag and placed it down onto the table. "The tox results came back as positive for Succinylcholine." She met Lavinia's eyes referring back to their conversation last night.

"A muscle blocking drug," Lavinia confirmed.

"It seems he administered the drug via a fresh strawberry milkshake as opposed to using strawberry flavoured syrup or powder. No injection marks were found anywhere on the body during the post-mortem examination. He gave them small doses over a very short period of time which would equate to a large fatal dose. Their body mechanisms would slowly shut down, and eventually those used for breathing. Without ventilation support, both victims died of asphyxia," Hayleigh explained.

"Why use fresh strawberries and not flavoured syrup or powder?" Norton asked.

"It would make it easier to break down and digest to get rid of any traces of the drug. The reason we were able to pick it up during the toxicology testing was by looking for breakdown products and even then, there are minute traces of it, but it was enough."

"So, should the killer have left his victims alive a little longer for no traces to be found?" Tom asked this time.

"Possibly, but it's hard to determine. The rates at which products get broken down and digested vary from person to person based on their metabolism. Some are slow and some are fast."

"Do you think the killer has had experience of working with this drug before? Daniel has previously said about him being a surgeon and it seems to fit the profile?" Morgan enquired.

"Again, it's hard to say, without knowing anything about him. Succinylcholine is widely used as an anaesthetic in hospitals so it wouldn't be hard to obtain. He may work in a hospital setting where he has unlimited access to it, or it might be that's he has been administered it himself during a surgical procedure and that's how he became aware of it and managed to get supplies."

"I suggest checking the hospital supply records to see if there has been an issue of missing drugs recently or an unusual reduction in stock," Wilson suggested. They were all thinking of the Armstrongs. Specifically, Greg, who worked as a neurosurgeon.

"Morgan and I spoke to the Armstrongs early on in the investigation and they were all genuinely shocked and upset. Susan went into hysterics, but it was a natural reaction I have seen so many times working this job. They all work at the hospital or have access to a hospital so every single one of them could have had access to the drug, but I don't feel like any one of them had anything to do with Isla's murder. They

CHAPTER 15

didn't have a clue what was going on," Norton persisted, knowing what everyone else was thinking.

"Thank you for that, Norton. We will, however, need to speak to them again about this drug, and this time, I'm sending Tom and Lavinia to re-interview them, to get a different perspective."

****

Tom and Lavinia were just as in awe of the Armstrongs' property as Morgan and Norton were. They walked in the same footsteps, up the stone steps and knocked three times using the lion brass knocker.

Susan and Greg were eager to hear of any updates regarding the case and Isla's murder, and welcomed Tom and Lavinia into their home, expecting to get a closure, and not asked more questions.

"I don't get it. You haven't got an update for us? Is that why you're here, to ask us more questions?"

"We have made progress in the investigation and wish to ask you about that."

"What progress?"

"Are you aware that another body was found Monday morning?"

"We heard about it, why?"

"We believe this woman was murdered by the same killer as Isla."

"So, the attack wasn't personal? This wasn't Carl's doing?"

"No, it wasn't, Carl's alibi checks out and he's no longer a suspect in our investigation."

"Are you aware of a drug called Succinylcholine?"

"Yes, of course, it's used as anaesthetic. I use it regularly during the surgical treatment of my patients," Greg informed Tom and Lavinia.

"Have you had recent access to it?"

"The day before Isla's death I performed four surgeries. I've taken bereavement leave, so I haven't been undertaking any surgeries since the news of Isla's death. I've only been going into the office once, maybe twice a week."

"Mrs Armstrong, have you been into the hospital recently to work?"

"I'm the same as Greg, only I haven't stepped foot inside the hospital since Isla's death. I can't face it."

"Have you taken any supplies of Succinylcholine either for yourself or on behalf of someone else?"

"What use would I have of Succinylcholine outside of the hospital?"

"We believe Isla was given several minute doses of this drug."

"You mean as a neuromuscular blocking drug? Not for anaesthetic purposes?" Greg's face was pure horror at the thought of what had happened to his daughter.

"I'm sorry to say, but yes we believe that was the killer's intention."

"Are you suggesting we stole supplies of this drug on behalf of the killer so he could kill our daughter?" Susan's voice was becoming higher pitched and more bitter as the interview went on.

"We are not suggesting you had anything to do with Isla's murder, but since you both work in a hospital, I'm sure you can see, for the purposes of the investigation, that we needed..."

"No! What we need is for you detectives to stop blaming our family. We've gone through enough as it is and we can't even grieve in peace, without you lot showing up and pointing the finger at us." Susan was now in hysterics, tears streaming down her face, which was red with anger.

"I think you should leave," Greg said as he tried to console his wife.

As Tom shut the door behind him, it was immediately reopened by Jack, who took him by surprise. "I'm sorry about my mother, I'm sure you didn't mean how it sounded."

CHAPTER 15

Both Tom and Lavinia had noticed how quiet he was in the interview, as he sat on the sofa, out of the line of question. "We're sorry for bringing up the subject. I can clearly see how the news of Isla's death has affected you all. Understandably. We weren't suspecting either of you had anything to do with it."

"You're only doing your jobs. I want you to find Isla's killer as much, if not more, than you do. I am also aware of the drug you mentioned, and understand why you would need to speak to us all, and I don't want to speak ill of my sister, but maybe it was Isla who stole the drug? Obviously, you can't speak to her, but I know my parents would not do anything like that. Isla had a rebellious streak in her."

"How was she rebellious? Has she stolen or taken drugs in the past?"

"She went off the wagon for a brief period. Smoking, drinking, drugs, partying and staying out all night. I'm not aware of her stealing, but I wouldn't put it past her then. It wasn't long after her relationship ended with Carl. I think she's always had that streak in her, and it came out when she was in a bad and broken place. She's not a bad person. She just needed a wakeup call and once that happened, she concentrated on her studies and left the old her behind. We haven't spoken of that period since. I can't imagine Isla stealing a drug like Succinylcholine though, but I thought you should know."

"Thank you, Jack. Again, we apologise."

****

"Well, it could have gone better," Tom said to Wilson. Tom and Lavinia were currently sat in front of Wilson's desk, opposite him, giving him an update.

"Jack thought Isla could have stolen the drug herself," Lavinia told Wilson. "Could she have signed her own death warrant?" Lavinia asked the question that hung in the air.

"God knows. Well, we can't ask Isla what happened," Tom heavily sighed, his frustration for the case evident. Lavinia looked over at him and his face showed tiredness and stress.

"And there's been no unusual activity regarding hospital supplies either. That doesn't mean that someone didn't steal doses of the drug on behalf of the killer, or the killer himself dressed in uniform and took supplies. But we have no evidence. There are no specific quantities of the drug stored at any one time and no significant decrease in stock over the past month. It's in high demand so constantly gets checked and stocked up. All supplies get checked weekly and a log gets filled out and orders placed if stock is running low from a healthcare equipment and supplies store online which then gets delivered. So, nothing further to report there either."

"Another dead end then. No pun intended."

CHAPTER 16

The time had come.
Another day. Another victim.
And nothing excited him more.

It felt like Christmas had come early and his present was waiting for him downstairs.

Once he was satisfied that his alias, Dean Hadley, had completed his task, he was able to let himself take over.

The subject of his thoughts was hovered in the corner of the cage, shivering with her legs hugged against her chest to keep in the warmth. The hand-me down tracksuit bottoms and t shirt had been worn previously by both Isla and Madison, and although washed, Anna could still smell the fear from them both; it was the same fear she was feeling right now.

She was fully aware of the recent murders, from the bare bones of what had been published in newspapers and broadcasted on the news. Not much information had been released, and the media were speculating all sorts, but she never thought that she would be living in Isla's and Madison's shadows.

The fear in her eyes were unmistakable but that only made him more euphoric.

She thought back to what she last remembered and that was sitting in the house she had gone to view with Dean. They had coffee and she was sat on the Chesterfield, chatting away until she couldn't remember anymore, and she woke up here, trapped in this cage. She had been forced to change her clothing and had been given a small portion of lukewarm lumpy porridge on a plastic tray with a strawberry milkshake in a plastic cup.

She was neither hungry nor thirsty but didn't know when her next meal would have been, so she forced it all down.

She only felt weaker.

Being alone in the dark made her thoughts go wild. How had she missed the warning signs? Were there any warning signs to begin with? Had he lured her to a false sense of security?

She wasn't sure. She wasn't sure of anything.

But she couldn't imagine Dean doing something like that. He had a gentle soul and was just enthusiastic and eager to find himself a house, a home he could call his own. Again, had that been a lie? Had it all been an act? Had he come up with an alias and a different life to make it seem that he was looking to buy his first house?

A web of questions tangled around in her mind, forming a net of uncertainty. She felt trapped. She was trapped.

He waited for a few minutes to heighten the suspense before he made his way down the steps, which made a thudding noise every time he took a step.

Anna's head snapped up at the noise and saw the light that filtered through from the top of the stairs. Her heart rate accelerated more with each step he took as he descended the stairs.

Thud, thud, thud.

The rhythmic beating of his footsteps matched the beating of her own heart.

She could not make out any details, like his height, his hair colour, what he was wearing. He was just a silhouette.

He strolled nearer to the cage, wanting to emphasise his every move as he approached her. Wanting her to feel his every step, feel the fear growing inside her, feel her heart hammering against her chest, feel her whole body shaking as he got closer.

CHAPTER 16

He pulled on the string and a small light bulb dangling above the cage came to life, putting Anna in the spotlight. She had to blink a few times to make her eyes adjust to the sudden brightness.

He stood watching her for a few moments, gauging her reaction and feeling her trepidation.

She slowly looked up at him, meeting his stare and his hard-cold eyes. She could make out his cropped thick dark hair colour. He was tall and slender and had a beard stubble. His facial expression was stony and shrewd, but he did not look out of the ordinary. Just someone who had lost his place and meaning in society.

That made her have the courage to stare back at him with all the will she had left in her, which took him by surprise. This did not go unnoticed, and she felt a slight newfound confidence in her ability to speak and talk to him. It came out as a whisper.

"I'm not afraid of you."

"You should be."

"I have friends and family who care about me, and they'll soon know something is wrong and call the police. People will be looking for me."

"And they will find you." Something about that sentence and the matter-of-fact way he said it sent shivers down her spine and something told her that they would not be finding her alive.

All that confidence swiftly drained from her body like a tap and all the amiable things she thought of him disappeared and was replaced by abhorrence.

The cold evil in his eyes were a true reflection of himself, devoid of any emotion.

He turned away into darkness. His footsteps echoed on the concrete flooring and bounced off the four walls. Another light was switched on above his head and illuminated the horror.

Anna could now see a small wooden worktop with a steel sink that went along the entire wall, along with a trolley parked to the side of it that held various stainless-steel instruments and equipment of pure torture.

Her eyes widened in terror.

He took his time, eyes grazing over the curves, the grooves, the sharp points and the smooth surfaces of stainless steel, like he was studying the textures of a grand painting.

He wanted her to be afraid of him.

And he knew just what to do.

CHAPTER 17

At ten o'clock the following morning, Wilson was sat in a meeting with Gerald Fischer, who was in charge of the crosswords, sudokus, wordsearches, word wheel, mathematical problems and quizzes that were published in the local newspaper, Scunthorpe Telegraph. Gerald explained that he received the crosswords at the start of the weekend with strict instructions to be published in Monday morning's paper. It had been a last-minute change, but he was able to publish them just in time.

"Do you normally take requests to publish puzzles?"

"Not usually, I have done a few times in the past, but this one was very unusual, and I was hesitant about publishing it at first."

"Why did you?"

"I got paid good money for it."

"Aside from the obvious points, why did you think it was unusual?"

"It wasn't a very challenging crossword and with only seven clues. Not your regular crossword puzzle. That's why I had to come up with the mini crossword section, so I had reason to publish it. The subject was rather sombre and with strict instructions, so someone was obviously really keen to have it in the paper."

"You said you got paid good money for it. Did you get a generous tip from the Anonymous writer of this crossword?"

"Yes, once I published it, I received payment."

"In what form?"

"Cash. In an envelope. Both were addressed to me personally."

"Do you still have the envelopes?"

"They're in my office bin but I can get it back for you if you need to fingerprint it. I don't think anyone else touched them apart from me and the receptionist. I imagine the person who delivered it wore gloves. Feels like I'm in a good old cosy murder mystery."

"Were the envelopes handwritten?" Wilson asked, as he ignored Gerald's previous comment. It may seem that this was fun to him, but to Wilson, it was a pure nightmare.

"No, typed onto a label."

"Did it look like it had been typed from a computer or by other means, such as a typewriter, for example?"

"Definitely typed from a computer."

"And did you become suspicious when the second one was addressed to you?"

"At first, I was confused, then I thought it might be a miniseries. We've had that in the past. All to do with the same topic. It was very similar to the first one only with seven different clues. Maybe there's seven separate crosswords."

Wilson's face barely registered what he had just been told. And the significance of the number seven. Wilson's brain went into overdrive, and immediately picked up his office phone and called an urgent meeting in two minutes. He then slammed the phone into the receiver and turned his attention back to Gerald Fischer. "Are you aware of the significance of the date the anonymous sender wishes you to publish these crosswords on?"

"Coincidentally, they seem to be published on the same day that a body is found."

* * * *

The short but significant meeting with Gerald Fischer swiftly came to an end, as Wilson was desperate to meet with his team and discuss the likely importance of the number seven, possibly meaning seven victims.

CHAPTER 17

"Even Daniel had said that the killer had only just started and expected him to kill more victims before the end of it," Morgan pointed out which made the possibility even stronger.

"Seven crosswords, seven clues, seven victims," Lavinia concluded.

"Why seven?" Harris contemplated. "It seems a random number."

"I agree," Morgan said. "Maybe it's his lucky number or something. He has a vision; he's orchestrating a play, and each kill is another act. He can see the end, the finale. Seven is enough to warrant him a serial killer but not too many for it to be an overkill. Perhaps that's what he sees."

"The whole crossword was a clue," Tom stated, overwhelmed with the recent news and not playing any mind to what Morgan had just suggested. "Not just about the killings themselves, but the seven clues were a reference to the number of victims. Obviously, we didn't think anything of it at the time, but now it makes perfect sense."

"We've only received two crosswords. So that means there's five more victims to come," Norton said with dread.

"Nothing gets past you, does it? You clearly didn't miss maths lessons at school," Morgan replied sarcastically, to which Norton mouthed 'fuck off' to her.

"What happens now? There's no pattern to his victims so we can't base any intel off that, can we?" Lavinia asked Wilson directly. She based her question on the fact that both victims looked different, had different occupations, and apparently moved in different circles so they did not know each other. They may have known the killer, and that could be the connection, but they didn't have a link as of yet. They knew nothing about the killer. It was all educational guesswork from what Daniel had profiled, but that did not help them at this minute. Jake had been their prime suspect, but what he had said when Harris interviewed him, did not sound like he had anything to do with her murder. He was still very much in the spotlight, and they kept a close eye on him and his movements and whereabouts, but nothing sent alarms going. When Wilson finally looked at Lavinia, she could see the bags under his red eyes, that clearly showed the lack of sleep and exhaustion. The whole team looked and felt the same.

"It explains a lot but it's not enough," Wilson simply stated. Each piece of new information was energising; however, it only added to the confusion and asked more questions than it answered. They were getting several pieces of a puzzle that did not quite fit together to make one big picture, and that was the issue. They couldn't do much with bits and pieces of information. They needed leads, witnesses, evidence, they needed a full picture. They needed a miracle.

"What about these tattoos. Does it explain anything further with this new information?" Morgan asked, clutching at straws.

"Nope, that's still very much unclear. We may see more of a pattern with his next victims and with that, he will think he is unreachable and out of our league, so he'll get confident and cocky, and that's when he'll make a mistake. That's when we nail him."

CHAPTER 18

Sarah Hayes was a Forensic Scientist who specialised in Fingerprints.

She had completed a Forensic Science degree at the University of Central Lancashire (UCLAN), before deciding that that was the area of Forensics she wanted to specialise in.

That was twenty-five years ago.

Sarah was currently using the chemical enhancement technique, ninhydrin, on the envelopes given by Gerald Fischer, who had also supplied exclusion prints for comparison. The receptionist at the newspaper, Paul Goulding, had also supplied exclusion prints since he had also touched the envelope with his bare hands when he passed it on to Gerald.

Ninhydrin reacted with the amino acids in the finger mark to produce a purple colouration, known as Ruhemann's purple. It was used on porous surfaces including paper and cardboard.

Sarah was stood by the fume cupboard with the glass screen open just wide enough to insert her hands through. She wore blue latex gloves, a white lab coat that was stained by various different enhancement techniques she had worked with over the years, her long brunette hair tied up in a bun and she had placed safety glasses over her eyes. Tom and Lavinia were stood nearby, also wearing a pair of safety glasses and a lab coat each.

They watched on with eager eyes as Sarah sprayed the envelopes in turn with the solution and transferred on to a shelf in the humidifier oven that reached temperatures up to 50°C and 90% humidity, which accelerated the chemical reaction from days to minutes.

They had to wait for twenty minutes.

Sarah opened up the humidifier oven door and took a look inside at the envelopes that were stained purple. There were a few finger marks visible, some with full ridge detail, others a smudge, but with experience Sarah thought they would most likely belong to Fischer and Goulding.

The killer was too meticulous to leave finger marks on an envelope. Or anywhere. Even if they weren't forensically aware, they knew that fingerprints were the obvious contact evidence scientists would look for.

Sarah then photographed the prints and processed them onto the Automated Fingerprint Identification System, known as AFIS.

AFIS was a database used to store and compare known prints with unknown prints. It analysed the minutiae of the finger mark to compare individual ridge characteristics.

A specialist scanner, which sat next to the computer, was used to upload a photocopy of the prints so they could be searched and compared against the finger marks already stored on the system.

Sarah had up on the computer screen, an image of the finger marks she had just uploaded with the comparison points marked up of the individual characteristics: core, delta, ridge endings, lakes and bifurcations; and next to that on the right side of the screen, the results of the searches, which unsurprisingly belonged to the elimination prints from Gerald Fischer and Paul Goulding. There were enough comparison points on each of the finger marks to confirm a match.

Tom and Lavinia were not completely surprised by the news as it seemed to have been a theme throughout the case, that the evidence did not belong to the killer, unless he allowed such a thing to happen. And in those instances, the evidence was not identifiable to the killer.

CHAPTER 19

It was early Monday morning when the bin men came around to empty the black general waste and the blue recycling bins. Being summer, with the heat and the longer, lighter evenings, and with people gathering with friends and family for BBQs, there was an extraordinary increase in the amount of alcohol people drank. Bins were full of cans and bottles, but it felt normal for that time of year. It also happened around the festive season. So, it was no surprise for brothers Arthur and Alfie Stockton when bottles clanked against each other as they unloaded them onto the back of the waste vehicle.

"You watch the footy match last night between Man U and Man City?" Arthur asked his colleague James, as he grabbed the bins from the houses opposite.

"What a close game. David De Gea saved some cracking goals," he responded.

"Bet Pep Guardiola is happy with that 2-1 win," Dylan, the driver, piped up through his open window that he leaned out of to speak.

"They wouldn't have won if they didn't get that penalty in the last few minutes. What a controversy that was," Alfie stated, who clearly supported Manchester United out of the two.

"The VAR stated otherwise," Arthur pointed out. They got into a discussion about the pros and cons of using Video Assistant Referees.

Their discussion continued until Alfie went to empty the black general waste bin but found he couldn't move it as it was unusually heavy. He opened the lid to look inside as if that would make it lighter but what he saw turned his face as pale as a ghost. It was the smell that hit the back of his nose and throat, and he bent over and vomited beside the bin.

"Can't handle that Manchester City won?" Dylan joked, receiving a round of laughs.

"Call...the...police," he managed to say in between breaths as he pulled himself together. The others noticed the change in his demeanour, he looked shocked and shaken up. He sat down on the ground, unable to move.

Concerned, Arthur moved towards him, apprehensive of the reason for his brother's sudden change. Arthur noticed the smell first as he got nearer and covered his nose. When Alfie pointed towards the bin to let him know that it was the source of the smell, Arthur carefully approached and looked inside.

"Jesus fucking Christ!" he swore as he scrambled backwards and got the attention of his colleagues. "There's a fucking body in the bin. Call the police. NOW!"

****

When Wilson received a phone call on his work mobile, it usually meant bad news. Either a body had turned up or the press were after a comment or a story of the latest case. With the press already hot on his heels, he was about to lose control with them. That was, until the person at the other end of the line, told him that a body had been found.

The blood from his face had drained.

If he wasn't as white as a sheet before, he certainly was now when he saw the body at the crime scene. Hayleigh had confirmed that it was the same MO as the previous victims, so it was most likely the same killer.

He had struck again.

Victim number three.

"No toes, fingers, left eye or left ear. Ligature marks on the wrists and ankles which indicate she was tied up. Clear

CHAPTER 19

sign of torture. And just like the previous two, this victim has also been stripped of clothing," Hayleigh recounted from the other crime scenes. It was a tick list.

The victim was slumped in the bin, with her back against one side, her knees hugged up to her chest, her arms hung limp on her legs and her head was slumped forward. Hayleigh was able to move her hair out of the way and spotted the all-too-familiar neck tattoo that she had expected to see. Again, it was different to the previous two as it had a small circle with three dots in a triangular formation in the centre of a bigger circle.

"Without understanding the meaning of the other two, I'm just as stumped on this one as I am for the rest," Norton admitted as the team took it in turns to look inside the bin at the body and the tattoo Hayleigh had pointed out to them. Marcus had snapped all he could in situ, getting every angle possible and overview, approach and close up shots, trying not to miss anything out. He would have to wait until the body was at the morgue to photograph it properly. By now the nearby residents had gathered on their driveways to look at the commotion and were gossiping amongst themselves. The waste vehicle blocked off one end of the road while PCs Polly Frances and Samantha Briggs were getting witness statements from the bin men.

Lavinia walked up the elderly woman living next door to the person whose wheelie bin had been used to dump the body in. She was stood at the bottom of her garden holding onto a Zimmer frame, as she looked concerned.

"The body is not my neighbour. I've just phoned her at work and told her what's happening and she's on her way."

"Thank you, Mrs…"

"Call me Joan."

"Thank you, Joan. What's your neighbour's name?"

"Debra. Debra Gill. She works at a Nursery in Scunthorpe."

"Does Debra live with anyone?"

"She's divorced and has no kids. Her parents visited last week, but there's no one currently visiting."

Lavinia stood talking and asking questions to Joan about her neighbour and if she saw or heard anything in the early hours of the morning. Not surprisingly, she did not. And soon, Debra arrived home, shocked at the scene that was playing out on her driveway. She dumped her car before the cordon and ran towards her house, demanding to know what was happening.

Wilson managed to calm her down and led her back to her car so she could sit down. He asked her several questions, but she was none the wiser, just like the whole neighbourhood. It was the same situation as with the previous two victims. No one had heard or seen anything or anyone. The news had already made its way onto Scotter News Forum Facebook page where everyone was astounded by what had occurred, but no one knew anything.

Hayleigh continued to examine what she could in situ but insisted she take the bin back to the examination warehouse to extract the body, in case there was evidence in or on the bin itself.

She drove ahead of the body recovery van, which fortunately was able to fit the entire wheelie bin in, with inches to spare. It was a tight fit but they taped the lid so it would not come open during the journey and release the aromas of death.

She parked in a bay behind the warehouse, close to the door and waited for the body recovery van to arrive before she got out of her car and unlocked the padlocked door of the warehouse using a small key that was placed around her car keyring.

The warehouse was an abyss of darkness, until Hayleigh turned on the lights which brightened up the room with a natural white glow. The warehouse was dull with no decorated interior other than a large equipment and PPE station in the far corner and a lime green Kia Picanto

CHAPTER 19

stationary at a designated workstation. It was a vehicle examination warehouse for those involved in hit and runs and burglaries, but since it had more space than the laboratories, it seemed like the perfect place to conduct the examination and extraction of the body in the bin.

Hayleigh set up a workstation in a separate area to the car and placed a plastic sheet on the ground for the bin to be placed on. She wore latex gloves and an apron to prevent contamination and to protect herself from potential hazards.

Marcus had also arrived, and together, with the body recovery team, he helped them extract the bin from the car and wheeled it into the designated space in the warehouse. Hayleigh had enough time to set up and prepare equipment before Wilson and his team arrived.

Lavinia knocked on the door before she opened it and put her head around to make sure it was safe to step in. Hayleigh gave her the go-ahead and made them kit up in PPE just inside the doorway before they advanced to the workstation.

The bin was currently laid down on its side with the lid open on the plastic sheeting. The body could be compared to a foetus, in the way that she was curled up inside. Marcus was currently on his knees photographing inside the bin, and every step of the extraction. He had to narrow the aperture to f/11 to get a greater depth of field.

Rigor mortis had set in on her arms and so Hayleigh had to dislocate them at the elbow joint in order to help get her out. The sound was deafening and sent chills up their spines.

"Did you really have to do that?" Tom looked disgusted and uncomfortable at Hayleigh's approach.

"If I am to have any chance of getting her out of this bin, then yes, I did. It'll make the extraction easier." With the help of Wilson guiding the other half of her upper body and Norton pulling on the bin with the opposite force to help ease her out of it, they swiftly achieved the desired result in a smooth operation and her body flopped onto the sheet.

Her arms were twisted in an unnatural way below the elbow as a result of them being broken and Hayleigh had to do the same thing with her legs, which again the snap and pop echoed around the warehouse. Again, Tom looked as if he might throw up.

Marcus was there to digitally document the entire process. And he was snapping away again as the body now lay fully exposed on the sheet.

"God has small mercies. At least she's not alive to witness the pain of broken arms and legs. Poor soul," Norton expressed.

"No, but she undoubtedly witnessed a lot worse," Hayleigh stated.

"You know how to kill the mood."

Hayleigh started her external examination of the body. She was looking for similarities between this body and the other two, although there had been plenty already to confirm it was the same killer. She would wait to do the internal examination back at the morgue.

She then examined the wheelie bin inside and outside. She wasn't expecting trace evidence or fingerprints to be left by the killer as he would not be that careless, or if he left evidence behind, like with the footwear mark, it was because he wanted to and knew they would not be able to identify him from it. She took swabs of areas inside the bin, in case there was a small chance of getting the killer's DNA that transferred from the victim to the bin since she was in close contact with the inside. Control swabs around the area were taken primarily, and all of them were labelled on the swab tube, with her initials, time and date of collection and description of swab, and placed separately into evidence bags.

She was about to give up with the external exanimation, when she had to double check that her mind and eyes were not playing games on her, but sure enough, there was a small cluster of fibres caught in the inside handle of the bin. They

CHAPTER 19

were dark in colour, possibly dark brown or black. Marcus struggled to get the camera angle right but after a few tries he managed to capture them in situ, as best he could.

Hayleigh collected the cluster of fibres with plastic tweezers and placed them into a vial and then packaged that in a polythene evidence bag, labelling the continuity label on the front first. She placed it into a brown evidence storage box, along with the collection of swabs, to keep them safe.

"Let's hope we can get something from these," Hayleigh said optimistically as she put the lid on the box and called the body recovery team to take the body to the morgue so she could conduct the post-mortem. She did all she could on the wheelie bin and cleaned up the workstation.

****

Daniel Hargreaves had been a key part of the team, and with his expertise and knowledge of offenders and patterns of crime, he was able to help everyone else understand it. He was, once again, briefing the team. "He seems to move from victim to victim extremely fast. The victim who he unloads is probably barely cold by the time he has claimed another one and that's even more frightening. It means he's hungry for more, hungry to kill, and he wants to cause more fear and more pain, which seems to escalate with every kill."

That prospect did not sit well with the entire team. And Daniel was about to make it worse, as he had not come empty handed. On his way into the station, he had purchased several copies of the local newspaper which was now open on the puzzle page with the crossword staring back at them.

Across:
  3. Hit Dead Centre (4)
  5. Look Alike (6)
  7. Septet (5)

Down:
   1. Human Digits (7)
   2. The _ _ _ _ Bible (4)
   4. "Little Piggies" (4)
   6. Feeble, or Powerless (4)

The answer to 1 down, Human Digits, went down the centre of the crossword, so they worked out that one first to get a few letters for the other clues.

"Fingers," Lavinia stated for the Human Digits clue.

Fingers fit the word count, which meant that 3 Across, started with the letter 'N', 5 Across ended with the letter 'E' and 7 Across began with the letter 'S'.

"7 Across is ironically seven. Seems to be the magic number," Norton said.

"2 Down, the Holy Bible," Daniel said.

"Which means 3 Across starts with an 'N' and ends with an 'L'," Tom observed, his brain cells ticking over, to work out the problem.

"I thought look alike would be twin, but it doesn't fit the six letters and end with an E," Morgan admitted.

"4 Down, Little Piggies, has to be toes," Lavinia stated.

"You're good at getting the body parts," Harris joked.

"It's like the nursery rhyme, this little piggy went to the market, this little piggy had roast beef and so on," Lavinia explained, ignoring Harris's statement.

"Look alike is double," Norton exclaimed, thrilled at himself that he had managed to figure out a clue.

"So that leaves 6 Down, Feeble, or Powerless and 3 Across, Hit Dead Centre," Daniel specified.

"Weak. For 6 Down and Nail for 3 Across," Wilson worked out.

They discussed the crossword further and what each clue and answer could represent and how to link it with the evidence they already had.

CHAPTER 19

They concluded that the killer thought of his victims as weak – maybe they were already weak in his eyes – but especially when they had been administered Succinylcholine. As Lavinia had previously stated, the reference to the fingers and toes were clearly from his MO. The Septet clue was undoubtedly a reference to the number of crossword clues and ultimately the total number of victims. The struggle came with the nail and Holy Bible answers.

Was the reference to the Holy Bible a clue in that the killings were religious based, or did he think of himself as Holy and a creature of God that he answered to? Did he think of himself as God?

That would explain the nail answer as Jesus Christ was nailed to the cross when he was crucified, again signalling a religious aspect to the crime.

"I don't know if I am reading too much into this, but Jesus died on the cross and then got resurrected. Is that the killer's way of saying he's bipolar or something? He has an alter ego that overtakes his normal being and gets resurrected as this other person, the killer, to get rid of certain people for God?" Lavinia inferred.

"How the hell did you make that inference?"

"Didn't skip any history lessons," she joked.

"That might help to explain the reasonings and behaviours of the killer and his crimes," Daniel replied.

"Well, we have always discussed the possibility of there being a religious aspect to these crimes and I think we can safely say that there is, especially now with these crosswords in the picture," Wilson explained. "Good work, everyone. If we keep working at it, and focus on this religious characteristic, who knows what other answers we may find."

CHAPTER 20

Nearly a week had gone by with little investigative leads. They hadn't heard from the killer all week since the third victim was found, and the third crossword published in the paper Monday morning. The team were working endlessly but to no avail. They were limitlessly searching for answers to the religious aspect of the crime, probing all religions to make the crime pattern fit with teachings and Bible verses from testaments, old and new. But they hadn't got anything more than they already had.

However, Friday night meant speedway night and for a couple of hours, Lavinia could enjoy herself without having to worry about the case. She was looking forward to having a night off, where she did not get home, exhausted and barely able to stay awake to eat tea. The case was very consuming, and she felt like it was all work and no play. That was exactly what Alastair was afraid of and he encouraged Wilson to let the team have the night off so she could relax for the first time since she had started work experience. He did not want her to fall into the same trap he had done countless times.

Mindi also left work on time, so she could attend the speedway meeting with her family ready for the 7:30pm start.

This time the Scunthorpe Scorpions were riding against Redcar Bears.

They were in the queue in the Trackside Café that was situated at the far end of the stadium, between the first and second bends, and ordered a cheeseburger with onions, chips and a cup of tea each.

CHAPTER 20

They sauced their burgers and chips, and milked their teas, before they walked back to the stands and took a seat to eat their food before the meeting started.

"Nothing beats speedway food," Mindi commented as she took a bite of her burger and ketchup oozed out the floured bap.

"You're right. Classic speedway grub," Lavinia agreed, munching on her chips that were lathered in BBQ sauce.

"How were both of your days?" Alastair asked his daughters, catching up with them.

"Clients were as useless as always. I asked for three months' worth of bank statements from all accounts. She gave me statements for only two accounts and claimed that's all she had, but there was another account in her name that she failed to disclose and said it was because she doesn't use it anymore. When I received that, there was a transaction going from that account into another one as recent as last week. She told me she's only recently starting using it again to transfer funds between accounts," Mindi explained.

"Clearly they don't want you to know about that one," Alastair stated before he shoved a few chips in his mouth and took a big bite of his burger.

"It would make my life a lot easier if I didn't have to chase them for it. Also, had a new client come in for a meeting and she was lovely. Thought we wouldn't get a case to court since the client wasn't answering her phone but finally managed to get in contact with her."

"Sounds like a nightmare of a day chasing clients," Lavinia said.

"It really was. Spend half of my time doing that."

"But you build a really good relationship with them, and you've only been in the job, what, six months, and you've already come so far and done so much. You are passionate about helping clients and it's lovely to see you so settled in a short amount of time," Lavinia told her sincerely.

"Aw thank you, sis. That means a lot." Mindi momentarily laid her head on Lavinia's shoulder, to hug her, before turning her attention back to her food. "What about your day? I can feel see you're a bit tense and your mind is preoccupied."

Lavinia gave her a look that said, 'did you really have to say that?' before responding: "The entire team is exhausted. We haven't had communication from the killer since Monday. We now think there is most definitely a religious aspect to his murders, but we don't know what yet. We have odd bits and pieces of Christianity teachings and Bible quotes, but not enough to paint the whole picture. We've got the crossword that gives more questions than actual answers. It's certainly slow progress." Lavinia unloaded.

"Surely no news is good news," Mindi suggested.

"Well not really, he could be stalking his next victim or worse, torturing his next victim as we sit here and we're none the wiser. Daniel, the criminologist, says the killer strives on his victim's fear and will cause as much fear as possible. And we've concluded that there are possibly seven murders in mind. And we have three victims. So, you can imagine how tense everyone is. We want to solve it before more innocent women are murdered, but at the moment, the killer is in complete control so my gut tells me we will only uncover the truth as more victims turn up." Lavinia took a breath. It was good to get her feelings and worries off her chest, even if it did not help the investigation. She knew she needed to relax more after work and to clear her mind before bed, but that was easier said than done.

"They all want to cause fear and are successful at doing so. That's why they like it so much, it's something they know they're good at and can boast about and get off on it. The moment you think or know you're going to die, everything just goes, your mind goes blank, you stop feeling, but fear is the only thing that remains," Alastair responded.

"What about the drug lead?" Mindi asked.

CHAPTER 20

"And the connection to the Armstrong family? Especially the father? He works in the hospital, doesn't he, and would have access to the drug?" Alastair added.

"They all work or worked at the hospital. Even the son is studying Medicine at university. Greg is a neurosurgeon and apparently uses it all the time. He is the one with the closest connection to the drug and while we haven't completely ruled him out, there's no evidence to suggest he ever did such a thing."

"It's a waiting game and that's the worst. But let's not think about the case tonight. Just take your mind off it and enjoy the racing," Alastair instructed.

They finished their burger and chips in time for the starting parade, where Robbie Williams' 'Let me Entertain You' played from the speakers as the riders walked around from the pits to the starting tapes and stood beside their bike, the fans clapping and cheering and sounding horns all the while. The riders then got introduced by the commentator in turn, starting at rider number 7 from the away team and then ending at rider number 1 for the home team. They did a few laps of honour on the track before the siren signalled two minutes until heat one commenced.

CHAPTER 21

The following Monday morning, Samuel Jackford was born.

He had altered his appearance to make him look like a completely different person. He was a different person, and he lived a different life. He thought he would try something diverse, something he had never done before, and from someone else's perspective. And today he was going to see Tracey Evans, a Child Protection Social Worker, about the possibility of removing his imaginary son from his imaginary abusive mother and temporarily placing him in care with his imaginary auntie, while he was able to sort custody of his child in court matters.

He had come up with the perfect alias and stood in the bathroom staring at his transformation in the mirror.

He did not even recognise himself.

He sat down at his kitchen table and poured himself a freshly brewed coffee from the machine, flicking through the morning's paper. He was transfixed on the article published by crime reporter and journalist Yvonne Webster, about the recent murder of Madison McKinley. His killings. He thought there was a lot of speculation and it angered him that he had been so misunderstood by the media, by the detectives, by the public, by everyone.

He swiftly finished getting ready and ventured out into the world of Samuel Jackford.

The morning felt different. The air felt lighter and warm, with a slight breeze. He closed and locked the front door before meeting the taxi that greeted him at the end of the driveway. He had locked his car away in the garage, so the

CHAPTER 21

number plate could not be traced back to him, the real him, while he was portraying Samuel Jackford.

He exchanged pleasantries with the driver and confirmed his drop-off point at the North Lincolnshire County Council building.

His mind was blank the entire journey, no thoughts processing in his mind, he didn't even need to go over his fake life, like going over revision notes immediately before an exam, no nervous flutters in his stomach, no sickening feeling. Just nothing. He watched the world float past his window from the back seat, at houses, at shops, at the traffic and at people going about their lives as if it was just a normal day in Scunthorpe.

The traffic was steady but slow moving at times where there were busy junctions and too much traffic approaching roundabouts, such as at the Queensway roundabout, with cars coming from four different directions but all seemed to be heading the same way. But they made good time as the journey took under half an hour. The driver signalled left at the traffic lights off Ashby Road and entered the car park, situated next to The Pods Leisure Centre. He pulled up outside the entrance.

Samuel Jackford thanked the driver, and paid cash before exiting the taxi. He stared up at the basic brown bricked building which loomed over Central Park for a few seconds before entering through the entrance doors.

He could not help but notice the musty smell of the place, which made it seem all the more unattractive if that was at all possible.

His expression changed from neutral to sombre.

He located the reception desk just inside the entrance and asked for Tracey Evans. The receptionist, who studied Samuel for a moment before speaking, directed him to the right side of the building and up the stairs to the second floor where her department was. He followed her instructions and was immediately greeted by Tracey, who opened the door to welcome him in. He recognised her from pictures he had studied beforehand when conducting his research.

She gave him a wide beaming smile.

He could have wiped that smile off her face there and then, but he had a job to do, and he had to do it properly otherwise his cunning and well thought out plan would not be completed. He had to mentally calm himself down and suppress the desire to react.

Tracey introduced herself before she took him to her office, which was spacious and felt more like a study room one would have in their house, with the plants decorated all around the room, on the windowsill, on the desk, on the table and on the bookshelf. Her desk was in front of the window with a gamers' style ergonomic chair sat behind it. The desk was neat and tidy, with a computer, a couple of files and a very organised stationery desk tidy on it. There was a small two-seater sofa placed to the right of the desk, in front of the bookcase, what Jackford presumed was for the client, and a reclining chair opposite it, with a glass table in between that had an aromatherapy diffuser placed upon it. Jackford had to admit that it was a cosy and very home-like office, a space where her clients could feel calm and safe.

And he indeed felt that way.

He felt calmer now than he had done in a while.

"Please take a seat and make yourself comfortable. Can I get you anything to drink?" she politely asked, as she stood in the doorway.

"Water would be great. Thank you."

She walked away, giving him a moment to get settled, and returned a short while later with a jug of cool water with ice and lemons floating in it. She closed her office door to give them privacy and poured Jackford and herself a glass before grabbing a notepad and pen from her desk and settling into her chair opposite him. She placed glasses over her eyes and looked up at Jackford as she was poised to write notes and listen.

CHAPTER 21

The meeting had just turned serious.

"Sam, I briefly know your situation, but I am going to need you to inform me of every detail starting at the very beginning. I understand that it will resurface feelings and relive details that you just want to bury, but it is necessary to tell me everything so I can assess your situation and take the appropriate steps. Is that ok?" she said softly and evenly.

"Yes, whatever you need."

"How did you and your wife, Sabrina, meet?"

"We met at school, about twenty-two years ago now I believe. We weren't really friends, but we had a few classes together. She was the popular, beautiful, rebellious student, and I was the quiet, hardworking, nerdy student that hung around with the five other rejects, those who were not classed as the popular crew. Complete opposites."

"Sometimes opposites attract. It's not always a bad thing."

"I never thought someone like her would even look at someone like me," he laughed at the memories and like he couldn't believe his luck.

"When did you start getting acquainted with one another?"

"It was in Art of all subjects. We were sat on the same bench, and I have always loved art and have always been quite artistic whether in photography, drawing or cooking. Art for me is another world, a place to relax and get lost in. I think the first time she ever spoke to me was to compliment me on my drawing."

"What did she say?"

"She was watching me for a while. I could feel her eyes, but I was too embarrassed to look up, so I just blushed and continued with my drawing. I tried to focus but she was putting me off. I dared to look up and our eyes met. She nodded towards my drawing and just said it was impressive."

"How did you respond?"

"I had started to say hers was impressive too, but it really wasn't. I don't know how I managed to get the courage to approach her, but I did, and I showed her the effect of shadowing on objects. I just rambled on but felt confident as I was talking about a subject I knew about. Apparently, I intrigued her, and we started to speak more and eventually we hung out at school and then after school. I felt euphoric. I was in love."

"Did she feel the same?"

"I think she always thought of us as friends. Especially at the beginning. She would never want to be with someone like me. She was dating the handsome cocky lads that were into fitness and gyms and working out. It was similar to the stereotypical quarterback American footballer going out with the head cheerleader."

"So, you continued hanging out, then what happened?"

"I walked her home one night after she had been to mine for help with an art project. She kissed me briefly and very lightly on the lips and I will never forget that moment. After that she turned cold and ignored me and went back to not acknowledging my existence. I was fuming and upset. But after a while, I found out it was more to do with her boyfriend. She kept giving me looks as if to say she was sorry. Her boyfriend knew troubled guys outside of school and he dragged her into late night drug dealings in supermarket car parks. She declined physically and mentally from then on. All these jobs were making her have problems. Drinking and smoking and wasn't eating or sleeping. Apparently, her boyfriend slapped her around and one time raped her and threatened he would give her to his mates if she didn't do what he said."

"And do you think this is why she became violent towards yourself?"

"We actually ended up at the same college and rekindled our friendship. It seemed she had got rid of her boyfriend and

CHAPTER 21

sorted herself out. Our friendship turned into a relationship and escalated from there. The rest is history."

"When did she start to become aggressive with you?"

"It was shortly after she became pregnant with our son, Charlie. It happened suddenly like a switch had gone off in her head and she just turned."

"Perhaps something from her school days resurfaced and she couldn't control her emotions? Wouldn't help being pregnant either with hormones or emotions all over the place."

"That's what I believed, and I thought it would just be a brief spell, but it continued and escalated."

"What happened after Charlie was born? Did she have any prenatal depression? Or did she have a great relationship with her son?"

"I guess she had prenatal depression. It wasn't formally diagnosed but she continued spiralling after he was born. It was like she didn't want him anymore. She didn't bother feeding him, changing him, paying him any attention. She was always out late at night, smoking and drinking, and I found out later, doing drugs as well. She had gone back to her old ways, and I tried to help, I really did. After all this, she would become aggressive and get violent. She would never hurt Charlie, so she took it out on me." His breathing became more erratic and as he took a sip of water; Tracey could see his hands were shaking.

"Sam, do you know what happened to make her switch?"

"I contacted one of her best friends from school, they are no longer friends now, but I asked her if anything went on at school that could have influenced her behaviour and withdrawal. She said Sabrina became pregnant after her boyfriend raped her and she couldn't physically abort it because she was so against the idea, but she didn't want it either and got desperate so that's why she drank and smoked and took drugs to get rid of it. I always thought she wanted kids but maybe being pregnant brought all that back up. She lost the baby at school."

"Did she ever express her views of having children? Either with you or in general?"

"We never really spoke about it properly. The topic kept coming up, but she would change the subject. I don't think she was fully ready or fully healed from her ordeal back then, but she didn't ever say she didn't want them."

"How did she react when she found out she was pregnant with your child?"

"We were both surprised but happy."

"And she never touched Charlie once?"

"She never hit him, no. But I just don't want Charlie to grow up in a hostile and violent environment and all he remembers from his childhood is his mother having problems and his father getting hit. That's no childhood for Charlie. It should be filled with happiness and love and cartoons and toys."

"I understand. Did she have any exchanges with the police at all?"

"A few I think, from her school days."

"All drug or underage drinking related?"

"Yes, as far as I am aware. I believe she was imprisoned for a short period and that's what made her change her lifestyle and she attended college and got her act together."

"Any for domestic violence?"

Jackford hung his head in disappointment. "I didn't want to admit, but I called them a few times because I thought they could help her like they did the first time. But they didn't do much. Just took a statement and that was it."

"What happens now?"

"I will write up my report and forward you the number for a Family Law Solicitor to contact. They will want a statement from you just like I have done today. They may want additional details but for me this is just the preliminary meeting to get an understanding of what has occurred and

CHAPTER 21

what help you need. I will need further details from you at a later stage but for now, what you have given me is sufficient. The Family Law Solicitor will assess you for Legal Aid based on your financial situation which will pay for the representation in court amongst other things, and then a judge will hear your case in court and get the relevant orders put in place. I'm afraid it is a lengthy process, but I promise you, we will do our best for you and Charlie."

He was on his way out of the office when he collided with another man who was entering the building. They both said their apologies before going their separate ways. Samuel noticed he wore a Wetherspoons uniform.

As he waited for a taxi to pick him up, he thought he deserved an Oscar for that award winning performance. It went even better than he'd thought it would and he'd surprised himself at just how good he had been. Just the right amount of sadness and tears to be believable.

Tracey had said it was a lengthy process, but he wanted to spend as much time with her as possible and was delighted at that prospect. He also realised that he would have to set his plan in motion before the Legal Aid assessment as he only had bank accounts in his real name. He could open another account in a different name if he wanted to go all the way. But he decided to hold off calling a Family Law Solicitor for now and just concentrate on the meetings with Tracey. After all, that was why he came up with this fake life and alias in the first place.

A taxi swiftly arrived and unlike the silent journey he had on the way to the meeting, he was extremely chatty with his driver now.

Lying came tremendously natural to him.

CHAPTER 22

Seven intended victims.
Three down.
Four to go.
One investigation.
No evidence, no new leads, and no suspects.

The bodies of Isla Armstrong and Madison McKinley could not be released to their families during an ongoing investigation. Especially since the case was far from being solved and closed with the recent discovery of a third victim.

However, to help the families grieve, they were able to hold a memorial service in their memory, where friends and family could pay their respects and say goodbye. It would not be of any consolation knowing that their loved ones had been murdered, and their killer was still out there, but it would help them find closure for now until justice could be brought.

So, at noon, on the warm and sunny Wednesday, all those who had known Isla and Madison gathered at the St Peter's Church in Scotter.

Some were dressed in black from head to toe, others braved bold colours. There had been no formal colour scheme or attire set out for guests, so they wore what they felt was appropriate for the service. Almost every guest had arrived with a bright bouquet of flowers clasped in their hand and laid it by the shrine amongst other flowers, messages, and photographs by the altar.

Wilson and his team also arrived to pay their respects but also felt obligated to the families to attend. Lavinia brought a sunlight bouquet forming of yellow roses and white freesias, sent from the team giving deepest condolences and prayers.

CHAPTER 22

She knew the flowers would not be of any consolation to the families, but to find the killer would be. Death affected everyone differently, but the lives of every person who attended the service would never be the same again. Their world had been turned upside down.

They followed the gravel path that led them to the entrance of the Church. Susan, Greg, and Jack Armstrong were stood to the left of the doorway while Bridget and Rick McKinley stood to the right, to greet and acknowledge their relatives that had arrived for the service.

Their families had been united in death.

"It's good of you all to come," Bridget said to the team in a shaky voice, a scrunched-up tissue clasped firmly in her hand so she could wipe her eyes every time tears threatened to escape.

"Of course," Wilson responded as they all headed inside.

The pews were quickly filled up and a small crowd had gathered by the altar with people reading heartfelt messages from other friends and family members while depositing their own bunch of flowers onto the shrine. Candles had been lit on the table where two photographs stood staring back at them. One was of Isla, the other of Madison. Both wore wide happy smiles as they looked into the camera lens, full of life.

It was touching to see so many people gathered but that made Lavinia realise just how many people their deaths had affected and that was hard to comprehend. They had to find the killer, not only for Isla and Madison, or their parents, or the third victim, who they were still to identify, but for everyone in the church.

Lavinia scanned the crowd and noticed Cassie Nolan sat with her parents on the second row, head down, looking through photos on her phone of the two of them. She thought that must be torture and wondered why she was putting herself through that, but then again people coped and dealt with grief differently. Maybe that was the way Cassie dealt with the loss of her friend and colleague.

She also spotted Harry Nightingale and Angela together by the shrine.

Grace Sanderson was sat next to Isla's grandparents on the opposite side, and they were hugging each other and holding each other's hand for warmth and comfort.

The service was beautiful and touching. There was not a dry eye, especially after the speeches from friends and family.

Jack read a poignant speech on behalf of Susan and Greg which lightened the melancholy atmosphere as people were greeted with old and new memories of Isla that they could smile or laugh at.

"Isla was always so full of life, joking around and never taking it seriously, apart from her job which was about the only thing she did take seriously, and I remember when we were young and messing around and she cut my hair with a pair of scissors. Mum had to take me to the hairdressers to sort out the mess and couldn't stop cursing but we couldn't stop laughing. It's one of those fond memories we continually reminisce. We may have fought like siblings do, but Isla was and still is my best friend, always easy to wind up and have a good laugh with. Sure, life wasn't always easy, but she always shone brightly. Isla only ever wanted to become a nurse to help those around her. She was always selfless and inspiring and so thoughtful of others. Heaven has gained another Angel. Until we meet again." Every time Jack said his sister's name, it was like the knife took one more twist into his heart. Susan was shaking in Greg's arm, a protective arm shielding her from the world, as if scared the killer would take his wife as his next victim.

Bridget and Rick took to the stand next as the church waited silently. Rick led the way, keeping his wife's hand gripped in his own for support. Cassie who was sat on the row behind them was nervous to hear their speech because she knew it would reduce her to tears.

The atmosphere had turned cold again.

CHAPTER 22

Rick opened up the folded piece of paper from his pocket and cleared his throat before starting: "Our darling Maddy, we are so proud of everything you have achieved from riding your bike for the first time… to your first and last day at school, graduating university and becoming a Paralegal. You always set the bar high and never failed to reach your full potential. From our intelligent and funny girl to the young mature independent woman you have become…you will always be the light of our lives. Watching you grow… has been the best privilege as a parent. Taken too soon, but never ever forgotten. You leave us with a huge hole in our hearts that can and never will be filled. We won't rest until we find out what happened, and justice has been done. Sleep tight, my darling… Love you forever and always." Rick's voice broke as he was on the verge on tears and had to take a few deep breaths during the speech before he was able to carry on.

"I just want my Maddy back," Bridget cried in between streams of tears and almost collapsed on the floor had Rick not been there to support her. Cassie ran up to them, her own tears streaming, and hugged them both before helping them back to their seats.

It was a heart wrenching scene and Lavinia wished she had brought tissues with her. Tom had noticed and gave her his handkerchief, which she was grateful for.

A poem was written and read aloud by Angela and Grace, Isla's co-worker and two close friends, which was beautiful, poetic, and well written.

At the end of the service, people dispersed slowly, wanting to say their final prayers and goodbyes.

Wilson and his team silently made their way out of the church, not wanting to overstay their welcome. Wilson had watched everyone during the ceremony to clock their reaction and it was the same everywhere he looked.

Sadness, hopelessness, and emptiness.

CHAPTER 23

The team made their way back to the station.
Even though Wilson had sent everyone home after the emotional afternoon, the service had made the entire team even more determined to find the killer.

Every second counted.

And they weren't going to lose any more time.

Service aside, they set back to work, going through the case files, and looking through crime scene photographs, reports, forensic evidence, and interviews. Everything they had so far in case they had missed something. They were looking for missed clues, new investigative leads, answers.

Anything.

Their new focus was on their latest victim, trying to identify her and add intelligence to the ever-growing information board.

Lavinia went upstairs to locate Elaine Deakin, the Trace Evidence specialist, regarding the cluster of black fibres found on the bin handle. The bin that was used to abandon the third victim.

The Trace Evidence Lab was full of microscopes covering every worktop space. They ranged from comparison microscope to polarised light microscope to Scanning Electron Microscope.

Elaine Deakin had short brown hair with blonde highlights that shone in the overhead lights. She had completed a degree in Forensic Science as a mature student at Lincoln University and went on to do her PhD, focusing her research work on this specific trace evidence type. Alongside her studies, she had undertaken the role of a Laboratory Technical Assistant to gain experience of working in a laboratory setting. She was offered the job at Scunthorpe two months after she graduated when the police located her thesis online.

Just by being present in the room, Elaine had a great sense of respect and authority. She was a lovely lady, always happy to chat and had built up great professional relationships with her colleagues and other police staff working in the building. The world was ever changing, and more women were becoming scientists, and being involved in crime scene and police work. The jobs that many thought were suitable just for men. It was hard to get acceptance at first but then people soon realised how skilled she was and she quickly became a valuable asset to the team.

Lavinia spotted her chatting to a colleague at the work bench who was taking tape lifts of fibres on a burgundy jumper and walked over to them.

"Hi Elaine," Lavinia greeted. When Lavinia had first arrived at the Major Crime Unit, she was shown around the different floors of the building and introduced to everyone. Elaine had greeted her with a wide familiar smile.

"Hello, love. How are you doing? Heard about the service earlier."

"Yes, it was lovely, and very emotional but I think it's just what the families needed. I'm here about the fibres found on the bin."

"Yes, I've just about finished the report, take a look." Elaine walked into her office and beckoned Lavinia to follow. She sat behind her desk, logged onto her computer, and located the file. Once opened up on the screen and a copy printed, she passed it to Lavinia, all the while verbalising the analytical techniques used along with her findings.

"So, I took a look at the cluster of fibres under the microscope, and they are all man-made synthetic polyester fibres. Black in colour. Polyester is a common fibre type used for many clothing garments, upholstery, and home furnishings."

"Meaning?"

"Not a lot, I'm afraid, especially since I don't have a suspect sample for comparison to link the killer to the crime scene or to the victim. He could have been wearing any item of clothing made from polyester and it's possible he caught the garment in the handle when he put her in the bin. Dead body weight is heavy so he may have struggled, got extremely close to the bin, and that pulled on his clothes hence the transfer of fibres. Or it could have been a case of secondary transfer."

"So, the fibres from another source transferred onto the killer's clothing which then got transferred onto the bin? How shreddable is polyester?" Lavinia asked, thinking back to her fibre lectures at university.

"I'm impressed. Regarding the secondary transfer, the theory you have is spot on. The primary source could be anything that he came into contact with shortly beforehand. It could have even come from the clothing that the victim wore, and fibres transferred as a result of a struggle. It also depends on what type of clothing he wore."

"Could the fibres have come from the bin men?"

"According to a description, none of them were wearing dark clothing. They were, however, all wearing high vis jackets which does have high shreddability, but since we're looking at dark fibres, I would say unlikely."

"Could the killer have left it there on purpose?" Lavinia thought back to the footwear mark they found in the woods near the body and how that was too generic for identification. She wondered if the killer had chosen a common fibre type to wear for the same purpose.

"It's possible if he wanted to be that clever. After all, it is common and used variably so would be hard to locate the origin," Elaine explained.

"He is that clever and that's the problem."

****

CHAPTER 23

Lavinia walked back downstairs, Elaine's report in hand, and sighed as she entered the conference room but was unsure where to step so she just stood in the doorway.

The room looked like it had been bombed, with papers scattered everywhere on every available surface. The team plus Daniel were haphazardly moving around, rereading reports, and locating photographs or interviews or statements that corroborated with that specific piece of information and cross referencing it with the other victims' case files. It was mayhem.

"Any luck with the fibres?" Morgan questioned when she looked up from the photograph she was studying and noticed Lavinia stood in the doorway. The photograph was of Isla Armstrong at the crime scene where her body was found, and Morgan was comparing it to Madison's and their third victim.

"Polyester, a very common fibre type used widely. Could have transferred from anywhere. No suspect sample to compare either, which doesn't help narrow down the source."

"Same conclusion as with the footwear mark?" Tom asked.

"Yes, very much so. Anything to report here?"

Wilson, who was stood by the whiteboard and crime scene board, cleared his throat. He highlighted each photograph of the victim along with the neck tattoo to illustrate his point. "Going back to the comparisons of all three victims, the neck tattoo ties them all together, but without understanding what they mean, we don't have the link. What we know is that they were all disposed of within early hours of the morning in darkness. Same MO throughout, so we can assume all one killer versus copycat or multiple murderers. He abducts them and keeps them somewhere for at least two days torturing them and then disposes of their body. All women. What is interesting is that no mobile phone has been found on either victim, near the crime scene or at the property they reside in when searched. Same with their purse, handbags, keys etcetera. Did the victims have these items on them? Did the killer take these items as a souvenir or dispose of them somewhere else?"

"With regards to the tattoos, I think it may be worth speaking to a Religious Education teacher or lecturer. They might recognise the tattoos and the meaning, probably more than anyone else," Lavinia suggested.

"Great thinking," Wilson responded, thrilled with Lavinia's suggestion but annoyed at himself for not thinking of that solution quicker. "I shall delegate that task to you. If they don't know, double check with the tattoo artists to make sure they are not covering up for themselves or someone else." Lavinia nodded in acknowledgement. "Now, anything from digital forensics?"

"They are currently looking at Isla and Madison's laptops for any interaction or communication between the victims and the potential killer, or anyone they had a disagreement with days before they were abducted. Along with any searches that may indicate where they might have gone and any activities they were doing before their death. They are looking into downloads, files, images, apps, search history. The lot," Norton explained.

"Great. Chase them up and see what they have. Ask digital forensics to look into any groups our victims may have been a part of, book clubs, sports clubs, extra-curricular activities, hobbies. Search their social media platforms. Did they have any mutual friends? Did the victims meet at any point in their life?"

"I'll speak to the parents again and see if they knew of any clubs their daughters were a part of. Might help speed up the process," Morgan offered.

"Good. And, Harris, chase Missing Persons and see if they can come up with a match to the third victim. Widen their search area and time since last seen."

"Yes, boss."

"Just throwing this out there, but does Debra Gill, the woman whose bin was used to dispose of the third victim, have any outdoor security cameras?" Norton suggested.

CHAPTER 23

"I don't think anyone checked," Tom admitted, the thought clearly overlooked by everyone.

"Homes nowadays are equipped with this type of technology, CCTV, motion censored cameras that can send an alert to your phone when someone is near your house, records video and even lets you talk to them without opening the door. I'm thinking it's worth seeing if she has. Might have caught something on camera," Norton followed through, explaining his thought processes.

"Anything from house-to-house enquiries?" Wilson asked.

"Just the usual. People were in bed, did not see or hear anything. Bins were put out in the evening. No one can recall whether they saw Debra's bin out or not when they took theirs out," Tom summarised from various notes that were taken.

"The killer had to empty the rubbish before placing the victim into it. He must have taken it back home with him and emptied in his own bin, or he dumped it somewhere else," Harris added.

"Where does Debra keep her bins? Are they in a garage, outside, easily accessible?"

"They are all accessible via a side gate that is kept locked. Only keeps it open for the window cleaner or gardener, but it was locked at the time of the incident. She must have put the bins out the evening before, so it seems the killer chose the bin at random. Anything else from forensics?" Morgan answered, making reference to the case notes.

"No fingerprints on the bin. Not even Debra's which we were expecting, and she provided us a sample of her fingerprints for exemption so it's possible the killer wiped it down afterwards."

"What about the bin men who handled the bin?"

"They were wearing gloves."

"Meticulous. Forensically aware. Daniel, is there a chance the killer could have OCD?" Wilson wondered as the thought popped into his head.

"The cutting off of the body parts would be a messy job, and as we have already established, he likes to prolong the excitement and fear. That would mean a constant mess that with someone with OCD would hate. He uses more force than necessary to kill his victims with only one objective in mind and that objective is simply to kill."

"Well, if he has never been arrested or provided the police with fingerprints, then no match would be found on the database."

"Maybe he has been arrested and that's why he doesn't want to risk leaving anything behind because we would be able to identify him."

"Look through the database of previous offenders and locate where they are now. We need to rule everyone out."

"The cutting of the fingers could be to prevent the killer's DNA from getting under the victims' fingernails. Especially if he's worried about being identified. We know from the purple bruising on the wrists and ankles that they were tied down, maybe they tried to fight back," Morgan suggested. All they had to go on were propositions.

Wilson's phone rang and he had to lift a few files and paperwork off the table to locate it. He stepped out of the conference room and took the call before it shut off.

Moments later he walked back into the conference room with an apprehensive look on his face. The team quietened, waiting to hear his news. "A retired detective is on his way up. He has information about an old murder that occurred when he was DCI which has similarities to our current murders. Start with the tasks we discussed, and I want a full update at this evening's briefing."

The team did not speak again until the retired detective entered the office. Wilson met him halfway and shook hands.

"Thank you for coming in, Mr..."

"Sebastian Cooper."

CHAPTER 23

"Walter Wilson. Would you like to follow me to my office? I would use the conference room but as you can see, it's a bit hectic at the moment."

"No problem. I remember those days well."

"How long have you been retired?"

"Going on eleven years now."

"Where were you based?"

"Nottingham."

Wilson directed Sebastian to his office and offered him a seat and refreshments, which he gladly accepted and asked for a glass of water.

"I drank extreme amounts of caffeine during my working days so I'm trying to cut back," he admitted.

"The job wouldn't be without its caffeine boost." He grabbed him a water and sat back down behind his desk. "So, this old case of yours?"

Sebastian reached into his briefcase and pulled out a thick file, containing all the documents from the original case. He passed the file over to Wilson who studied the crime scene photographs with recognition as Sebastian explained. "The killer, a Nigel Atterbury, killed and butchered seven women. He arranged their body parts in a symbol. All seven were arranged in a different pattern."

Wilson studied each crime scene photograph in detail and marvelled at the similarities. "Three of these same symbols are tattooed on the back of our victims' necks. Did you ever find out what the symbols meant?"

"We did."

****

Meanwhile, the team dispersed with their various tasks.

Morgan went to speak to the Armstrongs again, and Tom and Lavinia went to the McKinleys'. They also had to speak with Janet Haines, the Theology and Religion lecturer at the

University of Oxford, via Zoom, about the symbols. Norton went to speak to Debra Gill, and Harris had the task of chasing up digital forensics and Missing Persons. They had instructed the help of a couple of uniformed officers to check and locate previous offenders.

Morgan learnt that Isla had established and was an essential part of a charity group, set up over Facebook. She, along with many others, either work colleagues, parents and members of the public, came together every month to raise money for different charities involving children, such as the Great Ormond Street Hospital, NSPCC, Barnardo's, and Sense. They would do fun days for families and children to get involved in, with games and competitions, and various sporting activities and challenges. The summer months would include BBQs, tea parties and outdoor cinema events. It was a massive organisation that the whole community would get involved in and support.

It turned out that the McKinleys, including Madison, had been active members in supporting and taking part in the charity events, hosted by Isla Armstrong. They had never known Isla personally and never interacted with her.

But the link was there.

They just had to find out if their third victim had taken part or attended these events.

Janet Haines was a middle-aged woman, who wore glasses around her neck on a chain and her silver-grey hair styled neatly in a medium layered haircut that suited her thin face shape. She was well spoken, well-educated and as sharp as a needle. It showed that she looked after herself, with her natural flawless skin that aged her younger than she was, and toned arms that were visible in her short-sleeved blouse of her trouser suit.

Tom and Lavinia were sat at Tom's desk, calling from his computer screen. Janet was also sat at her desk in the lecture theatre at the university. A traditional blackboard was situated behind her.

CHAPTER 23

"As discussed earlier over the phone, we would like to ask you questions regarding a series of symbols we have come across during our investigation and wondered if you would be able to help us out. We conclude they may be of some religious meaning," Tom explained after introductions were made.

"Yes, of course. I would like to help in any way I can."

"I will show you a series of photographs, take as long as you need and tell me if you recognise them."

"Sure," Janet agreed.

Over the next few minutes Tom showed her a copy of the three tattoos each marked on the victims' neck. Janet did not take long to look over each one before saying, "Yes, I recognise all three of them, but there are seven in total."

* * * *

Debra Gill had taken a couple of days off work, to get over the shock of a body being found on her property.

Norton could see she was fearful as she hesitated to open up the front door to him before instructing to see the relevant identification. He posted it through the letterbox for her to look over and she clearly had made up her mind that he was all right because she opened the door and let him in.

"I'm sorry about that. I know I'm too paranoid, but if the killer can dump a body in my bin and not get noticed, he could do anything unnoticed. He trespassed onto my property. He could have been in my house; the victim could have been me."

"It's a shock, I know, and I'm sure your mind is running through all the different scenarios. We think he chose your bin at random; he won't come back."

"You can be 100% sure that he won't come back to revisit the crime scene, can you? I get goosebumps just thinking that he could be lurking in the shadows, watching the house, watching me."

"I think you've watched too many crime dramas. It was unlucky that he chose your bin, but I assure you, he won't be back to harm you. He just needed somewhere to dispose of the body." Norton knew that no matter what he said to reassure her, Debra needed to talk herself round.

She offered refreshments, but he declined, not wanting to take longer than necessary. He asked about outdoor security cameras, and she did indeed have one installed earlier in the month. It was a sleek Video Doorbell Pro camera on the wall beside the front door, which would go unnoticed by someone at the end of the driveway in darkness, who was occupied at the time.

"Does it only work when someone rings the doorbell?" Norton asked.

"No, it has motion sensors too, so detects movement up to nine metres. I have the video on all on all the time. Never thought to check it to be honest."

"That's all right. And do you get a notification every time it detects movement, or someone rings the bell?

"Yes, you can customise it to receive notifications when you want. I set it up for when I leave the house. Should really set it up at night-time too, but just never got round to it."

"So, it has night vision too. Great little gadgets."

"Yes, they are."

"Can you check the recordings afterwards?"

"Yes, via the Ring app. It saves videos to my account for thirty days."

Norton gained access to the videos taken by the doorbell camera and selected the relevant date. He was amazed at the quality and was impressed by all the features. It had a wide field of vision so he could clearly see the entire driveway.

The day turned to evening and the evening turned to night as Norton eagerly watched on, hoping to see something of interest.

That came at 3:32am.

****

CHAPTER 23

Digital forensics were unable to note anything of interest or value.

Both Isla and Madison had a search history for Amazon, various online retailers, health, and beauty stores, and the purchases were legitimate and ordinary. Isla had intermittent searches for different charity event ideas whereas Madison regularly researched criminal law legislation. Also, the week before she disappeared, there were many searches for evening gowns.

Social media platforms were searched for multiple times a day, but they were both logged out of them all.

They both had two email accounts, a work account, and a personal account. Isla did not have many emails in her inbox or sent folders, and there were none in her junk or deleted folders either. A couple of emails that were sat in her inbox were of staff meeting reminders and follow up emails of patients and new patients coming in, and then a few emails sent around the various wards inviting staff to attend the charity events that were being organised, which had a few responses, but nothing of interest. Madison's work account was chaotic with flagged emails stating the urgency of them, emails to and from various clients asking for appointments, call backs, clarification on their applications, other things they wanted to discuss, new cases needing attention, multiple emails to and from other colleagues, to police, Family Liaison Officers and courts. Again, there was nothing out of the ordinary, just the odd one or two strongly worded emails from clients but nothing threatening. Their personal email accounts also flagged up nothing as noteworthy; confirmation emails and parcel tracking information from recent purchases and advertising of new collections from stores they previously shopped at, online magazines and articles from the Nursing Standard and Law Review and Law Gazette, notifications from Virgin Experience Days and LinkedIn.

The last known location where they accessed their laptop was at their home address.

Harris enquired if they had set up find my iPhone or find my device on their laptop that could be used to locate their mobile phone if lost, but that was a dead end, since neither had it set up.

Next on Harris's to-do list was to check on Missing Persons to see if they had any hits. They were still filtering through the countless matches that came back from the search criteria.

However, he only had to wait a few minutes before a match came back as positive.

Their third victim was Anna Shaw.

CHAPTER 24

All the updates regarding the investigation were discussed in turn during the evening briefing.

Harris started by informing the team that their third victim had been identified as Anna Shaw. "Her parents reported her missing a couple of days ago when she failed to return their calls, which was out for character for Anna. She moved from up North from Bristol to Scunthorpe to pursue her career as an Estate Agent with Holmes Estate Agents but remained close with her family. They got worried after they had no contact with her."

"Why would you move to Scunthorpe from Bristol to be an Estate Agent? Surely Bristol has more going for it than Scunthorpe."

"Maybe there weren't any jobs going in Bristol that suited her, or maybe living costs were too expensive for her salary, or she could have just fancied a change. Endless reasons why."

"Did her workplace not find it suspicious when she didn't show up for work?"

"Speak to Holmes Estate Agents tomorrow after informing the parents. The parents will have to formally identify her."

"Ok, great work. Norton, what did you get from Debra?" Wilson diverted his attention.

"Turns out she did have a doorbell video camera installed earlier this month. It constantly records video that covers the entire driveway. I was able to access the footage." Norton stood up from his seat, walked over to the computer screen and inserted a USB drive. The projector was turned on and the screen ready to play. "She was able to download and send me the footage," Norton explained as he pressed play and set the video to just a few minutes before the event occurred. The others watched on eager for a lead.

The early morning was still in pitch black, but with the night vision feature, it made it easier to spot movement. A car parked up just after the driveway, out of view of any streetlamps and with the headlights not turned on. The number plate could not be seen, making it impossible to undergo an ANPR check. A figure dressed in dark colours exited the car and came into view, but it was not possible to get any intelligence, other than approximate height, but even that would be tricky to ascertain. The figure moved with ease and speed, gathering the rubbish out of the bin, and placing it into another bin bag which he dumped in the back seat of the car.

Next, he opened the boot and carried something heavy to the bin. That was their victim, Anna Shaw. He then placed her into the bin, closed the lid and scarpered out of sight.

The job had been an extremely swift task which he did at ease.

"So, that's our killer," Morgan stated, stunned as Norton turned off the video. This was the closest they had come to identifying him and seeing him in action gave everyone goosebumps.

"Yep. Won't be able to get any intel from that footage such as a number plate or a biological profile of the killer, but we've seen him in action so that's something to build the case with."

"He's strong to lift dead body weight so has to be in reasonable health and fitness."

"Something to add to the killer profile."

A further moment of silence was needed to let it sink in what they had just witnessed before Wilson moved on and grabbed everyone's attention as he began to explain his meeting with Sebastian Cooper. He compared the similarities of his old case and compared it to their current case.

CHAPTER 24

"The symbols that the body parts were arranged in matches that of the neck tattoos on our three victims.

"The Seven Deadly Sins," Lavinia cut in; realisation hit her that both Sebastian and Janet were able to identify the meaning behind the symbols. The team were finally able to understand more about the case. Whether that was a good thing or not, time would tell. But the more they delved deeper into the investigation, the more horror was uncovered.

"I take it Janet was able to identify the symbols."

"Yes, she was. She told us the sins were pride, greed, lust, envy, gluttony, wrath and sloth," Lavinia consulted her notes as she read them aloud.

"That corroborates with what Sebastian told me," Wilson confirmed.

"What do each of them mean?" Norton asked.

"Pride is about being too self-satisfied without any regards for other people. Greed is wanting too much. Lust is the fulfilment of intense desires, strong passion that kind of thing; envy is basically jealousy with an intense desire of wanting what someone else has; gluttony is similar to greed but is the action of taking too much, over-indulgence. Wrath is the feeling of strong anger and hatred towards another, often seeking revenge. And finally, sloth is the failure or laziness to act," Tom explained, referring to his notes from the meeting with Janet.

"Each one of his victims must have committed that sin that is tattooed on them," Harris concluded.

"That would verify the reasoning of seven victims."

"What's the origin of the Seven Sins? And was death the punishment for committing a sin?"

"They originated from Christianity and, yes, if you committed a sin, you were signing your own death certificate."

"Was the killer ever convicted in Sebastian's case?"

"Yes, Nigel Atterbury. He spent some time in Wakefield prison but failed to disclose any details of his murders to the police before he committed suicide in his cell, so everything died with him. He did have a fellow cell mate, though, going by the name of Kelvin Anderson. I have made an appointment with the Governor to speak with him tomorrow afternoon. Lavinia, I want you in attendance with myself and Daniel. So, in light of what has been discovered this evening, I want Tom and Harris to speak to Anna Shaw's parents in the morning and get them to attend the mortuary as soon as you can to formally identify her and interview them. Morgan and Norton, you will speak to Anna Shaw's colleagues and boss. Well done, everyone, on your findings, great work. Please go home ready for an early start tomorrow."

It seemed they had the leads they had sought, and the investigation could move forward.

CHAPTER 25

HMP Wakefield was a high security men's prison that housed high profile and high-risk sex offenders and murderers, alumni included Harold Shipman, and Mark Bridger, the abductor and murderer of April Jones. One inmate, dubbed as the most dangerous murderer, Robert Maudsley, lived in a glass box underneath the prison for 23 hours a day. It wasn't for the faint hearted.

Lavinia familiarised herself with Nigel Atterbury's case from the files left by Sebastian Cooper during the journey. They arrived at HMP Wakefield just after 9:30am, and Lavinia was feeling trepidation. Every mile closer, and Lavinia's heart picked up speed.

This did not go unnoticed by Wilson who noticed her fidgeting with her hands, the rings on her fingers and picking at her nails.

The visitor car park was situated around the back of the building with the entrance to the side, but they could not enter through the door until they were authorised to do so. A prison guard came out to them, dressed in uniform with a clipboard in hand and had requested to see their ID and the nature of their visit.

"Detective Chief Inspector Walter Wilson and Lavinia Newbourne with the Major Incident Team in Scunthorpe and Daniel Hargreaves, Criminologist. I requested an urgent visit with Kelvin Anderson yesterday."

Once the guard was satisfied and permitted Wilson's request after checking on his clipboard of the list of names, he reiterated the rules for once they were inside about going through security and no mobile phones allowed before he indicated the way to the visitor car park. Wilson thanked him before driving off and parking up.

Wilson turned to Lavinia and said, "I asked you to be here today for the experience, it's more than we normally would get our work experience students to do, but it's not every day you get to witness the interview of a high offender prisoner. Daniel and I will be in the interview room with Kelvin and you'll be behind the two-way mirror," Wilson briefed.

While the thought of what or rather who was waiting for their visit scared her, she was excited by the prospect and dared to ask if she could be in on the interview with either Wilson or Daniel. Wilson was firmly against the idea but after some persuasion from Daniel, he nodded in agreement before they climbed out of the car and together made their way to the entrance.

More ID checks were completed upon arrival. They swiftly made their way through security, bags searched and safely stored in a locker to be collected on exit and were given a visitor lanyard to wear around their neck, before being shown to the interview room by Anders Derrick, a prison officer.

They made small talk on their way, with Wilson and Lavinia asking what day-to-day life was like for the prisoners and what it was like to work in such a high security prison with high profile offenders. To Daniel, this was an all-too-familiar setting.

"The prisoners have access to a range of courses including English, Maths and distance learning open university. We also have several accredited courses in subjects such as hospitality and catering. It keeps their days occupied and filled with activities. There's also a library with a quiet study and group study area. Each prisoner has their own individual learning plan. There's also paid work in the kitchens, laundry rooms and workshops. A lot of the prisoners like to work out in the gym. I guess they can channel their anger and frustration

CHAPTER 25

out on the equipment rather than a fellow prisoner. They have a privileges scheme which includes more visits from friends and family, and they get to spend more of their money allowance each week and have access to a TV, but it all has to be earned. These are incentives to do well and stay out of trouble," Anders informed them.

"And what's the punishment if they break the rules? "Wilson questioned.

"Depending on the severity of the situation for which they are being punished, they are kept in their cell for up 21 days and can even have up to 42 extra days in prison on top of their original sentence in extreme cases. But it's mainly that we take away their privileges until they are earned again." Anders placed his ID card on the scanner, where the light turned from red to green to permit entry and they were buzzed through. He held open the gate for them, slamming it behind him afterwards, which automatically locked it again. They went through several secure gates before coming to a corridor that opened up to conference rooms, offices used by prison staff and psychiatrists, and three interview rooms.

He led them to interview room two, which was similar to those back at the station. The door opened to a small rectangular room, known as the observation room, with several monitors placed on the desk in the corner that showed different camera viewpoints in the interview room with recording equipment. A two-way mirror looked out into square room. A table was located in the centre with three chairs placed around it. It was very basic.

A door at the back of the interview room was pulled open and a prisoner tied in handcuffs walked into the room wearing a blue sweatshirt with matching joggers. He was closely followed by two prison officers who walked side by side and sat the prisoner down on the single chair. He remained cuffed and the officers dispersed to opposite corners of the room. They would stay present in the room during the interview, in case of any disturbance or violence that needed to be taken control of. It was for the safety and protection of Daniel and Lavinia.

Lavinia's breath hitched at the sight of Kelvin and goosebumps covered her arms.

What struck Lavinia was that he looked like an ordinary person, and at first glance, she could not believe that he was capable of murder; he had short black hair and was average height. He clearly worked out in the gym. Then she saw his eyes; the coldness and darkness in them that sent shivers down her spine.

He stared straight ahead, no emotion showing in his face.

Wilson stood next to her looking at Kelvin through the two-way mirror. "He is a classic psychopath and may try to get into your head. Do not let him. He also may say inappropriate things but do not react or show any response. Remain calm and collected. If you need to step out for any reason, give the table a tap and Daniel, who will be in there with you, will ask for a drink from the machine. It will mainly be you listening and observing but if you feel confident enough to ask questions then please do so. He's all ready for us when you're ready. Daniel will be beside you the whole time and I'll be here observing."

Lavinia took a deep breath and one last look at Kelvin before saying, "I'm ready."

Daniel opened the interview room door and held it open for Lavinia. The room remained silent as they took their seat. Kelvin's gaze never left Lavinia as it followed her every move. Lavinia could feel him watching her and her heart rate picked up, and she suddenly felt really hot and claustrophobic.

"Good morning, Kelvin," Daniel greeted him with.

"It is a very fine morning indeed." He smirked as he directed his response to Lavinia. She held his gaze. "What do I owe this pleasure?"

"My name is Daniel Hargreaves, a criminologist, and this is Lavinia with the Major Incident Team. Is it all right if we ask you a few questions regarding recent murders of ours?"

CHAPTER 25

"I don't know how I can help you. My alibi is watertight," he simply defended in a sarcastic tone.

"What can you tell me about Nigel Atterbury?" Both Daniel and Lavinia, and even Wilson, who was looking on in anticipation, were expecting some kind of response to his fellow cellmate's name but there was no sign of recognition or surprise shown.

"Now there's a name I haven't heard in a while." He sat back in his chair with his arms rested on his thighs. He was getting comfortable. "It has got to be a decade at least."

"You shared a cell together?"

"Yes."

"Did he ever tell you why he was sent to prison?"

"Doesn't everyone want to know that?"

"Did he tell you?" Daniel pushed.

"He might have mentioned it." Kelvin was trying to be clever, and Daniel knew that he would not give anything away unless he knew there was something for him to gain afterwards. It was a game; it was always a game.

"And what might Nigel have told you?" Daniel tried to push him gently, but it was like pulling teeth. He knew it was a waste of time, and he had no choice but to compromise, but Lavinia cut in before he had the chance to say anything further.

"Look, we have three dead women, and there's going to be more if we don't stop it. All of them bear similarities to yours and Nigel's murders, so you can see why we need to speak to you. We know you didn't do it, but someone did. We need your help, and that information might just help save lives. We are just doing our job and it would be easier if you could cooperate with us."

"Bit feisty this one, isn't she?" The stare and the smirk were back. He made a thinking face as if contemplating her words. "I'll make you a deal, if you speak to the prison staff and let them know I have contributed to your investigation and have them make arrangements for more privileges, then I will tell you what I know."

"We will speak to them, you have my word, but after you supply us with the information. Depending on how significant that information is, will depend on how high we sing your praises," Lavinia bargained.

"Where have you been hiding this one? I like her," he indicated to Daniel. "And I will speak to Lavinia and Lavinia only."

"You are not in a position to bargain with us," Daniel firmly stated. He knew that serial killers were tough cookies to crack but once they wanted to make a bargain or fixated on something, you had to go along with it and not try to change their mind. You had to play by their rules for a time or play into their hands and make them think that they are in charge and call all the shots, but this would end in both parties being successful. It might be the difference between getting information and not getting anything. He couldn't risk the latter.

"Well, my mouth is locked tight. Good luck stopping your killer."

"It's fine," Lavinia told Daniel. She didn't feel entirely comfortable being left alone with a serial killer, but the two prison guards made her feel safer and he was handcuffed so what was the worst he could do? If it was the only way to get information from him, then so be it. "Is there anything we can get you to drink?"

"How very hospitable of you. I could murder a brew, no pun intended."

Lavinia wanted to wipe that smirk off his face, he thought he was being clever, but he was nothing.

Lavinia indicated to Daniel to get the tea for him while she carried on with the interview. Daniel announced he was leaving the room to the recording equipment installed and slowly made his exit. He was hesitant to leave Lavinia on her own. It wasn't until he closed the door behind him that the interview carried on.

"So, it's just me and you."

CHAPTER 25

"Delightful." He grinned.

"How long was Nigel an inmate of yours for?"

"Don't know exactly. Have no sense of time in here."

"Approximately?"

"Couple of months."

"His suicide must've taken you by surprise."

"It's not uncommon for prisoners to take their own life."

"Do you know why he did it?"

Daniel returned to the room with a Styrofoam cup of steaming tea in his hand and placed it in front of Kelvin. He gave a reassuring look to Lavinia who nodded that she was fine, and he left the room once more. He would be watching tensely from the observation room with Wilson.

"The same reason why any prisoner commits suicide, so their secrets die with them."

"He must've been questioned?"

"Intensely, time and time again, but as I understand he only gave them what he wanted to."

"The evidence was there in black and white, he was guilty. Surely it would've been in his best interest to tell the police what they wanted to hear."

"From my perspective, I can understand why he kept quiet. Despite the myths that all psychopaths like to tell the police their story, relive the murders and get the recognition that they want, not everyone is like that. The police had found their killer, they just didn't understand why he did it or any of the specific details that only Nige knew."

"Did you know? Did he ever share any details of his killings?"

"Yes. We both did. It was a proud moment for us both when we realised that someone else was just as skilled and disturbed. We understood one another. You don't get that in the real world." He almost sounded melancholy. Almost.

"So, you swapped notes, for want of a better phrase."

"Everything, emotions, thoughts, feelings, tactics, killing methods. The lot."

"What were your killing methods?"

"Torture, drugs, you know, the usual," he shrugged it off like killing people by torture and drugs was normal. Lavinia's mind briefly reflected on their own case before reverting back to the present.

"Did you ever write any of it down? Keep a diary?"

"We created our own murder encyclopaedia." Lavinia could tell from the way he beamed that he thought it was a great achievement.

"Murder encyclopaedia? Fascinating. Do you still have a copy of that?"

"It's long gone by now."

"Where?"

"Nige gave it to his son."

"Nigel has a son?" This was news to Lavinia, there was nothing in his notes about him having a family.

"Yes, Benjamin. I don't know specifics, but Nige's wife left him and took their son with her and years later, Ben wanted to find his dad. Located him here." At the mention of his son's name, Wilson got on the phone to Harris back at the station and requested a comprehensive background check on Benjamin Atterbury. Could it be that Benjamin is trying to copy his father's murders?

Daniel was amazed that Kelvin had revealed so much to Lavinia and in a short space of time. The mind of a killer was complex and surprising.

"Did Benjamin ever visit his dad in prison?"

"Multiple times."

"Was Benjamin aware of why his dad was in prison?"

"Yes, he was. He attended this religious boarding school and I think he thought he could help his dad reform."

"What boarding school?"

"Something of God, a really fucking weird name."

"Do you know if Benjamin came back to visit since his dad died?"

"Not that I know of. He wouldn't have any need to."

CHAPTER 25

"Did you ever meet him?"

"Once or twice during visitation, just to say hello. Nige talked about him all the time. Sweet boy. No idea where he is today though. He would've left the boarding school by now I should think and probably making a life of his own."

"As I understand, Nigel butchered seven women and arranged their body parts in different symbols, known as the Deadly Sins. What do you know about the Seven Deadly Sins?"

"I know of all seven sins and what they mean."

"Did you learn all that from Nigel, or were you aware of them beforehand?"

"Nige told me everything I know."

"Did you tell anyone else?"

"Absolutely not."

"Do you know if Nigel told anyone else?"

"We swore to secrecy that we wouldn't tell. I kept up my end of the bargain, I expect he did too and killed himself before he had the chance to tell anyone else; the only other person who knows is his son."

* * * *

Anna Shaw's parents, Maria and Darren, and her two sisters, Christine-Maria, and Georgina-May, made the trip up to Scunthorpe to speak to Tom and to identify Anna's body. They met Tom at the hospital entrance, just up the road from the train station, where they silently made their way to the mortuary for the viewing.

The siblings, including Anna, all had the same grey eye colour and curled chestnut brown hair, although Christine-Maria's was longer in length than the others. They stood at 5'10" and had the same face shape and body shape, making it hard to tell them apart. There was no doubt that their victim was Anna Shaw. She was the spitting image of her siblings.

It was easy to see that they took after both their parents, the hair colour from Maria and the height from their father Darren.

Tom had to ring through to Hayleigh once they had reached the Pathology Department reception for her to come and meet them since she was the one with authorised access and her ID card would be required to grant them access through the doors.

At the end of the corridor, she led them through a side door to the mortuary which opened up into a small rectangular family room, with a vase of fresh flowers on the table, and scenic pictures hung on the walls. A scented candle was lit upon on a shelf along with a reed diffuser. It was to keep the smell of bleach and bodies of the autopsy suite away from the snug and comfortable family room. They took a seat on the sofa and declined any offer of refreshments.

Maria spotted the viewing window along the east wall and simply stared at it. The curtains were currently closed, but she would see her daughter on the other side of it shortly and that was hard to comprehend.

"When you are ready, Hayleigh will open these curtains and Anna will be on the other side of it. Take all the time you need. Afterwards, I will need to ask you a few questions," Tom explained.

"How will she be?" Georgina-May asked.

"She will be laid on a table, covered in a white sheet. Only her face will be visible," Tom reassured her.

After a few hesitant moments, Maria nodded her consent and Tom disappeared from the room. When he returned moments later, the curtains slowly opened, as if preparing the family an inch at a time as to what they were about to see.

At the sight of Anna's lifeless body, Maria broke down into tears. The others soon followed. Christine-Maria placed her hand on the window, as if trying to reach out to her sister. Georgina-May had her head rested on Christine-Maria's shoulder and their arms were wrapped securely around each

CHAPTER 25

other, not letting one another out of their embrace for fear that they would be gone forever if they did.

As Tom had said, Anna was covered in a white sheet, the ordeal of her last moments on Earth covered up to spare her family. Thankfully Hayleigh positioned her so they would not see her missing left ear either and her eyes were closed. Her hair had been washed and styled, and her face had been made up with a thin cover of natural make-up. She looked beautiful and peaceful, like she was sleeping. A sleep she would never wake up from.

"My b...b...beautiful Anna," Maria cried. Darren held her close as the tears fell down his face. Then the whole family hugged. It was an emotional moment.

Tom took himself out of the room to give the family a moment alone to grieve. He felt he was intruding and had he not stepped out, he possibly would have shed a tear or two himself.

He waited as long as he thought would be sufficient enough before knocking and stepping back into the room. Maria was sat on the sofa with her daughters either side of her, holding their hands while Darren paced the room.

Tom gave a nod to Hayleigh who closed the curtains.

"Can I have a glass of water please?" Christine-Maria whispered.

Tom disappeared once more and came back with a tray that held glasses of water for everyone and placed it down on the table. Christine-Maria reached over to grab a glass with shaky hands.

"I hope you don't mind me asking, but did Anna have a double-barrelled name?" Tom thought of the two sisters and how they both had and thought it was odd for Anna not to.

"Yes, Anna-Margaret. Anna was my mum's name and Margaret is Darren's mother's name. She didn't really like it, so everyone just called her Anna."

"I'm sorry to have to ask you these questions but when did you last have contact with Anna?" Tom started.

"A week ago, I think, not too sure, we kept in regular contact," Maria said.

"Did you notice anything odd about her behaviour recently?"

"No, she was a little busier than usual at work but nothing out of the ordinary."

"What made her move to Scunthorpe? Was it just about the job or was there anything or anyone that influenced her to move?"

"She just felt it was the right time to move, Scunthorpe was where the job was, it was good money, open to promotions and living costs were cheaper than in Bristol. It seemed perfect for her. Only now I wish she had never made the move; she would still be alive," Darren explained.

"What about any previous boyfriends?"

"She broke up with her boyfriend a month after she made the move," Christine-Maria informed Tom.

"Why was that? How long had they been seeing each other?"

"A couple of years. It was difficult for them both, being hours apart, not being able to see each other. They were always so busy with work. He wanted more contact, but neither could get the time off to visit. Chris was near promotion and so he had to be around and focused on his work. Anna knew it was a big time for him and I guess she didn't want to hold him back. They just grew apart and wanted to focus on their careers," Georgina-May explained.

"Was it a mutual decision to break up?"

"Yes, they remained friends. He'll be devastated," Georgina-May said again.

"What's Chris' full name and what does he do for a job?"

"Chris Sayles, with a Y. He recently got promoted to Business Development Manager."

"Do you know if Anna was involved in Charity work?"

"Not especially, she did a bit here and there like the Race for Life or donated items," Maria recalled.

CHAPTER 25

"She mentioned a Classic Car Night somewhere not too far away, a village that I cannot remember the name of; mind you, I hadn't heard of Scunthorpe before Anna told us she was moving there, but it was probably a fortnight ago. I remember her telling me about it because I'm a big lover of old cars. It's on this Friday 7th July and apparently, it's a big community event and very popular. It's also to raise money for the local park at the primary school, something about needing to make it safer," Darren notified Tom, relaying the last conversation he had had with Anna.

*****

Holmes Estate Agents were located on Mary Street, in the heart of Scunthorpe.

Morgan and Norton parked on the street outside the estate agents in a bay and made their way inside, where BBC Radio Lincolnshire was playing in the background.

They were instructed to take a seat in the corner of the room until the manager was available, in what one of the workers called a waiting room, where two single sofa chairs sat either side of a coffee table that was covered in a pile of housing magazines and brochures from Holmes Estate Agents.

There was a certain uneasiness in the room; aside from one worker speaking to a client over the phone, no one else spoke. Had it not been for the radio playing in the background, then the atmosphere would have been a very cumbersome one. The other three agents tried to concentrate on their computer, but Morgan noticed that they each glared in their direction every now and then. Norton wondered if they were aware of the reason for their visit, or if they at least knew it was to do with one of their colleagues, Anna Shaw, even if they were not aware she was dead.

Just for something to do, Norton picked up one of the brochures on the table beside him and flicked through it while they waited. He really wasn't interested in the details, but it allowed his eyes to focus on something other than the stern faces of the agents that were sat in front of him.

A few moments later, the manager came out of his office and strode over to Morgan and Norton, who then gathered themselves together and got up from the seat to greet him. They shook hands and introduced themselves before being directed to his office in private.

It felt like they were being called into the headmaster's office as they passed the agents' desks to get to the manager's office, all suspicious eyes following them. Oliver held the door open for them as they walked inside his office.

He walked around his desk and sat down on the chair, directing to Morgan and Norton that they should do the same, and clasped his hands together on the top of his desk. "What can I do for you?"

"We're here about one of your employees, Anna Shaw."

"Ah yes, no one has heard from her or seems to know why she hasn't come into work for the past few days."

"Is this unlike her?"

"Very. She's always punctual, professional, enthusiastic, dedicated, she really is one of our best." Oliver couldn't praise her enough.

"When was the last time you did see her?"

"Why? What's that got to do with anything?"

"If you could just answer the question please."

Oliver bought up his work schedule and scanned over the dates until he found what he was looking for. "Friday 8th July. We had a review meeting first thing before she went off to a house viewing with a client."

Morgan and Norton did not need to look at each to confirm the significance of that date.

"What was discussed during this review meeting?"

"Just a reflection of stats, client reviews, performance, that kind of thing."

"Any worries?"

CHAPTER 25

"None at all. She was efficient, all reviews were excellent, she loved the job and had settled in really well. I had no qualms, and she didn't have any issues either, so it was a very good review."

"Then you said she had a house viewing with a client afterwards?"

"Yes, at 11am."

"Do you know who this client was?"

Again, Oliver looked back over the schedule, but this time he looked at Anna's to confirm. "Dean Hadley. She had a viewing with him at 27 Waggoners Close in Scotter the day before, the 7th, and then the viewing on the 8th was at 5 Robina Mews in Scunthorpe."

"Have you had any dealings with this Dean Hadley?"

"No, none, it was all Anna."

"Did she have any issues with this client?"

"Again, none. She was quite taken with him; he was looking to buy his first property and she was enjoying the journey with him. First time buyers are usually the best clients."

"Did she have any more viewings that day or did she return to the office?"

"That's the thing. That was the only viewing she had that day. It was a last-minute viewing, so she should've been working in the office all day, but she never came back."

"I'm sorry, just to clarify, so she went to this viewing with Dean at 11am in Scunthorpe and failed to come back to the office afterwards, and you haven't seen her since?"

"That's correct."

"Why didn't anyone report her missing?"

"Well, I didn't think it had come to that."

"But this was unusual for Anna not to show up for work?"

"Yes."

"And she never phoned in sick or told you she was taking a few days off?"

"No."

"So, what did you think?"

"I don't know. Maybe she needed to take a mental health day or something."

"So was something bothering her?"

"Not that I know of."

"How did you come to the conclusion that she needed a mental health day, as you put it?"

"I have to look after my employees and if I do that, they produce good results and in turn make me money. I'd rather they had a day off than turn up to work not feeling 100% because their performance drops. I understand that they may need to take a day off for personal reasons and I don't like to push. Anna had a lot going on work-wise recently, so I thought she just needed time."

"Isn't that inconvenient for you if someone just decides to take a day off last minute and fails to mention it to you?"

"We work around it."

"Right." Morgan couldn't understand that, but she didn't manage the business. She thought of Wilson and what he would say if one of his team decided to take a random day off just because. He wouldn't be completely against it, and she would like to think he would encourage it, but not during a case like this one. Everyone sacrificed a lot.

"Can I go back to an earlier question and ask why you're enquiring about Anna?"

"The reason she hasn't turned up to work is because she was found dead on Monday."

Oliver's face went blank and for once, he was lost for words.

"I'm sorry to have given you bad news, but we should leave you to it. Thank you for your time," Norton said as they got up to leave; but before they did, Oliver muttered: "Anna really was the best thing to have happened to Holmes Estate Agents."

CHAPTER 25

****

Harris completed an extensive background check on Benjamin Atterbury.

He was born to Nigel and Clarence Atterbury, who resided in Bedfordshire at the time. From the updates provided by Wilson, Harris knew that Clarence had left Nigel and Bedfordshire for Cumbria when Benjamin was two years old.

Benjamin attended a local school for six months, before being transferred to the Grace of God Boarding School in the Berkshire Countryside.

The reason was no doubt to help his rebellious behaviour, where he had a few close calls with the police and official warnings. It seemed his mother could not cope and possibly feared he was turning into his father and tried to put a stop to that before he got too disobedient.

There was no recent record for Benjamin after 2012.

Next, Harris researched the Grace of God Boarding School. It was a 16th Century grand building with stunning architecture. The motto, *'For it is the power of God unto Salvation to everyone that believeth'*. The school was situated in the countryside, with acres of fields surrounding the building. The building had been dilapidated but was purchased and renovated by Jonathan Paxton, who later became the headmaster. The website was still up, allowing Harris access to the yearly student photographs under the archive heading. He selected the relevant year, the last year the school was open, and the picture appeared on screen. Underneath the picture was a list of students. He located Benjamin Atterbury's name, who was stood in the middle of two other boys, Aiden Brown, and Elijah Anderson. These three boys stood out because they were the only ones pulling a funny face at the camera. Harris concluded that they must have been friends.

The name Anderson rang a bell, but he couldn't fathom why.

He made a note of the two names.

A name check revealed why Harris had recognised Elijah Anderson's name. He was the son of Kelvin Anderson. With his father in prison and his mother having abandoned him, he was a revengeful boy, his care home and other residents not understanding his behaviour, took him to the school in hope that he could learn. He stayed there until the school closed. No record of him after that.

Aiden Brown was born to a Henry and Harriet Brown, but they had died in a car accident when he was six years old. A series of failed placements led him to the back streets of drugs and alcohol. But then he was fostered by Socialites Camille and Rupert Davenport and a few months later got enrolled at the Grace of God. Again, no record of him after 2012.

They all came from a similar unsettled background.

But what the hell happened to these boys after the school closed?

Why was there no record for either of them after 2012?

Those were the questions that Harris was eager to answer.

The news was full of old articles following the renovation work undertaken by Jonathan Paxton and publishing the school to potential students. In an interview, Jonathan stated that he had built the school to help troubled youths from all backgrounds find their way in life away from the pressure of drugs and alcohol and instead, make a difference to their life. It focused on giving them an education in a safe environment, a place they could call home since many had no home or no place where they could call home.

Harris came across other news articles of an incident that occurred at the school. It did not go into great detail, but there was a fatal accident involving a couple of the students which led to the closure of the school.

Were Benjamin, Aiden and Elijah involved in the accident, whether victims or perpetrators, and is that why there is no record of them afterwards?

CHAPTER 25

He also did a quick background check on Jonathan Paxton, who led a very religious life. He himself attended a religious school, became a member of the Church, helping with community projects and church services, but retired to be the headmaster of Grace of God. He taught others to believe in God, ask for salvation and forgiveness and allow God to guide them.

Once the school closed, he moved to Dartmouth, Devon, where he currently resided.

Maybe it was worth speaking to him.

CHAPTER 26

Today was Samuel Jackford's second meeting with Tracey Evans.

Samuel Jackford did the same routine as he had previously in preparation to enter the outside world.

He hadn't expected another meeting so soon, but it seemed luck was on his side.

Maybe he wouldn't have to wait as long for his next kill as he thought.

She had written her preliminary report, had meetings with other agencies to discuss his case and had asked him in for a follow-up appointment to review a couple of things in greater detail, which would help his case move forward.

So, at 10:55, he strolled into the council building. He now knew his way up to her office, so he did not need to stop by reception to ask for directions, but because he was in a good mood, he greeted the man behind the desk.

The meeting was a swift but very informative one, he believed.

Samuel didn't really take note of what happened during the meeting, he would get a follow-up letter anyway, he was too busy studying Tracey in detail. The shape of her ears, the way they curved in proportion to her face, the elegant way they looked as the light caught the zircon studs placed delicately in her lobes, the way her writing curled as she gripped the pen with her long slender fingers or the way she swiftly typed on her computer using all of her fingers to reach the letters, enjoying the way they worked and the way her eyes moved as they saw everything.

CHAPTER 26

Samuel could not contain his excitement and decided that he would stop by Wetherspoons in the town centre for a bite to eat. He hadn't realised how hungry he was until he exited the building and heard his empty stomach growl in protest of hunger.

The sky was fairly cloudy, but the sun was warming and shining, making the air a pleasant temperature, so, he decided to walk to Wetherspoons. He was surprised at how easy it had been to become someone else. With his disguise, he was free to walk anywhere unnoticed, just another face in the crowd, just another member of the public. It wasn't far and the walk would do him good.

Once inside Wetherspoons, he located a table in the far corner, away from everyone else. The pub was filling up with people come for brunch or an early lunch. He scanned the menu and quickly decided what he would order. He used the Wetherspoons app to put his order through.

In the meantime, he scanned every table in his view, people watching. He thought people were very interesting to watch, the way they communicated, their response to someone else's comment or opinion, the way they expressed themselves through movement. He became lost in watching a group of elderly men and women and did not see his food arrive.

"Oh, sorry I was miles away," he apologised to the waiter when he exited his trance. He recognised the waiter as the man he'd bumped into by the entrance to Tracey Evans' office. What a coincidence. Only not really. He took note of his uniform when they collided and read his name badge.

Greg.

"Hey, aren't you the man I bumped into the other day at the council office?" Greg asked.

Samuel took a moment to study his face, as if pretending to search his distant memory for his face. "So it is. Sorry about that. I always seem to be distracted recently. The name is Samuel." He held out a hand to shake his.

"No worries, mate, I'm Greg. Enjoy your food and I'll see you around."

"Yes, you will," Samuel said under his breath as Greg walked away, clearly busy. He was disappointed not to have spoken more to him.

But it's a name and a face he would not forget. He will come in handy one day, Samuel thought as he downed half his pint of beer before tucking into his Brie and Smoky Chilli Jam Burger.

CHAPTER 27

The team got caught up with the daily updates during the evening briefing in the incident room. Wilson agreed that it would be beneficial to speak to Jonathan Paxton, the former Headteacher at the Grace of God boarding school, as he was their only source of first-hand information with anything regarding the school. He instructed Tom and Lavinia to take the trip down to Dartmouth the following weekend.

Morgan and Norton informed the team of their interview with Oliver, the manager at Holmes Estate Agents, and highlighted the house viewing Anna had had with her client, Dean Hadley, at 11am on the morning that she was last seen.

But they could not find anything on Dean Hadley.

"We all know the killer moves around society as a normal person so this Dean could have been the killer acting as a buyer," Morgan finished explaining.

"I would bet good money on this being the case," Harris agreed.

"He never stops," Lavinia sighed in defeat.

And the team never seemed to stop either. Due to the hard and constant work over the past weeks, Wilson gave each member of his team the option to either work from home, be on call or come into the office. Wilson did not mind, as long as they were around and available if needed. No one would be able to take time off with an ongoing investigation, but he thought they deserved a little break and to cut them some slack. Especially since nothing was happening any time soon. If it had, then it would be a different story.

Tom and Lavinia were going to make the most of the early finish, and with no Speedway that week, there was only one place to be.

The Classic Car Night situated around the Centre Green in Scotter was, as Anna had told her father, very popular indeed. It was heaving with locals. There was a sense of community with everyone coming together to share common interests and show their support.

Tom and Hayleigh parked up at Alastair's so they could all walk down together.

As they turned left around the corner by the local Chinese takeaway to enter The Green, they were met with a fleet of cars parked all around. From Jaguar EType, Ford Capri, 1973 Triumph Stag and Ford Anglia to Porsche 911, Ford Model T, Ferrari 250 GTO and Aston Martin DB5. There was even a Renault Type CB Coupe de Ville and Renault Saloon 1932 on display. They were all stunning and very classic indeed.

A gazebo offering pulled pork and apple sauce hog roast was situated by the hairdressers on the outskirts of The Green. The smell followed them as they walked around admiring the cars and chatting with the owners.

"I had a MK2 Volkswagen Scirocco just like this one as my first car," Alastair stated when they came across one. He recognised the make and model by sight before the owner was able to tell them what it was. The car they saw had actually been the owner's first car. He explained that he had always wanted a MK2 Volkswagen Scirocco as a young boy and was determined to get one. He kept talking for a while, giving a history of how he came to own his prized possession. Alastair had found it a fascinating story and was happy to listen.

The others slowly milled around nearby checking out the other classic cars while waiting for Alastair to catch up with them.

CHAPTER 27

To help raise money for the local park, there was a raffle stall, a hook-a-duck, and various items including furniture and children's toys up for sale that were donated by local residents.

It was a good night to somewhat relax and empty the mind of thoughts about the case for a short time.

Only that did not work; Lavinia could not help but think of Anna. Had she not died at the hands of her killer, she would have been there, they would have walked around the same space, admired the same cars, maybe have even acknowledged one another as they passed on the street, as many people did. Anna may have even queued up to buy a hog roast, perhaps standing in front of or behind Lavinia as she queued up with Hayleigh, Mindi and Tom. Alastair was still talking. Lavinia felt the need to look behind her, feeling a chill creep up her spine, as the memory of Anna lingered.

Had the killer been here? Was he around now?

Lavinia would not be able to pick him out if he had been, he was just another face in the crowd, another person, another resident. He was just another member of society, which is why he had evaded them this long.

Alastair soon joined them in the queue and as he rambled away, all thoughts of Anna evaded Lavinia's mind, if only temporarily.

CHAPTER 28

He watched in the shadows.
Tonight, was the night.

She had rung her husband from the office, apologising for having to stay late and catch up with paperwork.

That old and well used excuse.

He knew Greg would come in handy one day, and today was that day.

When he had returned to Wetherspoons, he engaged Greg in a longer conversation, and had learned a lot. He realised that people loved talking about themselves and would offer their whole life story if asked the right questions.

Which he had accomplished.

His disguise had not failed him and he felt that Samuel Jackford had become good friends with Greg, the Wetherspoons waiter.

His plan for that evening formed while he was listening to Greg pour his heart out.

****

Tracey made her way to Greg's apartment.

He had learnt that Tracey was having an affair with Greg, but they had argued when she told him it was over between them. Greg hadn't told him outright, but he was able to read in between the lines. On Samuel's way home, he purchased a burner phone and sent a message to Tracey pretending to be Greg, begging to talk to clear the air.

As he expected, Tracey fell into his trap like a fly in a spider's web.

CHAPTER 28

Oh, how the human race were ever predictable.

He waited outside, lurking in the shadows, and followed her route on his phone from the tracker he placed under her car.

He would then know when to act.

He saw her park up and make her way to the second floor, going up the stairs while he took the lift.

He had to get the moment timed perfectly if he were to execute his plan without any interference.

He stepped off the elevator as Tracey had her back to him and was approaching Greg's apartment door. Her hand was raised to knock on the door, but her knuckle made no sound as he crept up behind her.

She struggled against the attack at first, eyes wide in surprise, arms and legs flaying trying to escape his ever-tightening grasp, but he had put a cloth over her mouth, so she began to lose consciousness and her body felt heavier by the second. Samuel Jackford led her down the elevator, placed her in the back seat of his car where he would drive her to his house. All in the dead of the night. Coincidentally, the streetlights outside the block of apartments were out of order. Oops. He closed the car door, where the world was shut out on the events that would occur in darkness.

CHAPTER 29

After a quiet and uneventful weekend, Monday bought mayhem as Tom and Lavinia had been instructed to meet the team at The Green in Scotter, by the War Memorial.

When they arrived, it was a hive of activity.

SOCOs were like white clouds floating around the scene, cars and vans were parked up nearby, cordons were placed around the perimeter, the team, Hayleigh and the Senior SOCO were huddled together in a group discussing the body and the scene, and a small crowd had gathered outside of the cordons where police were politely directing people away from the scene.

The memorial, used to commemorate the men who had served, died and survived the Great War, was placed in the centre of The Green, directly opposite a few houses, and homeowners had gathered on their front garden or by windows on upper floors to get a good look at what was happening on their doorstep.

"What's happened?" Tom asked as they approached the team. His voice faltered at the prospect of a fourth victim. But the look on the team's faces confirmed his suspicions.

"We have our fourth victim," Wilson confirmed.

"Same MO, same estimated TOD, same body positioning, and a neck tattoo is present," Hayleigh listed. "But what's interesting with this body, which is absent in all the others, are the letters written on the memorial, presumably the victim's initials in a red substance."

Tom and Lavinia took a closer look at the memorial, and added to the bottom of list of names were the letters written in red capitals, 'T.E.'.

CHAPTER 29

The victim was propped up against the memorial, naked, with her head slumped forward. The similarities were unnerving. This victim looked older than the previous three, with her age estimated at mid to late 30s. She had medium length brown hair that had been styled into a graduated long bob.

"Any forensics at all?"

"We have taken a swab of the writing to confirm, a, it is blood, and b, if the blood came from the victim or from another source. We will be able to obtain a DNA profile from the blood sample and match it. Similarly, with the first victim, there appears to be dark fibres in her mouth, perhaps from a cloth that was used to render her unconscious when he abducted her or put in her mouth to keep her quiet during the torture process. Other than that, there seems to be no forensic evidence on or around the body or scene, as usual with this killer, but we are looking extensively as you can see," the Senior SOCO surmised.

"Seems like this killer doesn't have weekends off either."

* * * *

Missing Persons could not find a match.

No one had reported their victim missing.

Did she have any friends and family, either in the UK that she kept in contact with or anyone local who had failed to notice she had not returned home?

Wilson had ordered a check on everyone living in the Lincolnshire area with the initials TE. It would be like finding a needle in a haystack but at least it was one way they could locate the identity of their victim and tick off those on the list that were accounted for.

It would be a slow process.

The search came back with nine hits.

Thomas Evans, Tristan B Evans, Timothy R Evans, Terence Evans, Tracey Evans, another Tracey Evans, Teresa Edgehill, Tracy Eustis, and Tamara Evers.

It seemed Evans was a popular surname in Lincolnshire.

They immediately discarded male names since their victim was female.

The list was reduced slightly.

Tracey Evans from Grimsby, Tracey Evans from Scunthorpe, Teresa Edgehill from Louth, Tracy Eustis from Gainsborough, and Tamara Evers from Boston.

Three women who were less likely to be their victim were the persons from Grimsby, Louth and Boston since the location was further out of range for the killer. The victims seemed to either live in Scotter or Scunthorpe and were found in either of those places.

The team divided up the remainder of names and underwent further searches, to locate home addresses with co occupants, their occupation, and a telephone number.

Tracy Eustis from Gainsborough was 18 years old, was on the electoral register and was at John Leggott's College in Scunthorpe. They ruled her out due to the estimated age of the victim being older.

Tracey Evans and Teresa Edgehill.

Tracey Evans from Scunthorpe lived with her husband, Collin Evans. Tracey was a Social Worker and according to her date of birth, fit the victim's approximate age.

The telephone number was answered by a man named Collin, Tracey's husband. When Harris explained the reason for his call, Collin got suspicious and informed Harris that she had failed to return home Friday night.

"She sent me a message to say she had to stay late at work. When it got to nine-thirty and she still wasn't home, I rang the office and then her mobile. She messaged me later and said she bumped into an old friend, and they had gone for a drink to catch up," Collin told Harris.

"Was this an unusual thing for Tracey to do?"

"Working late, no, but making last minute plans, yes. She's never been one to be spontaneous."

CHAPTER 29

"So, were you then suspicious when you received the message from her about meeting up with an old friend?"

"More confused at first because like I said she wasn't as easy going as that, but never suspicious. Should I have been?"

"No. Do you know who this friend was?"

"No idea at all. I've tried to think who it could be ever since she said it was an old friend."

"Any idea where they might have gone for a drink?"

"They could have gone anywhere. The Queensway pub is near her office but that doesn't mean they went there."

"We'll look into it. Did you hear from Tracey after the last message?"

"Yes, hours later, saying she had had a few drinks, it was late, and her friend had offered her to stay so she accepted."

"We will need a list of any old friends you can remember and if you have a recent photo of your wife it would be very much appreciated if you could forward that on to me."

****

Wilson obtained a copy of the morning's newspaper, and sure enough, in the puzzle section was the all too familiar seven clue crossword.

The investigation became a repetitive cycle, but that was the job. A body found, same findings reported for all victims, no significant forensic evidence, crossword published in the paper, briefings and interviews with relatives and colleagues with no real leads or answers. New information always seemed to lead to a dead end. There were more people to interview, and a constant review of the case seemed to be the only way forward, looking for any scrap of information that had somehow been missed. That was the routine that had consumed their lives.

A briefing took place in the incident room, as it always did, and the team were currently working through the crossword.

"Here we find ourselves again," Wilson sighed as he began the briefing. "You know the drill by now."

Wilson admired his team from the front of the room as they were busy discussing the clues and answers to the crossword. They were all hard working, talented and sacrificed so much for the investigation which he was very appreciative of. He could not imagine working alongside a better team.

Across:
2. All-Knowing (10)
5. Women (7)
6. Bodies (7)
7. Clue (4)

Down:
1. Anagram (8)
3. Killing (9)
4. All-Powerful (10)

(Omniscient, Bitches, Corpses, Hint, Initials, Slaughter, Omnipotent)

CHAPTER 30

"We have a possible ID for the victim. Tracey Evans from Scunthorpe. Lived with her husband Collin. Tracey was a Social Worker and worked in the North Lincolnshire County Council building on Ashby Road. She was apparently working late and, according to her husband, she had bumped into an old friend, they went for a drink and Tracey stayed over after drinking over the limit. Collin hasn't seen or heard from Tracey since. He will compile a list of possible friends she could have gone out with and in the meantime will supply me with a recent photograph of her," Harris informed the team.

"We were just at The Green on Friday night for the Classic Car show," Lavinia said in reference to the killer's chosen disposal ground, bewildered that so much could change in a couple of days. It seemed coincidental.

"If the killer was present at the shows, he may have seen you there and that's why he decided to use that specific place as his disposable ground. Or he had already decided to dispose of Tracey there, heard about the event and attended what would soon be his victim's graveyard. Like Daniel said, he is confident enough to walk these streets and interact with people like an ordinary being. It would excite him that he was the only one that would know what would happen hours later," Wilson inferred.

"So, we have to establish if he planned the Memorial as his place before or during the event. I guess the only one who knows that is the killer himself. And unless we catch him, we may never know that either, amongst other things."

"Did you see anyone you recognised?" Norton asked.

"About half the village," Lavinia replied sarcastically.

"Was the event on all weekend or just Friday?" Norton asked again, ignoring her previous sarcastic comment.

"Just Friday."

"We know Tracey didn't attend the Classic Car event because she was either with a friend like she stated or with her killer," Tom surmised, as if that singular piece of information might aid in eliminating all the possibilities the team had come up with to explain the reasons for the Memorial being the killer's latest depository site.

"Great work. Visit Tracey's colleagues and get copies of her clients' files. There may be an angry client out there somewhere wanting revenge."

****

Morgan and Norton, along with a team of three uniformed officers, arrived at the North Lincolnshire County Council building with a warrant in tow to legally obtain Tracey's client's files.

Colleagues were either gobsmacked, hysterical or extremely upset, or all of the above, about the intrusion and to learn that she was dead. They were all shocked at the news.

A separate office was used to interview the colleagues in turn by Morgan and one of the uniformed officers, while Norton and the other two uniformed officers searched the cabinet in Tracey's office and removed every file she had pending. They also searched around her office for any other potential evidence, but all looked ordinary, and nothing stood out. The computer on her desk was switched off and password protected. Norton would arrange digital forensics to take a look at it and see if they could access it. Any communications with clients via email may prove useful. Her calendar would be an interesting read to see when and where she met clients, how often and what other events she had scheduled.

CHAPTER 30

Six cardboard case file boxes were filled with the files obtained from Tracey's office. Each box was alphabetically labelled. They were removed from the premises and placed into the boot of the squad cars. When they arrived back at the station, the team would search through each file and contact the client for anything that may have put Tracey in jeopardy or anyone that had a reason to want revenge or sue Tracey.

"Every single one of Tracey's colleagues were just as dumfounded about her death as each other. She met with various clients a day, sometimes in her office, sometimes elsewhere in a public place such as a park or a coffee shop. Generally, clients were well behaved, respected Tracey, she had a good professional relationship with her clients and there wasn't anyone she had a particular problem with. Tracey had a soft spot for children, and it was always those she developed a personal relationship with. Still contacted a few old clients to check in on them from time to time. One client, however, went off the rails. Shouting abuse, threatening her, trashed her office and stalked her, but the police soon sorted that out and no one has heard from him since. The reason for that was because he was placed in a psychiatric hospital. He's still a patient there." Morgan consulted her notes as she summed up the information from the interviews with Tracey's colleagues.

The team were in a briefing in the incident room, once again. The incident room felt like it was a second home since they spent many hours in that room, getting to grips with the case, understanding motives, establishing investigative strategies and updating each other on newly found information.

"What's the client's name?"

"Shaun Saunders. He had mental health issues, and his child was taken from his care and placed with the mother. He clearly wasn't happy with that arrangement, but it was in the best interest of the child while he got the help he needed."

"We will split the files between everyone based on alphabetical order. Each box has been kindly divided up into these sections. Harris take A-D, Morgan E-H, Norton I-L, Tom M-P, Lavinia Q-T and I will take the remainder U-Z files," Wilson directed.

They each retrieved the relevant assigned box and laid out the files in front of them to go through them one at a time and those that had been dealt with would be placed back into the box.

Coffee was supplied on refill from the machine, and the incident room was silent, only the shuffle of papers, conversation exchanges with clients over the phone were heard or the sporadic discussions between the team were occasionally conducted.

Every document in each file was verified and confirmed with the client. They were asked the reason for their meetings with Tracey, and some were more forthcoming with the information than others. Some played the confidentiality card but were reminded that they had legally obtained each file by warrant and anything they shared might prove useful in an ongoing murder investigation. That seemed to alter people's perspective. They were also asked how many times they visited Tracey's office or met with Tracey to discuss their case. It was difficult to find a client who had any issue with Tracey, significant enough to warrant her death.

Besides, even if there had been an angry client who had threatened to kill Tracey, or had even gone ahead with the action, it would not explain the link to any of the previous victims, therefore, it was unlikely that it had been a client; but they had to venture down every avenue in search of any potential leads and investigate every possibility.

The link between the victims were still missing.

Was there a hidden link that they had not found yet? Or were they just chosen at random?

CHAPTER 31

The week had been draining.

It felt like it should have been Friday two days ago.

But thankfully it was, at last, Friday today.

The team were officially looking for a serial killer, and the investigation had scaled immensely in terms of paperwork, case files and victims. The amount of work had significantly increased as a result of more bodies, more reports, which made for a more detailed investigation into each victim's life and death. The team were working more hours and definitely felt the added pressure.

They also had to deal with hundreds of complaints from the public.

The media had broken out over the latest news of a body. They were blaming the police at the lack of investigation for the reason that the killer was still out in the public, killing. It had created mass panic amongst women especially, and they had resorted to buying pepper spray, never being out late at night, but always going out in the company of another person, working from home and staying indoors. That was understandable in the circumstances, but Wilson had wanted to avoid the panic, the confusion, and the interference.

The killer would be ecstatic to learn that he was the talk of the town.

The families of the victims were very much in the public eye, reporters stationed outside their property trying to snap pictures or get a statement from them. They too blamed the police for their prolonged heartbreak and grief. From the lack of justice their loved ones received to the length of time their bodies were held for, so relatives could not say goodbye properly, lay them to rest and grieve normally. No one seemed to know when they would be released to their families and that was always on Wilson's conscience.

Wilson's wife, Denise, had never seen Wilson so hopeless and defeated. He would come home in the early hours of the morning when she was asleep and leave early the next day, before she awoke. Or he never came home at all, he would sleep in his office. They hardly saw each other. He looked exhausted; she knew he wouldn't be eating properly but would be having at least one tumbler of whisky every night instead.

Denise knew the consequences and expectations of marrying a detective. It was like three of them were in the relationship. Denise, Wilson and his job. She always knew how much the job meant to him and could never ask him to give it up. Cases always consumed his time and his private life, but he had always managed to make the effort to come home in time for tea, or even occasionally, come home early enough to make Denise tea. They saw each other in the mornings, had breakfast together and left the house at the same time. Sometimes he would have to go into work early, but they found a routine that worked for them. It saved their relationship, and it was healthy for them both.

That was before this case. And ever since, he had returned to his old habits. Denise was worried for him, but she knew he was just doing his job, and for that, she could not argue. Alastair had arranged a dinner for them all to hopefully take Wilson's mind off the case for a few hours. Of course, he would still be thinking about it, he was always thinking about his cases, but he could have an evening to somewhat relax, enjoy good company and conversation away from the case, and just remind him how important friends and family were.

Until then, the investigation required attention.

Daniel Hargreaves had joined the team in the incident room.

CHAPTER 31

"We need to know the who, the what, the when, the where, the why and the how," Daniel emphasised. "We don't know the identity of the killer as of yet, but we do know who the victims were. We can give an estimate as to the timescale when they were killed and when the killer disposed of them. Where did he kill them? We also don't have this information but from the evident torture each victim went through ante-mortem and for the duration he kept his victims, we can suggest it was somewhere remote, in an abandoned warehouse or even in a basement nearby, perhaps in an empty house, but whichever option, it would be locally based, more convenient for our killer. And we also know the various different locations where the bodies were found. We don't know why he chose these locations, and we are also unsure as to the reason for killing these specific women. We can only suggest it was to do with the deadly sin that was tattooed on their necks – did the victim commit that sin and is that why they have been branded with it? And finally, how. We know from the postmortem that they were drugged with a neuro-muscular blocking drug, which eventually caused asphyxiation. The recent crossword clues support our theory that he has a strong dislike for women, referring to them as bitches. To him, he feels powerful over them, they are helpless, worthless, and he is in control, they are better off as corpses that he has slaughtered than beings," Daniel was able to sum up.

In the meantime, they started by creating a timeline of events for all victims when they were last seen and found.

"Isla was last seen by Harry Nightingale on their date Friday 3rd June. They went to Miller and Carter in Bottesford, he dropped her off at approximately 10pm and she went missing at either some point that night or in the early hours of the morning, before her shift at the hospital the next day. Failed to show for work. Not reported missing by friends or family, neither realised she had gone missing. Found the following Monday 6th June in the River Eau in Scotter," Wilson began.

"We know Madison was reported missing by her friend Cassie on the day that she was found at Scotton Beck on Monday 27th June. She was last seen on the Friday before, the 24th of June, at the Parker, Prescott and Skinner event, by Jake Higgins. She had left his apartment later that very same evening, time is unclear, but she failed to make it back home. She got picked up in a taxi to the station but there was no sign of her on the station's CCTV, so some point on her journey to the station, she must have been abducted.

"Anna Shaw was last seen at work on Friday 8th July. She was showing a client around a house in Ashby and failed to report back to the office. It would seem she was abducted by her client, going by the alias Dean Hadley, whilst still at the house. Found the following Monday 11th.

"And Tracey Evans. Worked late, and then met an old friend at the Queensway pub, who, according to the messages sent on her phone to her husband, whether it was her or someone else, decided to stay over at this friend's house because she drank too much to drive home on Friday 29th July. Whoever that friend was could have been the last person to see Tracey alive. We know she never returned home. Found Monday 1st August."

They reflected on the information.

"The killer doesn't tend to keep his victims for a long period; to say that he wants to prolong the pain and the fear," Tom observed.

"There's a pattern. The victims are always last seen on a Friday and then found the following Monday. It fits the theory that he could work a normal 9-5 job. It would look too suspicious if he kept taking leave from work around the time when each victim was last seen or found," Harris added.

"He must be exhausted. He finds time to stalk his victims, abduct them, torture them and then dump them in the early hours of the morning on top of working a full-time job. I barely

CHAPTER 31

have time to eat some evenings before I'm asleep," Morgan exclaimed, wondering how the killer has managed to get away with it for so long without making even the slightest of mistakes. "Also, how does no one notice them missing before the weekend is over? The victims can't have made plans."

"Harry got suspicious but just thought Isla was ignoring him, Cassie also got suspicious but due to the circumstances didn't think anything of it at the time. Collin is another one. He was more confused than suspicious of this friend Tracey was with as it was unlike her to make last minute arrangements. All seem like innocent explanations. It would be worth checking the pub's CCTV for confirmation and start getting a picture of her movements," Lavinia added, trying to comprehend the chronology.

"We also need to speak to Chris Sayles, Anna Shaw's ex, just to ask him some routine questions," Harris recalled.

"Ok, Harris, you get on with that and Norton, check the CCTV at the Queensway pub for any sightings of Tracey Evans and her friend. If we get all that done, plus the reports written, we may be able to leave on time tonight. I know we all have evening plans."

****

Chris Sayles was in the midst of writing a report when his desk phone rang. He sighed before accepting the call, as it had interrupted his thoughts.

"Good morning, Chris Sayles speaking," he answered in his most upbeat professional tone. He stopped typing and sat back in his chair, hoping the call would not take too long.

"Mr Sayles, it's DI Harris Forster speaking from the Major Investigation Team in Scunthorpe. Is it a good time to ask you a few questions about Anna Shaw?"

"I suppose so, guess there's never going to be a good time. Maria and Darren informed me of her death. It's still a shock when I think about it now. Just can't believe it."

"I am very sorry for your loss, but when was the last time you spoke to Anna?"

"The day before she was found. I phoned her in the evening. I was just checking in with her, making sure she had settled into her new house and her new job."

"How did she seem?"

" Really happy. She was ecstatic about the job, she absolutely loved it and the move had been tough on us both, but she had really settled into it." He smiled at the memory, and he was genuinely happy for her.

"She didn't seem distracted by anything or anyone?"

"No. I mean we didn't talk like we used to on the phone when we were together, and it got a bit awkward and silent at times, but nothing seemed to unsettle her."

"I heard you continued to be in a relationship when she made the move to Lincolnshire, but soon after it was a mutual decision to break up?"

"Yes, neither of us found time to see each other. We were hours apart and it had seemed like she moved on and found a life for herself. That's all I ever wanted. Sure, it was hard and upsetting, but we remained friends and I still had her in my life and that was the important thing."

"Did you speak to each other much? I know she rarely spoke to her family."

"Not really. The odd phone call or text here and there."

"And you didn't see her after she had moved?"

"No, I wanted to visit but I wasn't sure if she would have wanted me there considering we were no longer seeing each other."

"Do you know if she was seeing anyone else after she moved?"

"No, I don't think so. If she was, then she moved on pretty quickly but that wasn't Anna. I know she would have wanted to focus on her career, which is why she made the move in the first place."

****

CHAPTER 31

The Queensway pub was located on the right of Queensway roundabout and accessed from Ashby Road.

Being 10:12am on a Friday morning, the pub was very quiet. There were only two small groups, sat at opposite corners of the pub, tucking into a full English breakfast.

It was an average English pub with carpeted floors, several wooden tables with either two, four or six seats around it and booths in the upper area. The bar was the first thing they saw when they walked through the entrance door.

Norton and Morgan beelined for the bar. A middle-aged woman in black uniform was stood behind the bar, tapping away at the screen. She didn't notice the detectives until they approached her.

They showed her their ID badges and introduced themselves.

Her face did not give anything away, nor did she seem surprised by their visitation. But Morgan guessed that from working in a pub, she was used to all kinds of people coming and going, and all the troubles punters brought with them.

"Can we speak to the manager please?"

Moments later, a short young-looking man with brown hair and a stubble, wearing grey trousers and a blue striped shirt with the sleeves rolled up, appeared. The badge attached to his shirt said, 'The Manager'.

He greeted them with a business-like smile, but it wasn't quite friendly. "What can I do for you?" he said in a polite tone, although Norton guessed he wanted to be anything but polite.

"We would like to take a look at the CCTV from last Friday evening that could help with our inquiries." Norton got to the point.

"May I ask what it is in relation to? There have been no recent altercations so I don't think I would be able to help."

"We believe that someone related to our investigation visited this pub with a friend last Friday evening for a drink. We need to look at the CCTV to confirm her movements as it could be vital to the investigation," Morgan explained in a professional manner, and tried to be as equally polite as the manager had been moments before.

He looked between them for a moment, and then caved in. They followed him to his office where he set up the CCTV for them to watch.

"Do your employees have access to the CCTV?"

"Only I do as it is kept in my office, which I lock when I vacate the room," he said matter-of-factly, as if he was the one being interrogated.

The manager rewound the footage to the night in question and then got up from his chair behind the desk to allow Norton and Morgan better access and a better view of the computer screen.

They watched on, expecting a woman matching the description of Tracey Evans to walk through the door. Being a Friday evening, the pub was packed with people starting their weekend as soon as the clock hit 4pm. People came and went, but Tracey Evans was nowhere to be seen.

She never entered the pub.

"That's odd," Morgan voiced what they were both thinking.

"So, it seems Tracey lied when she sent that message to her husband."

"Or it was sent by someone else." Morgan shuddered at the thought as they both knew the person she was thinking of.

****

Dinner at the local pub had been arranged by Alastair, before he was to depart for his two-week annual fishing trip to Whitby, as it had been a tradition to go out for a meal the night before. Marcus was to join a couple of days later, not wanting to take a full two-week holiday all at once. Hayleigh would get Zoe to cover and assist with the digital

CHAPTER 31

documentation of the crime scene. Marcus had offered to cancel the trip, but Hayleigh was adamant to let him take it. Mainly so he could look out for Alastair. Usually Wilson went along, but there wasn't anyone else to take the Detective Chief Inspector's role in Wilson's absence, especially with the required experience, expectations and pressures of the case. But they could just about manage with the absence of Marcus.

The Gamekeeper was always busy on a Friday night where locals gathered with friends and family, finally toasting the weekend ahead. Live music would start at 9pm by local singers.

The seven of them were sat around a large table near the window looking out onto the street. Alastair, Wilson, Denise, Hayleigh, Mindi, Lavinia and Marcus. Tom had arranged to see Jess before the weekend trip to Dartmouth, and the rest of the team had their own plans to eat out together. They had to persuade Wilson to leave his work and take one night off. He always put his team first, granting them time off to rest, but he knew if he pushed his team too hard, he would not get results.

The drinks were flowing, several conversations were being exchanged around the table, and it became a relaxed atmosphere. Wilson felt the most relaxed that night than he had done in months. Alastair had done his job, and he was pleased to have his old friend and colleague back even if only for one night.

CHAPTER 32

Ruth Damson was a natural with children. She loved to see them progress with their spelling, punctuation, grammar and witness their social development improve as they made friends and gained more confidence.

When she first started teaching her Year 1 class at the beginning of the academic year last September, they were all shy and timid. No boy or girl wanted to speak to their new 'scary' teacher who had been a stranger at the time. Over time, more students gained confidence to put their hand up and speak in class, more students trusted the other children to play in the sand pit with, or sit and draw together. It took some children longer than others to gain that social skill, but once they had, there was no stopping them.

By the end of the year, they were all very talkative, very engaging and enthusiastic with the lessons and the work. It made Ruth's heart swell, and she was extremely proud of each and every one of her students. They all loved Ruth and their assistant teacher, Hilary Ferguson, after seeing that they weren't scary at all, but very patient and caring people.

Ruth was in her early 30s, with ginger locks and forest green eyes. Teaching had been a passion ever since she undertook work experience at her old primary school, back when she was in college. Before that, she had no idea what job she wanted to pursue. She went on to study Primary Education at university, undertaking more placements with several different year groups, before gaining her PGCE and teaching full-time, at Scotter Primary School.

At first she felt weird returning. The corridors, the assembly hall, the classrooms were the same and, even some

CHAPTER 32

of the teachers and dinner ladies were still there from when she attended, and it felt like she was back to being six years old again. It did have a sense of familiarity about it though, and that's possibly why she had settled so quickly.

She had been teaching at Scotter Primary School shy of five years. She absolutely loved her job, and it made it easy for her to get up in the mornings or complete lesson plans in the evening or at weekends, when she should be relaxing or doing other things with friends, family or even her husband.

Ruth was doing exactly that now.

She was researching a lesson plan on the five-times-tables, trying to come up with a fun practical but educational activity to keep the children engaged and learning. The children loved to do practical work more than sitting down at a desk and writing out sentences, or maths puzzles. The lesson wasn't until the following Monday, and since it was Friday evening, she had all weekend to think of something.

Right now, her husband, Duncan Jennings, was becoming impatient. Ruth, had said she would be ready for their date night by six o'clock on the dot. It was now getting on for half past six, and Ruth still had not moved from the dining room table to get ready.

Luckily their table at The White Swan wasn't booked until 19.30 and was only a short walk away from their house, but Duncan had wanted to them to have a drink at the bar beforehand. They were celebrating. It was their four-year wedding anniversary, but also Ruth had recently discovered that she was pregnant. Duncan had invited friends and family to have a surprise joint anniversary and baby celebration at The White Swan, but she was even going to be late to that.

"The table isn't booked for another hour; we'll make it in plenty of time," Ruth defended when Duncan persuaded her one more time to get ready.

"I know, but I wanted to have a drink at the bar beforehand, to make more of a celebratory evening."

"Why don't you just have a drink here? You're the only one who can have alcohol at the moment. I'd just be sat at the bar drinking tonic water, pretending it tasted like gin."

"There is such a thing as non-alcoholic gin nowadays," Duncan tried to persuade her.

Duncan sighed and sat down next to Ruth. She looked up from her computer and into his eyes, placing a hand on his thigh. He held her hand in his.

"I know, it's just been a long road for us to get here, and now we have, and I feel it's a miracle. I just want to celebrate this little miracle. Our little miracle. You've been so occupied with work and worrying about the baby; we both just need a night off from it all and to just focus on us. For one evening," he pleaded.

Ruth had had a series of miscarriages that felt like a stab in the heart every time it happened. Duncan knew that teaching twisted that knife in deeper, but it was her passion and her job. She would come home crying, exhausted and shut off because she desperately wanted to have children, but somehow the universe was against it. She would never change jobs, no matter how many times Duncan tried to make her see that it might have been the best thing for her at the time. She was told the heart-breaking news that she would never be able to have children. After attempting seven IVF treatments in the hope that the doctors were wrong with the word never, they finally struck lucky. They would take it one day at a time, and it scared the hell out of them both. But working too much was not healthy either.

When Ruth was told she could not have children, her best friend of thirty-two years, Chloe Ashford, had already had one child, Hazel, and another girl since, with another one in the planning. While she was thrilled for her friend, she was also jealous. Jealous that they could have as many children as they wanted without the worry or stress of whether it would live past a few weeks. Jealous that they could breed so easily.

CHAPTER 32

So jealous that after one night of babysitting Hazel, Ruth kidnapped her. That was two years ago.

When Chloe and Martin came back from their anniversary weekend, they found the house empty. Ruth and their baby daughter were not present in the house. They noticed some of Hazel's clothes and toys had disappeared. As a mother, the first thought is always the worst. They phoned the police. After searching for two hours, they had found Ruth on a bridge a couple of miles away, watching the sunset, with Hazel content in her arms. Ruth was telling her a story as Hazel's eyes felt heavy and struggled to stay open as she dreamed of unicorns and princesses dancing at the ball in the sunset. Once the sun set, stars shone brightly against the dark sky. So peaceful and carefree. The world seemed simple in times like that, but in reality, it was depressing, hard and brutal. Chloe and Martin thought she would jump into the water with their daughter, and maybe Ruth had been contemplating that, but Duncan had talked her round. And all charges were dropped.

The aftermath of that incident had been punishing enough for Ruth as her and Chloe's friendship became non-existent because Chloe no longer trusted her. Martin had forgiven and was civil to Ruth, but he would never forget. Ruth had been seeing and was still seeing to date a psychiatrist. She was mentally healthier. Her job at the school had been momentarily put on hold but after she proved she was capable and got it signed off by her psychiatrist that she would be well enough to return to teaching, she got her job back. Despite working with children, she had never felt happier than when she was teaching.

Since Martin was still a great friend of Duncan's, he had invited them both that evening. However, Chloe politely declined, making the excuse that she would not be able to get a babysitter for that evening. Duncan knew she still wanted to avoid Ruth.

After contemplating Duncan's argument, Ruth agreed to get ready. She closed her laptop and quickly kissed Duncan before going up the stairs to get changed. Duncan cracked open a cold beer from the fridge while he waited.

By 18.55, Duncan heard the plod of footsteps coming down the stairs. They lived in a three-bedroom house, with a garden, in the heart of The Granary housing estate in Scotter.

Duncan and Ruth had met at the school. Duncan was a teaching assistant before Hilary in Ruth's class, but after the struggle with not being able to have children, and the brief spell they had split up because of that, he thought it was better to move schools. He knew it was too much for Ruth to be in each other's company 24/7 and that had turned their relationship sour. Duncan thought the best thing he could do for them both, to save his relationship, and support Ruth, was to move to a school in Scunthorpe. He did just that, and slowly they were able to reconcile. They became stronger for it.

As he looked at Ruth in awe, with amazement and affection as she descended the stairs, he knew that it was all worth the pain, the stress, and even all the arguments, which thankfully were no longer a regular occurrence.

Since she was only eight weeks pregnant, Ruth was not showing just yet, and she could get away with wearing her own slim fit jeans for now, rather than maternity jeans. Although she knew that time would swiftly come. She wore slim blue demin jeans, a white linen blouse with gold buttons and her black chunky heeled boots. She knew she wouldn't be able to wear heels for months either.

"I thought you were going to wear that maxi dress you decided this morning?" Duncan asked, although not surprised that his wife had changed her mind on what she would wear. It happened all the time.

"I was. Just thought I'd wear my jeans and boots while I still can," Ruth simply replied.

"Well, you look stunning in anything." Duncan downed the remaining beer, threw the bottle in the recycling bin,

CHAPTER 32

and held the door open for Ruth to exit before locking up behind himself.

They walked hand in hand to The White Swan and to Duncan's amazement, they had made it with seven minutes to spare. The waitress took them through to the main dining room, where they were met with the bang of party poppers, the echoes of people shouting 'surprise' and 'congratulations' and the amused looks from both Ruth and the guests as she was genuinely surprised.

"Was this your idea?" Ruth turned to Duncan with an amazed look, who was stood behind her, grinning like the Cheshire Cat at how seamless his plan had gone.

"I had help from Martin, and your parents, but yes."

"It's perfect. Thank you." She leant in to kiss him, receiving whistle reactions from their guests. They laughed in response.

The crowd dispersed and went off to talk in their own groups, while Duncan and Ruth made the rounds, to catch up with people they hadn't seen in a while and to thank everyone for coming. Firstly, Ruth went up to her parents, Desmond and Betty, and hugged them tightly, giving thanks for helping Duncan pull it off.

"It was all Duncan really, we just kept you occupied while he went out and organised it all with Martin. We only really sorted the cake and added a few guests to the list."

Ruth's eyes landed on the cake, and it was magnificent. It was a recreation of their wedding cake four years ago, but with blue and pink ribbons and decorations to represent their unborn baby. Her mother was a professional cake baker and decorator, so she had designed and made their wedding cake, and now the celebration cake. It was perfect. Ruth's eyes watered and she blamed the hormones for being emotional. She spotted her brother on his way back from the bar, whom she kept close contact with, but hadn't seen for over a year. He had moved to London to study law and become a renowned criminal barrister. He had had cases in the Caribbean and the British Virgin Islands, so his work took him all over the country for extended periods of time. He was aware of the hardships that had occurred in Ruth's life, but she hadn't told him about the full extent in not wanting her to burden him or even distract him from his job. It was good to see him in the flesh.

"Hey." They hugged each other. She only realised after seeing him there, just how much she had missed him.

"It's great to see you. When do you go back to London?"

"Charming, I've only just arrived and you're already asking when I'm going back. Sunday evening," her brother joked.

"Shame you can't stay for longer, but you're here now and that means the world to me. We will have to go for lunch tomorrow and spend the day somewhere. All of us." She turned to her parents to include them in her plans.

"That would be lovely," Betty responded.

"There's a vintage fair and food festival in York on tomorrow," their father Desmond suggested.

"Perfect. Be great to have the four of us together again. Like old times." Ruth beamed as memories of family outings and holidays flashed across her mind.

Ruth moved on to chat with three friends from university: Abbey, Naomie and Clarice. Again, it was about a year since she had seen them. With everyone having families of their own, working full-time, and being at opposite ends of the country, it was hard to find time for all to meet. They had all studied the same course and had lived together throughout their time at university. They spoke pretty much every day in their group chat, or Facetimed regularly to maintain contact, but like with her brother, it was good to see them in person again. They screamed with joy, and laughed with each other, taking selfies. She made a mental note to make an effort to see more of her friends and brother. It was at times like this that she appreciated the people around her and realised how lucky she was to have them in her life.

CHAPTER 32

Martin approached Ruth and they smiled awkwardly at each other. He felt like he was betraying Chloe's trust by talking to her, and forgiving her, and he only really attended the celebration event for Duncan, but he felt he had to say something.

It was Ruth who spoke first.

"Thank you for helping Duncan organise this, it means more to me than I can ever say. I know I don't deserve it, but please just know I am grateful," Ruth said genuinely. It still felt more like an apology than a thank you, but Ruth would be apologetic to the Thompsons for the rest of her life for what she did and what she put them through.

"You're welcome. And congratulations. I know how hard it's been on you both and you deserve some happiness. I did try to persuade Chloe to come, even just for half an hour, but you know how stubborn she is. She knows she shouldn't have rubbed the pregnancy in your face. It was wrong of her to do that, and it only made matters worse between you both."

Martin could see the disappointment in Ruth's face. "I know. And it's fine, I never expected her to come anyway. It would have been nice to hear that from the horse's mouth though. What she did was spiteful, but what I did was unforgivable."

"Give it time, I know it's already been a while, but you know Chloe. You should pop round some time."

"Chloe would love that. She would love you more for even suggesting that," Ruth replied sarcastically, laughing slightly at the absurdity of the idea.

"I'll talk to her. Maybe the first visit should just be in the garden without the kids."

"That sounds like a marvellous idea." The booming voice of Chloe interrupted their conversation. She strode over to them ostentatiously, swinging her hips as she went, making sure that every eye was upon her. Her wide Ray Ban brown sunglasses were sat in her blonde curled hair. The mini skirt she wore showed off her long slim model like legs, and her four-inch-high heels showed how toned her calves were. She beamed, but there was no warm emotion behind it.

"Chloe" was all Ruth said in response, more surprised than anything else. The room had grown quiet, guests listening in eagerly at the exciting or catastrophic moment that two ex-best friends finally met again after not speaking for more than two years under an unjustifiable situation.

"I thought I would drop by, show my face, and congratulate Duncan for putting up with you for four years." Her smile was fake, put on for show. Chloe loved to be the centre of attention, and by making a grand entrance and a scene, she was doing just that. And she would be the talk of the event for weeks afterwards too. "Just kidding," she laughed, tilting her head back as she did so. No one else, but Chloe, had found that hilarious.

"Well, you put up with me for thirty-two years, so four years is no comparison," Ruth bit back bluntly.

Martin walked close to Chloe's side and whispered something in her ear. He was the only one who could rein her in, and he told her to leave if she was only here to cause trouble, or be civil to Ruth. She took her pick and turned to Ruth, all serious. "Congratulations, Ruth. Pregnancy is a horrible cycle of needing to pee every five minutes, being overly hormonal and craving food that's not in the house. But it's worth everything in the end. And I know you'll make a great mother." It looked like it had pained her to say all of that.

"Thanks. I remember." She knew what being pregnant was, first and foremost from her own pregnancies, but from witnessing it all from Chloe. She was a nightmare. They couldn't go out anywhere without seriously thinking of the logistics first. If there were toilets nearby, taking snacks with them, looking at restaurant menus beforehand to see if there was anything Chloe could stomach, or scouting a restaurant that served that specific food. She cried at dogs walking in the park due to their cuteness, she cried if Ruth said something

CHAPTER 32

supportive. At the time, Ruth had laughed at it all, at the silliness and the annoyance of it. Now she was beginning to understand and could even, to some extent, sympathise with her.

Ruth excused herself to use the bathroom, but she didn't need to pee. She locked herself in a cubicle, sat on the toilet, and took a few deep breaths. She was overwhelmed. That Martin was being nice, that Chloe had showed up out of the blue, that Chloe had even spoken to her. And even congratulated her. Ruth knew she didn't really mean a single word that came out of her mouth, unless it was to hurt.

But why now?

And why here?

The bathroom door squeaked open and she could hear the slow clop of heels collide with the flooring, like someone was waiting for Ruth to evacuate the cubicle. Ruth hitched her breath in anticipation and her whole body froze.

"I know you're in here, Ruth," sounded the familiar voice. There was no affection in it.

Ruth knew she would not be able to stay in the cubicle much longer, so she swore under her breath, took a deep breath and flushed the toilet before unlocking the door.

She came face to face with Chloe who had her arms folded against her chest and again beamed her fake smile, which only made Ruth want to punch her in the mouth to stop her smiling. Instead, Ruth walked straight past her to the sink and was busy washing her hands for something to do, more so she wouldn't have to look at Chloe.

Chloe walked to stand beside Ruth, her back leant against the sink as she faced the cubicles. Her presence was unnerving. Ruth could not remember Chloe ever being so intimidating, and never would have thought she was capable of being so cold. How she had changed.

It was the first time they had spoken since the incident.

"What are you doing here?" Ruth asked, surprised that her question sounded more malicious than she intended. She leant over the sink with her hands on either side for support, still trying to avoid looking at Chloe.

Chloe turned her head to look at Ruth and simply said, "Your husband invited me." She watched Ruth closely for a reaction. "You can ask him if you want, but I'm sure you can appreciate that as a surprise I had to keep it hush hush. Wouldn't be the first time."

"If you're looking for a fight you have come to the wrong place," Ruth defended, knowing that Chloe would try to wind her up.

"I came to celebrate your fantastic news!" she exclaimed.

"Like hell you have." This time Ruth looked directly at Chloe, her ice blue eyes frozen like her heart and soul.

"I don't think you'll ever know how it feels to think you've lost a child. At the hands of someone you thought was your best friend, to make it worse."

"I have miscarried before, so yes I am aware of the pain."

"The embryos you lost were barely formed as a human being. It doesn't compare."

"You have always thought your life is better or worse than mine. You have always thought you were a better person than me, the one with more drama, the one who needs all the attention, the helpless one who wants everyone else to feel sorry for her, the selfish one who only really cares about herself and her own issues. Well, this time you are the one no one asks after, the one everyone has forgotten even if just for a night. That spotlight that always shined over you has gone dark, and there's nothing left but bitterness and emptiness so go the hell home." Ruth didn't know where that confidence had come from to do a speech like that in front of her ex-friend, but it felt like a massive weight had lifted from her shoulders. Once upon a time, in another life, they were best of friends who had always dreamed they would be in each other's lives always and forever. But life happens and Ruth just now had realised how much she had been hiding under Chloe's shadow, the whole time, and felt

CHAPTER 32

free to let her go. All this time she felt bad for ruining the friendship and letting one of the best things to ever happen to her walk out of her life, but Chloe hadn't gone anywhere. It was Ruth who finally found the courage and the strength to walk away.

The silence and the tension between them was only disturbed by the drip of a leaking tap. Ruth was about to walk away when Chloe grabbed her arm and slapped her so hard across the cheek, that it not only pierced the air with an agonising sound, but it also knocked the wind out of Ruth. She had stumbled backwards but managed to grab onto the edge of the sink to steady herself. She was in shock at what had just happened, and it took her a few moments to catch her breath.

As she got her breath and her balance back, Ruth's rage had been released as she lunged forward at Chloe and they both hit the bathroom floor with a thud.

After a few minutes of them squabbling on the ground, the door burst open and they were being pulled apart from each other by Duncan and Martin.

"What the hell?" Martin was flabbergasted at the sight and restrained his wife.

"I think it's time you both left," Ruth managed to say in between gasps as she was getting her breath back.

"It would be my pleasure. I wish you were out of our lives for good and went to hell," Chloe spat back, tugging at Martin's hand that held her down and stormed off. Martin did not have to say anything but gave a nod of the head to Duncan and followed his wife out.

"What was all that about?" Duncan asked Ruth calmly.

"What do you think?" Ruth replied bitterly. She turned to face the sink, hands steadying her once again.

Duncan stood beside her, rubbing her back in comfort. "I should never have invited her."

"I can't and won't stop you being friends with Martin, so she would've shown up anyway, invitation or no invitation.

Addicted to the drama." Ruth could not be upset with her husband, so took a deep breath and hugged him tightly.

"You all right?" Duncan asked concerningly.

"I will be when I can relax in my pyjamas and not feel guilty about eating a whole tub of ice cream."

Duncan laughed in response, holding her close.

"I'm just so tired," she sighed.

"We can leave, everyone will understand."

"It's not that, really. I'm just tired of fighting. I don't want to do it anymore," she said, referring to Chloe.

"Then don't. You've tried to fight for your friendship but it's time to stop and let go. You have more important things to worry about now and our son is going to need all of your love and attention. Close that chapter in your life because we have another exciting chapter starting."

Ruth looked up at her husband. "Son?"

"I can just feel that our baby is going to be a boy."

"Wishful thinking more like," Ruth teased.

"We should go otherwise everyone is going to wonder why we've disappeared and start talking."

"That's not a bad thing."

They laughed, kissed and exited the bathroom hand in hand. The rest of the celebrations went by quickly with no mention of Chloe.

Duncan and Ruth left the celebrations shortly after.

Duncan knew that Chloe had ruined the night for Ruth no matter how persistent she was in saying it was the pregnancy that made her tired for the reason to leave.

Little did Chloe know that her wish would come true.

CHAPTER 33

People were so gullible and too trusting. And she had been the easiest so far.

It had been a week since the party and subsequently Ruth had been extremely tired, constantly stressed and had regular pains. She climbed into bed, in her pyjamas, with her feet up.

Duncan was away all weekend on a school PGL trip with the Year 6s. He had volunteered to go a while back, only now he had regretted that decision, but after some persuasion from Ruth and reassurance that she would be fine, he had gone. He loved the outdoors and outdoor activities so she knew he would enjoy teaching the children to abseil down a wooden tower, or how to hit the bullseye with an arrow during archery, or how to read a map and compass.

Ruth fell into a deep slumber thinking about Duncan but suddenly woke up from a sharp pain. She was immediately worried that something bad had happened and grabbed her phone on the bedside table. Her finger hovered over Duncan's number but she couldn't take him away from the trip, so she scrolled further down her contacts to 'Katy Midwife' and dialled her number instead.

After a few rings it was picked up but the voice on the other end of the line was not the light soft feminine voice she had expected. Instead the voice belonged to a male.

"Hello, Dr George Roberts."

"Hi, I was expecting to speak to Katy, my midwife," Ruth answered, confused.

"Ah, yes, I'm the on-call doctor for this evening so all of her calls have been redirected to myself as she is currently unavailable. Is everything all right?"

Ruth didn't know if she should voice her concerns to Dr Roberts. She didn't know him nor had she dealt with him before and wasn't exactly comfortable explaining her issues.

He seemed to have noticed her hesitation and reassured her that he would try and assist as best he could and hoped to match Katy's enthusiastic and professional approach.

Ruth explained her sharp pains and her history of miscarriages, admitting the tense scenes at the party might be the reason for it. Apparently, the doctor lived locally and within minutes he was on his way to check her over and reassured her that it was most likely stress that had caused the pains and he ordered her to rest and not do anything strenuous as a precaution. Ruth felt better already.

She quickly changed into yoga leggings before she heard a knock at the door and answered to his dashing smile as Ruth invited him in.

She offered refreshments which he gladly accepted with the condition that he would be the one to get the drinks. He grabbed two glasses from the cupboard and filled them both with cold water.

He walked back into the living room and handed Ruth a glass which she half downed while he retrieved the blood pressure machine from his bag.

He was chatting away, asking simple questions as he placed the band over her arm and pressed the button on the machine which sucked the band tighter around her arm.

He was so concentrated on the machine reading that when Ruth failed to answer his latest question, he looked up and smiled.

She had fallen into a deep sleep.

CHAPTER 34

The sun barely had time to rise before Tom arrived to pick up Lavinia.

Lavinia had woken Mindi up with a cup of tea in bed and they sat for nearly half an hour chatting the morning away. But they both had to get ready. On her way out, Lavinia hugged Alastair tight, and told him to catch a lot of fish.

"I will miss not coming home to vent or discuss things with you," Lavinia said.

"I will miss not waiting for you and Mindi to come home from work and telling me about your day, but you'll both be busy with work and I'll only be away for a couple of weeks. It will go quick. We can go back to being normal afterwards. But I hope you get what you need from this interview."

"I hope so too. But I don't think this family was ever normal."

"You're right there," Alastair joked, giving Lavinia another hug before she left. "If you need anything, either for the investigation or in general, you know I'm only a phone call away," he added.

"Thank you, love you, Dad, and you too, Mindi."

"Love you too," they both shouted back in unison as she shut the front door.

The journey would take just over five and a half hours covering 323 miles, via the M181 and then the M1, M42, and M5 to Devon. They had factored in one planned half hour stop. It was a lot of driving for a weekend but before they could suggest to speak to the headmaster over the phone or even via Skype, they were told he had no social media, no immediate family nearby that could help him out and he rarely used a mobile. He was on a pay as you go and apparently hadn't needed to top up credit for five years. He was old fashioned and resorted to writing letters by hand or by typewriter if he wished to communicate with anyone, but that would not work for the interview. Wilson therefore instructed a face-to-face meeting with him at his home address, and that's what Tom and Lavinia set out to do.

Lavinia had packed up a picnic and snacks for the journey. They agreed to have a McDonald's breakfast since they were setting off early, but Tom would not permit Lavinia to have a McDonald's lunch in the same day, so she'd arranged a picnic for them instead. They would either wait until they arrived at Dartmouth around midday to eat before speaking to Jonathan, or have lunch when they stopped.

"I have created a Spotify playlist specifically for this trip, mainly a mixture of 80s songs because I know that's the era you like, along with some more modern music. We can either play that or listen to CDs. That is up to you, DJ Newbourne," he said to Lavinia as he set up Google Maps on his phone.

Lavinia looked through his CD collection even though she had been through it before, but he had recently purchased the Now That's What I Call Power Ballads album Lavinia had recommended.

"We'll start with CD, one of the Power Ballads then." She inserted the CD into the player and Bon Jovi's recognisable instrumental introduction to *Living On A Prayer* began blasting out from the speakers as Tom reversed out of the driveway.

"How was your date night with Jess last night?" Lavinia asked casually.

"It was great. Just got a takeaway, had a couple of drinks, nothing fancy. How was the pub?"

"Everyone was just so relaxed, especially Wilson. Haven't seen him that relaxed in... well I've never seen him relax. But the food and the company was great."

"Sounds good. The others went out in Scunny."

CHAPTER 34

"Yeah, Morgan kept me updated throughout the evening. Apparently, it was an eventful night with a marriage proposal and a fight across the road where a police van showed up to arrest them. But everyone deserved to have a proper night off after everything with this case."

"Certainly. Is Alastair looking forward to his trip?"

"Always. He says it's the best two weeks in the year. I think he's a tad disappointed that Wilson isn't going with them this time, but I'm sure he'll enjoy it regardless. Do you know where we're staying, or even Jonathan's address?"

"In the blue wallet on the back seat. Wilson has sorted it all out for us."

Lavinia reached over to retrieve the blue wallet and opened it up to find information about the hotel, taken straight from the website, booking confirmation emails and Jonathan's address. Plus a map of Dartmouth, with the hotel and Jonathan's address highlighted on it, a printed copy of the background check on Jonathan, and information about the Grace of God boarding school.

"Wilson certainly made sure we were prepared for this trip," Lavinia observed.

"Indeed."

The hotel was more of a Bed and Breakfast, named Capritia Guest House. Just a short walk from the river front and the town centre with restaurants, shops and galleries. Breakfast was included and they had two adjacent single rooms. Both rooms were complete with a bathroom, TV, bed linen, large soft towels, toiletries and a hospitality tray.

"Oh wow, we even have free use of the Dart Marina Health Spa and 10% off treatments."

"Don't get too carried away, we're not there long enough to go sightseeing or visit tourist attractions."

Lavinia read aloud from the description taken from the Visit Devon and Dartmouth Visitor Centre Websites. "Dartmouth is a beautiful historic harbour town, situated on the banks of the River Dart. From glorious coastline and countryside walks in the magnificent gardens, parks and nature reserves available all year round to the public, to the museums, galleries, shopping centre and ancient ruins, there is something for everyone. The trip would not be complete without visiting Dartmouth Castle and Agatha Christie's former home. Also worth noting are the Devonshire Cream Teas widely available at local restaurants and cafes, and the local markets that sell amazing fresh produce sourced locally from fruit and veg to freshly caught seafood and locally grown meats." She continued to read the documents, reading out the odd sentences that caught her attention. "The town was used to import cloth and wine in the Middle Ages. Stunning Medieval and Elizabethan houses and streets. The Britannia Royal Navy College, is recommended a visit. From the map, it's an eight-minute walk via Victoria Road from the B and B to Jonathan's address. By the looks of it, there's a couple of pubs nearby, The Dartmouth Arms and The Dolphin. So is the museum, a Dental Practice, a Pizzeria, a gallery, another bed and breakfast, Dartmouth Harbour and the Royal Avenue Gardens."

"Sounds a great place. We will have to return and visit Dartmouth properly."

"Definitely. Dartmouth Court where Jonathan resides looks pleasant. A white building with four floors. Has four flats on each level with a balcony overlooking the River Dart. Seems he chose the right place to retire after his school closed. Lots of churches around the town. Wilson has even supplied us with a list. Dartmouth Church, St Saviour's Church, St John the Baptist Roman Catholic Church, Flavel Church, St Petrox Church, St Clement's Church and the Church of St Thomas of Canterbury. For a small town, they certainly have a fair share of churches."

"I didn't realise it was such a religious town."

"Me neither."

"I'm sure Jonathan will be able to enlighten us with that knowledge."

CHAPTER 34

Once Lavinia was caught up with the information supplied by Wilson, she turned her attention back to the music. CD one was playing, *'The Final Countdown'* by Europe, as Lavinia was singing along and getting ready to change it over to CD two.

The sun was becoming brighter and warmer through the glass in the car. Tom put the air conditioning on to circulate cool air inside the car and Lavinia shed her hoodie and just wore a short sleeved navy sports top and matching tropical leggings. She wore her usual striking red sunglasses while Tom wore brown Aviator glasses. He also wore tanned cotton trousers and a white short sleeved Fred Perry t shirt.

They stopped for a half hour at the Services, to stretch their legs and have a quick toilet break. They snacked on the picnic provided by Lavinia, but the stop went by too quickly before they were on the road again.

By midday Tom was parked up outside the cream and green building of the Capritia Guest House on Victoria Road. The green sign across the doorway and on the wall stood out from the row of other B&Bs and guest houses.

They grabbed their bags from the boot of Tom's car and entered through the gate onto the property. There was a small rectangular patio out front, which sat a couple of chairs and a table under the window. A pair of bay trees, and pyramid shrubs in flared black planters, and hanging baskets adorned the front garden.

Inside was very welcoming and homely as they were greeted by the owner sat at the front desk, watching an episode of a series on Netflix.

She greeted them with a beaming smile and was a very chatty middle-aged lady with a brown perm.

After they had freshened up, and Lavinia changed into a red and white flowered cami dress with bamboo buttons, white converse trainers and a three layered necklace, they headed out towards Dartmouth Court. They walked down Victoria Road and merged onto Duke Street where they reached several pubs and shops that adorned both sides of a narrow street. From Joules, Mountain Warehouse, Cancer Research, Dartmouth Ice Cream and Dartmouth Deli, there were independent shops, amongst well-known names and brands. There was a wide variety of shops that suited everyone.

Across the road from Duke Street, they spotted the arched entranceway to the Royal Avenue Gardens, but they turned right along The Quay, and walked along the harbour. A wide orange bricked and cream Elizabethan building, now home to a Jack Wills store, was sandwiched in between two grand black and white Tudor style buildings, which added character to Dartmouth, and these old fashioned buildings were seen throughout.

They continued straight onto Fairfax Place, which, again, was a narrow street with various shops, restaurants and pubs open to the public, and merged onto Lower Street. They then turned left into Oxford Street, and already Tom and Lavinia had a view of the horizon. They were impressed. The further they walked down Oxford Street, the more scenery was revealed of the harbour and the hills, which stretched from one end of Dartmouth to the other, creating a panoramic view. The place was packed with people walking along the harbour, and seagulls cooed above as they circled the public sourcing food. Lavinia took a picture of the stunning view.

Tom indicated the building that was stood to the left of them, and they both recognised the cream colour of the walls and the balconies of Dartmouth Court.

Access to the property was around the side and up several stone steps, or via a ramp, where they buzzed for Jonathan's flat by the entrance. Tom and Lavinia introduced themselves as Jonathan's voice sounded on the intercom. As he was expecting their visit, he buzzed them through, and the front door opened up to a carpeted hallway. A cabinet of numbered slots for post was to the left, and access to two lifts or the stairs were to the right.

CHAPTER 34

They took the stairs to the third floor.

Once his apartment was located, they knocked on the door to Flat 10, which was swiftly answered by Jonathan. Judging by the walking stick clasped firmly in his right hand and the way he shuffled to the side to let them in, he had waited by the door and listened out for their arrival, so they would not be kept waiting.

As they entered, both Tom and Lavinia glanced around the apartment. It was open plan, with the living room being the first room they came to. A two-seater Chesterfield sofa and a matching Chesterfield chair sat around a carved oak coffee table. Upon the table sat a reading book, today's newspaper open and folded on the crossword section, and with reading glasses perched on the top of it. A vase of freshly cut lilies added colour and fragrance to the room. An empty mug sat towards the edge of the table, on a dark purple amethyst coaster. The TV and stand was against the opposite wall. Landscape paintings hung proudly on the walls all around. The sizeable kitchen curved around the far corner of the large room, with a breakfast bar, and a circular table and chairs sat in front of it. A door to the left opened up into a master bedroom, with floor to ceiling wardrobes and a chest of drawers and a bedside table on either side of the bed. The bathroom was an en-suite with a wet room, a power shower and all the usual necessities, although Tom and Lavinia did not see those rooms.

The balcony, fully opened, offered stunning views of the harbour. Lavinia was drawn to the view and immediately went outside to take in the surroundings. Two iron Bistro chairs and table were in the centre of the balcony, with herb plants that adorned every available space. It was magnificent.

"What a view," Lavinia commentated contentedly as Jonathan and Tom joined her outside.

"It looks different every day and that view is one of the many reasons why I purchased this apartment."

"How long have you lived here for?" Lavinia queried out of interest.

"Going on ten years now."

"I see the appeal."

"I like to sit out on the balcony for hours just minding my own business, being in my own world and draw the view, the sunrises, the sunsets, the seasons. Here, come into my sitting room, I can show you my work if you'd like."

"I would love to." Lavinia gladly followed him into the other room that looked more like an organised warehouse than a sitting room when she entered. All painting supplies, paint and paintbrushes were placed neatly in labelled cupboards and drawers. Canvases of all varying sizes were propped up against the wall. Some of the paintings he had already completed were placed against the wall or hung up on the walls. He had also taken several hundred photographs which were neatly stored in one of the drawers.

He beckoned her to the completed canvases that were propped up against the wall and flicked through them.

"This was just last winter; the water was iced over and snow topped the hills and the roofs of houses in the distance over the other side of the harbour. And then in contrast, summer. This is the most recent one I have completed just over a couple of weeks ago."

"You capture the bright and vibrant colours of the boats and the houses so perfectly," Lavinia observed.

"We all have hidden talents," he joked, placing the paintings back, and they exited the room.

"This seems a very religious town from the many churches around the area, which neither myself nor Tom realised. Is that why, apart from the view from your apartment, you moved here?" Lavinia took that opportunity to steer the conversation in a different direction.

"Yes, there were many opportunities to get involved in the local community, volunteering at the churches or the upkeep on the grounds several days a week. There's always

CHAPTER 34

something to do and that keeps me busy. Overlooking the lower town, you have St Clement's Church, which dates back to the 13th Century. St Saviour's Church, built in the Middle Ages closer to the waterfront, was used instead of St Clement's when Dartmouth started to develop as a town and people no longer wanted to trek to the upper town to St Clement's Church. St Petrox is one of the oldest in the town, dating all the way back to early 1190s and overlooks the River Dart, next to Dartmouth Castle. Flavel Church is a Methodist Church named after The Flavel arts and entertainment centre nearby. St John The Baptist Catholic Church was built from local limestone and Bath stone dressings in the late 1800s. Then you have a couple of churches in the nearby villages of Kingswear and Stoke Fleming. St Thomas of Canterbury Church, in Kingswear, looks out over the River Dart on the opposite side to Dartmouth and St Petrox. The church was demolished but later rebuilt, leaving the 12th Century Tower as it was back then. And St Peter's Church in Stoke Fleming also dates back to the 13th Century. The tower stands at 83 feet high and was used to help sailors find their way to Dartmouth port," Jonathan informed them as if he was a tour guide or still the Headmaster at the Grace of God and was relaying the history of Dartmouth's churches to his audience.

"You have a very in-depth knowledge of the local churches. I'm impressed," Lavinia responded.

"Thanks, love. Some will find it wearisome but it's a hobby of mine to visit churches wherever I go and learn their history and origin. I've been religious my entire life and Church has been an important aspect of it. I guess that never went away. Well after all, God is omnipresent, his presence and guidance never go away, so our belief in Him shouldn't either."

"No" was all Lavinia could think of to say in response.

"Are you both religious?"

"I'm not, no."

"Same, but I was christened."

Lavinia looked at Tom, who looked to be trying so hard not to laugh at his own comment or die of embarrassment. He cursed himself. Lavinia would remember to bring it up later.

"Right. That's a shame. I guess society has made it normal for people to be atheists. When I was younger, you belonged to a religion no matter what and you were brought up on it."

"Is that something you taught your students at the Grace of God boarding school?" Tom found the right opportunity to start their line of questioning.

There was a very slight flicker of sadness that briefly washed over him and then Jonathan's whole body tensed at the mention of the name. Even though he had expected them and knew the reason for their visit, it was still emotional for Jonathan to talk about. He had spent many years of his life devoted to that school and the students in it, and had worked tirelessly to help them get an education and off the streets, all for his efforts to be reversed.

"Yes, amongst other things."

"Did you teach other subjects, or was it just Religious Education?"

"All the core subjects, English, Maths, Science, along with Languages, Physical Education and Art. And obviously Religious Education as a separate subject, but there was also an emphasis on Religion in each subject. For example, in Art, they had projects where they completed a painting, a sculpture, or a drawing, on what they perceived to be the meaning of God. In English, they read passages from the Bible and did comprehension exercises to understand the language and the teachings, and books with a religious meaning or religious teachings amongst learning to read and write properly with all the usual lessons on grammar, spelling and punctuation. Physical Education was just for them to get fresh air and exercise, doing rounders, athletics,

CHAPTER 34

football, rugby. Science was just science, but some people are naturally scientific so we wanted to do a range of subjects to see if anyone possessed specialist skills and help them advance towards that career choice. And we taught the usual languages, French, German and Spanish, only when they advanced in English. They got to choose which one they wanted to pursue, but I believed it was important to be international."

"How long was it after the Grace of God closed that you decided to retire and move to Dartmouth?"

"Think it was just over three months after. The incident at the school, the reason for the closure, gained a lot of media attention and journalists were hassling myself, the teachers and the pupils. I had had enough. Nothing was the same after the school closed."

"What happened to the pupils after the school closed? Did their education continue after?"

"I'm afraid not. I tried but it didn't quite work out. I put them up in temporary accommodation but that wasn't fit for teaching, and we didn't have access to desks, textbooks, etcetera, and we couldn't split the pupils up into manageable class sizes so in the end some stayed, and some left, but the learning stopped." There was emotion in his voice as he said it. He wanted to do good by the young people, and had succeeded in doing so, but it was not enough to keep them off the streets for good. If the school had remained open, then it was possible that many would not have gone back to the streets and sought out good jobs and lived their life away from the streets, and away from the drugs and gangs.

"What was the purpose of The Grace of God school? Where did that name come from and what was your main focus for opening a religious school?"

"The Grace of God motto from Romans 1:16 states, 'For it is the power of God unto Salvation to everyone that believeth.' Salvation is based on Grace and we help students find that Grace, and only when they understand, it releases

God into their life. The aim is to help troubled youths understand religion, beliefs, teachings whilst maintaining a proper education and steering them away from drugs, alcohol, gangs and violence and let God guide them in the right direction. That's where the salvation and the belief in God comes in."

"Is there specific criteria that these children need to meet to be eligible?"

"No specific criteria, but if they have previous drug, alcohol abuse, gang violence, or had parents that were involved in any of the above, or were neglected as children, then they would automatically be enrolled if they came forward. Those students who had wealthy parents, but were just rebellious children, we interviewed them first to see if they would benefit from being enrolled in the school."

"But if they had parents who made the effort or were sober enough to attend the interview, surely that inferred they cared for their child and they would not be eligible to join the school?"

"Yes, that's why we interview those children, to get an idea what their home situation is like. Some parents love to attend because they think they can influence myself and others to take their child. Some parents are just too full on and controlling. Others just want their child out of the way but we're not childminders."

"What type of questions would you ask during an interview session?"

"I would enquire about their upbringing, about their childhood and what that was like. I would ask about their home situation and whether that was happy, or disruptive. I would ask how they became so frayed from family and home life and what influenced their rebellion. That type of thing."

"So very personal matters." It was more of a statement than a question.

"Yes, but it's impossible to take on every student that may have dabbled in a little heroin, got themselves expelled

CHAPTER 34

or suspended from school but still had a healthy relationship with their parents, a roof over their head, phone contracts paid for, food paid for etcetera. It's about those who have lost their way in life, who have nothing and want to be on the road to redemption."

"Were parents ever present during those interviews? Some questions you ask are personal and the children's answers may have been influenced by the presence of their parent or guardian."

"I always asked the child whether they wanted their parents, guardians or carers present or not, but out of those I did interview, none of them actually did want their parents there. There was a reception area where the parents were requested to wait."

"How many students did you interview?"

"From what I can remember, 24 or 25."

"How many of those were enrolled?"

"Only a handful. Like I said, I didn't accept students who had a little disagreement with their parents but still had everything handed to them on a plate."

"Did you interview Aiden Brown, Benjamin Atterbury or Elijah Anderson?"

Jonathan's demeanour changed again at the mention of those names. "Now those are three names I haven't heard in a while. Out of the three, only Aiden."

"Who was present with him? His parents died in a car accident when he was a young boy, before he came to your school. Was it a carer or a guardian?"

"They said they were his guardians. They're socialites and very wealthy people."

"Sorry, who are?"

"Rupert and Camille Davenport. Everybody knows them. Mayors, top dogs in the public services, the prime minister, even your DCI has been invited to a few socials at their estate."

That took them both by surprise. And neither had heard of Rupert and Camille Davenport. They sounded like the type of people who would do good, solely for their image in society and to get the publicity they desire. It was all for show. The type of people that could pay millions for a cover up."

"Were you ever invited to one of these social events?"

"Yes, when I first opened the school, and it was all over the news. I was their special guest. That's how they knew about the school and why they enrolled Aiden."

"What was their reason to enrol Aiden?"

"I was aware that his parents died, and he was put into care but after a series of failed placements, he just left. He was on his own, on the streets. From there, he got into petty crime, drugs, alcohol and violence. The usual. He would use money to fund his addiction which turned him violent. He crossed Rupert and Camille Davenport, but after speaking directly to Aiden, they realised he was just a lost soul, they felt sorry for him and wanted to give him a better life. They are well known for becoming guardians for orphans, so he was just the latest project for them, for want of a better word. Due to his troubled time, and the objectives of the school, they thought it would be perfect for him."

"How well did he perform?"

"He improved as time went on. He was a very bright young lad. All of them are when they realised they could actually do the work and were good at it. He was very sporty, very attentive. But he got in with the wrong crowd, with Benjamin and Elijah, and his performance deteriorated. He got into trouble a lot, with Benjamin and Elijah. They were all disruptive, they all encouraged each other to misbehave. But it changed Aiden, he was more confident, he had friends, just the wrong ones I guess."

"Can you tell us what happened to Benjamin and Elijah?"

"Aiden said they dared each other to drink acid. It was a terrible accident and he said it was only meant to be a couple of drops mixed in with water, nothing lethal or damaging, but still not a clever thing to do. I guess they got too cocky

CHAPTER 34

and the amount of acid they drank killed them. They were excused from their science lesson to have a drink. All bags are placed in a locker in the corridor outside of the labs for safety reasons, but they never returned. A 13-year-old girl found their bodies, on her way to the ladies. Her scream could be heard from the labs and everyone went out to see what had happened. They were ushered back into the classrooms and I was called for. I phoned the police and the ambulance, but it was too late by then. They were declared dead at the scene and the conclusion was tragic accident."

"What was the benefit of closing the school? Their deaths weren't your fault, no one else was hurt in the process. You were doing a good thing by giving these people an education, a second chance in life, why was that just abandoned?"

He sighed with regret. The school had been his life, his calling from God and he had failed everyone who had been a part of that school. "Negligence. I had a duty of care to each and every student that was under my care as their headmaster. And I failed. The options were to close the school, where I could hope to find another job, or retire. I thought the best thing I could do was close the school and enrol the students in a grammar or comprehensive school, or just set up another establishment and carry on. None of it went to plan of course, and retirement was the only option left."

"There was only the mention of a tragic accident in the media. Did anyone else bar yourself know what actually happened?"

"Agatha Phillips, the science teacher. She was questioned about the acid of course, she just put two and two together. She confronted me about it, I was upfront with her. Nothing was mentioned about it since."

"What happened to Benjamin and Elijah's personal possessions at the boarding school?"

"I thought it was only natural to allow Aiden to take what he wanted, for his own use, for memoirs, whatever his reasons may have been. They were his only friends."

"Were you or was someone else present with Aiden when he went through their things?"

"I was with him at first but thought it was courtesy to allow him to do it in private."

"Do you know what he took?"

"Erm, all I remember is a comic. It broke my heart what he told me about it. He said they all liked to read it together and imagine they were each a different character and make up their own stories. That was definitely sentimental."

"Did you ever see this comic for yourself?" Lavinia thought back to the interview with Nigel Atterbury and knew that Benjmain had the murder encyclopaedia in his possession. Is this the comic that Aiden had found?

"No of course not. I have no idea what these boys had in their own possession. I know they didn't have drugs, guns, alcohol etcetera, but as long as they didn't have any of the contrabands, they could have whatever they liked."

"So, you only have Aiden's word that it was a comic?"

"Yes, I didn't go snooping if that's what you're suggesting."

"We're not suggesting anything, Jonathan, we just need to be thorough in our investigation."

"I never heard any of them talk about a comic, apart from that one time Aiden did, nor did I ever see one. But that doesn't mean there wasn't one."

****

The interview continued for a while longer and the leads they did have seemed promising.

"So you're not religious but you were christened?" Lavinia queried as she brought up and laughed at his earlier comment. They left Jonathan's flat, crossed over the road and walked further along the harbour.

"Shut it, you. Why couldn't I have just said no and left it at that?" He shrugged and laughed along. "I guess he was so

CHAPTER 34

hopeful that we were religious, that I felt I was disappointing him by not being and just added that I was christened so he knew I wasn't a complete arrogant arse who turned their noses up at religion."

"But you did make an arse of yourself by saying that."

"All right ha ha. It was hilarious," he replied sarcastically and held his hands up in surrender. "I bet you couldn't wait to bring that up afterwards."

"I was hurrying the interview along just because I could not wait to laugh at you."

"Thought so."

Tom's phone buzzed in his pocket and he looked confused when he read the message that flashed up on his screen before relaying it to Lavinia. "It's Wilson. He forgot to mention that he made reservations for us at Taylor's restaurant for 8pm. Order what you want and send me the bill, he adds."

"That's nice of him to do that."

"I guess we have travelled all this way for work." Tom consulted the clock on his phone: 16.07 "We have a couple of hours before we need to be there, so where do you want to go?"

The Royal Avenue Gardens sign arched over the entrance and was situated at the heart of Dartmouth. It was named as such to commemorate Queen Victoria's visit to the town. At the centre of the gardens stood the impressive cast iron bandstand, surrounded by the serenity of nature.

Situated across from the bandstand stood the triple tier stone fountain which was added to celebrate Queen Victoria's Golden Jubilee in 1897. Twisting paths led to several different gardens, including a herb garden, a rose garden, a Mediterranean garden and a memorial garden. Also featured within the gardens was a community greenhouse and a small pond.

Tom and Lavinia meandered around the gardens, following wherever the winding paths led them, taking in the dazzling flower beds that emitted floral fragrances.

They took a seat on a bench near fruity peach, pearl white, bright yellow, dashing red and pretty pink rose beds, which reminded Lavinia of the rose bed at home in memory of her mum. Cherry blossoms adorned the outside of the beds, adding to the colour and the sweet floral scents.

Lavinia did not want to ruin the tranquillity that the gardens offered, but as she sat in silence on the bench next to Tom amongst the roses, with her thoughts whirling around in her mind, she had to break the silence.

"Jonathan is a sweet gentleman. Seems lonely and regretful and that's sad," Lavinia reflected.

"Yep, but he seems happy enough here. As long as he has a church and a view to paint, he's more than content with life."

"I know, just feel so sorry for him. We should probably update Wilson though."

Tom sat undisturbed for a moment. He was marvelling in the stillness of the gardens and how clear his mind was, and how relaxed and calm he felt amongst the array of flowers, their colours, their arrangement in the designated spaces and their fragrance.

"You're right, we should. Let me enjoy the roses and the cherry blossom a tad longer before delving into work mode again," Tom suggested.

Lavinia could not argue with that.

After ten more minutes, Tom sighed and Lavinia knew that he didn't want to but knew that they had to speak to Wilson about the interview with Jonathan. He would be expecting their call any minute. He retrieved his phone from his pocket and dialled Wilson's number, turning up the volume and holding it up close between his ears and Lavinia's so she could hear as well, but not putting him on loudspeaker, in case anyone nearby could overhear their exchange. The gardens were busy, but where they were sat, it was near empty and they hadn't seen many people pass whilst they had been sitting there. Still, Tom did not want to take any risks, especially with such a high profile case.

CHAPTER 34

"Tom, thanks for ringing. I've been expecting your call. How was the interview?" Wilson greeted as he answered Tom's call and got straight to the point.

"It was interesting to say the least. Jonathan was able to inform us of the event that closed the school. Benjamin and Elijah were in a science class and went out to the lockers in the corridor just outside the laboratory to have a drink. The teacher thought they had bunked off, but they were found forty-five minutes later by a girl on her way to the ladies' bathroom. They were pronounced dead on scene. Jonathan said they were constant troublemakers, always showing off and getting themselves into trouble. So it was no surprise to Jonathan when he found out they had drank a lethal dose of acid."

"So they must've stolen supplies from the laboratory. Also, would the acid not be diluted or used in minute doses to make it safe for pupils to work with?"

"I guess they did, yes but it was never proven that they had stolen the acid. Even if it was diluted, too much of it would be lethal. It's not for consumption so any amount wouldn't do you any good. So, Jonathan agreed to close the school after it was deemed a tragic accident by the investigative team at the time. No details were ever released to the public other than that, so it was kept covered up even until now."

"Is it just Jonathan who knows what actually happened?"

"Jonathan and the science teacher, Agatha Phillips. She only knew because she was questioned about the acid after the incident and put two and two together."

"And no one else knew?"

"Not that Jonathan was aware of."

"Where is Agatha Phillips now?"

"As far as Jonathan is aware, she tried to get another job afterwards but no one wanted to employ her, so she retired. Haven't seen or heard from her since."

"Who was the Senior Investigating Officer?"

"Anna Longfield. But apparently she died in the line of duty some years ago. Jonathan tried to contact her about the investigation only to hear the news of her death."

"That's all we need. But we should be able to locate old case files from storage. We can go through the case, read up on the findings from the investigation and see if there is anything more suspicious to their deaths than a tragic accident."

"I'm not sure that would help the investigation. Benjamin and Elijah died. Elijah's father is currently serving time in prison for murder, Benjamin's father the same thing, but he committed suicide in prison. Kelvin told us that Benjamin visited his father in prison and his father gave him their murder encyclopaedia, or whatever you want to call it, who was residing at the Grace of God at the time. He had to have that in his possession at the place of his death."

"What happened to their things?"

"Jonathan let Aiden Brown, Benjamin and Elijah's only living friend, look through their personal effects and decide if there was anything he wanted for himself for keepsake, for memoirs, for his own use."

"Was Aiden alone or did he have company when this occurred?"

"He was alone. Jonathan thought it wouldn't have been right for him to have been there. It was an emotional time for them all, especially Aiden. I mean it's hard enough losing one friend, but two at the same time in the same horrific circumstances, that's hard for anyone to comprehend, never mind a young boy."

"So, Aiden could've come across that book and took it for himself. Did Aiden mention a book of some kind to anyone?"

"There was mention of a comic. Whether that was an actual artefact taken by Aiden or just a cover up for the murder encyclopaedia, who knows. But it's not unusual for boys that age to be into comics, so it wasn't suspicious."

CHAPTER 34

"Did Aiden leave any of their possessions behind?"

"Yes, there wasn't a lot to begin with, but he left an Aston Martin DB5 toy car replica, a couple of postcards, unwritten and of scenic views, no mention of the place on them, and some games. They were given to other pupils that wanted them."

"Does Jonathan know what happened to Aiden after the school closed?"

"There was no record of him a few months later."

"After the incident, the media were hassling him, the pupils and the teachers, all trying to get information from them about the incident. Jonathan stuck around for a few weeks, making sure everyone was cared for and set up in temporary accommodation, but it was difficult to keep up with the education. There were no classrooms, they did not have access to any teaching equipment, so many just left and went back onto the streets of drugs, homelessness, crime and alcohol again. He guessed that that's what Aiden did. That would explain the lack of record. Clearly he did not get a job, or bought a house, because we would have been able to locate him from employment or housing records. Jonathan retired to Dartmouth shortly afterwards."

"What was interesting though, was that socialites Rupert and Camille Davenport were Aiden's guardians and it was them who enrolled Aiden in the school."

"He didn't ever go back to stay with them after the school closed?"

"Doesn't seem like he did, there's no one under that name registered at that address."

"Well Rupert and Camille are well known people, they do Charity work abroad and in refuge centres. They host several social events throughout the year, I get invited to a few. They're doing a Hollywood themed Charity Gala next month," Wilson stated.

"Yes, Jonathan mentioned that you knew them. Jonathan got invited when he first opened the school as their special guest. And that's how they knew about the school."

"What about the other teachers? What happened to them afterwards?"

"They moved onto other teaching jobs or retired themselves. One of them became a refuge support worker and managed to help a few of the ex-pupils."

"It was like the Grace of God boarding school never existed after it was closed."

"What happened to the building and the land that surrounded the school?"

"Turned into a modern housing estate."

"Our priority is to locate Aiden Brown. He may have even changed his name and that's why we cannot locate a record for him. I will try and speak to Rupert and Camille, see if there is anything they can tell us about Aiden specifically, especially where he went after the school closed. In the meantime, I will organise an artist to draw up an impression of what Aiden may look like now and circulate that to the media. If no one, apart from the Davenports, recognise his name, someone somewhere has to recognise his appearance. Anyway, thank you for the work and the update and go and enjoy Taylor's. You both deserve it." Wilson hung up.

Taylor's Restaurant was modern, classy and distinctive. The décor was completed with a monochrome finish.

All the waiters and waitresses were dressed in smart uniform from the brogues to the crisp freshly washed and ironed pearly white blouses or shirts, and moved around with confidence and pride as they attended to their guests.

The young woman that looked to be older than her eighteen years, had her silvery blonde hair up in a neat high ponytail where the curls swished with every movement she made. Her face was covered in a thick layer of make-up. You could tell she took pride in her appearance with her trimmed and dyed eyebrows, lip fillers, highlighter and bronzer, and white teeth. She was average height and very slim. She was waiting by the bar to take drinks over to a nearby table, but as soon as she saw Tom and Lavinia enter the restaurant,

CHAPTER 34

she sauntered over to them, smiling brightly, with her upper teeth on full display, to welcome them.

"Good evening. Do you have a reservation with us?"

"Yes, I believe it was made under the name Wilson?" Tom replied, as Lucie, according to her name badge, took the highlighter pen that rested on the top of the desk, her eyes scanning down the page at the list of names and highlighted through the reservation when she located it.

"Yes, if you would like to follow me, please. You are at table four this evening, over by the window so you have a great view of the sunset while you are eating. I'll give you a moment to get settled and then I will be with you in a few minutes to take your drinks order."

"Thank you," both Tom and Lavinia said in unison as she left them to it and disappeared off elsewhere. Once she had left the table, Tom went around to Lavinia's side and pulled out the chair for her, which took her by surprise.

"Oh, you don't have to do that." She turned around to face him.

"I know, but I treat all my dinner guests with the same courtesy, so it's only fair I do it for you as well."

"Well, if you insist, thank you. What a perfect gentleman."

He pushed the chair under her as she sat.

"That's me." He grinned as he took his place opposite Lavinia.

"So, how many dinner guests, as you put it, have you done that for then?" Lavinia asked casually as she opened the wine menu and turned to the red wine list.

"That would be telling. But that's how my grandad told me I should treat a lady and I've done it ever since. Call me old fashioned, but in my opinion, that's how every man should treat his guest, with respect and be courteous."

"Wise words to live by."

Lucie had reappeared at their table and asked if they were ready to order drinks. Tom and Lavinia consulted each other on what to order, and swiftly agreed to a bottle of Brunito Rosso Toscano from Tuscany, Italy. Lucie handed them the food menu and disappeared again.

"This restaurant is incredible," Tom admired, looking out the window and gazing at the fiery sunset.

"You should come here with Jess. Make a weekend or a week of it after the case. Do Dartmouth properly," Lavinia suggested. She too admired the blazing sunset and snapped a picture as it engulfed the horizon in a hot pink, flaming orange and intense yellow glow.

"Great idea. Jess wants to meet you actually," Tom stated casually, his attention back on the food menu.

"Meet me? Why?"

"She wants to meet the woman I always run off to on our dates."

"Funny." She looked up at Tom whose face was serious. "Oh, you're not kidding? But that was one time, maybe twice. And that's work related."

"I know, but I agree with her. It's only natural for my work partner and friend to meet my girlfriend."

"I have met her already in case you've forgotten."

"Once. And I mean properly. Not when she's at work and we've gone to interview her colleague who happens to be the victim's friend."

"That's why I'm not sure it's a good idea to see Jess now, in the middle of the investigation."

"We don't talk about work, or the case, or if it does crop up, I give her the bare minimum. She understands that I cannot talk about an ongoing investigation."

Lavinia sighed. She was glad Tom had found someone and was happy, but her first impressions of Jess were not that great, and she didn't think they would get on that well since she saw them as completely different people. They did have one thing in common though: Tom. Maybe they would have more. And he wanted Lavinia to meet her properly, as he wanted Jess to meet Lavinia properly. He was right. As

CHAPTER 34

much as she did not want to agree, she knew she had to, for Tom's sake. And their partnership, but more importantly, their friendship.

"Ok, yes. I agree to meet Jess properly."

"Great. And I appreciate this more than you know."

"I know."

"And who knows, you two may just become the best of friends."

"Don't get too ahead of yourself."

Lucie came back with their bottle of Tuscany wine and apologised for the wait. She then took their food orders. Tom started with cured salmon teriyaki with picked ginger and then opted for the pan roasted noisettes of lamb with deep fried cauliflower, redcurrant and wine sauce, and dauphinoise potatoes for main. While Lavinia ordered the seared scallops with garlic, parsley and lemon butter for starters and then confit of duck with honey roasted vegetables, sweet and sour black cherry sauce and also dauphinoise potatoes. Lucie disappeared once again.

The conversation flowed easily and comfortably between work, Jess, Alastair, their trip and general topics of conversation. They naturally enjoyed each other's company and both said how nice it was to be away from the office, even if they were in Dartmouth for work officially, but still felt like a very short break. A change of scenery, as Tom had said. Their starters arrived which were devoured in a short amount of time. The presentation was spectacular and looked more for show than to eat. Their mains soon followed, with the same artistic presentation, like the empty plate was the chef's canvas and the food was his paint. With dessert Tom ordered a pint with his pear, almond and amaretto tart, while Lavinia ordered a glass of vintage ruby port to accompany the Eton Mess. Again, the food was a masterpiece.

After the bill was paid for, they exited the restaurant, bellies comfortably full with incredible tasty food and wine, and slowly headed back to the guesthouse. The evening air was muggy, but with a constant cooling breeze, which made Lavinia's hair and dress blow gently in the breeze.

Jonathan was right, the view did constantly transform. At night, the wavy turquoise blue sparkling water, turned a deeper shade of midnight blue to a smooth sheet of black, the reflections sharper in the water as Dartmouth came alive like it was the Diwali festival, and the orange glow of house lights became one big flame. The sky made the transition from cloudy white and blue topaz by day, to a luminescent burnt padparadscha orange during sunset to a London blue topaz by nightfall.

****

The pain was unbearable.

Tears streamed down her face as she could no longer hide from the pain that was tearing her soul apart.

The sound of the saw tearing through bone was earth shattering.

She wished he would just hurry up and quickly finish the job to put her out of this miserable existence.

She knew she was going to die.

It took her all of an hour to realise no one would be coming to her rescue. Duncan would not be her knight in shining armour because he was away on a PGL school trip with his Year 6 group. He was clueless and did not know she was on the verge of death.

She was alone.

She would die alone.

Well not completely.

She has the little plum she was growing inside her, but that little plum would die with her and the thought of that was heart breaking. Even though the baby was not fully formed, it did have a heartbeat, and she found some comfort in knowing that she wasn't somewhat completely alone.

CHAPTER 34

She was finally able to have children and now that would be taken away from her and they would both be taken away from Duncan.

She knew she had done a terrible thing in her past, but why her?

Was she finally paying for her actions?

Would Chloe and Martin stoop to this level?

Even though she knew that Chloe would dream of killing Ruth every night, she knew she would never act upon it. She was capable of doing a lot of things, but killing another human being was not one of those.

Or was it?

Her heart was hammering out of her chest and her breathing laboured as the next wave of pain crashed over her and momentarily numbed the pain as it drowned her until she resurfaced and gasped for air.

* * * *

The journey back home felt long but it had been a successful trip.

They left Dartmouth just after nine o'clock and made it back into Scunthorpe in time to pop into the station. The team were still there when they entered the office, all wanting to know the details of their trip.

"Jonathan is just an old man who has a good heart, sees the potential in people and wants to help them achieve that. Just a shame it came to what it did," Lavinia answered the various chorus of questions that came their way about Jonathan.

Wilson came out of his office and greeted Tom and Lavinia. He called a briefing so the team could get up to date with the latest developments. Tom and Lavinia took the lead and told them everything they had found out.

"Woah, so much information. So this Aiden boy vanished without a trace. Could he be our killer or just have ended up dead in a ditch somewhere?"

"Either scenario is possible. Just because there's no record of Aiden, doesn't mean he's not out there. We will need to set up a meeting with Rupert and Camille, Aiden's foster parents, and see what they know. Maybe they can shed some light on Aiden, his upbringing, or where he disappeared to," Harris concluded.

Wilson piped up, "I couldn't get through to them when I tried, something about a charity lunch. They're not easy people to contact and arrange meetings with but I'll keep trying."

"What's this annual event they host?" Norton asked.

"It's a massive publicised event where local heroes, local public service workers and local celebrities attend for a fundraising event. It is a fabulous evening, but they keep doing it to uphold their status if you ask me. All for show. They're doing a Hollywood Themed party next week."

"Interesting."

"What are they like, Rupert and Camille?"

"I haven't had much contact with them personally. They are professional people, like to think they are important people in society. They like to think they ARE society. They do a lot of work overseas, working in refuge shelters, working with children, fundraising for animal sanctuaries. They love being in the spotlight but at the same time they are very private people."

"So, snobs basically," Norton summarised.

"The work they do is incredible and it helps so many people and charities. It's certainly not a bad thing what they do, quite the opposite actually, but the reason they do it is wrong. For power, for wealth, for their image, for recognition, for fame."

"Well, they sound like lovely people. Anyway, it's great to hear the trip has been a success."

CHAPTER 35

The following day did not bring good news and were the words that the team now dreaded to hear.

Another body had been found.

They were all huddled by the navy double doors that signalled the Main Entrance to the Scunthorpe General Hospital.

To an ordinary person, the victim just looked like a sleeping patient, outside for some fresh air sat in a wheelchair. Where the other three victims were naked, this one was wearing a hospital gown and covered in a blanket. But exactly the same missing body parts as the rest.

She was a white female with ginger locks, in her early 30s.

By now, it was evident what they were about to witness, but that still did not stop the stillness.

"Same MO?" Lavinia asked quietly, even though she already knew the answer. Just from the looks on everyone's face was enough to confirm her suspicions that it was the same killer.

Hayleigh nodded. Nothing else needed to be said.

Lavinia didn't realise she had been holding her breath until she released a sigh.

"What do we know about this victim, if anything?" Tom asked.

"Same as the others, apart from the obvious signs of torture, there is nothing. Although I expect to find the same during the post-mortem. By now, I can take samples to test right away now that I know what we're looking for. But right now, she's just another Jane Doe in the system."

"All the others were not wearing anything but this one, why alter it?" Morgan asked.

"A person in a wheelchair outside the hospital donned with a patient gown wouldn't look out of place. That's why no one questioned it. She looked like a patient who had gone out for some fresh air and fallen asleep. It wasn't until someone had checked on her that they realised she was dead and everything else became apparent, but even then, a dead person in a hospital is not unusual."

"Who found her?"

"Some nurse who had gone out for a cigarette break, works in ICU. Said she had left her jacket hung over the railing and went back to collect it. She noticed the woman in the wheelchair again who didn't seem to have moved an inch."

"Did the nurse recognise the woman?"

"No."

"Why the hospital? Did this victim work here? Or was it just the luck of the draw where the killer dumped her?"

"We know Isla worked at the hospital but she was found in River Eau in Scotter so I'd hazard a guess and say it's unlikely she did work here."

"But I'd still say the location is relevant. As you've just said, Isla worked at the hospital but was found in the river. Madison worked in Sheffield but lived in Scunthorpe and was found at Scotton Beck. Anna was found in a wheelie bin outside a home in Scotter but lived in Scunthorpe. Tracey Evans was found by the Memorial at The Green in Scotter but lived in Scunthorpe. And I know we don't know anything about this one, but I have a feeling it's all linked. I think these victims are dumped where another victim worked or lived."

"So he knows who his victims are way in advance?"

"Well it's certainly a link we should look into more closely."

CHAPTER 35

"What about the tattoo?"

"Same story as with the previous victims, same place on the back of the neck, same colour ink and recently done, botched job like the others but this time the mark is a smaller circle with an arrow inside a larger circle." Hayleigh showed them the tattoo on the back of the victim's neck, allowing Marcus to photograph this crucial piece of evidence that may help to determine the reason for the killing.

"What does it mean?"

"This time, envy," Lavinia recounted.

"Any suspects or people of interest?"

"None."

"Anyone reported her missing or identified her yet?"

"Not yet but we will circulate her image to Richard and Kathryn to look through Missing Persons. Hayleigh will be doing the post mortem first thing tomorrow morning. Tom, I know how much you like to attend autopsies so thank you for volunteering," Wilson directed.

"I guess we should also stop by the newsagents on the way back to the station. See what the latest crossword has in store for us," Harris mentioned.

****

By the fifth victim, everyone knew the drill: it was the same story each time, and as expected, the weekly crossword was no exception.

Norton did not bother reading the headlines or the articles in the paper, but instead went straight to the puzzles page.

There at the bottom was the small-scale crossword they had all become accustomed to during the course of the investigation.

Same title, just seven different clues.

Across:
  3. Lack of Light (8)
  6. Intense Jealousy (4)
  7. Cat and Mouse (4)

Down:
  1. For a Secret Never to be Told (4)
  2. Underground Level (8)
  4. Public Entertainment or Spectacle (4)
  5. Be Frightened (4)

(Darkness, Envy, Game, Five, Basement, Show, Fear)

CHAPTER 36

Wilson contacted Rupert and Camille's agent and managed, with some persuasion about assisting in an ongoing murder inquiry, to set up a meeting with Rupert and Camille at their home estate the following morning. He did not expect to meet with them so quickly, but guessed they had more important things to do and wanted to get this interview out of the way.

So Wilson and Harris found themselves entering the elaborate entrance to the Davenport Estate with stone pillars on each side and a wrought iron gate. Wilson had visited there on numerous previous occasions, but it was always for an evening do, and always at night. This time, with daylight enunciating the mansion, he was able to take in the sheer size and was in awe at what his eyes were seeing, and it looked even more impressive than before. And somehow it felt wrong to be there during the day on official business.

He pressed the buzzer and announced their name and rank, showing their ID badges at the CCTV camera and were permitted entry. The gates slowly opened to reveal a long, winding, smooth tarmacked road.

"Follow the yellow brick road," Harris joked, making reference to *The Wizard of Oz*.

Rupert and Camille were stood on the balcony outside the first floor main windows. As soon as Wilson's car came into view they made their way down the steps with their chocolate brown Labrador called Jasper at their heels.

The magnificent mansion loomed behind them, making them look like miniatures in a dolls' house.

As they came into view, Wilson could see that Rupert wore retro golf clothing of maroon knickers with matching cap, and a maroon, navy and grey matching sweater and socks. He didn't have to go far to play golf as they had a course made in their own garden. Camille's attire was more sophisticated and consisted of dark blue denim jeans, brown leather Barbour boots, fresh from walking the grounds with Jasper, and a navy Joules body warmer. Despite it being summer, it was the UK after all, and the temperature had dropped significantly with a forecast of rain.

With them, they carried the aura of power and wealth.

The uneasy look in their eyes did not go unnoticed by Wilson nor Harris as they drove to a halt and turned off the engine.

"They look nervous. Probably worried about what secrets we're about to uncover," observed Harris.

"Probably more worried what people might say regarding police presence on their grounds."

They both exited the car to be greeted by a sniffer dog.

"Jasper," Rupert called out and the dog responded by sitting down.

"Such an obedient dog," Wilson greeted, patting Jasper on the head.

"After rigorous hours of training with a specialist," said Camille.

"It paid off," Harris added.

"Yes," Camille simply replied.

"Forgive me for not officially introducing ourselves," Wilson started, "I'm Detective Chief Inspector Wilson and this is Detective Inspector Harris."

"Happy to make your acquaintance. I'm Rupert and this is my wife Camille."

They all shook hands.

"According to Bertha, our agent, I understand your visit is in relation to an ongoing investigation?" Rupert asked the inevitable question.

CHAPTER 36

"Yes, that's correct. Is there somewhere we could talk?"

"The drawing room. I'll get Gail to make us some tea."

Wilson and Harris both felt they had stepped into the 19th Century but with a house as grand as the Davenports', they were not surprised that it still contained the original drawing room.

The drawing room was a magnificent room with intricate décor. The original fireplace was positioned at the foot of the room and a large mirror with a gold frame hung on the wall above it. Two 2-seater sofas sat parallel to the fireplace, facing each other with an oak table positioned in the middle. A chaise longue, covered in silk with intricate sewing detail, a mahogany frame and horsehair cushions was placed against the wall opposite the window which displayed red and gold curtains neatly tied up with elaborate rope. A pristine white grand piano sat at the top of the room and did not look touched in all the years it had been in that room.

Wilson thought that the room, especially the chaise longue, complemented the Davenports' high place in society.

Rupert and Camille gestured to one of the 2-seater sofas for Wilson and Harris to take as Rupert and Camille took the one opposite.

"So how may we assist you?" Camille asked as she crossed one leg over the other and clasped her hands together on her lap.

"We're here to ask you a few questions about someone you have fostered," Wilson started, treading lightly: Rupert and Camille were powerful people and he did not want to cross the line with them.

"May I ask who you are enquiring about?"

"Aiden Brown."

It was very slight, but Wilson caught the startled look in Camille's eyes before she swiftly recovered, regained her posture and cleared her throat before she carried on. "We haven't seen Aiden for a while so I'm not sure there's anything we can tell you."

"When was the last time you did see Aiden?"

"I don't remember. Years ago."

"Have you spoken to him more recently?"

"No, we haven't had any contact with him for years. Do you know where he is? Do you think Aiden has some relation to your ongoing investigation?"

"His name has popped up but we're just following several lines of enquiries at the moment." Wilson simply stated the bare minimum, not wishing to delve into specific details of their investigation. Rupert and Camille would no doubt be aware of the horrific murders Wilson and his team were currently investigating.

"What was it about Aiden that made you want to foster him?" Harris asked gently just as there was a soft knock on the drawing room door.

"That'll be Gail," Rupert announced, standing up and walking to the door to open it for her. Carrying a tray of teacups, saucers, milk, sugar and a teapot was a petite middle-aged woman. She smiled politely at no one in particular, concentrating all her efforts on the tray. As she approached the coffee table, she bent down and slid the tray onto the wooden top. Camille smiled and exchanged thanks before Gail quickly and efficiently evacuated the room. Rupert poured the tea for everyone while the others watched on in silence. He asked if Wilson or Harris took sugar, to which only Harris replied 'one'.

When it felt right to do so, Camille answered Harris's question. "In answer to your question, Detective, I suppose one could say we felt sorry for him. He was a very troubled person, but I can only assume it's because he was left an orphan after his parents tragically died in a car accident. I'm sure it affected him in different ways. No boy should have to go through what he went through."

"You thought you could help him?"

"It's what we do," Camille defended.

"What exactly did you think you could do for him?"

CHAPTER 36

"Help him turn his life around. Give him a stable home surrounded by people who cared about him. Stability, guidance, love. Everything that was missing from his life." Camille was almost teary as she reflected.

"So, nothing that children's care homes couldn't do for him?"

Camille looked aghast at the thought. "Care homes don't care for young people, despite their name, they don't help anyone, not in the way we do anyway. We're not a care home, for starters."

"We know Aiden attended the Grace of God boarding school, under the former Headmaster, Jonathan Paxton. How did you come to know about the school?" Wilson took over once again, feeling Harris had hit a nerve.

"Who didn't? It quickly received a good reputation. Jonathan's view was clear and supported by many good friends of ours high up in Society. Everyone was talking about it, so much so, that it became a well discussed topic during our dinner parties."

"So word was going around about this school and you thought it might help Aiden because he was still getting himself into trouble even after you tried to turn his life around?"

"Are you insinuating that we had failed?"

"Not at all, some people just cannot be helped."

"And you think Aiden was one of those people?"

"Perhaps."

"We spoke to Jonathan on many occasions and discussed in detail what he could do for Aiden and it was an offer we couldn't refuse," Rupert piped up to explain.

"We really thought it would make a difference," Camille added, uncrossing her legs to lean forward and pull out a drawer attached to the coffee table. She produced a brochure but Wilson and Harris did not know what the brochure contained until Camille held it out for them to take. On the front, was displayed an old style building, comparable to Rupert and Camille's mansion, with the words "*Grace of God*" displayed on the front with the motto, '*For it is the power of God unto Salvation to everyone that believeth*' underneath. "Jonathan gave us this brochure of the school to read before we made our decision," Camille explained.

Wilson quickly flicked through; the brochure detailed Jonathan's ideology and views, it followed the journey from abandoned building to Jonathan purchasing the land and stages of improving the building, from it being covered in scaffolding and then the refurbished school as it became. Towards the end, several students' testimonials that illustrated their journey and jobs they had landed after graduating. All extended their appreciation to Jonathan. He was a Saint in their eyes, could do no wrong, only right. This had been Jonathan's life for numerous years.

When Wilson had finished, he looked up and met Camille's eyes. She did not need to explain to him why they sent Aiden to the school. It had seemed the perfect place, perhaps too perfect.

"How did Aiden react when you told him you were sending him away to a boarding school to straighten out his behaviour?"

"Well, we didn't put it quite like that, but he was furious. He resisted and argued at first, but I think that's a natural reaction. I don't think he ever came around to the idea, but he didn't have a choice. Jonathan kept in contact with us to inform us of Aiden's progress and eventually he had made friends and seemed to settle, although still causing mischief."

"Did you know who his friends were?"

"Just two boys who took the same classes and were in the same dorm as each other. I asked about them, but Jonathan did not disclose any details."

"We received one letter from Aiden during the time he resided there," Rupert informed them.

"Can you recall what this letter said?"

CHAPTER 36

"That he was doing well, he hated the idea at first but told us it was the best thing we could have done for him and he even thanked us for putting him on that journey. It seemed he had really mellowed and realised the error of his ways and was reforming. He could be a polite gentleman when he really tried to be. It seemed Jonathan had worked his magic and he really was going to turn his life around afterwards. We were so proud of him," Camille recalled, a tear rolling down her cheek.

Wilson was slightly confused at Camille's words and wondered if she had recalled them correctly because the Aiden they had been told about and the Aiden he had built a picture of inside his mind was still mischievous and still caused a lot of trouble with his friends. He may have mellowed slightly but it did not seem he had fully reformed to have made his own successful way in life. He guessed they would never fully understand or know what had happened or what would have happened unless Aiden was able to tell his own version of his story.

"But that never happened?"

"After the incident that closed the school, he never returned home, we don't know where he's gone or what he's doing but we never spoke to him again, it was like he just simply vanished."

****

Tom and Lavinia found themselves back at the mortuary where they saw all five victims splayed out on the gurneys once more with Hayleigh in the middle of cutting out skin from the back of the victims' necks.

"Are you doing what I think you're doing?" Tom questioned, announcing his arrival but disgusted at what he saw.

"If by that you mean cutting the tattoo out from the victims' necks to send to the labs for analysis, then yes, you are spot on."

"Why are you always in the middle of some horrific cutting when we arrive?"

"It's my work, so this is probably what you would find me doing 80% of the time. The other 20% in meetings and doing tedious paperwork."

"Good point."

"I thought you had already sent samples off to the labs?" Lavinia wondered.

"I did, but it was only a swab of the area, they need the full sample apparently."

"So, you're hoping to get intel from the ink and the needle used?" Lavinia asked.

"Correct, but I'm not hoping for much if the killer's previous reputation is anything to go by."

"Don't remind me."

"Have you done the postmortem on our latest victim yet?"

"Not yet, but you might as well stick around because I'm going to do that after I've got these samples."

"Oh boy." Tom's face dropped.

"You can wait in my office if you want," Hayleigh suggested, smirking.

Tom did just that and took a seat on the comfortable sofa in Hayleigh's office, checking and responding to several emails so he didn't feel completely useless.

That morning, Marcus had left for the fishing trip, so Zoe took over the photography. She did a couple of practice shots of the mortuary to make sure the settings were correct and when she was satisfied, she approached the victim and began snapping away. As she approached the gurney, she studied their victim with a sombre expression, how and why had this woman's life ended in being tortured and murdered? Lavinia could imagine all the future plans she had made like concerts or holidays, career prospects, even choosing her next car. All of which she would never get to do. Other than being a female, she bore no other resemblances

CHAPTER 36

to the others. Lavinia's eyes landed on her hand, where once-long slender fingers typed on the computer, played the piano, held someone's hand, had now been replaced by ugly stumps where blood had dried around the wound. Lavinia could not begin to contemplate the horrors that this person entailed during her last moments on this Earth and her eyes automatically cascaded down to her toes, where the same ugly blood-dried stumps now appeared. The victim's hair covered her missing ear and with her eyes closed, you would never know her left eye had been extracted. That, at least, made her look peaceful.

Hayleigh interrupted Lavinia's thoughts and asked if she was all right to continue, to which Lavinia nodded. As with all of her autopsies, Hayleigh began with the external examination, all findings spoken to her Dictaphone. Lavinia followed Hayleigh's narrative methodically from head to toe.

By this stage, Lavinia had become extremely familiar with the killer's MO so it did not come as a shock when Hayleigh described in detail the ghastly wounds.

But the shock came from Hayleigh's next words: "She was pregnant."

CHAPTER 37

"We need to get onto that guest list."
"We can't just show up at their house and go snooping, they probably have hundreds of cameras in their home and tight security. We would never get away with it," Norton's sensible head reasoned.

"Lavinia's right, it's the only way we can get in and have a legitimate reason to be there. If we get caught, we'll just say something classic like I was looking for the toilet," Morgan argued.

"Why not just wait and get a warrant to search their home, or ask them if we can take a look. Surely that would be better and safer than snooping and getting caught? They haven't given us permission, we'd be breaking the law that we're supposed to uphold. Besides, if we find any evidence, it would not stand up in court. How do you think we would explain how we obtained it. We abused the power of Wilson to get us invited to that party so we could search around their estate and hopefully find something incriminating that we would not be able to use against them in this scenario. What would be the point? Our jobs and reputation ruined," Norton added, astounded at the idea.

"As soon as our names are on that guest list, we have permission to be in their house so we would not be trespassing. We may not find anything, but if we do, then we would take the necessary steps. It could help us solve this whole mystery and, more importantly, our investigation. It might steer it in the right direction or down another long winding road that leads to somewhere we never thought of. And later down the line might allow us to obtain a search

CHAPTER 37

warrant because of its relevance. It's definitely worth a try," Tom tried to sway Norton.

"It's the perfect opportunity. Think about it, Rupert and Camille are going to be distracted by the whole evening, mingling with the guests, putting on a show, whatever they need to do. They have to be present the whole evening since it's their event. Which means we can sneak out at the most opportune time. Think of it as going undercover and we have reasonable doubt that they are hiding something that might just be the key to these murders," Lavinia reasoned.

Wilson just sat and listened to the exchange between his team, mentally writing a pros and cons list in his head as they voiced their opinion on the matter. He had to agree with everyone, they all had valid points and that only made his decision tougher. It wasn't by the book, but sometimes you had to bend the rules slightly to get results and push the investigation forward. Look at Alastair, he barely stuck by the rules his whole career and is one of the best detectives Wilson has ever worked with. He's pushed boundaries but it got results. It could have serious consequences, not just for the entire investigation but everyone's reputations would be in jeopardy. And if they did find something, Norton had a point, that evidence couldn't be used in court or couldn't be used against anyone, but there was a possibility that it could assist the investigation and open up more doors. They really did not have much, or anything, to go on at all and even the slightest of things could change the investigation for the better. It could be the difference between finding the killer and solving these murders, getting justice and closure, or letting the killer walk free.

It was a huge risk.

"Right, I've heard quite enough of this," Wilson interrupted, getting up off his chair and walking to the front of the room, with the authority he always had. "I think it's quite clear that it would be a huge risk to everyone and everything involved in this investigation. But I think we need to do this." Everyone but Norton's response was excitement. "We will have strict conditions all of you must agree to and follow. It will be an undercover operation but must remain within the law. On arrival we will be greeted by Rupert and Camille and their family, whoever is there at the time. We smile, say good evening, shake hands and that's all. We follow a red carpet into a hall where several tables are laid, there's a stage, a bar and usually a photo booth. There is a bathroom at the end of the hallway on the same floor, purposefully built next to the hall so no one gets lost or wanders around aimlessly. We are never allowed to leave that floor. There are security guards everywhere, manning each floor and CCTV cameras inside and outside the hall, so it will be a very difficult operation," Wilson recounted from having been invited to these events on a couple of previous occasions. He continued, "I will be in the hall monitoring the evening from there and Rupert and Camille. You five, the famous five, will be able to get away with being absent for most of the evening so you will be doing the legwork. I will signal to you when it is good to go. I know we are odd numbers, but I need two groups of two to stick together at any one time. I don't mind who those groups are. Be mindful, be wary and look out for each other."

"Could we get digital forensics to tap into the cameras?" Morgan wondered aloud.

"What about earpieces? Be useful especially if we need to communicate with the others to warn them," Tom added, finding his inner James Bond and thinking what he would require.

"I'm not sure what digital forensics can do, but I will have a word and see if they can assist us in any way. I will do all the planning, you guys just trust each other, be prepared, turn up, do your thing and not get caught."

****

CHAPTER 37

In the week they had to prepare, Wilson made them consider all the different scenarios that could arise and how to deal with them. It was a useful exercise but only made Norton more apprehensive than before.

Digital forensics could make the cameras go down for a maximum of half an hour before someone could reboot the system and get them back up and running again. It wasn't a lot of time, but it could be enough. They could make the system go down a couple of times if they required more time, but only if necessary. Wilson was interested in how they could hack into the system, but he didn't want to know at that point. He was taking a huge risk by agreeing to this operation, the fewer people he involved the better and the less that they knew the better.

The moment, the cameras were down, Wilson thought that that would be the time for them to sneak upstairs. Perhaps it was too big of an ask for them to have a look around and be back downstairs in the hall before that half hour was up. It would be a difficult task, but not impossible. Half an hour would be better than nothing. He trusted his team and knew they were good at their jobs.

While Wilson battled with his thoughts, planning everything down to the fine line, one exciting preparation step, for Morgan and Lavinia mostly, was outfit shopping and one evening after work, they all headed to Oldrids department store as they had a good selection of evening gowns and suits that would be perfect for the event.

"So, the theme is Hollywood. Basically, we need to go elaborate, sophisticated and over the top. Men I'm thinking black tie, aim for James Bond lookalike and for us women, the more glitz and glamour, the better. Sequins, sparkle, the lot," Morgan briefed as the men and women went their separate ways to shop.

Two hours later, after trying on what felt like hundreds of gowns and jumpsuits, and trying to match with accessories, clutch bags and shoes, they all came away with a perfect Hollywood themed outfit each.

"Think it's time for a drink after all that shopping," Norton said, exhausted. Shopping was hard work when you had to try on loads of different outfits to find the perfect one.

"Agreed, all that shopping has made me thirsty for a G&T," Morgan insisted.

"Or a bottle of wine," Lavinia agreed. "But we have plans for tonight so we'll love and leave you and see you tomorrow."

Morgan's eyebrows rose and a mischievous grin spread across her face in a suggestive way. Lavinia was quick to pick up on her trail of thought and immediately dismissed the idea. "Not like that. We're having dinner with Jess," she clarified.

Tom and Lavinia met Jess at Queensway pub since it was close to the town centre and on the way home.

Lavinia felt strange entering the pub as it had featured in the investigation with Tracey Evans. And although CCTV footage had not captured Tracey in the pub the night she was murdered, as first thought by her husband, it had still been investigated.

Tom led the way to the table and as soon as Jess saw them, her face lit up. She got up to kiss Tom and gave Lavinia a hug, which she was taken aback by.

"So great to see you again and meet you properly this time," Jess beamed. She was dressed in denim jeans, an olive green A-neckline bodysuit that showed off her slim figure and wedges. Despite Queensway being a casual pub, Lavinia had to admit that she looked stunning. That was just Jess, she was always dressed so fashionable. She would make a black bin bag look like a designer dress, Lavinia thought.

"You too. How's Grace doing?" Lavinia thought back to the first time they met. Tom and Lavinia had gone to Specsavers in the town centre to speak to one of Jess's colleagues, Grace Sanderson, about Isla, who had been their

CHAPTER 37

first victim. After everything that had happened in recent weeks, that felt like a lifetime ago.

"Not great. She returned to work after you interviewed her and had a complete breakdown, hasn't been to work since. I've stopped by a couple of times but she's so broken it's hard to know what to do or say."

Tom, who was sat next to Jess, took her hand in his and gave it a reassuring squeeze for comfort. Jess smiled slightly at the gesture and appreciated his action.

"I'm sure just by being there for her is more than enough and Grace will appreciate that more than she's letting on."

"Yeah, just got to keep being there for her and being her support and hopefully she'll see some light at the end of the tunnel. It's going to take time but I know she's strong and she'll get there. Anyway, I've heard so much about you, it's great that Tom has someone like you as his friend and partner."

"The pleasure is all his," Lavinia joked.

"Lucky to have you on board," Tom added, making eye contact with Lavinia longer than he should have done.

"Tom told me your father is also a detective?" Jess cut in.

"Not currently on this case, but yes he is."

"That must be amazing to have that support and someone to look up to."

"Well, he's the best at what he does. Everyone respects him, everyone admires him. It's quite intimidating having such big boots to fill and expectations are high, but I don't know anyone who works as hard as he does. He's inspired so many people and generations of police officers and detectives. What about your father?"

Jess listened intently, smiling at the way Lavinia talked about her father who clearly meant so much to her. It was both heart-warming and upsetting at the same time. "My dad died a couple of years ago from a motorbike accident."

"Oh shit, Jess I'm so sorry. I didn't mean to talk about my dad like that, it was insensitive."

"No, it's okay. It's so lovely to hear the way you talk about him and you clearly have a great relationship and he's a big part of your life."

"Well my mum died when I was young from breast cancer, so I do know how you feel and what it is like to lose a parent."

As the evening wore on, Lavinia realised she had more in common with Jess than she had originally believed and hadn't thought they would get on as well as they did tonight. However, Lavinia was still not completely sure about Jess. She had slowly warmed to her throughout the evening and was pleasantly surprised by her, but there was just something about her that Lavinia was not sure of. What, she did not know, but if they didn't have Tom in common then Lavinia was sure her and Jess would not be friends. Maybe it was all in her head. She had only agreed to meet Jess for the sake of Tom and had been apprehensive about it all day so perhaps she was just looking for an excuse not to like her. Jess paid for the meal with the promise from Lavinia that the next one was on her. They exchanged numbers and agreed to meet again soon, just the two of them, for lunch or as Jess suggested, a spa day.

Tom drove Lavinia home and he had a triumphant smile on his face. Lavinia noticed, narrowed her eyes at him and asked why he was smiling like he had won the lottery.

"I told you that you two would get on. Thank you for this."

Lavinia didn't know what to say in response, so she just smiled and the rest of the journey home was in comfortable silence.

As late as it was, Lavinia decided to Facetime Alastair.

He answered after three rings. He was clearly in the lower deck, eating his catch of the day, and looked confused. "Hey darling, everything ok?"

"Yeah, Dad, everything's fine. Just wanted to check in, see that you're behaving and having a good time."

CHAPTER 37

"I'm the parent, I should be making sure you're behaving, at least temporarily anyway."

"You know me, Dad, best behaviour."

"That's my girl. What's up?"

"Another body was found the day we got back from Dartmouth. Same MO, same everything. Seems we're back to square one with it all. The more bodies we get, you would've thought the easier it would be, but it doesn't feel like we're getting anywhere. I met Tom's girlfriend properly this evening. We're also attending the Davenport's annual themed party in a couple of nights. I expect you've heard about it, but we've managed to get onto the guest list, if only to search the premises."

"Blimey, need to get anything else off your chest? You just have to be patient and keep doing your job. I know that doesn't seem like great advice right now, but trust me it is, and it is all you can do. And yes, Wilson likes to vent about the whole Davenport thing the night after over a pint, or a couple. That should be interesting."

"Why'd you say it like that?"

"Like what? It will be an interesting evening, I'm sure. They're interesting people who do a lot of interesting work. I won't be bailing any of you out of jail, just remember that."

"Hopefully it won't come to that."

"I'm guessing you have interviewed the Davenports already and they haven't given much away or you think they are hiding something?"

"I think there is more to that story that they're not telling us. Wilson and Harris went to interview them, and they seemed to be cooperative and forthcoming with information, but I guess you could call it gut instinct, Wilson thought they were holding back."

"Maybe they are trying to protect their reputation, their integrity."

"Well, I hope we find something."

"I have every faith that the missing piece of the puzzle will turn up for you, you are my daughter after all and if I've taught you well, you'll be fine. I'm going to finish eating my trout. Caught fresh today, very tasty. Enjoy Friday, good luck, and stay safe. Pass my love on to the right people."

"I will send Wilson your love," Lavinia joked. "Love you, Dad.

"Make sure you do! Love you too."

CHAPTER 38

As the days until the party loomed closer, it was all anyone could think of, and with the investigation going as slowly as it was, it served as a distraction to the lack of evidence they had so far.

"So, are we all getting ready at mine after work? Then the limo can pick us all up after Wilson and then head straight to the Davenports'?" Morgan queried, spinning around on her chair from the desk to face everyone.

"Sounds like a plan to me!" Lavinia agreed, getting excited as she looked over her computer screen. The others joined in, singing a chorus of agreement.

In the meantime, they had work to do.

It sickened the team that the killer had murdered a pregnant woman, not only taking one life, but two, and that had turned the investigation sour.

The photo given to Richard and Kathryne in Missing Persons did come back with a match.

Ruth Damson.

Her husband, Duncan Jennings, had reported her missing Monday afternoon, when he came back from a school trip to find the house empty.

As Tom had previously mentioned, telling relatives their loved one had been killed, never got any easier, but over time, he accepted it would be something he would have to do countless times in his line of work and dealt with it accordingly. Lavinia had just started to understand that fact, as they were on their way to inform Duncan of the bad news.

They parked up and walked down the driveway. Lavinia's knuckle was raised and poised to knock on the door but it didn't make a sound. She realised her hand was shaking. She thought she'd got over the nerves but clearly she hadn't, but there was no going back now. She took a deep breath and knocked.

They waited a few minutes before the door was opened by a dishevelled looking man who clearly had had no sleep. His hair pointed up in all directions, he was dressed in lounge wear, and his eyes were red and bloodshot from crying.

When Tom and Lavinia introduced themselves, it was like the world had turned to slow motion. They didn't need to say anything for Duncan to know that it was bad news. His confused look turned to surprise turned to realisation turned to heartbreak and melancholy. Every transition captured by Tom and Lavinia. He started crying again and stumbled backwards until Tom's lightning speed reaction caught him.

It took a while to calm him down. Duncan turned hysterical, he broke ornaments, threw chairs across the room, punched a wall and then collapsed on the sofa, crying and exhausted.

This had been a new reaction for Lavinia to witness and, in some ways, it had been harder to watch.

Tom skipped the tea with sugar and went straight to the brandy, which Duncan gladly accepted and downed in one and then asked for a top up.

He seemed slightly calmer after his outrage, which Lavinia couldn't blame him for, but she was cautious about asking questions until Tom handed Duncan his second brandy and he asked, "So you were away all weekend, Friday to Monday, and Ruth was home all weekend? She didn't go anywhere or have any visitors that you're aware of?"

"Erm, no. I don't know."

"Did you check in with her at any point during the weekend?"

"Yes, I messaged when I could, when I got signal."

"And she replied?"

CHAPTER 38

"Of course she did," he snapped at Tom who became cautious with his next question.

"We just need to get a timeline of events, that's all. When was the last message you had received from her?"

"Sunday afternoon." Tom and Lavinia knew that that message was most likely sent from the killer himself pretending to be Ruth as he would have abducted her on the Friday so she wouldn't have been able to reply.

"What was the content of the message?"

"She's pregnant, I guess you already know that, and just said that the baby was requesting a Sunday roast and both were looking forward to having me back to boss around. I've not only lost my wife but my unborn child too." Duncan teared up again, and this time Tom handed him a tissue.

"I'm very sorry." Lavinia didn't know what else she could say.

"Do you know if she contacted the midwife at all over the weekend?" Tom asked after giving Duncan a minute.

"Funnily enough, I thought the same, and contacted Katy, the midwife myself, but she didn't receive any calls from Ruth."

"Were you aware of anyone that may have wanted to harm Ruth?"

"If I thought that, do you think I would've left her on her own?" Duncan snapped once again.

"I don't think that at all."

Duncan's head snapped up as if he had suddenly remembered something, "Wait, there's Ruth's friend, well they're not friends anymore, but there was an altercation a couple of years ago which Chloe never forgave Ruth for. She wouldn't have done this, would she?"

"I don't know, you tell me, what's this Chloe like?"

"A bitch. Self-absorbed, attention seeking, spiteful..."

"We get the idea," Tom interrupted.

"What was this altercation that happened?" Lavinia asked.

"Erm, Ruth and I struggled to have children, Chloe didn't, so I think she bred just to rub it in Ruth's face. One night Ruth babysat and ran off with Chloe's daughter. She didn't go far, and both Ruth and Chloe's daughter were completely safe, but Chloe exaggerated and thought Ruth had kidnapped her daughter, which she kind of did, but never would have caused her harm."

"And that caused the end of their friendship?"

"Yes."

"Did the police ever get involved?"

"Yes, but Chloe dropped all charges, at the persuasion of myself and Chloe's husband."

"And Chloe kept a grudge against Ruth for this?"

"Oh yes, Chloe never let it go and likes to remind Ruth every now and then."

"So they still have contact with each other?"

"Not really. Chloe has sent the odd letter here and there, and she showed up to Ruth's surprise anniversary party and baby shower and it all kicked off."

"How?"

"Chloe's husband and I caught them fighting in the bathroom."

"You still have contact with Chloe's husband? Sorry, what's his name?"

"Martin, and yes I do, we remained friends. It's just hard with the situation."

"Do you think Chloe would be capable of harming Ruth?"

"I think Chloe is capable of doing anything once she gets it into her head."

****

They left Duncan nursing the brandy, against the advice of both Tom and Lavinia, which he happily ignored, and they were on their way to Chloe and Martin's house, which was only a few minutes away.

CHAPTER 38

"If I had done something that my ex-friend never forgave me for and made my life hell, I think I would move further away."

"They're probably both just as stubborn as each other and fail to move not to give the other one that satisfaction."

"Village wars."

"Do you think Chloe could be responsible?"

"She doesn't fit the killer profile. I think Chloe could easily threaten to do something like this, and would get a thrill from doing so, but I don't think she would have the guts to ever act out on it. All mouth and no trousers kind of thing."

"Interesting take," Tom replied as they pulled up to Chloe and Martin's house.

When Martin politely opened the door to them, he thought Chloe had done something that Ruth or maybe even Duncan had called the police for.

"I'm afraid we're here about a different matter."

A playful scream filled the house followed by laughter. Martin explained that it was the kids messing around and invited Tom and Lavinia into their home.

"Is there somewhere away from the children that we can talk with yourself and Chloe?"

"Yes, the children are in the playroom, so we can go in the lounge." Duncan called to Chloe who appeared in the doorway to the playroom and was just as confused at the intrusion as Martin was.

"The police? Well I don't know what lies Ruth has told you, but I haven't done anything." It seemed both Chloe and Martin were on the same wavelength and thought that Ruth and Duncan had something to do with the police turning up on their doorstep.

"They didn't call us. If we could talk?"

Chloe shut the playroom door to, and Martin gestured to the lounge where they all took a seat. Martin sat back while Chloe, Tom and Lavinia, all sat on the edge, not wanting to get too comfortable.

"So, why are you here?" Chloe asked impatiently.

"Ruth was found dead on Monday morning."

"Dead? Well, I had nothing to do with that," Chloe assumed.

"When was the last time you saw Ruth?"

"At her surprise party a week ago."

"You two were seen fighting."

"Yeah."

"And just over a week later she's found dead, so you can see how that looks, especially after your history."

"You've spoken to Duncan, haven't you? Did he accuse me of murdering his wife? Bastard."

"So, you haven't thought about killing Ruth at all after what she did?"

"Yes of course I have, but I would never actually kill anyone, not even Ruth."

"Have you ever threatened to kill Ruth?"

"I might have done. You're making out like she was the innocent one in all of this. She's the one that kidnapped my child."

"That's another matter entirely. We're just interested in this one. Where were you last Friday?"

"I was here with my family."

Martin nodded to verify.

"Did you have any contact with Ruth over the weekend?"

"No, I wouldn't waste my time on that woman. We, the family, went out for the day on Saturday and then we spent the day baking on Sunday."

"What about you, Martin. You've been quiet?" Tom asked, snapping him out of his reverie.

"Well, Chloe can verify where I was all weekend because we were together with the kids."

"I understand that you are still friends with Ruth's husband?"

"Yes."

CHAPTER 38

"How is that considering the bad blood between your wives?"

"I won't lie, it's difficult at times but we try not let that affect plans. We try and talk about other things."

"How did Ruth die?" Chloe asked.

"I'm afraid I can't disclose any details," Tom replied. "Do you have any idea who may want to harm Ruth?"

"You mean aside from myself?"

"Chloe," Martin warned, "I can't think of anyone sorry. I know we're the number one suspects considering what happened, but I can assure you that neither of us would hurt a fly. Chloe does have a short temper on her at times, and never has a good thing to say about Ruth, but neither of us would ever go that far."

"Martin's right. I have voiced my dislike for Ruth and that I want her dead, but they're just words to hurt her, I wouldn't actually do anything. Not when I have my own family to think of, she's not worth losing all that for."

****

Lavinia needed to get out of the house, take a walk and breathe in the fresh air.

Her mind was distracted but her legs took her to the riverside. She gazed over the other side of the bank and watched the ducklings. Another group of ducklings were in the river, their little legs going a million miles an hour to keep up and swim against the current.

It was peaceful and her mind was able to shut off from the case and focus on the scenes in front of her. The trees blew gently in the light breeze, the sun glistening in the water. Her mind took her back to when Mindy and Lavinia were children, they used to come to the riverside with Alastair and a picnic basket filled with sandwiches and cakes, and enjoyed those summer days. It was where they would come with a bucket of seeds to feed the ducks, throwing handfuls in the air, scattering the food for the ducks to swarm over.

Now all she could see was Isla's lifeless body floating.

She didn't know how long she had been stood there for, but jumped when Mindy interrupted. "Thought I might find you here." She had a tight hold of Star's lead as Star had bounded towards Lavinia, tail wagging. Lavinia turned, smiled at her sister and gave Star a stroke who then went back to smelling the grass.

"Just needed some fresh air."

"You couldn't have taken Star for a walk with you." There wasn't any malice in Mindy's tone at all, she was just joking, hoping it would earn a smile or even a laugh from her sister. All she got was a look, followed by a slight twitch of the lips. Mindy's smile quickly faded as her face turned to worry. "What's up? Are you okay?"

Lavinia took a deep sigh, walked over to the nearest bench and sat down, beckoning Mindy to follow. "I didn't really know what to expect, but this wasn't it. The emotional roller-coaster. One minute the adrenalin is pumping through your veins and you're excited because of a breakthrough, a piece of information and you think that's it, then the next thing your heart catches in your stomach because another body has been found and it's back to square one again. Then frustration because the case is going nowhere, the desperation to find a needle in a haystack because it makes you feel better that you're trying to do something even though you know it won't lead anywhere or there's nothing there to find but you keep going anyway. Hope in that you come across something. Sad because you witness the victim's families collapse and breakdown in front of you and you realise their lives are never going to be the same again. Anger at the killer for torturing innocent women. I could go on. I never knew one person could feel so much all at once."

"You feel all that because you care. You don't have to keep working on it."

CHAPTER 38

"I do."

"You need to do what's right for you."

"I am. I am doing it for myself because this is what I want to do. How could I be a detective if I just gave up at a moment of weakness? I'm doing this for Dad because he gave me this opportunity and I can't just throw that away over some emotions. I'm doing it for the victims and their families who need answers and justice. I need to help get that for them."

"Everyone in the team has had prior training and experience. You haven't had either. They get used to dealing with these situations and that comes with experience that you haven't had yet. But this is your experience. Everyone has to start somewhere and it might not be on a serial killer case, but once you deal with this, you will be able to deal with anything. As for Dad, I think he was just desperate to go fishing."

This earned a slight laugh from Lavinia.

"I can't tell you everything Dad would be able to, because I haven't been through it myself, but I shall channel my inner Alastair and say something wise. You have it in you and I know you would never give up until the end because you care too much to let it go. We are human, after all. You let your emotions show outside of the job, but you never let them cloud your judgement, you get on with it and all that are qualities for a great detective. You just need to believe it, believe in yourself, because I certainly do and I know Dad does too."

"You know it's scary."

"What is?"

"How much you sound like Dad."

Mindy laughed and Lavinia joined it too. They looked at each other and Mindy held Lavinia's hand.

"You'll always be my baby sister and I'll always worry about you, but you've grown up so much in so many ways since this case and I've watched you blossom into this inspiring investigator who didn't know what skills she had until they were tested. They should be proud to have you in their team."

Lavinia's eyes clouded over as she listened to Mindy's words.

"Thank you. You, me and Dad are each other's support bubble, I wouldn't know what to do without you both."

"Well, we're not going anywhere."

"It's selfish. You always seem to be sorting me out that I never ask you about your job or how your day has been."

"I'm used to that by now," Mindy joked, then went on to talk about her day and her job in general. They were sat there for a while, Lavinia's turn to listen.

CHAPTER 39

The evening of the Davenport Party.

Since the start of the case, the team were in high spirits as they had something else to focus on and look forward to. It was a mixture of apprehension and adrenaline.

Work came by and went and before they knew it, they found themselves at Morgan's house. She lived in a three-bedroom semi-detached house with a small square garden at the front, a paved driveway for her Vauxhall Astra and larger garden at the back. The rectangular patio area sat grey outdoor furniture, complete with sofa, cushions, matching round table with two chairs and a firepit. A washing line stood in the centre of the garden, and a small shed was packed away in the corner.

The open plan kitchen/dining area led out into the garden via two double doors. They were sat on the sofa outside eating nibbles that Morgan had prepared earlier, and popped open a bottle of champagne. They toasted to the evening ahead, and even though they were still technically on duty, Morgan believed that one drink before would be acceptable to steady the nerves.

Music was blasting through the speakers in Morgan's room where she and Lavinia were getting ready. Norton and Tom were still sat outside, adamant it would take them half the time to get ready as the other two. Which was a fair comment considering Morgan knew she took a while.

Morgan was sat at her dressing table facing her mirror to apply a thin layer of make-up while Lavinia was sat on the bed, in a dressing gown, sipping the remaining champagne in her flute and chatting away to Morgan.

"We better get something from tonight after all this."

"There will definitely be some good gossip to make up for it."

"I think we can count on that."

* * * *

The limousine's horn sounded from the driveway.

"Taxi's here," Norton shouted up to the women who were putting the final touches to their outfits.

Norton and Tom were about to head outside and wait in the limo when something caught Tom's eye. He had to do a double take when Lavinia descended the stairs.

The black sparkly dress accentuated her tall slim figure, the side slit and heels showing off toned calves and her wavey hair added the finishing touch.

"Don't you two scrub up well," Lavinia observed as she saw Tom and Norton dressed handsomely in their tuxedos.

"I can say the same for both of you," Norton replied.

"Stunning," Tom agreed, not taking his eyes off Lavinia, who blushed when she caught his eye.

Tom held his arm out for Lavinia who took it gladly, and Norton followed suit with Morgan and made their way to the limo.

The ride was filled with talk, laughter, alcohol and music.

Even though Wilson had recently visited the Davenport Estate to interview Rupert and Camille regarding Aiden Brown, he was always still amazed by the sheer size of the building, the grand architecture and the decorations that lit up the estate like a Christmas tree.

Garden lights lit up each side of the driveway like cat's eyes on the motorway, guiding vehicles down the long road to the house.

"This feels very much like the extravagant show that Parker, Prescott and Skinner put on in June," Lavinia

CHAPTER 39

commented, remembering the CCTV footage from the night Madison was last seen alive.

"Very much so," Wilson agreed before adding, "I'm hoping nobody turns up dead the next morning."

"You and me both," Harris added.

The limo slowed behind a queue of traffic and when it was their turn, the doors were opened, allowing them to pile out one by one.

As Lavinia exited the limo, she looked up and gasped at the sight of the mansion, her eyes widened in bewilderment. The mansion was lit up like the Blackpool Illuminations with orange, yellow, red and blue coloured lights, giving off a retro Hollywood colour scheme.

There were stars on the ground and up the steps, representing the Hollywood Walk of Fame, to guide visitors to the entrance of the property where they were greeted by Rupert, Camille and the family.

Lavinia took Tom's arm once again as they made their way to join the queue of people waiting to be welcomed into their home. They looked a million dollars, with the lavish emerald green gowns Camille and presumably her foster daughters wore with matching emerald accessories, where the size of the emerald gemstone hung around Camille's neck was bigger than Lavinia's head. Lavinia was certain their whole outfit cost more than her house, and the impeccably crisp and well-tailored matching emerald three-piece suit Rupert wore. They were certainly the definition of Hollywood and for the reason of them being the hosts, failed to conform with the stereotypical gold and black theme that everyone else seemed to adhere to.

Lavinia surveyed the way the family interacted with their guests, and could see why they were the faces of society. They took their time with everyone, smiling, shaking hands, French kissing both cheeks and having a chat as if they had spotted them on the streets coming back from a jog, buying the morning's newspaper from the local shop.

She could see the respect the public had for them and vice versa.

Wilson took the lead when it was their turn and he greeted Rupert and Camille like old friends. The previous meeting all but forgotten.

"Walter Wilson, what an honour it is to have you attend our ball this evening." Camille spoke with the softness and gratitude after they kissed her both on the cheek and shook hands with Rupert. To Wilson, it was almost like the previous interview had never happened. How quickly they could pull a wall up and act completely different.

"The pleasure is all ours," he replied. It was strange hearing him speak so formal and he turned to the team behind him as he introduced them, "I would like to introduce you to the Major Incident Team who have been working tirelessly over the past weeks on the latest case. We are thankful for your extended invitation and I'm sure they are grateful to have a night off."

They took it in turns to greet Rupert and Camille and give their thanks for the hospitality and in return they were appreciative of the time and effort they had all put into the case that had made gossip around the town several times over.

As standard, they greeted Lucia and Luisa from the refuge centre in Spain. As the two women greeted the team, they were clearly related: they had the same figure, the same fearless dark eyes that had seen too much pain and the long dark hair that gave them that Latina look. Even though they still had a heavy Spanish accent, their English was understandable.

"Showing off their latest projects," Tom whispered to Lavinia as they had finished greeting the hosts, walked over the threshold and continued to follow the Hollywood Walk of Fame stars that guided them to the hall, but this time they were walking on a red carpet under an arched tunnel of lights.

CHAPTER 39

"They're clearly proud of the work they do and they should be. Giving underprivileged people a chance at a better life, I'm all for that, even if they do it for all the wrong reasons," Lavinia replied, thinking back to the conversations they had had about Rupert and Camille and their motivation being for publicity and for their high place in society.

There were even more lights at the end of the tunnel.

The big circular golden arch on a stand made the entrance to the hall stand out and added more class and elegance to the evening as it provided the perfect backdrop for photographs. It was decorated with white artificial flowers and a silk curtain that was draped in an upside-down V shape and hung down at the sides. Fairy lights hung vertically across the front.

Two matching golden tables were placed to the left side of the arch, holding a Moet and Chandon champagne bottle and two crystallised champagne glasses on them.

The whole scene was from a fairy tale.

Guests were having their pictures taken by the professional photographer who manned the stand upon entering the hall, using the crystal glasses and champagne as props.

The big oak doors were pushed aside to reveal the layout of the evening's events.

A seating chart had been made and was placed strategically by the door for the guests to search for their name and find their table. The tables were dressed in a white cloth, where gold and black light up balloons decorated the centre. Hollywood-themed confetti of stars, film reel, clapper board and camera cut outs were spread across the table and small Hollywood party popcorn boxes, filled with popcorn, were placed at every seat. Also on the table was an ice bucket filled with two bottles of complimentary champagne.

The stage at the front of the room was completed to look like a red carpet moment, with the 'Hollywood' sign written in silver against the dark blue backdrop and silhouettes of paparazzi taking pictures with the flash of their cameras. The red carpet was placed down the centre of the stage trailing down the steps. Red movie curtains with gold tie backs framed the screen on the stage.

Lavinia's eyes were darting left and right to take it all in. The hall was beautifully decorated and fitting for the theme. She noticed a photobooth in the corner of the room along with a miniature replica of the Hollywood sign, life size Oscars and a LED Lights, Camera, Action box. That was clearly the photo corner.

"You don't think this is a Hollywood themed party by any chance, do you?" Norton joked as he too, took in the scene around him.

"What gave you that idea?" Morgan replied in the same sarcastic tone.

They located their table (number 4) and took their places. Wilson did the honour of popping the champagne open and poured a glass for everyone. They toasted to the evening ahead.

The hall quickly filled up as more guests arrived. Wilson knew several people across the different public service sectors that he had met at this event before, or had had the pleasure to cross paths with whether in everyday life or during a previous case. Being top dog, they knew all the important people.

They introduced everyone around the table, and asked the usual introductory questions.

When the conversations stopped and people had gone back to their tables, Wilson was in work mode.

"Right, speeches from Camille, Rupert and their special guest will be coming up soon. After that, everyone will mingle before food arrives. That is your opportunity to go looking. You'll have around half an hour, maybe a little longer so do what you can in that time and I expect you all back here before that half hour runs out."

He received nods of understanding from Morgan, Norton, Tom and Lavinia in response. Harris decided to stay

CHAPTER 39

behind with Wilson so as not to draw too much attention to the half empty table.

Sure enough, twenty minutes later, Rupert and Camille, followed by their clan, received claps and cheers as they walked on stage. They loved being the centre of attention, revelling in the spotlight.

Their smiles greeted their audience in delight, but that was just for the photographer who was stood by the stage, capturing the Davenports in their element.

Rupert opened up the evening by thanking his guests for coming and reflecting on the magnificent year the public service sector had. Camille then took over and described in detail, the magnificent year they had had working alongside charities in the UK and overseas, raising millions for cancer, refugees, children and those with life changing illnesses. Which led up to a speech conducted by their latest fosters, Spanish twins Lucia and Luisa. They were first hand witnesses of the work Rupert and Camille did and had been two of the many who had benefited from it, so of course there was nothing to say but how great they were as people and as fosters, feeding their ego an eight-course Michelin-starred meal.

Camille soaked up the attention by shedding a few tears and making a fuss of it, ruining her make-up.

"They sure know how to boast about their wealthy life and fortune, don't they?" Tom whispered to Lavinia, but not so subtly as the whole table heard.

"Ssh. I agree."

"I'm not discrediting their work, just the publicity seems a bit over the top."

"That's the way it goes. We do good, it has little effect to the world. We send £3 a month to help children in Africa get clean water, no one knows but us and has little effect because we do that for years and still see it advertised all the time. When someone like Rupert and Camille do good, they can go over to Africa and install fresh water pumps for all the communities along with a load of other things, like supplying equipment for schools. Massive impact and the whole world knows because they get the publicity and sponsors and then they can't stop."

Tom was about to reply but the whole room erupted in applause and people headed to the bar or another table to exchange in conversation with others.

Wilson gave them a knowing look.

This was it.

CHAPTER 40

While people were distracted, Morgan, Norton, Tom and Lavinia scarpered from the room and piled into the corridor.

There were a few people milling around, either heading to the toilets or heading outside for fresh air. Morgan, Norton, Tom and Lavinia pretended to do the same whilst surveying the area.

Their hopes were dashed when they saw security guards manning the entrance to the upper floors.

They were not allowed anywhere else in the house but this floor. Which wasn't news to them as Wilson had previously warned them, but it didn't help them.

Then Lavinia's eyes widened as a thought shone in her head.

"I have an idea. It's a bit out there but I have nothing else. Tom and Norton, you guys could head into the men's room. You could use my pepper spray in front of the fire alarm to set it off. The security guards will be busy ushering everyone outside so when they have vacated we are free to access the upper floors."

"Why do you have pepper spray?"

"Where the hell are we going to hide?"

"Why use the men's room?"

These questions were darted at Lavinia at the same time, so she looked at everyone with an impatient look.

"I thought the reason for the pepper spray was an obvious answer, although not important in the scheme of things. We could hide in the crowd then veer off after, I don't know, I've accidentally lost my shoe from rushing out or

Morgan left something in the bathroom, for example. As you two are accompanying us, you follow to make sure we are all right as the gentlemen you are. The men's room is never busy. There's always a queue for the women's so we can hide in there until everyone has vacated."

A pregnant pause kept Lavinia in suspense as the others pondered the idea. "Unless anyone has a better idea," Lavinia felt the need to add.

"I think that might just work. You are incredible." Tom beamed at Lavinia's idea, getting excited that they had a decent plan that might actually work.

Morgan and Norton nodded in agreement.

"Okay, POA. Morgan and I will hang around inside the women's bathroom. As soon as the fire alarm sounds, wait until I come in and get you guys out from the men's. I leave a shoe near the stairs as we slide into the crowd and then at the right time, which I will signal, I will realise I have lost a shoe and Morgan, you will realise you have left something in the bathroom. The crowd continues to pile out, and we sneak off."

"It looks like we can access the top storey from these sets of stairs, so we all enter these stairs and go our separate ways. Tom and Lavinia, take the second floor, and Norton and I will take the third," Morgan added.

"Good luck," Lavinia told Morgan and Norton.

"You too." Morgan gave Lavinia's hand a nervous squeeze, but that seemed to fill Morgan with the confidence she needed. Still holding hands, they gave a nod to their partners and headed to the women's bathroom.

The plan was about to commence.

****

As they entered the bathroom, Morgan had a new profound confidence as she started up a random conversation with Lavinia to act normal, as if they had been talking about it all night and was continuing their conversation in the bathroom.

CHAPTER 40

"Did you see that dress, would love to know who designed it," Morgan said, with passion.

"Probably costs more than my rent," Lavinia laughed.

As expected, there was a small queue for the ladies with a few reapplying lipstick or mascara at the mirrors.

Luckily, they managed to get two cubicles next to each other and just waited it out.

They overheard several interesting conversations and gossip while the wait felt like forever when a piercing sound made them jump. A few women screamed at the sudden interruption. Then they heard a man yell from outside the bathroom that everyone was to vacate immediately.

Lavinia looked through the tiny gap between the door of her cubicle and the wall that attached the cubicles together and witnessed a mosh pit as the women scrambled to leave, thinking they would burn to death if they stayed a moment longer. That was when Morgan gave three knocks on the cubicle wall that separated them and they vacated the bathroom.

Lavinia retrieved her mobile phone from her bag and pretended to call Tom, a worried look on her face when he wouldn't answer. "Come on, pick up," she said aloud to no one in particular. She then put the phone back in her bag and entered the men's bathroom, calling out Tom's name to make it seem like she was looking for someone, just in case anyone noticed.

Their eyes met in acknowledgment that the first part of their plan had worked.

"Right, let's go," Tom said, taking Lavinia's hand in his and exiting the bathroom.

There was a stampede of people exiting the hall with an annoyed look on their face.

They joined the edge of the crowd so Lavinia could kick her shoe by the step as they passed.

A bit further on, when the majority of the guests had vacated, and Lavinia could see the entrance to the stairway was clear, she cried out once she had realised what she had done and insisted it was in the rush of getting out that she forgot to tie the strap on her shoe around her ankle properly and it fell off in the hustle of the crowd. Onlookers did not care what she had said as they just wanted to leave the building as quickly as possible in case of a real fire.

Turning back, and feeling like salmon going against the current, they made their way back through the crowd that had started to disperse. Lavinia picked up her shoe and they ran up the steps with Morgan and Norton in tow, with just enough people to cover them but not enough people to notice them.

Tom and Lavinia headed right at the top of the stairs, while Norton and Morgan veered left and disappeared out of sight.

With a huge sigh of relief, Tom laughed in hysterics that the plan had actually worked. Seamlessly.

"Not out of the woods yet," Lavinia informed him, getting her breathing back to normal. With nerves, she had forgotten to breathe when they turned back through the crowd and did not realise until she had reached the top of the stairs and her lungs were burning from the lack of oxygen.

They went along the corridor, peering over the edge of the balcony every once in a while, and tried the doors.

All of them were locked and they were just about to lose hope that they had done all that for nothing, when, with the turn of the handle, the door clicked open.

Lavinia looked at Tom in wonder.

They had no idea what they were going to find, but there was only one way to find out.

Slowly they crept inside and shut the door behind them.

****

Wilson smiled to himself with pride, as he had the gut feeling his team was behind the disruption.

CHAPTER 40

The piercing scream of the fire alarm filled his ears as Wilson, along with everyone else, made their way back outside to the front of the house.

The security guards ushered the guests out with real urgency, but at least they were distracted, Wilson thought to himself, which would have given his team a chance at gaining access to the upper floors.

Whatever got the job done.

He now started to sound like Alastair.

Wilson made a mental note to never mention this to Alastair otherwise he would not hear the end of it. Allowing his team to bend the rules to unlawfully access personal artefacts of a family potentially connected with an ongoing murder investigation. Yep, Alastair would have a field day.

Wilson, however, would not.

This would be an epic disaster on all proportions, not to mention a media frenzy and a mass firing.

Wilson's morals were torn. Well, after this he didn't have any morals, he was just as bad as those criminals he helped to convict.

But he would stand behind his team, always, whether it was the right or the wrong thing to do. And if they came out of the other end of this successfully, they would just as act clueless as everyone else.

CHAPTER 41

Norton and Morgan did not have the same bad luck in finding an open door.

It seemed the entire third floor was dedicated to Rupert and Camille themselves. It was like an entire separate apartment within the house.

They had a fully equipped kitchen, gym, library and study room, a sitting room, a massive bedroom, linked by an ensuite and a dressing room with a walk-in wardrobe.

"Woah, I did not expect this," Morgan said in astonishment as they entered the lush modern and spacious but cosy living room. Throws and cushions decorated the two-seater sofa and two separate chairs that were all sat facing each other in the centre of the room with the original feature fireplace to the right. In between, a rug was placed on top of the oak wooden floors and with two small coffee tables. The room was light and airy with floor to ceiling windows overlooking the horizon.

A glass table which was placed in the corner of the room, with six chairs sat around it underneath the rustic wood panelling.

Bookshelves adorned the south wall and many interesting paintings hung all around the walls, both traditional landscape and modern art.

The apartment was very modern in contrast to the dated character found around the rest of the mansion.

"This feels like I've just stepped through the Narnia wardrobe and into a completely different place."

Norton's analogy was spot on, thought Morgan.

CHAPTER 41

Morgan walked over to the bookshelves and scanned the titles of the books. She came across a few leather-bound classics that she recognised, by Charles Dickens, Jane Austen, William Shakespeare, John Steinbeck, and also others she had never heard of. She picked up a few random books and tipped them upside down and leafed through them in case anything was hidden inside.

Nothing.

She was going to move on when she tried one last book.

As soon as she turned the book upside down, something fell out of it and landed face down on the floor.

To Morgan it looked like a photograph, with the white side of the back facing upwards.

She bent down to pick it up and turned the photograph over.

She studied it carefully before realising it was a photo of the young Rupert and Camille.

Camille had not aged a day since the photograph was taken – obviously she had the money to buy all the expensive designer skin care products and probably adorned strict skin care regimes that made her look ageless. However, the man in the photograph had changed a lot and Morgan did not recognise it to be Rupert. He looked too young, compared to Camille, to be in the photograph but he looked very much like Rupert.

She took a picture of the photograph on her phone, slotted the photograph back into the book and placed the book back on the shelf.

Norton started to get distracted and instead of searching for evidence, he was just searching to be nosey, looking in every cupboard in every room. And the kitchen was no exception and just as impressive as the living room.

Marble worktops adorned the space, with plenty of storage areas so it was very clean and tidy. Stools sat around the breakfast bar and three ovens lined the wall.

But they both agreed that if there was anything to hide, Camille and Rupert's walk-in wardrobe or dressing room was the most likely place.

If they were impressed with the living room and kitchen, then they were most certainly impressed with the bedroom/ensuite/dressing room.

The bedroom was just as grand, modern and as expensive looking as the rest of the apartment. A statement-piece superking-size French style bed was the centrepiece, with an eye catching chandelier hanging above; a sofa suite took up the rest of the room and a grand flat screen TV hung on the wall opposite the bed.

The ensuite looked that of a five-star hotel bathroom, with a monochrome colour scheme. Every surface gleamed and designer toiletries were on display. A black grid pattern walk-in shower complete with glass screens stood in the corner with a graphite grey slipper bath on the opposite side overlooking a window.

Rupert and Camille each had their own dressing room that doubled up as a walk-in wardrobe. His and Hers.

They were searching Camille's walk-in wardrobe and both were impressed with the colour-coded theme and the amount of designer shoes all lined up in place and the several two-piece matching suits of all colours for every occasion.

Morgan looked through one of the drawers, expecting to find the usual but instead felt like she had been transported onto the set of Princess Diaries, when the Queen showed Princess Mia her own walk-in wardrobe where drawers of sparkling diamonds were revealed. Morgan's eyes widened in awe. That drawer held more diamonds than a high street jeweller's.

Norton's eyes lit up as they landed on something that could contain the answer.

A safe.

****

CHAPTER 41

Lavinia scrambled to find the light switch. She ran her hand along the wall to try and find a source of light.

Her hand made contact with a switch and illuminated the room to reveal that they were in a bedroom.

The red blackout curtains had not been opened, hence the room was submerged in darkness.

Photographs pegged up on fairy lights on the wall showed them that they were in Lucia's room.

"We've been transported to España," Tom commented, looking around at the Spanish décor and homely touches of bedroom. The red and yellow Spanish flag was used as a tablecloth over her desk, with another hand-held flag placed in a flower vase on top of the chest of drawers.

Lavinia headed straight for the wall with the photographs and studied them. There weren't any childhood photos but then again to have lived in a refuge, she didn't think that Lucia and Luisa had the best upbringing. Apart from the flags and a flamenco dress that Lavinia later found hanging in the wardrobe and looked to have belonged to a relative as it was a couple of sizes too big for either Lucia or Luisa, there was nothing else to indicate her home country. The photographs were more recent ones, since they came to live in the UK. Probably the happiest memories they had.

Lavinia recognised some of the UK's most iconic landmarks in the background of a few pictures including Buckingham Palace, Windsor Castle, Stonehenge and Edinburgh Castle. They were all taken with Luisa.

Whilst Lavinia looked at the photographs on the wall, Tom started rummaging around in the desk drawers which were empty aside from the stationery essentials and a laptop.

Tom took the laptop out from the drawer, opened it up and turned it on. The laptop came to life, showing the desktop image from Bryce Canyon National Park in Utah. To his surprise, it wasn't password protected so Tom was able to gain access.

"Didn't Camille ever tell Lucia to use passwords," Tom said aloud to no one in particular, but Lavinia heard him and came to stand beside him.

Tom looked at the search history, in file explorer and email but it was all empty.

"Maybe she never uses it or doesn't know how to," Lavinia suggested with a plausible answer.

"Or she knows how to cover her tracks. What about the possibility that there could be a hard drive somewhere. If this laptop is not password protected anyone can access it, to do exactly what we're doing now and if Camille wants to take a snoop around on it, then you would have to be smart and back up everything and delete from the laptop."

At that moment, Tom and Lavinia both looked at each other and smiled, both knowing what the other was thinking.

"That's what we have to find," Lavinia said, excited, as she bounded for the chest of drawers. But she was disappointed when she did not find anything in the knicker drawer. "I always thought a woman's secret weapon lived in the underwear drawer."

"That's such a cliche. First place everyone looks." Tom got on his hands and knees to look under the bed but there was nothing there. He also looked under the mattress but the same thing happened. Nothing.

He looked confused. He thought he would at least have found something under the mattress. But again, was that too much of a cliché? Maybe there was nothing to find in the first place, they were just clutching at straws.

Tom looked at his watch.

Ten minutes gone.

While she was searching through the tops and t shirts drawer, Lavinia realised that she wasn't taking the tops or t-shirts out to search them properly as they were neatly folded and she didn't want to disturb the clothing, but someone could easily store a photograph or a document in between the folds. Unfortunately, no photograph or document was

CHAPTER 41

between anything when she had searched the drawer properly and folded the t shirts and tops as neatly as she could to make it look like no one had been through it.

She moved onto the jeans and trousers drawer.

As she took out a pair of jeans, she caught sight of a hidden photograph.

Tom drew closer to view the picture.

* * * *

The safe was locked.

Both Morgan and Norton really wanted to break into the safe but the sensible side of Morgan reasoned that they couldn't for obvious reasons and didn't know why she had to explain it to Norton.

"How would we explain the broken safe? Rupert and Camille would immediately put out a red flag, and we would be investigated."

"But whatever it is we're looking for is most likely to be in this safe. If we could just get access without it looking like it was a break in," Norton replied, frustrated.

"It could just also be the biggest carat weight of diamond you've ever seen that's worth millions." Morgan sighed, also defeated but still in shock from seeing the diamond drawer.

Silence hung in the air for a moment while they battled with their thoughts and decided what to do.

"We don't have much time, we should just continue searching," Norton decided.

"Yes, you continue here and I'll search the dressing room."

The dressing room held three full length mirrors against one wall with a black cushioned chair at the side of it. This was obviously where Camille checked her outfits out for approval.

A long rectangular dressing table with another smaller three-way table mirror placed on top was where Camille applied her make-up. Morgan sat down on the plush chair and stared at her own reflection. This seat was occupied by Camille during her morning and evening routine and Morgan could not imagine the life she led. On her days off, Morgan would lounge around the house in loungewear, catching up on programmes or chores around the house. She would tie her hair up in a messy bun and wouldn't put make-up on. When she has a few consecutive days off, she would go and visit family or have a short staycation. But she knew Camille would not be seen dead in tracksuits and a hoodie. She guessed Camille had never worked round the clock on a job before. Being a detective had, at times, very harsh hours, but she loved her job. They were completely different people and led different lives, but circumstance had brought them together in the same house and now Morgan found herself searching Camille's home.

She opened the drawers of the dressing table and was disappointed not to find more diamonds sparkling back at her, but instead loads of expensive creams and serums, then a make-up drawer with every colour of lip gloss, lipstick, nail varnish and eyeshadow she could imagine, a make-up brush drawer and then reusable eco make-up remover pads and make-up remover micellar waters in the other drawer.

She closed the drawers and stood up to leave the room, when a thought occurred to her.

She turned back and reopened the make-up drawer and picked out a shade of black eyeshadow.

She then reopened the brush drawer and ran her hand over the bamboo handles and picked up a few during the selection process to run her fingers through the soft bristles to decide which one would be best to use. She settled for the blush brush.

Happy with the selection, she made her way back into the walk-in wardrobe via an adjacent doorway and found Norton combing through the endless handbags and clutch bags.

CHAPTER 41

"I may have found a way into the safe," Morgan announced, making Norton jump, unaware that she had entered the room.

"Jesus," Norton exclaimed, hand over his chest.

"Sorry, but look what I have found." She held up the eyeshadow and make-up brush.

Norton's confused face said it all.

"It's a very long shot but I am going to attempt to use this black eyeshadow as a fingerprint powder along with this brush to see what numbers Camille has touched when punching in the code to the safe."

****

The photograph Lavinia held in her hand was taken at autumn time as the ground was littered with brown and green crunchy leaves, the sun shone in the cloudless blue topaz sky, but Lucia, who was clearly identifiable in the photograph, was dressed in a thick coat and a bobble hat, giving the illusion that it was chilly. Lucia's face was beaming, her red painted lips separated showing white teeth.

But Lucia was not alone: there were two people in the photograph.

At first Lavinia thought it could have been Luisa, but when she looked closer, she noticed dark denim jeans and brown brogues, attire that appeared to be more masculine. The stance and stature of the mystery person did not match Luisa and therefore, Lavinia believed it to be a man.

Lucia and a man.

But the man was a mystery.

The picture looked to have been taken in the back garden of the mansion, Lucia was facing the camera, but what looked to have happened was that the man grabbed a handful of leaves from the ground and at the exact moment the camera snapped to take the photo, he released the handful of leaves over Lucia. Lucia's face was somehow clear, but the man's back had been turned to the camera, the back of his head covered by the falling leaves, only his arms visible in the air at the precise moment the leaves fell from his grasp.

"Who is that man?" Tom asked the inevitable question, the one that was on both their minds.

"No idea. We might have to get this blown up to get a better view of him, but even then I think that would be impossible." Lavinia brought the photograph to within inches of her screwed up eyes, once again, to get a better look at the man, but it was pointless.

"Maybe it was someone she met at one of these events that she became acquainted with, or a fellow foster."

"It looks like they were well acquainted. They don't look as if they've just met, they look like they know each other well. We need names of everyone Rupert and Camille ever fostered and see if we can get photographs of them."

"I'm sure if we just googled Rupert and Camille, all that information would appear and then we wouldn't be breaking any laws," Tom answered as a matter of fact.

Lavinia just looked at him. "No point in getting sensible now."

"True, but then we can just say we got the information online from a simple internet search, wouldn't be breaching data protection laws. They don't need to know we only googled their fosters from a photograph found in Lucia's room, do they?"

"I guess not." Lavinia took a picture of the photograph on her mobile phone, and placed it back in the original place. Still searching the rest of the drawer in case anything else of interest was found, but when she had exhausted all the jeans and trousers, she closed it shut.

Lavinia still had one more drawer to look into. But they already had a minor lead that they could investigate and she wasn't hoping for anything else.

Until she opened the last drawer.

****

CHAPTER 41

Norton looked excited but sceptical. "Long shot indeed, I don't think it will work but I guess it would be worth a try." Norton's shoulders shrugged up and down.

They made their way back over to the safe where Morgan broke up the eyeshadow into a fine powder in the pallet and loaded the brush. She knew it wasn't the most professional way of dusting for fingerprints and the issue of cross contamination was major, but it was all they had in that moment. She then took a deep breath and began dusting over the numbers.

Morgan and Norton held their breath.

Just like a black fingerprint powder, the eyeshadow powder adhered to the latent finger-mark that was deposited when contact was made.

And sure enough a finger-mark was developed.

They did not know when Camille, or even Rupert, last had contact with the safe. It wasn't a good quality finger-mark but it did show signs that contact had been made. And for this purpose, that was all that mattered.

The look on their faces was pure amazement that the technique had worked, and so Morgan dusted the rest of the safe keypad.

Slowly but surely more finger marks were uncovered.

It was easier to guess the first and last digit due to the amount of residue deposited upon contact and the detail recovered by the powder.

3 and 0.

They didn't know if the passcode to the safe was a four or a six digit number but once they recovered the fifth finger mark, they made an educational guess that the code was six digits.

"Now the impossible tasks of working out the code," Norton said sceptically.

"Well at least one digit has to be repeated, we will just have to try different combinations and maybe we will strike lucky." Morgan sounded more confident than she felt.

"Well, we've come this far, might as well try. Any idea how many guesses we can make without being locked out?"

"Only one way to find out." Morgan retrieved her mobile phone from her bag and handed it to Norton with the notes page open. "So the numbers in the code are 01357."

As she read out the numbers, Norton punched them in the phone for them to visualise.

"I doubt they would go in that order, too easy. But I think we've already established and agreed by the ridge detail that we think 3 is the first number and 0 is the last," Morgan said aloud.

"Maybe 357100. Got to start somewhere," Norton suggested.

Morgan tried, but without any success. They both wracked their brains thinking of combinations that could work.

Norton wrote several ideas on the notes page of Morgan's phone.

01357:
3....0
~~357100~~
355710
357710
357110
310570

"It would make sense it was a date. A birthday like 31st May 1970. That makes them 52 years old which we know they are, or the day they fostered Lucia and Luisa, the date of their first tour. Something that means something to them," Norton suggested.

Morgan tried 310570 for the birthdate as that was the most logical.

The safe did not open.

"A birthday would be too easy to guess. You should never have a birthday as a password, it would be too easy to

CHAPTER 41

find, especially if it's on social media. But yes, I agree it needs to be something meaningful," Morgan reasoned.

"Can we tell if a number has been repeated? That would really narrow down the guesses."

Morgan looked closely so that her face was nearly touching the keypad. She gestured to her phone and Norton handed it over. Morgan pressed the torch button and shined it at different angles.

"I'm looking to see if any prints are smudged or if I can see a duplicate of ridge detail but it's really difficult."

To Morgan, time had slowed down drastically and it felt like they had been there hours.

She was looking so hard that she nearly gave up because they were running out of time, when she told herself to look one more time.

She nearly missed it.

She went back over the 5 once more and could just make out a smudged finger mark that looked slightly too wide to be from one deposition, unless Rupert or Camille really made the point of pressing the finger down for a couple of seconds and moving it from side to side to make sure the detail got deposited onto that number. But that did not seem likely.

"I think it might be the five," Morgan announced after what felt like an eternity. "When you enter in a code, your finger presses on that number but doesn't linger. The detail on five, although smudged, suggests the most or longest contact than the other numbers."

"I'll go with that."

Morgan handed Norton her phone back for him to note down combinations.

375510
371550
355710
317550
371550
315570

"That still creates a lot of possibilities," Norton observed.

They both looked at the list and thought it would be like looking for a needle in a haystack and wished they hadn't started this process.

"Which one looks more like it could be a date?" Morgan started down that line of inquiry again.

"Well there's only two which start with 31 but then then there's not 75 or 55 months in a year so that doesn't work but 1970 or 1950 could be a date," Norton worked out aloud.

"Unless it's something like 31st of July 1955, but not in the usual format of date, month and year, or 31st May 1957," Morgan added.

"Well, someone would have to be either 67 or 65 years old and we both know that's not Rupert or Camille and I don't think it could be either of their parents either, unless they had a child at 13 or 15," Norton pointed out.

"Could be someone else? Someone they met on their travels that inspired them enough to have their birthdate or a date related to them as their safe code?"

"You do know we could be here forever just making guesses."

"I know."

They became silent as their minds worked at a million miles an hour.

"Try 317550 and 315570 for the dates you mentioned. God knows we haven't got any other ideas," Norton sighed.

Morgan tried each of those codes.

Nothing.

375510

371550

355710

~~317550~~

~~315570~~

Norton crossed those off the list.

CHAPTER 41

They were slowly narrowing down the possibilities but they did not know how many chances they had left to enter the correct code and couldn't risk another wrong one in case they became locked out and it was all a waste of time and effort.

They both stared at the safe as if it would just open for them like magic, or at least reveal the code.

"Just a random thought and going way back, but you know back at school when people used to mess around on a calculator and typed in a load of numbers that spelt out a word if they turned the calculator upside down, what if that's the case here?" Norton suggested. "But obviously not turning the safe upside down," he felt he needed to add.

"You mean like how you did that, no doubt with rude words."

"I think everyone did that."

"Well dates didn't work so let's try this."

Norton used the calculator on his phone and tried typing in the remaining codes and turning his phone upside down to see if it made a word.

375510 = ELSSIO

Morgan googled each word to see if it existed.

Elssio showed results for the name 'Alessio' meaning defender.

"Doesn't seem to be this one. You would probably use a 4 for an 'A', wouldn't you, rather than a 3."

"Yeah 3 is normally used for an 'E'."

Norton crossed that one off the list.

~~375510~~
355710
~~317550~~
371550
~~315570~~

They had two more to try.

355710 = ESSLIO

"Only search result is an Italian word 'Esilio' translating to banishment. But that repeats the 'I' which would mean two ones instead of two fives."

"How confident are you that the number five was repeated on the code? I fully trust your judgement by the way."

"Thanks for the added pressure there. I'm fairly certain."

"Thanks for the extreme confidence there."

Morgan gave him a look. "Okay, I am 80% sure that the number five is the repeated number." She said it with more conviction in her voice. "But we can search the last remaining possibility and decide which one would more likely fit and take it from there."

Norton nodded as he tried the last one on their list.

371550 = ELISSO

"Shit."

Both Morgan and Norton looked at each other with eyes wide in disbelief.

****

The drawer revealed the thing they had been searching for.

In a back pocket of one of the pairs of jeans held a small external flash drive.

Lavinia held it up to the light so Tom could see what she had found.

"This could be the key to everything we've been looking for. Plug it into the computer."

Tom almost galloped to the laptop that was on the desk and began to open it up when Lavinia looked at the time on her phone.

"That will have to wait, we really need to go."

Tom looked disappointed but understood. They couldn't leave the memory stick, not now that they'd found one, so Lavinia pocketed it, in the hope that Lucia wouldn't go searching for it until they could return it to her. How they

CHAPTER 41

would explain that one, Lavinia did not know, but thought she would cross that bridge when she came to it. Now they had more pressing matters to deal with.

As Lavinia opened the door just a crack to peek in the hallway, she signalled the all-clear and opened the door wider so they could slowly creep out from the bedroom.

As Tom shut the door behind him, he heard Lavinia swear under her breath.

They saw a guard making his way up the stairs and in a few seconds, he would see them and Lavinia did not how to blag her way out of this one.

Until it suddenly dawned on her.

She turned around and captured Tom's lips with her own. He was hesitant at first then went along with the plan and melted into her.

He turned her around so that her back hit against the wall and he could keep her stable.

His touch was light but electric and sent shivers down her spine.

Her mind went blank and it felt so natural, too natural, as his lips moulded perfectly to hers and their tongues fought for dominance.

They were so wrapped up in each other that they did not hear the guard approaching and did not, at first, hear him clear his throat until he did it louder the second time.

They soon parted and looked embarrassed.

"You two should not be up here, upstairs is not allowed for guests. I'm going to have to tell you to leave and head back downstairs."

"Sorry, we took the opportunity when the place was empty. Won't happen again." Even though they were both naturally embarrassed, they did look the part and played it well.

"It better not. And you two should have been outside when the fire alarm sounded. Luckily it was a false alarm, but you might not be so lucky next time. You've been told."

"Understood, apologies again." They scuttled across the hallway but before they descended the stairs, the guard spoke to them again.

"No damage done, just remember to stay downstairs next time."

They nodded and could not leave quick enough.

The guests had been given the all-clear to head back inside and a steady stream were making their way back into the hall, so Tom and Lavinia joined that crowd.

"Jeez, that guard is a bucket of laughs, isn't he?" Lavinia joked.

"Thank God he let us off with a warning, eh? I wonder how Norton and Morgan are getting on or if they have already left."

"I guess we'll soon find out."

****

"Elisso means 'God is my salvation'," Morgan read aloud from the Google search page.

"Well, it has to be that."

Morgan entered the code: 371550

The safe opened.

"I cannot believe we solved that code."

"Neither can I but we better hurry, we need to go very soon or our heads will be served for the main course."

Inside the safe were bundles of documents.

Morgan took them all out and gave some to Norton to rifle through.

Adoption papers.

Morgan's phone pinged with a message from Lavinia.

'We got caught. All good but guard on second floor. HURRY but be careful.'

"Shit, we need to go. Lavinia just messaged saying guards are looking round. Take pictures of what you can and let's go."

CHAPTER 42

Lavinia's heart was racing and her leg was anxiously shaking, waiting for Norton and Morgan to return. She had half expected them to already be sat at the table waiting for them when they had arrived back into the hall, but there was no sign of them.

She wondered if they had been caught, but hopefully her message had warned them and they were able to leave undetected.

Lavinia's mind was too busy wondering and too focused on the doorway, that when Tom put his hand on her leg to stop it shaking, it made her jump.

"They'll be fine," he whispered. It was obvious that she was nervous, awaiting their return.

As soon as she spotted them, she gave a huge sigh of relief.

Norton and Morgan casually sat down and nodded at Tom and Lavinia.

Morgan was sat next to Lavinia. "Thanks for the message. I think that saved us."

"You're welcome."

"So what happened with you guys? You got caught but did security say anything?" Morgan wondered.

"We just blabbed our way through it and got off with a warning."

Morgan and Lavinia began to feel calmer.

Wilson came strolling in with Harris amongst the crowd slowly piling back into the hall, and nodded to his team in turn. The looks passed told him everything he needed to know. The operation had been a success.

It took another fifteen minutes before everyone had returned and settled back into their seats.

Rupert and Camille conducted another speech, apologising for the interruption and carried on the evening.

Norton, Morgan, Tom and Lavinia could relax and enjoy the evening properly, knowing that their task had been completed and would give an update to Wilson and Harris tomorrow.

The evening turned out to be fun and filled with endless photographs taken in the photo booth with different props, many refills of champagne and a Michelin-starred five course meal fit for Hollywood Stars.

CHAPTER 43

Sunday, the day after the Rupert and Camille event, was a day of rest.

A day of rest after the amount of alcohol consumed between the members of the Major Investigation Team.

Morgan suggested that they met at hers for breakfast, some needing a greasy bacon butty and others just needing coffee and paracetamol. But it would allow them the chance to discuss what had happened without having to worry about prying eyes or ears, and allowed them to talk freely.

By the time they all met up at Morgan's it was more of a late lunch. But the award-winning Lincolnshire sausages were in the oven, the water slowly warming up to boiling for the eggs, the bacon grilling and the fresh coffee brewed, by the time they arrived.

Lavinia and Morgan were looking and feeling less hungover than Norton and Tom, but all dressed in equally comfortable loungewear clothing: tracksuit bottoms or leggings, hoodies and trainers.

"Has anyone heard from Wilson yet? Thought he would call a meeting to discuss what happened."

"Nothing. Maybe he's feeling the after-effect of the alcohol just as much as we are," Tom suggested, turning his nose up at the smell but his stomach rumbling at the same time.

"You mean Norton and yourself," Lavinia teased.

"We did tell you to drink at least three pints of water and eat some bread before you go to sleep. But then again, if I was as intoxicated as you were, I wouldn't have remembered to do that either," Morgan added, opening a can of beans.

Tom just made a face.

"Would you like us to do anything?" Lavinia asked politely, watching Morgan do all the cooking and feeling useless watching her.

"Not really, got it all under control. You could get the plates and cutlery out and place on the table if you like, along with the condiments which are in the fridge," Morgan directed.

Lavinia set to work while Norton and Tom slumped on the sofa, demanding coffee, and Lavinia obliged, feeling slightly sorry for them at feeling unwell.

The food was ready five minutes later and was a massive hit as they all started to feel much better after eating, especially Norton and Tom. To say they weren't feeling hungry, they sure did devour their plate.

"That was exactly what I needed, thank you so much," Norton said appreciatively, sitting back on his chair, nursing his full stomach.

Norton and Morgan were dying to know what Tom and Lavinia had found and vice versa and so it was the moment of truth. The unanswered question that hung between them all, neither of them sure how to approach the topic.

Since Morgan had brought them all to her house, not just for an English Breakfast, but to talk about what had happened and what they each had found, if anything, she decided to open up the conversation.

She started by telling them everything from when they first entered the apartment, what they had seen, the layout of the apartment, the eyeshadow turning into a fingerprint powder and dusting for prints on the safe code.

"That was brilliant thinking," Lavinia commented.

"Great use of your initiative," Norton piped up condescendingly, but Morgan knew he was only being sarcastic with a hint of truth at the same time. That was Norton all over.

"I still can't believe it actually worked," Morgan added, still in awe.

CHAPTER 43

Morgan went on to show Tom and Lavinia the pictures of the documents on her phone.

"Adoption papers?" Lavinia asked, bewildered.

"There's one for each of the people she fostered," Norton told them.

"Do you think they know that they're adopted?" Tom asked, taking it all in and studying Luisa's name on one of the many certificates.

"I don't think so."

"Shouldn't they have a right to be told, or asked if they want to be adopted, rather than Rupert and Camille going behind their backs? Surely that's not legal?"

"Somehow, I have a feeling Rupert doesn't know."

"And she has money and contacts so I guess it wouldn't be hard for her."

"Isn't it risky having a safe in her walk-in wardrobe, where Rupert could stumble upon it, it's not the most camouflage thing, rather than keeping it somewhere else, in one of the many unused rooms, for example?"

"She would be able to keep an eye on it, have it close to her. Besides, Rupert isn't likely to go into her walk-in wardrobe unless he was a cross-dresser or something.""

"There's more."

"I didn't realise until I had a proper look through the photos as we were in a bit of a rush, but one of those certificates has the name Aiden Brown attached to it."

"Aiden Brown? That name rings a bell but my mind is still a tad foggy," Norton tried to connect the dots.

"The boy from the school," Lavinia suddenly spurted out.

"What school?"

"The Grace of God boarding school. His friends Elijah and Benjamin both died in the accident that closed the school," Lavinia recounted.

"We know they fostered him, but I didn't realise they had adopted him."

"I have a feeling no one did, apart from Camille herself."

"There was no record of him after the school."

"Well, there wouldn't be, would there, if Camille adopted them in secret. She certainly wouldn't want an official record kept and risk people finding out."

"We didn't see anyone who looked like him last night."

"A very interesting twist to the case."

"And it's about to get more interesting because that's not all," Morgan began. She then showed them the picture she took of the photograph found in the pages of the book.

"The guy isn't Rupert by the way," she told them, reading the questioned expressions on Tom and Lavinia's face. When she'd first laid eyes on the photograph, she wasn't sure if the man had been Rupert. Upon closer inspection, she came to the conclusion that it wasn't.

"Who is it then?"

"We would have to ask Camille that because we don't know, but there seems to be more to Camille than meets the eye."

It was Lavinia's turn to show Norton and Morgan the images she took on her phone.

It was the photograph they had found in the chest of drawers in Lucia's bedroom.

"They look like they're well acquainted."

"That's definitely Lucia. Even though her and Luisa are twins, there is a distinction and the fact that you found it in Lucia's bedroom."

"Doesn't tell me much but maybe I'm missing something?" Norton admitted.

"Well, like with your photograph, it's the man that we need to identify. Perhaps it's the same person in this photograph and is in yours. Maybe it's someone else entirely. We don't know, but we need to find out who he is and what connection he has to Camille and Lucia."

"That will be more difficult. You can't see his face."

CHAPTER 43

"You can get an estimate on the biological profile, but again, how identifiable would that be? Could be he fits the profile of the average male which doesn't narrow it down."

"Surely the most obvious choice would be to ask Lucia directly. She might even be able to shed some light on who the man is in the photograph with Camille."

"Then we're going to have to explain how we came to be in possession of the photographs and that won't look good for us."

"That seems to be the only option."

"Well, we're not completely out of options," Lavinia drawled out, as they all turned their attention to her. From the pocket of her leggings, she produced the flash drive that was found in the pocket of a pair of Lucia's jeans. "We also have this." The small black memory stick was laid in the palm of her hand and on display to the others.

"USB? What's on there?"

"I don't know."

"I'll grab my laptop." Morgan got up from the table and left the room. Moments later she was back at the table and logged on before Lavinia handed her the memory stick. She slotted the stick into the correct port and opened file explorer. There on the left hand side at the bottom, was the name, USB E, which she double clicked onto.

The others watched on eagerly awaiting news from Morgan. "Ok, so there's two separate folders. One titled 'Emails' and the other titled 'Responses'."

Chronologically she opened the 'Email' folder first. "There's twenty-two emails."

"What do they say?"

Morgan opened up the first email read it out. "My Dearest Lucia, they say that absence makes the heart grow fonder and indeed it does. If only you were enough to calm my ways, we could have been together for all the days to come. She has put a stop to that and instead I am stuck here in this place, but I write to you with dear fondness. It is the thought of you that gets me through the days and the nights. The thought that when I get out of here, we can have a proper life together away from them and away from everyone. We could live in the countryside in a big house, no one around but fields for us to enjoy our long walks and picnics, walking hand in hand. Keep that image alive and one day it will come true. Always yours."

"What a load of sloppy bollocks." Norton said.

"It's well written. Whoever the author of that email is could be the man in the photograph?" Lavinia suggested.

"I think that is a strong possibility," Morgan agreed.

"The email doesn't really give much away. They talk of a 'she' and 'this place' which could mean anyone and anywhere. What's the response?" Tom added.

Morgan clicked out of the Email folder and selected the Responses folder. Again she opened the first one and read out loud. "I always look at that photograph with so much love and imagine our life together. The countryside sounds perfect. We can just be ourselves, no one to keep us apart, no one to judge. Just us. That image is keeping me sane and getting me through the trials and tribulations of everyday life. She has done a lot for me, and for you, and we have to be thankful for that. For one, we wouldn't have met. She brought us together. Think of it as the starting phase, keep your head down and after you return, we can leave. Hope you email soon. Always yours."

"Not as sloppy but still bollocks," Norton couldn't resist commenting.

"You don't think the 'she' and the 'this place' referred to in the first email relates to Camille and the Grace of God school, do you? The photograph mentioned in the response could be the one Lavinia and I found. The only other photographs were of her and Luisa around the UK," Tom concluded.

The table became silent while they pondered the possibility that Tom was right.

CHAPTER 43

"Are you suggesting that these emails could have come from Aiden Brown?" Morgan asked.

"I reckon so."

"Until the Grace of God, Aiden wasn't very well educated, got himself into all sorts of trouble. He wouldn't have been able to write like that," Morgan debated.

"Well, he went to live with Rupert and Camille for a while before they sent him to the school. All you have to do is engage in one conversation with either of them to pick up on their well-spoken English," Tom considered.

"What about the last email and the last response?" Norton asked, breaking up the ping pong match between Morgan and Tom.

Morgan located the relevant folders and selected the last email and read that out loud before moving onto the last response from Lucia. "My Dearest Lucia, life is good here. My friends and I seem to have more and more in common as each day passes. I long for the day that we can all be reunited. Until then. Always Yours."

"That was much shorter the first one," Norton noted and added, "but not as cringey."

Morgan went on to read the response, "You will have to tell me more about these friends of yours, I am so glad you are not alone. Just remember you are never completely alone. Ever. Some days are harder than others but there's a light at the end of tunnel. Our story continues. Hope you email soon. Siempre Tuyo."

"Siempre Tuyo?" Tom questioned, not sure he pronounced it correctly.

"Always Yours," Lavinia translated.

"And that's it," Morgan ended.

"The documents on the USB, are they copies directly from the email with all the original information or has Lucia just copied the wording onto a separate document and labelled in date order?"

"The latter, I'm afraid. No trace of Lucia's or the mystery man's email address. No time or date stamp. Just as you said, a word document with what appears to be a simple copy and paste of the original," Morgan confirmed.

"What if she wrote them to herself pretending to be this mystery man?" Norton suggested.

"Doesn't sound likely. The last email talks of friends, that could potentially be Benjamin and Elijah, right? Camille told Wilson that Aiden hated the school at first but then mellowed and settled down. What if it was because of his friends? Maybe he didn't need to rely on Lucia as much or didn't need her and that's why the emails stopped," Tom followed through on this theory.

"Or Benjamin and Elijah died soon after and he never got a chance to email again," Lavinia offered. "We really need to speak to Lucia to confirm our suspicions," Lavinia voiced. Even though Tom's theory was logical, it was all guesswork and circumstantial until Lucia would be able to confirm.

"Camille probably won't let us anywhere near her."

"Wilson got through to her once before, so maybe he can do it again."

CHAPTER 44

The sun had begun to set, light turning into darkness as the day turned to night.

Alastair and Marcus had been anchored at the same spot since dawn and both had had a good day. The full ice bucket next to him was proof that there was plenty of fish in the sea. Alastair's rod was still in the water, hoping for a last try before it got too dark to continue. They only had one more day on their trip before returning to land and reality, and Alastair wanted to make the most of it.

Alastair was sat on the deck, beer in hand, as he listened to the peace, the calm and the quiet before the storm. He knew all too well how quickly the weather could change out at sea. The sea was tranquil, the sound soothing and the freshness of being out at sea was why he loved fishing so much.

While Alastair was on the top deck, watching his rod for any indication of movement, Marcus was below deck, in the kitchen, preparing their dinner.

Despite eating fish for dinner every night, they were not deterred from it just yet. There was so much variety you could do, including fish tacos, fish and chips, fish with mash and veg or couscous, fish curry. They had stocked up on basic ingredients before they left so they could enjoy fish many different ways. Tonight, Marcus was preparing a classic: fish and chips, and was gutting the fish before cooking. He was probably going too hard at the fish, his annoyance clear at Alastair whom Marcus thought was asking too many questions about the case. He knew Alastair was gifted when it came to his job, but Marcus thought he wouldn't have had that much to say of his theories and input, not having worked the case. Of course, Lavinia would have told him everything.

Marcus put his annoyance down to the fact that they had spent all day every day in each other's company for the past few days.

The sea air made Alastair's mind clear as he kept wandering to the case. He knew the forensic criminologist, Daniel, had helped to build up a picture of the murderer, but he had his own idea. He knew this had been in discussion multiple times, but he could just see it in his mind. He believed it to be a man in his early thirties, fit enough to move the dead weight of his victims and young enough to have lived through trauma and have anger and resentment build up inside of him for years. Someone who lives on their own in an old house due to the amount of time the murderer assigned to each of his victims and the basement where they think his victims are tortured and killed. A man who is handy with a knife. The cuts to the victims aren't amateur cuttings, maybe not as skilled as a surgeon or a butcher, but certainly someone who is confident with a knife. The one factor Alastair is confused with the most, though, is the awareness of forensic science. Clearly, the killer is educated about such things.

When Marcus was invited on the trip with Alastair and Wilson – who couldn't make it in the end due to the case and work commitments – Alastair knew only too well, he didn't know much about Marcus and thought this would be the perfect opportunity to get to know each other. Especially since they have a mutual friend in Hayleigh. Alastair thought that that would be a starting point of conversation, but he realised, towards the end of the trip, that he still did not know much about Marcus at all. Not that he hadn't tried to ask, but Marcus seemed closed up. Perhaps he was just shy or felt that he didn't know Alastair well enough yet to divulge personal information. Those were the simple explanations and the most logical to anyone else. But to

CHAPTER 44

Alastair he thought it was strange and there was something about Marcus that didn't quite add up.

He would talk to him this evening so they could go home and tell Hayleigh and everyone else how great the trip had been for them both.

Alastair was so deep in his thoughts that he did not hear movement creep up behind him or the soft, quiet voice that spoke. "Dinner is almost ready."

Alastair jumped in response, an involuntary movement of his hands shot to his heart, as if it wasn't enough to hear the pounding of his heart, he had to feel it to know he was still alive. "Jesus, you nearly caused a heart attack," Alastair exclaimed, laughing.

"A penny for your thoughts."

"That's what I always say to Mindi or Lavinia whenever they're deep in thought." He smiled at the mention of his two daughters.

"It must be nice to have family, to have that support bubble, someone close to share your thoughts, fears and successes with." There was a melancholy to Marcus's voices, and a hint of jealousy that Alastair had never heard before. He knew that sadness. He had come across it countless of times in his job.

Marcus was an orphan.

"No brothers or sisters?"

"Nope, my parents didn't even want me." He laughed but there was no happiness or warmth attached to it. His laugh was cold and unforgiving. That was when Alastair noticed how cold the air had become.

"Do you mind me asking what happened to your parents?"

"They died when I was young."

"I'm sorry, Marcus. That's hard for anyone to deal with, never mind a young boy. Did you go to a grandparent's house or a family friend?" He knew Marcus was reserved and he now understood why. Alastair was intrigued by Marcus's past and wanted to know more but he didn't want to push Marcus too far. This is the most he has said about his past and Alastair knew he needed to tread carefully so Marcus doesn't shut down again.

"I was an orphan, so I went to a place where orphans go." There was now a bitterness to his voice. He resented his parents for dying, he resented his past. Marcus has probably felt alone all his life and realised his passion for photography gave him comfort.

The wind had picked up a few notches and the sea was becoming rougher. It certainly reflected the atmosphere.

There was a silence.

"So, what were you so deep in thought about that I nearly caused a heart attack?" Marcus's voice had changed again. It was louder, lighter and more relaxed. The same could not be said for the weather.

Alastair was unnerved by how quickly Marcus's voice had changed tone and pitch, it was like a switch in his brain and the change had not got past Alastair.

"Just the case on my mind," Alastair answered passively.

"What is the great detective thinking?" Marcus pushed.

"Just killer profile. You know someone who lives alone, works in the law enforcement industry or has an unusual obsession with forensics, someone who has a hatred toward young women, someone who lives in an old house with a basement. Easier to keep his victims there than going to a separate warehouse or abandoned building. The killer won't have time for that. That kind of thing."

"Oh," was all Marcus responded; he didn't expect that answer.

Alastair looked at Marcus and was about to suggest they shut up shop for the night as it would be a rough night, but he stopped when he noticed Marcus had gone pale and looked a bit seasick.

"Are you all right?" he questioned concernedly.

CHAPTER 44

Just as Marcus was about to answer, they heard a pull of his rod. Alastair's reflexes were second to none and he started reeling in his catch. As he turned his head to look at Marcus, the triumphant smile that lit up his face quickly disappeared when Marcus was not in sight.

CHAPTER 45

Alastair realised he was all alone on the deck, suspecting that Marcus had disappeared as quietly as he came up on the deck moments ago, to check on dinner.

He felt a heavy movement of his rod and was quickly bought back to the attention of his rod and the fish on the other end of it.

He faced out towards the sea, the boat rocking, reeling the line to unhook the fish.

His back was turned to the rest of the boat.

To what was happening behind him.

The wind was picking up, sending a chill down Alastair's spine. At least it hadn't stopped him enjoying and chilling in the sea breeze.

Nor had it stopped Marcus.

In fact, it was the perfect condition.

As the pole swung around, Alastair did not have time to turn around and look at the source of the noise as he was too engrossed in what he was doing to register that the pole had hit him hard on the back of the head.

The momentum of forward force and the element of surprise had knocked him off balance as he tumbled overboard into the sea. The rod and the fish fell with him.

He was knocked unconscious.

Marcus had quickly retrieved the rod from the sea and unhooked the fish. Despite the fish being no longer alive, Marcus released it back into the sea.

He had had enough fish to last him a lifetime.

As he released the dead fish, he smiled at how symbolic it was.

Alastair floated face down in the water.

CHAPTER 46

Marcus arrived back in sunny Scunny two days earlier than scheduled due to a forensics conference he had wanted to attend the following day. He was on edge but had to remain calm if his plan was to work.

He had heard about the conference in passing but hadn't been interested in attending until he realised that he could use that as an excuse to leave Whitby early.

More importantly, there was a forensic photography session and workshop that Marcus had said would assist his job by enhancing his skills and keeping up his knowledge.

His plan seemed to come together and was easy to execute.

Alastair was due back Tuesday, a couple of days later, so no one would wonder why Marcus had returned alone. He could be in complete denial when the news about his body turns up.

If it ever would.

****

Marcus caught the early Monday morning 07:08 train to London King's Cross, and catching the several underground lines until he reached the venue on Royal Albert Dock.

The conference was due to start at 10am but thankfully they were running late as it was 10.23 when Marcus finally sat down for the opening remarks, which this year was from Harry Graeme, the Forensic Science Regulator.

Marcus wasn't really listening to Harry Graeme as he gave his welcome speech. He talked about the upcoming events and the structure of the day's schedule. He also gave a presentation on how forensic science had developed and adapted over the years as science became more advanced from the first use of DNA to ever growing digital forensics, and the conference was a reflection of that growth and celebration of forensic science. While the speech was happening, Marcus studied the schedule.

10-10.15	Welcome Speech	Harry Graeme	Forensic Science Regulator
10.15-10.45	Inside The Mind: Serial Killers	Robert Carter	Criminology Lecturer at Teesside University
10.45-11.15	Just How Unique Are Our Fingerprints? Case Studies	Angela Pugh	Specialist Fingerprint Examiner for Staffordshire Police
11.15-11.45	Post Mortem: Hidden Secrets	Professor Gary Suslow	Pathologist
11.45-13.15	Establishing a Cause of Death from Ancient Remains	Dr Susan Lodge	Anthropologist
13.15-13.45	Workshop	Ethan Samuels	Bomb Disposal Unit with London Metropolitan Police
13.45-14.15	Digital Documentation from Crime Scene to court	Laura Nixon	Specialist Forensic Photographer for Merseyside Police
14.15-14.45	Digital Presentation for the Courtroom	John Stubbs	Digital Presentation Officer with West Midlands Police
14.45-15.15	Quality and Accreditation ISO 17020 and ISO 17025	Brenda Godfrey	United Kingdom Accreditation Service
15.15-15.30	Closing	Harry Graeme	Forensic Science Regulator

He wasn't interested in any of the sessions, but had to make the most of being there, especially if his plan was to work. That's what he kept telling himself. He really needed to make

CHAPTER 46

out that he had wanted to attend the conference by choice. So he agreed to attend the only two sessions that he found remotely interesting.

Inside the Mind: Serial Killers and the Bomb Disposal Workshop.

He didn't need to attend the Forensic Photography sessions as he was the best at what he did. He knew that. He knew all there was to know about a camera as he had studied photography for years. He was used to more nature photography than forensic photography, but how different were they really? The principles regarding aperture, ISO and shutter speed were all the same, and he photographed species. The only differences were that his subjects were dead and he photographed for digital documentation, and integrity for the purposes of the law.

The round of applause interrupted his thoughts as he was brought back to reality. The applause slowly died down and a mass of people vacated the room, to either use the bathroom or to grab another drink and a snack before making their way to the next talk.

There were welcome signs stationed outside each of the rooms signalling the topic of the session and the scheduled time that that session was due to take place.

The doors were open for the next session, Inside the Mind: Serial Killers, and Marcus went in and took a seat in the middle of the back row directly facing the board at the front. The room was filling up quickly.

He loved to people watch and noticed that all those who had entered the room were not a certain type of person he had expected to see. There were middle aged professional workers dressed in suits, groups of adolescent students with an interest in the criminal and forensic world who were dressed in jeans and trainers, and newly recruited eager forensic specialists in uniform who wanted to impress their employees. Marcus realised he did not fit into any of those groups.

As Robert Carter entered the front of the room, where a PowerPoint presentation was displayed on the screen, the room quietened.

He introduced himself and gave a brief overview of his background before introducing his topic.

****

As believed, Wilson was able to persuade Rupert and Camille to allow him to interview Lucia and Luisa. She had asked on what grounds, but Wilson avoided the real reason and instead simply replied, "for routine questioning". He doubted that that was what swayed Camille to agree but instead believed Rupert had had a word with her.

As ever, they were in the driving seat and Camille only agreed if she could be present in the room. Wilson initially agreed as he didn't want to face the challenge of getting a warrant, but would find a way to get Lucia and Luisa on their own. More importantly, Lucia.

So when Wilson arrived with Harris, driving up the all too familiar driveway, he felt a sense of déjà vu.

Camille looked very stern and upright as if her spine had turned into a metal rod since the last time he had visited on official business.

Wilson and Harris found themselves, once again, in the drawing room.

Lucia and Luisa were sat opposite Wilson and Harris, where Rupert and Camille were only days ago. Camille was stood right behind them, one hand on each of their shoulder as if they needed protecting. Wilson thought harshly that maybe they needed protecting from Camille.

After introductions were made, Wilson started asking questions. "Whereabouts from Spain are you both from?"

"Seville, but our accent seems to be fading after three years living in the UK," Luisa replied. Only certain

CHAPTER 46

words, especially when announcing their home city, were pronounced with the Spanish twang.

"Only slightly," Wilson agreed.

"What is it you wanted to ask?" Camille piped up. This is why they needed Camille to leave the room because she would put words in their mouth and be a constant interruption.

"How old were you when you left Spain and came to the UK?"

"Nineteen. Many people do not want to foster adults."

"Which was partly why myself and Rupert wanted to help them. The forgotten ones," Camille interrupted again.

"So it was only when Camille and Rupert agreed to foster you both that you came to this country?" Wilson clarified.

"Yes, and we are grateful to them for giving us the chance. We would still be in that refuge centre had it not been for Rupert and Camille. We have a good life now."

"Were there any other fosters at the time you arrived?"

"Yes."

"I don't see why you need to ask them the questions that I can answer myself," again Camille interfered.

"Just need to get their point of view on the subject," Wilson tried to explain as loosely as possible. Camille seemed to straighten her back as if the lengthening of the spine would add to her authority and presence, but it did no such thing. Wilson continued. "How well did you get on with the others?"

"At first we were the new kids and kept ourselves to ourselves, only really connecting with each other, but Camille likes to do these exercises with us all, like an ice breaker, team building activities and such, and we became better acquainted with everyone," Lucia explained.

"From then on, we were all friends and did things together. We became a part of the family," Luisa added after her sister.

"I always encouraged them to think of this as their home and it's big enough to give everyone their freedom," Camille piped up once again.

Wilson was starting to get frustrated but ignored her input and carried on.

"Is it currently just the two of you?" Harris asked for the first time during the interview. He recalled that at the Hollywood event, they only met Lucia and Luisa. There was no one else on parade.

"It is," Luisa confirmed.

"Would I be able to have a word with each of you separately?"

"Why would you need to do that?" Camille asked in a bitter tone.

"It's just better for the investigation if we can corroborate what each person says."

"But if it's just routine questions, I'm not sure how they can assist with your enquiry." Camille was not letting things go.

"It's fine by me," Luisa said. Lucia remained silent but nodded in agreement.

"Fine, but I still require to be present."

"That's not necessary, Camille, I'm sure these routine questions won't take long and are easily answerable but thanks for being here," Lucia stated.

After what Wilson and Harris knew, Lucia probably did not want to reveal her secrets to Camille. It worked in Wilson's favour as he had wanted to get rid of her from the beginning.

Camille looked a tad offended and Wilson had to cover up a smile. He thought she would put up a fight but it seemed only her fosters and her husband were the ones that could put any sense into her mind.

Camille curtly left with Lusia to leave Lucia alone with Wilson and Harris. She looked different than before, Wilson noted. Almost as if keeping up appearances whenever

CHAPTER 46

she was with Camille but looked deflated and upset, as if foreshadowing the interview.

Wilson waited until he was sure Camille had left the vicinity before saying softly, "What can you tell us about Aiden?"

Lucia knew this was coming and did not look surprised at the question. She hung her head low as if shameful before answering Wilson's question. "He was a fellow foster of Camille's. He was already here when Lusia and I arrived. He was blunt and liked to stir things up. Very troubled, always causing mischief and getting into trouble. He was cheeky and liked to push boundaries. But whenever I was with him, he calmed. It was like I was with the real Aiden Brown, sincere and gentle and kind, not the Aiden Brown that everyone else seemed to know. He refused to take the ice breaker activities seriously, always ending in an argument with Camille over something stupid. But he was just like the rest of us. The forgotten ones, as Camille likes to describe us. We had all been in a similar boat and I felt sorry for him. We got more acquainted with each other and the more time we spent with each other the more I liked him." Lucia was fiddling with her fingers in her lap as she relayed the past.

"You became more than friends, isn't that right?"

Lucia nodded.

"But even you couldn't stop his troubled behaviour completely?"

"No, it would seem I didn't."

"We know Rupert and Camille sent him to the Grace of God boarding school. That must have been hard on you both?"

"It was."

"Did you ever stay in contact while he was there?"

"We sent the odd email to each other."

"Can you recall what was said in these email exchanges?" Wilson knew exactly what has transferred between them as he had read them himself, but he wanted Lucia to confirm the contents.

"Just that we were planning our life together after he graduated from the school. He hated it there at first and then I think he made friends, after which he became happier and a bit more withdrawn. He would always send regular emails, but they became shorter and less informative."

"Did Aiden mention anything about his friends?" Wilson had been through the emails several times, looking at them too hard, trying to read between the lines to see if there was a hidden message, nothing about Aiden's friends and nothing but innocent emails between two people.

"No, I asked about the friends, but I never received another email." Lucia looked sad.

"Why was that?"

"The last email was sent shortly after the incident at the school. It was everywhere, all over the news, in every newspaper. After it closed, I tried to reach out to Aiden. I sent more emails, I got the number from the website and rang the headmaster, I even went out looking for him on the streets, but he was nowhere to be found. He just disappeared without a trace." Lucia transitioned from sad to resentment. "I thought he would come back for me. After a while, I learnt to accept that he had gone and left me behind. He never intended to follow through on our plans. It was never about us; it was always about him. He didn't have room for anyone else."

"And Camille was still none the wiser about anything happening between the two of you?"

"Yes, Aiden taught me how to cover my tracks and keep secretive. That's the only thing I'm grateful to him for."

"What do you think of Camille?"

Lucia sighed. Wilson saw her straighten up as the topic swiftly moved on from Aiden. He could tell that it was still emotional for her to talk about him. Even after all these years. "Overly protective, like we're made from glass and

CHAPTER 46

could shatter at any moment. Her work is inspiring and I owe her everything. She really helps us and I really am grateful."

"But?" Wilson sensed.

"It can be suffocating."

"Is that why you kept the emails on a memory stick?" Wilson wanted to tread carefully and not get her worked up that they had gone through her things without permission.

Lucia looked blank while she soaked in the question. "How do you know about that?"

Wilson simply admitted, "We found it in one of your drawers."

Lucia looked aghast at Wilson's admission. "You went my things? When was this?" Her head was going from side to side, accentuating her movement as her eyes landed on Wilson and Harris in turn.

This was do or die for Wilson and his team, but he had a trick up his sleeve. "At the Hollywood event. We're sorry for doing that."

"You really should've got a warrant. If Camille finds out, she'll sue you," Lucia said matter of fact, although this wasn't news to Wilson.

"Well, I think it's in both of our best interests if we kept quiet about it all." This was the statement Wilson hoped would save them all. After all, if Lucia blabbed to Camille that they had been snooping, news would eventually come out of what they had found and all of Lucia's secrets would be revealed. He knew that she did not want that to happen and had worked too hard to cover them up.

After a moment's pause while Lucia pondered over Wilson's statement, she replied, "Suits me fine."

That was the desired outcome and Wilson could relax knowing that whatever was said between them all would stay in that room and between them. If he wasn't mistaken, he saw Lucia slowly draw out a breath and thought she had begun to relax slightly. It had turned into a safe space and so he continued on with the interview. "So you kept a memory stick so Camille wouldn't catch you communicating with Aiden?" he clarified.

"I guess you've seen the blank laptop then as well." She didn't attempt to hide anything now there was a mutual agreement that both parties benefited from.

"It's possible."

"She gave each of us a laptop and a mobile phone as a welcome gift. It was actually Aiden that was sceptical and suspicious about Camille and suggested not to put anything that we wouldn't want her knowing about on the laptop. So I didn't."

"Why was Aiden so suspicious?" Harris asked.

"He never said. He definitely had trust issues so maybe it was just that he didn't trust her. Something from his past I expected but never questioned."

"Were you aware of Aiden's past?"

"Briefly. The little pieces of information I got out of him. I know his parents died when he was little, and he was in the care system for a long time and was never able to settle anywhere."

"What was different about Rupert and Camille's?"

"Despite all the negative comments I've said about Camille, they really did care about every single one of us. They got us anything we asked for. They gave us cooking lessons and paid for a private tutor and took us to many different places around the UK on holidays. They really helped us apply for jobs, with job interview practice, they put us on a path to success. Aiden wasn't bothered about any of that. When they heard what the Grace of God could do for Aiden it was a no brainer for them. They just wanted to help. I think they were the first people who actually cared about helping him."

"I'm going to show you a couple of photographs. I want you to say, firstly, if you recognise the photograph and then if you could tell me about the people in them."

"Ok."

CHAPTER 46

Firstly, Wilson showed her the photograph of Lucia and who they now believe to be Aiden, in autumn. "Wow you guys really miss nothing do you? I thought I hid that well," Lucia said in astonishment.

"We're used to looking in all the secret places. Can you tell us who this person is?" Wilson pointed to the man throwing the leaves up in the air.

Lucia confirmed Wilson's suspicions, "Aiden. He wanted me to have a picture when he went away."

"It's not the usual couple photograph of you both standing side by side smiling into the camera as one would expect."

"But that was just him. It would've been weird if we did that. No, that picture sums up Aiden to a T." Lucia had a smile on her face as she recalled the memory. "Seems a lifetime ago now."

The next photograph was of Camille and the mystery man that Morgan had found hidden in the pages of a book. They were standing side by side, arms around each other and smiling into the camera.

"Do you know who this man is with Camille?"

"May I?" Lucia asked, pointing at the picture laid on the table in between them.

"Of course," Wilson indicated to her and she picked up the photograph.

After studying it for a few minutes, she replied, "No idea, I'm sorry. If it's not Rupert then I don't know." She placed the photograph back onto the table and Wilson picked it up to place it back into his jacket pocket.

"Do Camille and Rupert ever talk about their past?"

"Not to us they don't. We've heard all about their previous charity work of course, but I'm afraid that's about it. As far as they're concerned, they never existed before we knew them."

****

Luisa did not take as long to interview as they weren't aware of any secrets she kept hidden from Camille and admitted she didn't have anything to hide and was not aware of her sister's and Aiden's complicated relationship and communications.

Luisa did admit that she thought Lucia's emotions were a bit over the top when Aiden was never seen or heard from again, when they found out about the incident at the school and all the events that unfolded as a result. "I guess it makes sense now," she spoke.

It wasn't up to Wilson to share Lucia's deepest and darkest secrets. That was for Lucia to unfold when the time was right, if she ever wanted to, but he had to inform Luisa of the bare minimum to understand what Lusia knew, which turned out to be nothing. He could gather that they would be having a heart to heart sometime soon.

Although not surprising, when the interview was over, Camille stuck her oar in and asked what took so long to answer a few simple routine questions. She gave off the scent of paranoia, but Wilson simply reassured her there was nothing to worry about and they were simply just chatting. Whether Camille accepted his answer or not, he didn't care.

Wilson and Harris could not get out of there quick enough.

"Somehow I don't think we will be on the guest list next year," Harris said as they got into Wilson's car. He was, of course, referring to Rupert and Camille's annual party event.

"After this case, I don't think I want to be." He put the car into first gear and drove away down the long thoroughfare.

****

The conference was in full swing.

Marcus had a long break until the bomb disposal workshop he wanted to attend. Maybe he could use this as

CHAPTER 46

inspiration for future kills. But then again, he didn't want to take the shine away from these recent murders, he wanted to sign his name in recognition of them, he wanted people to think of him when they thought of the murders.

In the meantime, Marcus grabbed a coffee and a sandwich, reflected on the first talk that featured serial killers and thought it was insightful.

It was amusing at how much he could relate to the majority of factors Robert Carter had talked about. Common traits, personalities, abuse, lack of emotion and lack of social development and social skills, lack of feeling and emotion, lonely people as they were unable to form lasting relationships and friendships.

It was sad really.

But Marcus knew that serial killers were some of the cleverest and creative beings out there. A fact that was, more often than not, overlooked. The case studies Robert Carter mentioned in detail were proof of that. The images shown were inspiring and Marcus was entertained at the in-depth discussions with the audience. He just sat back in his chair, arms crossed, thinking how right or wrong they were. Some of them really did not know inside the mind of a serial killer.

After all, there had been a killer amongst the audience and yet no one knew or suspected.

When it was time for the workshop, Marcus made his way into the designated room to see a 'bomb' had been placed in the centre with chairs and tables arranged in a square around the room, facing the bomb. He took a seat and admired the subject of the talk.

When the workshop got going, Ethan Samuels explained the make-up of a bomb using diagrams to illustrate, explained how they were built, how they were detonated, but more importantly, how they were diffused.

He demonstrated on the made-up bomb, that was completely safe, and used for training purposes, how to diffuse it. He then used a mock scenario and a timer to engage the audience and selected two members of the public to act as the bomb disposal experts to diffuse the bomb within the given time or it would detonate in a busy shopping centre.

The mock scenario really had people tense and it didn't appear that the chosen members of the public were going to diffuse the bomb in time, but they just managed to cut the right wire before it detonated.

All thoughts of murder and Alastair gone from Marcus' mind.

CHAPTER 47

Lavinia, Mindy, Hayleigh and Wilson were all excited at the return of Alastair and had organised a special meal upon his return.

However, they had all received a message from him saying he was to extend his trip by a couple more days because he was just loving it and wanted to carry on.

So they all sat at the dining room table, with the exception of Wilson, gorging on takeaway pizza, trying to hide their disappointment that he wasn't coming home that evening, but trying to remain happy that he was really enjoying the time off and his trip.

"I just think it's weird that he didn't call us," Lavinia thought aloud, taking a bite of the BBQ chicken pizza.

"Maybe the signal wasn't that great and he only just managed to send a text," Mindy argued.

"It didn't have the usual warmth behind it, I will agree with Lavinia, but then again, he probably just wanted to send a quick universal text while he could, to let us know of his plans," Hayleigh added, trying to state the most reasonable explanation she could to stop everyone worrying.

"I'm not the only one that's thinking it's odd."

"Let Dad have his fun while he can. He hasn't had a break in a long while, let's not ruin that. And it's only a couple more days. We can put him under house arrest then," Mindy reasoned.

****

A couple more days went by without the return of Alastair.

Tom and Lavinia were grabbing a coffee at Costa before heading into the office one morning.

"It's fine if he wants to keep extending his trip, but he hasn't let us know like he did last time. I'm just really worried about him," Lavinia admitted as they were stood in the queue, Lavinia scanning the menu for her choice of beverage.

"Maybe he doesn't have service and will let you know as soon as he can."

Lavinia just looked at him.

"What? I'm just saying there could be a simple explanation for it, that's all."

"For a detective, you have really missed the cue there."

Tom just laughed in response.

"I'm serious. What about gut feelings and all that?"

"What is yours telling you?"

"That something doesn't quite add up, something is wrong."

Tom studied Lavinia's face and he could clearly see the concern in her eyes.

"I'll contact Whitby's coastguard and RNLI and check there's been no incidences or anything. But Marcus should really be the one to talk to."

Lavinia nodded and sighed. "Thank you."

****

Wilson called Lavinia into his office and asked her to close the door behind her.

"What can I do for you?" Lavinia asked as she turned around to face Wilson, who was sat behind his desk, after she followed his instruction to close the office door.

"Just wondered if you have heard anything from your father?" Wilson queried.

"I'd like to say yes but I'd be lying," Lavinia sighed and slumped down in one of the chairs placed opposite his desk. "It's not like him to go radio silent."

CHAPTER 47

"I agree."

"Have you tried contacting him?"

"I have and no response."

"Everyone seems to think it's the lack of service."

"My messages have gone through all right."

"Mine too."

Silence stilled the room.

"I was thinking of talking to Marcus to see if he can shed any light on the matter."

"Good idea. Let me know what he says. I'm just as worried about him as you are."

****

Hayleigh was surprised to see Lavinia in Zoe Collins' office as she was not expecting any visitors either dead or alive.

She had to do a double take when she passed their office to check that she wasn't imagining things. "Lavinia," she simply said with a tone of surprise.

"Hey," she simply answered in response.

"Wasn't expecting anyone today." Hayleigh's brows creased together in confusion.

"I'm here to speak to Marcus."

"Oh."

"Just wondering about Dad, that's all."

"Aren't we all?"

Marcus returned to his office with a brown manila folder in hand from another ongoing case in addition to a confused look upon his face, like Hayleigh moments before.

"What can I do for you, Lavinia?" he greeted. Marcus could guess the reason for her visit but kept a neutral face so as not to give anything away.

"No one has heard from Alastair in a couple of days, and I just wondered if you knew anything?"

"Last I heard he had extended his trip by a couple of days but I'm guessing that's the last you heard too."

"Yes, it is. Did he mention anything to you about doing a longer trip?"

"Nothing past the couple of days he already extended. He was absolutely loving the trip so I'm not surprised he decided to carry on. I would have loved to as well but duty called."

"You don't seem surprised that he hasn't contacted anyone in a couple of days."

"I'm not. If you had been there with him, then it wouldn't be a shock to you. The fact that he hasn't rung or messaged shouldn't worry you either, service was really sporadic so he's probably anchored in a spot with no signal. It's Alastair, and if I know one thing about him then it's that he's the most responsible and careful adult I know, he can take care of himself and he will let you know he's okay when he can."

"Do you have any idea where he could have gone?"

"Somewhere in the North Sea."

"That's helpful."

"I'm sorry I can't be of any more help. I really wish I could. We were just off the coast of Whitby. He's probably still around that patch of water, or he sailed somewhere either further into the North Sea than where we were."

"So you expect me to just wait for a call or a message?"

"Yes. He didn't mention to me where he was going. I don't think he fully knew himself; he just wanted to sail and fish for a bit longer. Can you blame him? He hasn't had time off in years, it's the first time I've seen the real Alastair come out and a relaxed one at that. Let him have some fun. He'll be back in no time."

Lavinia was about to leave his office subdued, but before she vacated the room, she asked, "How was the conference by the way?"

"Huh?" Marcus looked up confused as if she had asked a maths question that he didn't know the answer to.

CHAPTER 47

"You know the forensic conference in London that you came back for?" she explained as if the answer to the maths question had been the most obvious.

"Ah yes, sorry, it's been hectic since getting back as you can imagine. It was insightful," Marcus recovered.

Lavinia remained quiet, expecting Marcus to expand on his response but when he said no more she turned to leave.

"Will you let me know if you do hear anything?"

"Of course I will."

"Thank you." With a smile, Lavinia turned and left feeling deflated.

****

Lavinia was sat outside in the garden on the patio step getting some fresh air.

She had a cup of tea in one hand and a family picture of Alastair, Maire, Mindi and herself taken in the same back garden that she was sat in now, in the other hand. It was one of her favourite pictures and she found that she couldn't take her eyes off of it. It was the last photo of the four of them. Alastair was stood behind Lavinia and Maire was stood behind Mindi, one arm around each other and the other hand on each of their daughters' shoulder.

She was so lost in the picture that she never heard Tom approach and sit beside her.

"That is one great photograph," he said, making her jump slightly and turn her head to the source of the voice that startled her. Their eyes met and she just looked at him, not able to say anything in return for a moment.

"I thought you and Jess were going to her grandparents?"

"We are. I just wanted to pop by on my way to pick her up."

"She lives closer to you than I do."

"I was going a very roundabout way to her house."

Lavinia just shook her head and smiled. "You don't need to check up on me."

"I know."

"And there's also a fairly new phenomenon where you can send a message from miles away electronically that reaches me in a split second. Very clever technology really."

"I know."

"Then why are you here? Did Mindi tell you to come here?"

"No, she didn't, not this time. Do I need a reason to see my friend?"

Lavinia shrugged. "I guess not."

"How did it go with Marcus earlier?"

"I knew that's why you came here."

"I didn't come here just to ask that. I know how worried you are about Alastair. I also didn't ask you earlier because I thought you would tell me in your own time, but you never mentioned anything."

"That's because there's nothing to tell. He doesn't know where Alastair is. No one does. He told me not to worry and that he will be back at some point. But do you ever get a feeling that something just isn't right?"

"All the time, comes naturally with this job; but I spoke to the coastguard earlier today."

"Oh yeah?"

"Alastair rented another boat. It's anchored just a few miles from the coast of Whitby, further north to where he was with Marcus. He's further from the coast so signal isn't great there and the coastguard told me you can get cut off for days, that's why they recommend not fishing in that part, but you know Alastair, he has his own rulebook. He's got the boat for another three days."

Tom heard Lavinia let go of a breath she had been holding and her eyes fell on the picture once more.

"He's all right."

CHAPTER 47

"He's all right," Tom confirmed, even though he knew Lavinia had not asked the question. "If it was the other way around he'd be doing the exact same thing."

"What's that?"

"Worrying."

Lavinia let out a little laugh at the accuracy of Tom's statement. "He would, that's true." And then added, "Things must be getting more serious between you and Jess if you're meeting the grandparents."

"They are, but don't get jealous – you'll always have a special place in my heart too." He put his hand over his heart as if to emphasise his point.

"Not the jealous type."

"But Jess is, so I better go before she suspects anything."

"I wouldn't like to get on the wrong side of her."

"No, me neither."

They both stood up and headed back inside.

"Tom?" Lavinia asked just before he opened the front door.

"Yes."

"Thank you."

"What for?"

"For always being there even when I didn't realise I needed it."

He pulled her into his arms and gave her a long hug. Tom didn't need to say anything in response.

CHAPTER 48

They spoke too soon.
The RNLI base at Whitby docks received an urgent call from a boat out at sea regarding a body that had been found floating face down in the water.

The adrenaline hit instantly as the crew immediately responded to the call, getting kitted up, briefed and all resources were deployed in a matter of minutes.

****

One of the RNLI's crew members, John Payne, took a deep breath as he picked up the phone with a shaky hand.

This was the part of the job that he did not enjoy.

It was euphoric when they were able to save a life, the relief for the team and the person being saved was what made the job worthwhile. You were making a difference to somebody's life, not just for the person being saved but for their friends and family too, but he also knew that sometimes it was just a tad too late and there was nothing the team could have done.

This was one of those times.

****

When Tom's phone rang on the bedside table, he was still asleep and woke up groggy, rubbing his eyes to open them before grabbed his phone and crept out of the bedroom, trying not to wake Jess, who slept peacefully beside him.

"Apologies I'm calling this early, but is this Tom I'm speaking to?" Tom's eyebrows creased together in confusion

CHAPTER 48

– he didn't know who was calling at this time as he'd failed to check the caller ID before answering.

"It is yes. May I ask who is calling?" he answered in his most professional tone.

"My name is John Payne and I volunteer with the RNLI at Whitby. I believe you called yesterday enquiring about Alastair Newbourne and any incidences we may have recently dealt with."

Tom's brain suddenly woke up as he put the pieces together. If the RNLI were calling, at 6.30am on a Sunday morning, it certainly wasn't for a chat and something had happened. He had made calls like this one several times during his career.

"I think you need to come to Whitby, I'm afraid it's not good news."

"I'm a Detective, just tell me," he said, bracing for the blow.

"We have found a body this morning…"

That was all Tom needed to hear before he cut off John mid-sentence.

"I'm on my way."

Tom's body went numb, it was only his brain overriding that kept him moving. He didn't remember getting dressed, writing Jess a very brief note or driving to Lavinia's.

He rang Lavinia several times, not wanting to bang on the doors or windows and waking Hayleigh and Mindi.

She answered after the seventh call.

"Blimey whatssup?" she answered groggily.

"You need to get dressed and come with me now," Tom demanded.

"What's going on?"

"I'll explain later. I'll be waiting in the car."

Tom hung up and Lavinia just looked confused at the phone. He was speaking cryptically but whatever it was sounded urgent, so she got up and dressed quickly before making her way downstairs and left a note.

Lavinia locked the front door and slid into the passenger seat.

"Are you going to tell me what's going on now?"

Tom was silent while he concentrated on reversing out of the driveway. He was just stalling, not knowing what to say or how to start the conversation.

Instead, he just replied, "I'll tell you when we get there."

Lavinia knew from his demeanour and tone of voice that it wasn't a social call.

"Why can't you tell me now?" Lavinia pleaded.

"I know you have a million questions but please just trust me. I need to wait until we get there to be sure and then I can tell you."

The rest of the journey was ridden in silence.

Tom parked his car and looked over to the passenger seat to see Lavinia sleeping peacefully. He just stared at her for a few moments, not wanting to ruin the serenity before her world came crashing down. He sighed and exited the car, gently shutting the door, not wanting to wake Lavinia. He decided it was best she stay here while he checked out the scene.

****

Lavinia awoke twenty minutes later, instantly refreshed after her deep nap.

She looked around at her surroundings and realised she was in a car park overlooking the harbour she recognised as Whitby. Tom's vacant seat left her confused.

She unbuckled her seat belt, opened the car door and exited the car, greeted by the salty smell of the sea air, and took a deep breath inhaling the all too familiar scent.

She looked around for Tom but couldn't see him anywhere in the car park. She looked in the window screen and spotted a paid ticket.

Nothing added up.

She called him a couple of times, but it went straight to voicemail.

CHAPTER 48

Should she wait by the car in case he returned in a few minutes with a greasy bacon butty and a steaming cup of tea? Or should she start walking, hoping to catch him up?

She battled with her brain but decided to start walking.

* * * *

Tom was currently stood by the edge of the harbour, waiting nervously for the boat to return.

He was just looking out at the vast sea, time ticking away slowly, mind full of thoughts but not able to concentrate on any of them.

He wished with everything he had that it would all just be a mistake.

That the body was someone else's.

But then he knew that if it was, that body was also someone else's father, someone else's son, and even if it meant that Lavinia's world was still okay, it meant that someone else's wasn't.

But he didn't care for anyone else at that precise moment. No one else in the world mattered.

Minutes felt like hours before he finally heard the distant hum of the boat engine speeding towards the harbour.

He took a deep breath and prepared himself for what was about to come. He thought about it just being another job and tried to remain as professional as he could, even though he had some level of personal interest in the matter.

It could all be a misunderstanding.

But the reality of the body being Alastair's was high, he knew that.

Tom walked towards the boat as it was being secured.

He could tell by the dejected expressions of their faces it wasn't good news.

Just as Tom was about to say something, he heard his name being called.

CHAPTER 49

Tom recognised who the voice belonged to and cursed. He had hoped Lavinia wouldn't wake until he had had the chance to survey the situation first and foremost.

John Payne had started talking to Tom, but he had zoned out and asked him to repeat what he had said.

"We have a body. The police, pathologist and crime scene guys will be here any minute. We do not know if this person died from a boating accident or in more suspicious circumstances, but the pathologist will know. We are not saying it is suspicious but as you know the possibility needs to be explored. The police may also want you to identify the body if you can, to confirm it's the same person you think it is or not. I apologise it's not better news."

"I understand. Thank you, John."

John nodded his understanding and walked away to join his team who were unloading the boat. They wanted to wait until the crime scene investigators arrived to move the body.

Lavinia stood beside him. "What's going on?"

Before Tom had an opportunity to answer, North Yorkshire Police had arrived. Tom and Lavinia stood out of the way to allow them to conduct their jobs. Police unravelled crime scene tape to keep the public out of the immediate area with an officer that stood guard to control entry and exit. The crime scene investigators got kitted up beside the van with coveralls and grabbed their required equipment before they headed toward the boat. The officer held up the crime scene tape for them after they had signed the logbook and they ducked underneath.

A couple of investigators had erected a blue tent beside the boat which blocked the scene and so Tom thought that

CHAPTER 49

that was the best opportunity to explain to Lavinia what was going on.

He took her aside and held her hands in his. He could tell by the expression on her face that she knew. He hated to be the one to confirm it for her.

"They've found a body out at sea. I don't know any more than that but there's a strong possibility that it may be Alastair's." He didn't know how else he could have told her, and so perhaps being direct was the only way to do it. Tom had been in this position multiple times in his job, telling a relative that their loved one had passed away, or had been murdered, and it was always heart-breaking, but Tom remained professional, he had a job to do and had to remain in control and head strong. However, this was by far the hardest thing he had had to do in all his years of working with Lincolnshire Police. He still had to remain strong, now more than ever, for Lavinia.

Her eyes glassed over, her stare filled with emptiness and her expression vacant as Tom said those words to her.

The pathologist stood behind Tom and cleared his throat to get noticed, which was the only way he could think of to get Tom's attention.

Tom spun around and the pathologist immediately held out a hand and introduced himself as Dr Adrien Banksy. Tom thought the exchange was fairly awkward, with Banksy's receding hairline adding years to his youngish face, his glasses unnaturally magnifying his eyes making them pop out, and his inability to stand still and talk jargon in his area of expertise.

"We would require you to formally identify this individual," Banksy continued.

Tom nodded and made sure Lavinia was looked after by a nearby officer while he followed the pathologist to the tent.

Dr Banksy talked through the procedures of identifying a body in situ as if he was reciting from a textbook. Tom zoned out as he had heard and seen it all before, but he let the man do his job.

When the entrance to the tent came into view, Tom could not see the body for the crowd of crime scene investigators conducting their jobs, just like he had seen many times previously, only this time felt surreal. It felt like an outer body experience, he was watching from above while someone else was walking in his shoes, telling him what to do and what to say, he didn't have any control.

Once the CSIs saw Tom approach with Dr Banksy, both in coveralls, they moved out of the way so they could get a better view of the body in situ.

When Tom walked in, his brain went into automatic overdrive and scanned the body for potential evidence. He noticed that his hands had been placed in plastic evidence bags, tied with cable ties and his clothes had been disturbed to look for any personal possessions he may have had on him. His skin looked wrinkled in appearance.

He forgot that Dr Banksy was still present in the tent until he had heard him speak. "The body was found face down in the water, which is a standard drowning position; however, I won't know more until the postmortem."

Tom knelt down beside the body and forced himself to look at the face.

It was a face he had seen many times, a naturally aged face that showed years of dedication and hard work to service with bags under the eyes, deep laughter lines and deep forehead wrinkles. Showing he was always either deep in thought, or smiling and laughing.

It was a kind face, an approachable face, a face Tom had looked at many times for guidance, for reassurance, a face that belonged to an authoritative and fatherly figure.

Tom's head bowed in respect and sorrow before looking up at Dr Banksy who was eagerly awaiting his confirmation. To him, it was just another body.

Tom nodded and barely formed the words. "Yes, this is Alastair Newbourne."

CHAPTER 50

Lavinia was perched in the boot of an officer's car. The officer, PC Clara, had given her a cup of tea with two sugars in it but Lavinia had only stared at the brown liquid in the polystyrene cup bought from the local fish and chip shop just yards from the harbour.

Her mind couldn't quite comprehend what Tom had just told her, and out of instinct she had decided to call Alastair fifteen times, only to get voicemail.

To her, it had felt like an eternity since Tom had left her with PC Clara. She was only a few years older than Lavinia and had recently joined the North Yorkshire Police from College. Lavinia had learned she was born and bred in Whitby, North Yorkshire, her thick accent a giveaway. She knew Clara was only trying to make conversation, but Lavinia just zoned out and let her talk.

She didn't know what was taking Tom so long. Surely he was able to take one look at the body and say it wasn't Alastair? That would only take a matter of seconds, but when Lavinia looked up, Tom was still nowhere to be seen.

She was becoming agitated.

She spotted movement in the distance and together Tom and Dr Banksy had vacated the tent and were in discussion. The look on Dr Banksy's face was solemn, a look she had seen a lot of recently and immediately her stomach tightened and her heart fired rapidly because she knew what that meant.

With the speed of light, she dopped the cup to the floor and ran, not hearing Clara yell after her. She had tunnel vision and focused on running towards the tent, unaware of what was happening around her.

Surprise lit up on his face at seeing Lavinia racing towards them. He took control of the situation and ran towards her before she could get to the tent in an aim to prevent her from seeing Alastair's body inside.

They collided.

"Woah woah woah," Tom said as he blocked her path and held his arms out to stop her and to steady himself when she crashed into him.

"Is it him? Is it Dad?" she cried out.

Tom did not need to say anything, just the tear that slid down his cheek, the dip and then the nod of his head confirmed it for her. Lavinia stood silenced, paralysed with shock.

At this point Tom had let go of her to wipe his own tears away and Lavinia took that chance to dart past him and enter the tent.

Tom cursed himself and dashed after her.

Lavinia was stood, her back to Tom, gazing down at the lifeless body of her father that was laid in front of her on the ground. Blankets covered him, making it seem he was at ease, sleeping peacefully.

She felt Tom's presence behind her, but he did not approach her straight away, he held back slightly, giving her a minute.

For Tom, it all happened in slow motion.

Lavinia's knees buckled under her, no longing supporting her, letting her collapse to the ground. Tom was there to catch her fall and he held her tightly as he felt her whole body shaking and his t shirt became soaked with her tears.

They stayed like that for fifteen minutes.

CHAPTER 51

After the interview with Wilson and Harris, Lucia was unsettled and could not get it out of her mind.

She constantly kept replaying the scene. It seemed she wasn't the only one keeping a secret.

She deeply respected Camille and her work and understood the need to keep secrets; after all, Lucia had kept things from her so it wasn't that that was bothering her.

It was the identity of the man in the photo.

The photo had clearly been taken when Camille had been slightly younger, that much was evident; however, the man in the photograph did not look like Rupert. Surely people don't change that much over the years, so that they are unrecognisable in earlier photographs?

She didn't know what either Rupert or Camille had looked like in their younger days, perhaps late 20s, but the fact that she was able to identify Camille so easily bugged her that she couldn't identify the man just as easily.

So if it wasn't Rupert, then who was it?

It could be something so innocent such as a past boyfriend, but the fact that the photograph was hidden inside a book suggests that Camille had recent contact with it and needed somewhere to hide it, most likely from Rupert finding it. It was that thought, together with the fact that the photograph, taken some years ago, was no longer in a photograph album in a box in the attic or a disused room, where they kept other old things, which was suspicious.

That was why she was on the mission to find out.

Luisa was walking somewhere around the grounds with Jasper before an interview video call with a university. She was inspired by Rupert and Camille and her own story, and wanted to study social work, with the hopeful view that one day she would become a social worker. She wanted to help people the way she was helped and given a second chance. So, she would be occupied with no chance of being disrupted.

Rupert and Camille were out at lunch with someone important. She didn't take much notice of who they mixed with, but it was always someone important and those affairs took all afternoon. Lucia was glad that they hadn't wanted to show her and Luisa off. The lunches were so boring and there were always so many rules; never slurp, never eat quickly or shove food into your mouth, never take too long to chew just in case someone asks a question and expects you to respond right away, sit up straight, always smile and seem engaged, no elbows on the table. They ate at fancy places where caviar and champagne were on tap and were always served on the side, like someone ordering fries as a side to accompany a meal. Even after they had returned home, they always enjoyed a digestif in the form of brandy or loose leaf herbal green tea. So she was safe from them disturbing her too.

That made up her mind.

She snuck quickly out of her room, closed the door quietly behind her and found herself tiptoeing down the corridor. She didn't know why she did that as no one was around and wouldn't be present for a while, allowing her free roam of the house at her own leisure. So, she began walking normally, ascending the stairs to Rupert and Camille's apartment.

Even living in a mansion with endless rooms, many used for a different time of the day or for different visitors, but most of them unused, left to go cold, dusty and haunted, and Rupert and Camille still decided to convert the top floor as their apartment. Probably giving the illusion that they were giving their fosters complete privacy and a 'safe space' where they could be anytime of the day or night without interference, Lucia thought. Not that that had worked, of course, but she admired Camille for trying.

CHAPTER 51

She stopped at the door and tried the handle. It wasn't a surprise to find that it was locked but she hadn't thought about what she would do. She looked around as if there would be a spare key hidden under a mat or under a plant pot. But there was nothing there outside the door and nowhere to hide a key.

Failed at the first hurdle, she cursed at herself.

Lucia was having a mental battle with herself inside her head when a thought occurred to her. She turned around and descended the stairs away from the apartment to return to her own room. She opened her bedside drawer and searched around for a small coin purse. When she located the item, she took a moment to admire it, remembering the treasured memories she had with her grandmother back home in Spain. The coin purse had been hers when she was a little girl and passed it on to Lucia. When she opened the item, she found several black hair pins laid inside it and removed a couple before returning it to the drawer.

She had once caught Aiden trying to access a locked room using a pair of hair pins to trick the lock and decided it was worth a try. She didn't know what to do or whether it would work but she had nothing to lose.

Hair pins in hand, she returned to the apartment door. As she approached, she thought that it would be weird to call it a front door when it was inside the house but it was technically the front door to the apartment.

She knelt down on the floor so she was face to face with the lock. For a moment, she just dubiously stared at the hair pins lying in the palm of her hand and wondered how she was going to manipulate the lock.

Thinking back to when she caught Aiden red handed, she tried to visualise what he did to the hair pins he showed her and realising that one had been distorted, she bent the first hair pin into a 'V' shape and removed the rubber piece at the end using her teeth. It took a while and she thought during that process she would either break a tooth or Rupert and Camille would return, but it came away before either scenario happened. Discarding the rubber piece on the floor, she took the second hair pin and inserted it into the base of the lock feet first. She bent it towards the left, applying constant pressure before inserting the first hair pin at the top of the lock. All she had to do now was keeping jiggling until it eventually opened the lock.

That was the plan anyway.

The jiggling started to make her hands ache after a while, and trying not to concentrate on the lock and aching hands, she let her mind wander as to what she might come across. For one, she knew where to start and that was the bookcase where the photograph of Camille and another man was found by the detectives. Only, what use would that be? She had already seen a copy of the photograph and burned it to memory so she didn't need to see it again. She guessed she would search in the bedroom and through the drawers. After all, speaking from experience that was where she herself hid things. Would there be more photographs? Would she find photo albums of their childhood, their adolescent years, their young adult years of finding themselves and their place in the world? Mementos and keepsakes from their childhood or from their travels that reminded them of a specific person or a specific place or a familiar scent. Similar to how Lucia's coin purse that held the magic hair pins came from her grandmother. She recalled the familiar scent of paella cooking in the deep pit of the wok that she used and then handed meals around to their community and other happy memories associated with her. Her grandmother's house always smelled of cooking and the floral scents of her perfume.

Lucia was getting distracted by her own thoughts and barely heard the click. Before she realised, she was keeping the same amount of pressure on the hair pins so that it forced the door open just enough for her to notice and gasp in response.

CHAPTER 51

"Shit," she muttered to herself, realising what she had actually done. She had just broken into Rupert and Camille's apartment and the shock was just sinking in. Would they notice? What would they say? But then euphoria kicked in after realising she had just used two hair pins to pick a lock. She had done it! Oh well, too late to turn back now.

She extracted the hair pins from the lock and stood up from the kneeling position she was in previously, her knees protesting at the movement.

Using just the tip of one finger, as if more force might break the door, she pushed it open further to reveal the majestic apartment. Lucia had only been there on a few occasions so she wasn't stunned to witness the grandeur before her. Well, she did live in an equally ostentatious mansion.

She closed the door behind her and with her back leant against the door, she just stood there and looked out to the apartment.

Lucia had always thought of it as more of a show apartment than a place where someone lived because it was too clean and tidy and everywhere had its place. Of course there were personal pictures hung up on the walls or framed and displayed pictures on worktops, but that was the only thing that made it look lived in.

As she walked around the room, she glanced at the photographs. They told a story of a couple who liked to travel and get involved in charity work, helping animals or children, or even the community. There was a picture of what looked like an African community, with children, parents and teachers all gathered around Rupert and Camille, every face illuminated by their smile, in front of what looked like a modern building. Judging by the young age of the majority of people in the photograph, Lucia guessed that Rupert and Camille helped build a modern school facility, no doubt complete with equipment and furniture. Another photograph was taken at an elephant sanctuary in Thailand,

Camille wearing overalls and wellies, hugging an elephant. She couldn't imagine Camille getting down and dirty with laborious work, but there was the picture to prove that. Other photographs were closer to home and of their fosters. Lucia saw one of her and Lusia, in the first few days of them arriving at the Davenport Estate. She remembered feeling overwhelmed at living in such a place and the generosity of Rupert and Camille still touched her heart today.

Lucia took the drawer out of its slot, turned it upside down and emptied the contents onto the floor for her to search through thoroughly. She did this so she wouldn't miss anything.

Just the usual crap, she thought, and put everything back in its place. She knew that Camille was meticulous and would notice if an object had been moved out of place even with something as little and insignificant as a crumpled piece of paper in the drawer that hadn't been put back properly.

There were a pile of receipts that still needed to be checked and accounted for, stationery, invitations to various events, brochures of charity programmes. Nothing out of the ordinary.

She spotted the bookcase where the photograph of Camille and the younger man was found by the detectives. Temptation gnawed at her to go searching through the books to see which one she hid the photograph in, but her mind ruled over her heart as that would have been a pointless exercise and the sensible side of her moved on to the upstairs section.

She felt invasive searching through the bedroom, but other than a bed, a sofa suite and a bedside table each, that held, on Camille's side, a reading book, reading glasses, prescription and vitamin tablets, lip balm, hand cream and tissues, there was nothing of note.

She went into Camille's walk-in wardrobe. From the number of years living at the Estate, she knew Camille had great fashion sense, always dressed appropriately for whatever the occasion. And she had an outfit for every occasion, with shoes and accessories of every colour to match, same styles

CHAPTER 51

of two-piece suits, jackets and trousers, again, all in different colours depending on the mood of her soiree or meeting.

Lucia shuffled through the wardrobe and drawers mainly just to be nosey. She probably had a different outfit for every day of the year, with matching accessories. How one person needed so many clothes, she did not know. There was a smaller section for leggings and jumpers, more casual and comfortable clothing she wore sporadically.

The room was lit up with mood lighting, a soft dim ceiling LED strip going around the perimeter. Lucia felt inside the jacket closet hoping to find a light switch that would either illuminate the closet itself or the room. As she flicked the switch on the wall inside the closet, nothing happened. At first she was confused and flicked the switch from off to on again. Still nothing happened.

Lucia thought that perhaps the light needed replacing. As she went to take a better look, moving the jackets slightly out of her way, she noticed a hole in the wall. It was more than a hole, it was an opening, like someone had physically just opened the wall up.

Her curiosity overruled her sensible mind and she took a closer look. She saw there were a pile of leather bound books inside the hole in the wall. Carefully reaching into the opening as if it was a booby trap, she took out a book and opened it up.

It was Camille's diary!

She smiled and nodded her approval to no one in particular but at the secret place in the wall opened by an inconspicuous light switch. She made a mental note to herself as it was a genius idea.

One by one she took out six diaries and flicked through them all in turn. She noticed that there was an entry for every day of the year. One diary per year, all dated within the last six years.

She didn't know Camille six years ago.

She made herself comfortable and started to read the diaries beginning at the start six years ago.

CHAPTER 52

Wilson's phone rang and when he looked at the caller ID, it read Tom. He immediately vacated the incident room to go into his office, shutting the door behind him, before pressing the green button.

"Tom?"

Tom's voice was full of mourning over the speaker and as soon as Wilson heard it, he knew. The words, "It's him," that Tom had whispered would forever be etched in his memory. It was all he needed to say. It's the words every person dreads at the thought of losing a close and dear friend or loved one. Now silence out of mutual respect hung over the line. Wilson didn't need to say anything to Tom so he hung up to let his words sink in, if they ever would.

He collapsed in a state of shock in his chair and could not begin to comprehend what had just occurred.

His face, now drained of colour, was in shock as his eyes grew wide and his hand went to cover his mouth in disbelief.

He had to tell his team and Tom had asked him to inform Hayleigh and Mindi while they were still in Whitby so they had someone there for them, and for the first time in his life, he was lost for words.

He opened the bottom drawer to his desk and retrieved a bottle of whisky and a tumbler. He filled the glass to just under halfway and raised his glass in a silent toast to Alastair before draining the liquid in two gulps.

"Shit!" he exclaimed before throwing the empty tumbler at the wall. The shatter echoed as fragments fell to the ground.

****

CHAPTER 52

Tom's phone was constantly buzzing in his pocket.

It was Jess but he didn't want to speak to her, so he declined every call. He knew he should explain but he didn't have the words to say anything. He knew Wilson would take care of everything back at the station and with Hayleigh and Mindi. He had to take care of everything here, and in that moment, his number one priority was Lavinia.

Lavinia was sat in the back of the police car that was driven by PC Clara, after being carried there by Tom. Lavinia's legs would not work and every time she tried to stand, her legs gave way and she collapsed again. She was weak and had vomited a couple of times. Her eyes were red and swollen, her cheeks were tear stained and her face was ghostly pale.

Tom was speaking to the Senior Investigating Officer, Detective Chief Inspector Jerome Blackburn, of the North Yorkshire Police.

He assured Tom that he would get the pathologist to conduct the post mortem as soon as he was able to do so and ensured that they would do everything they could to find answers. Being a detective himself, Tom appreciated those words and knew they were sincere. It didn't matter how many times they said it over their career, they meant it every time.

"I will keep you updated with any developments and send over any reports," DCI Jerome Balckburn added.

"Thank you." Tom nodded and they shook hands after there was nothing left to say. Tom walked away leaving DCI Jerome Blackburn at the scene. He hadn't been the most empathetic person Tom had met in the police, but that was how some people dealt with scenes of sombre.

On the way to PC Clara's car to collect Lavinia, Tom looked up to the sky. It was as grey as he felt, the salty sea air filled his lungs as he took a deep breath, the breeze dried the tears that escaped.

****

Wilson faintly heard a ringing noise in the distance, but it was like hearing a sound with ears full of water. After the noise momentarily stopped, it began again and that was what made him snap back into reality and realised it his office phone ringing. He just stared at it like it was a foreign object he didn't know how to work.

After constant ringing, he picked it up without saying anything into the receiver.

"Wilson? Is that you? I've been trying to ring you and I'm sorry to bother you, but I have someone in reception demanding to speak to you and you only."

It took a moment for Wilson to register what Dorsi had said, but when she called out his name again he answered, "Who is it?"

"Lucia. She said you would know who she was."

"Yes. I'm coming down," he replied faintly before he replaced the receiver. He just stood there like a statue for a while longer. He didn't how much time had passed but then it was like time had started again as he carried on, picked up his notebook and pen, exited his office and headed downstairs into reception.

As soon as he entered into reception, Dorsi pointed towards the set of chairs where Wilson could see a nervous looking Lucia sat there with crossed legs and fiddling with her hands in her lap. Wilson headed over and Lucia's head snapped up as she heard someone approach her. She shyly smiled at Wilson with recognition and Wilson got the feeling no one knew she was there.

"Sorry to keep you waiting."

"Not at all. I understand how busy you are."

Wilson just smiled in response, busy getting nowhere, he thought, and directed her to an interview room along the corridor. He opened the door and they sat down opposite each other. "Apologies that the interview room may seem a bit too formal, but I understand you wanted to speak to

CHAPTER 52

me about something?" he asked once they were settled into their places.

"If I tell you what I found out, will you keep my name out of it should it ever crop up again?"

"I will do my best."

That reassurance from Wilson seemed to have been the response Lucia was looking for as she carried on. "I came across Camille's diaries. Six of them to be precise. One diary per year dating back the last six years."

Wilson did the maths in his head. "2017 to 2023."

"1st January 2017 until the latest entry yesterday."

"Why did she start in the New Year of 2017?"

"Well, when you begin reading the entry on 1st January of that year, she talks about the diary as a way to grieve, to write her thoughts and feelings down as a coping mechanism. It was a gift from Rupert."

"So something must have happened the year before."

"She doesn't say until much later on what, but I think she gets to 2018 before she mentions his name."

"Whose name?"

"I've got an image of the entry. Hang on." She dug her phone out of her pocket, unlocked it and scrolled through her photos before selecting the entry in the dairy she was looking for. "'12th February 2018," Lucia read aloud, "this would have been his 28th birthday. His name means gift from God and he certainly was that.' She goes on to wonder what he would be doing with his life, imagining him in all sorts of roles, doctor, lawyer etcetera, but expects he would be successful. She mentions that he was the best mixture of both Rupert and Camille, her hair, his eyes, and hopes he would still have those attributes. I looked up names that mean gift from God and Nathaniel was the first hit."

"Rupert and Camille had a son named Nathan?" Wilson said in awe. He hadn't realised that fact.

"Something happened to Nathan in 2016. She records how heartbroken she is, how guilty she feels, how distraught she is."

"Anything else of interest in the diaries?"

"Yes, towards the end of 2019, that's when she starts to write about her guilt. It seems guilt of not being able to help her son. And then beginning of 2020, she talks about New Year's resolutions, no longer feeling guilty and channelling that guilt to helping others. That's when they go abroad and help in a refuge centre. She writes that she wouldn't have let her son live a life of pain and hardship, and that's why she did everything she could to help him. She hopes he can forgive her because she can never forgive herself. She documents her charity and volunteer work. Later that year, Lusia and I get fostered by her. She writes about that. Saying she hopes he would be proud of the work she's doing to help and if only her son were alive now, she would've been able to help him as much as she's helping other people. She wishes he was there etcetera." Lucia looks up from her phone at Wilson who is taking it all in. "It seems the diaries actually helped to her to process the death of her son. The first two years are more depressing than Anne Frank's diaries and then it seems she finds a purpose in the world again," Lucia adds.

"You think her son died?"

"I know he did. She eventually opens up and wrote that he had a rare form of cancer and they couldn't afford the specialist treatment to save him and when they did raise the money, he died before he got the treatment. They waited too long."

"That's why she feels guilty. My team searched her apartment and never came across any diaries."

"I only found them accidentally."

"Yeah, how did you find them?" Wilson asked intrigued.

"Like your team, I searched the apartment, wanting to find more about her life after you showed me the picture. Tried to switch on a light in the jacket closet which happened

CHAPTER 52

to be the opening for a secret hole in the wall where these were kept."

"She hid the diaries?"

"Rupert brought her the first diary to help, I don't think he's aware of the others. She basically says that Rupert believes she got over it."

"You said they raised the money for the treatment but he died before he could have it? What did they do with the money?"

"Donated it to charity. That was the start of their reign, for want of a better word, they received media attention for the money they were raising. She mentioned that she did not want the media snooping into their lives but then soon realised it could be used as a good thing to boost awareness and get more sponsors which worked. The media followed their story and the people admired them."

"That's when their lives changed for the better. But it wasn't until a few years later that they went and did all that charity work aboard."

"They did loads in the UK before getting the opportunity to go abroad and that was that. That reminds me." Lucia searched through her images again and turned the phone around to face Wilson. The image on her phone was taken from a picture in the diary. "The man in the photograph you showed me appears to be the same man in this photograph. It's Nathan."

"Thank you for bringing these to my attention. Is there anything else she may have mentioned?" Wilson was thinking that she may have written about the secret adoption of her fosters but didn't want to say anything in case Lucia hadn't read anything about it and was still as clueless. Turns out he was wrong.

"She...um...she writes that she not only fostered us but adopted us as well."

"My team came across adoption papers in the safe."

"And you didn't think to tell us about it?"

"It's not my place. I'm sure Camille has her reasons."

"She says here actually. The good she was doing for charity wasn't enough, not even the animal sanctuaries or volunteering in refuge centres. So she went to the next level and fostered. She thought we were able to fill that void that was left by her son but no one ever could. She believed that by adopting in secret we could never fully leave her."

****

When Tom finally arrived home after what had felt one of the longest and most emotional day in his life, Jess was not as pleased to see him as he had hoped. Seeing the look on Jess's face he knew that he was in trouble.

"You weren't picking up when I called, you left a very vague note this morning, you were gone all day. I was worried." Jess got straight to the point.

Tom was not really listening, he didn't want to hear it. He had had enough for one day and wanted to curl up in bed with alcohol, he knew he wouldn't be able to sleep, but he wanted to wish the nightmare had never started. And to wake up tomorrow morning and it had all been a bad dream.

"You always put Lavinia first. It's like a third person in our relationship and I'm always the other woman. Do you have any idea how that makes me feel?" Jess continued.

Tom did not expect to hear this argument.

"We're work partners, if I have to answer to anything work related then it usually involves Lavinia as we work together," Tom said weakly.

"Okay fine then you put your job before us. Every time."

"That's just the nature of the job, what do you suggest I do?"

"I don't know, make a work contract that states more sociable working hours perhaps?" she said sarcastically and then went on to suggest more reasonable options. "Or just

CHAPTER 52

make the effort to be home on time. Or to actually make it to or even through our dates. That would be a start."

"Okay," he simply replied, resignedly.

"And I don't want you to work closely with Lavinia anymore."

"What? You can't be serious."

"If you want this relationship to work, then yes I am serious. If you can't compromise then I guess we're over."

"There's compromise and then there's being ridiculous."

"How many times have you chosen work over me?"

"That's just the way it is. I thought you understood and accepted that?"

"I do, sometimes, but how many times is too many? And how many times have you chosen Lavinia over me?"

"I admit a couple of times. Work related."

"Finally, we're getting somewhere." Jess threw her hands up in the air exasperated.

"But I've always made it up to you," defended Tom

"That's not the point. The point is I am your girlfriend and I shouldn't come second best to some other woman, no matter if it's your work partner or friends or whatever it is, and I shouldn't come second best to your job either, but I have made an exception with that. The least you could do is meet me in the middle. I don't feel I am being unreasonable here."

"So let me get this straight: if I got a call about work in the middle of our date and it's Morgan, and I had to leave to go to Morgan, who I was working with, you would be fine with it?"

"I would feel better about it, yeah."

"How does that work?"

"Because I know you and Morgan would strictly be professional partners. You and Lavinia, I don't know how to describe it, but you two have a connection that runs deeper than professional and that makes it worse that you are so blind you can't even see it for yourself."

Tom stood there in silence, not knowing what to say. He knew Jess got jealous, but he thought she and Lavinia were friends.

Jess sensed this and said in a low flat tone, "I suggest you think about what I've said. It's because I love you that I'm saying these things and I want to make this work between us."

"Shit timing. Lavinia has just lost her dad. She needs my support now more than ever."

"And I don't? You can support her, in a professional capacity. Besides, she has all the support she needs from everyone else around her."

"That's not for you to decide."

"That's not for you to decide either. You're not her boyfriend, you have no obligation towards her." Jess's tone had raised a notch again as she was becoming frustrated. "We keep going round in circles. I don't think we're going to agree on anything tonight. Let me know when you have made your decision." Jess went to collect her belongings and head out.

Tom stopped her before she opened the front door. "You're asking me to choose between you and Lavinia?"

"I guess you finally understood." And with that she vacated the premises, leaving Tom dumbfounded on the doorstep.

CHAPTER 53

Wilson told everyone to have the day off after the shock of finding out about the death of Alastair. Being on the same team as Alastair had been an honour for all, he brought the laughter, sarcasm, guidance and wisdom. They had all learnt a lot from him and he was the detective they all aspired to be. They had lost not only a colleague, but a dear friend.

After Jess had left, Tom hit the alcohol hard and had fallen asleep on the sofa, only woken up to run to the bathroom to be sick in the toilet. He looked as rough as he felt; his hair dishevelled, dark shadows under his eyes from the lack of sleep and his face pale from the shock of the past 24 hours.

He splashed cold water on his face and then rested his hands on the edge of the sink, head bowed and he sighed before he looked at himself in the mirror.

He did not like what he saw. Or who he saw. He couldn't even begin to imagine what Lavinia was feeling but he felt his whole world had collapsed in one day.

****

Wilson did not get any sleep; instead he rummaged through the attic to retrieve old photos of back in the day of the early years when he and Alastair started working together and the family holidays they took.

Alastair had been like a son to Wilson. He had taught him everything he knew and Alastair had been Wilson's right hand man from the beginning. Wilson had passed his experience and wisdom onto Alastair, who had then done the same with other members of his team including Tom and Harris.

Their families took camping trips together in Scotland and The Lake District, telling stories over a bonfire and toasted marshmallows. They had dinner parties, summer bank holiday BBQs and day trips to the beach, piling deckchairs, blow up floaties and a couple of cool boxes with drinks and a picnic into the back of their cars.

A bottle of whisky sat beside him, and Denise on the other, tears never stopped forming in her eyes, but offered support for Wilson the best she could.

In all his years on the force, police and detective, working up the ranks, he had never had a worse day. The previous bad days seemed good in comparison to this one.

The task of informing Hayleigh and Mindi was by far the worst thing he had had to do in his career to date.

His world felt empty, he had lost an adopted son, a work partner, a friend.

He had one more obligation to Alastair and it certainly wasn't going to get any better sitting in the attic crying over past memories. So he downed the last of the whisky he had in his glass, packed all the photos away and together, with Denise driving, went to inform Hayleigh and Mindi.

* * * *

Hayleigh, Mindi and Lavinia stayed downstairs, cuddled up on the sofa, comforting each other for hours after Wilson had left.

They had no concept of time, but it was in the early hours of the morning by the time they vacated to bed.

Lavinia and Mindi had shared the same bed that night, neither wanting to talk but neither wanting to be alone either. They just held onto each other and grieved, the warmth and extra body comforting.

CHAPTER 53

The day had been exhausting for Lavinia, who had managed a couple of hours more sleep than Mindi had got.

Hayleigh just lain awake, time frozen, crying into Alastair's pillow, smelling him and yearning for him.

She got out of bed at 6:17am and crept into Lavinia's room to find her and Mindi cuddling and wrapped up in blankets. They were sleeping soundly and peacefully, and it broke Hayleigh's heart to know that when they woke up, the nightmare would still be very much real.

Hayleigh had to be strong for the both of them – she wasn't their biological mum but she had always felt a maternal pull towards them, and had done throughout their lives. She had been present for the majority of their years, and never wanted to take Maire's place, but she knew that fulfilling that role was more important and significant now more than ever.

****

Marcus was sat alone in his office, just staring at the unwritten report on his computer.

He didn't want to go home.

He didn't want to face anyone else.

He kept telling himself he did the right thing, that Alastair was getting too close to the truth and he had to kill him to protect himself. No one would understand.

Alastair hadn't been a part of his plan.

But he must lay off for a while until things cooled off, then he could resume.

That would be difficult, but he knew that everything would fall into place.

He just had to be patient.

Everything happened for a reason.

CHAPTER 54

The world felt at a standstill, like it had stopped spinning on its axis, like night and day had no distinction and all time had stopped ticking.

That is what Lavinia's world had been reduced to.

She only got a few hours' sleep, exhaustion taking over momentarily, but then her brain kicked into action, analysing the situation, using her investigative skills she had learnt over the course of the past few months to delve deeper into the circumstances.

Something just did not feel right.

Last time she had that feeling, Alastair was dead.

She wondered why she was having a similar feeling.

She would struggle to grieve and mourn the loss of her father, wearing a body of armour to hide her emotions after the day he was found, to be strong for Hayleigh and Mindi. She had had her time and now she had to think.

Lavinia saw her father as the most vigilant person she knew, always completing risk assessments in his head and being cautious before entering into any situation, always having a back-up plan and an escape plan if things didn't pan out the way they were supposed to. And so she just could not believe that an accident had led to his death.

She didn't know if this was her way of grieving, not really believing that he was gone, not really believing he had had an accident and trying to find an alternative explanation. One that actually made sense, because her world did not make any sense at the moment.

Despite this, there was still a serial killer on the loose, there was still an active murder case ongoing and the killer

CHAPTER 54

wouldn't stop just because of a personal tragedy within the team; it would only make the killer stronger, feeding on the weakness of the detectives.

With the absence of Lavinia, Wilson had called a team meeting in the incident room.

The dynamic had changed, for obvious reasons, but rather than coming together, no one knew what to say or how to deal with the situation and so the air was heavy with silence and sadness, and it was left to Wilson to address the elephant in the room.

"We have all been affected by recent events and if anyone needs more time or needs to talk about things, then please come and speak to me. We need to support each other now more than ever but we also need to do our jobs. This killer will not stop because we lost a colleague and a dear friend. The best thing we can do for Alastair is to carry on and bring the killer to justice. That is what he would have wanted and that is what we will do."

The team agreed to carry on.

Wilson retrieved copies of the photographs Lucia took on her mobile phone of the diary entries and the image of Nathan. He put it up on the whiteboard and explained the meeting he had had with Lucia.

"I feel like I've said this before, but it all keeps coming back to Camille," Norton stated, adding, "so that man in the photograph we found hidden in the book is Nathan?"

"I would say with certainty that yes it is. Lucia has confirmed it's him."

"How did it end up in a book?"

"No idea, I guess we'll never know that."

"Unless Camille was using it as bookmark."

"I feel so sorry for Lucia. She found out so much so quickly. It must be hard for her," Morgan sympathised.

"Especially about not being able to fill the void. As if she hasn't felt unwanted all her life and finally thought this couple did, only to ruin it," Norton added.

"Lucia was perfectly ok about it all. She understood and didn't really care, if I'm honest. It was hard for her to take in when she first read it but then saying it aloud allowed her to process it and it hasn't changed a thing for her. Camille has never resented any of her fosters for not being the son she so desperately misses. Both Rupert and Camille weren't trying to be parents to their fosters, they were just helping them and that they did." During the meeting with Lucia, after she had told him everything, he encouraged her to talk to Camille about it all. Wilson told her to implicate him and his team and to never let on that it was she who had found the diaries as a result of interfering. Wilson was pleased to have received a message from Lucia saying how relieved she was to have spoken with Rupert, Camille and Lusia. It was now all out in the open, they had a heart to heart, and actually felt closer because of it. She joked that Camille seemed less anxious as if the weight of it all had lifted from her shoulders. Lucia and Luisa would formally and legally, going through all the correct channels, be adopted by Rupert and Camille. Lucia signed off with *'Btw, Camille won't sue for illegally searching her property and you'll be pleased to know that you're still on the guest list next year.'*

Wilson wondered why everything else wasn't that straightforward.

****

Tom had to brave the mortuary on his own for the first time, and despite the many previous visits he had undertaken, he would never be able to get used to them. But it was better than staying in the office. He needed to get out.

He always felt he needed a shower afterwards, the smell of bleach and bodies getting on his clothes and up his nostrils so it was all he could smell for the rest of the day. Not pleasant.

CHAPTER 54

Tom hadn't seen or spoken to Hayleigh since the news of Alastair's death, but the investigation needed her just as much as it needed the detectives so here they were.

It was Hayleigh who approached the topic first.

"I just wanted to say thank you for what you did yesterday, not just with Lavinia, but the whole thing." She didn't know how to describe it without mentioning his death, which she wanted to avoid.

Tom had nothing to say in return so just nodded in acknowledgement to her kind words and stayed silent. He wanted to ask after Lavinia but as he knew she would not be okay, he felt it was pointless asking.

"I received a call from Jess this morning, giving her deepest sympathies."

Tom's face was full of surprise. He hadn't spoken to her since their disagreement, wanting to have space to cool off and reflect. But it also felt like it had happened weeks ago but was in fact only a couple of nights ago. His head space was full.

"Trouble in paradise?" Hayleigh asked Tom when he didn't respond to her comment.

Tom's confused face that she knew something was off, gave it all away. "I've had my fair share of love quarrels to know." She answered his unasked question.

"We had a disagreement."

"Oh, sorry if I had known, I wouldn't have said anything."

"It's fine. She doesn't want me working as much."

"That old line."

"How did you and Alastair make it work?"

"We had a mutual understanding what his job entailed and yes, it is hard to get used to and every time you plan something, you always half expect them to ring up and cancel or to leave halfway through because of work. It's something you don't have a choice but to get used to, always disappointed but you do it especially if you love that person.

It is like there is a third person in the relationship but when you're as old as we are you don't beat around the bush." Hayleigh's face grew sad at the thought.

"That's what Jess said. About there being a third person."

"You never know when it's the last time. If I did, there's so much I would've said. Just to hold him one more time, tell him I loved him once more, but you never know. Life is too short to argue. I am sure Jess will come round but the best thing you can do is to prove to her how serious you are about your relationship. Make the effort. Actions speak louder than words."

"She also doesn't want me to work with Lavinia anymore."

"Ah, you two remind me of Alastair's and my younger self."

"Oh yeah?"

"The banter, the chemistry, the bond, being young and alive. I'm not going to tell you how to live your life, that's for you to decide, but Lavinia is in a fragile state at the moment, we all are and I'm sure you are as well, so don't go playing with her emotions. I think she just needs you there as a friend when she's ready."

"I care about Lavinia deeply, I would never do anything to hurt her."

"I know, I see that you do and you're a decent human being, but all I'm saying is that she has lost enough without losing someone else too."

"So you think I should work it out with Jess."

"That's up to you."

"Amongst the angry exchanges she inadvertently told me she loved me."

"You don't feel the same?"

"I don't know. I don't feel like I'm ready to say it yet, but I like her a lot if that counts for anything."

"It counts for a lot. To love someone you have to like them first. Jess saying that to you, I think, has told you

CHAPTER 54

everything you need to know but don't do it just because you feel it's the right thing or you'll feel bad if you do, do it for you, do it if it feels right. Jess is a lovely person and you make a good couple. Don't throw it all away."

Tom sat there in silence; he had to admit his head was all over the place at the moment with Alastair's death, the investigation, the argument with Jess etc. He needed his head to be clear so he could think rationally and sensibly.

"Alastair was lucky to have you all by his side," Tom finally said and when he looked up, he saw Hayleigh broken and in tears. He rushed to her side to comfort her.

CHAPTER 55

Tom popped round to see to Lavinia with a pot full of slow cooked chilli.

She was dressed in an olive-green baggy jumpsuit, with her hair up in a small bun and a pen threaded through. She looked tired and exhausted, and Tom guessed she hadn't eaten much, if anything, for the past 48 hours.

"I'm busy and not hungry," was all she said as Tom stepped through the threshold into the hallway.

"You will be when you taste this chilli," Tom thought optimistically as Lavinia shut the door. She didn't have any energy to object and Tom took the door shutting as the invitation to stay. He advanced towards the kitchen, popped the pot down on the kitchen worktop, grabbed two bowls from the cupboard and dished out portions. He then warmed pitta bread in the toaster, dolloped sour cream and guacamole on the chilli and sprinkled grated cheese on top before presenting to Lavinia.

She had just stood in the kitchen doorway and watched him the whole time.

Lavinia took a small bite of the chilli which had awakened her taste senses that she had forgotten about.

"What do you think?"

"It's good."

"It's better than good, it's delicious."

"Thank you."

"My pleasure." There was silence as they both stood in the kitchen eating the bowl of chilli. "What are you busy with?" Tom asked eventually, using pitta bread to scoop some of the chilli into his mouth.

CHAPTER 55

"Trying to make sense of my dad's death," she replied bluntly, to which Tom had no response. It took him a moment to comprehend what she had said before he replied.

"And how are you doing that, may I ask?"

"Come with me." She put the bowl down on the table and beckoned Tom to follow her to her bedroom where he would see her wall turned investigation web. She had put a whiteboard up on her wall that had several comments and lines going to and from suggestions, pictures of a boat, Alastair and Marcus. He was astounded at the work she had done.

"In answer to your question, I'm looking at all the facts," she simply stated as if it was the most obvious answer.

"Investigating, you mean?"

"I'm not getting any answers from the police so I'm doing it myself."

"They're not going to come up with answers overnight, you know that."

"I can make a start."

"And what do you hope to find?"

"Answers. Reasons. Everyone I have spoken to so far thinks it was a bloody accident, there is more to it than that."

"You need the answers from the pathologist first before you delve into anything deeper, not to mention evidence."

"I don't think Alastair would have been that laissez-faire about boating. He would've been cautious, he would've been alert, he knows what he is doing, he's experienced, so why did he have an accident?"

"Accidents happen even to the most experienced."

"It just doesn't feel right. There's something strange about the whole set up, about the circumstances, I just need to find out what."

"You've lost me."

"Well take this for example: Marcus was the last person to see my dad alive. They were both on this fishing trip together, Alastair takes it every year, Marcus joined this year. Marcus came back a couple of days early to attend a conference, leaving my dad to his own devices. Marcus is seen on CCTV cameras at Scunthorpe station boarding a train at 07:08 and changes at Doncaster to go to King's Cross. The boat hire company says that my dad contacted them on his mobile to hire the boat for another couple of days. The phone records check out – there was an outgoing call from my dad's phone number to the boat company which lasted just over three minutes on the day that Marcus supposedly left. However, we didn't hear anything from Dad after he had sent us the message to say he was extending his trip for a couple of days. Triangulation of the phone shows that message was sent near the harbour with signal. The harbour is constantly busy with boats going to and from and nobody saw their boat near the harbour. So where did it go?"

"My theory is that my dad was already dead on the boat and the boat was in the original spot and Marcus, from my dad's phone, spoke to the boat company and sent us that message when he got signal. He would've had to use the blow up emergency dinghy to paddle his way to the harbour for signal, paddle back to replace the phone to make it look like Alastair was the one using his phone and paddle back to leave to attend this conference. Making it seem like Marcus was nowhere near the body when it was found. He created an alibi for himself. Lots of planning but genius."

"What? That's crazy!"

"No it isn't. It fits, it points to Marcus."

"You're just trying to make it fit Marcus because he was the last person to see your dad alive."

"Do you not see the theory fits?"

"It's a far-fetched theory; what happens if it was just an accident and that's all there is to it?" Tom's voice had raised a notch at the surprise of hearing such a statement.

"I'm sick of hearing that it was an accident. I guess we have to wait for the pathologist's results before assuming anything." Lavinia bit back an earlier comment Tom had

CHAPTER 55

made and her voice was raised a little higher as if they were in competition with each other at who could raise their voice the loudest.

"Exactly."

"I'm not assuming anything, the pieces fit, it all makes sense."

"No evidence? And the evidence you do have clears Marcus."

"That's exactly what he wants!" Lavinia's voice had raised again to try and get her point across to Tom who was not getting her side of things.

"You need to stop accusing someone of something they didn't do without the evidence to back it up!" Tom was hysterical at this point, not believing what he was hearing and not believing that Lavinia would try and pin a crime of an innocent man, yet to be proved guilty.

"You don't believe Marcus could've done it?"

"No! In all honesty I don't. He's a part of the team, he is one of us, but more than that, his alibi checks out and you've already checked that. You're just trying to prove something that isn't there. You are morphing the facts so it fits your theory. Does Mindi and Hayleigh know about this?"

"You're the only one, I thought you of all people would back me up." Lavinia had tears in her eyes as she slumped on the edge of the bed.

"You know I would back you with anything, but not this! You're hurting and wanting answers and someone to blame, I get that, I really do, but this is not the way, Lavinia." Tom sat beside her, his voice had softened. "Blaming someone is not going to bring him back."

This had clearly struck a nerve with Lavinia as she whispered to Tom, "Just go."

"Lavinia, I want to help, but not this way." He reached for her hand but she had retracted and would not look at Tom.

"Then leave, go, I don't want to see or speak to you right now. Or ever. I don't want your pity, I don't want your sorrow or your support. I was fine before I met you and I don't need you so please just leave," Lavinia pleaded in a harsh tone.

"I'm sorry," was all he could think to say and turned to look back at her before exiting the room.

She heard his feet descending the stairs, and when she was sure the front door had closed, she sat back on the bed, with her back leant against the bedframe, hugged her knees close to her chest and cried.

CHAPTER 56

As promised, Tom received an email from DCI Jerome Blackburn from North Yorkshire Police.

He hesitated to open the email afraid of what it would say but he needed to know.

A quick read of the email itself gave a summary of the pathologist's results in layman terms and the conclusion of the investigation into Alastair's death.

Tom thought it hadn't taken them long to conclude the investigation. Therefore, it had to be a straightforward open and shut case.

That meant that whatever the outcome was, it was final.

As he read the email, the word accidental screamed out at him.

'*Due to where Alastair had been standing at the time, and weather conditions, the force of the blow by the pole knocked his balance, as it was unexpected, and he fell into the sea. Unconscious but still alive upon entering the water so he continued to breathe. As a result water got into his lungs and he drowned.*'

According to DCI Jerome Blackburn, the weather conditions had been against him. On the night of Alastair's death, the sea had been very choppy, the wind reached speeds of 40mph and rain was due all through the night and into the early hours of the morning. In addition, Marcus's alibi checked out. He attended the Forensic Science Conference in London on Monday 22nd August, train fares were checked and verified, CCTV was checked and he was seen at both Scunthorpe and St Pancras train stations. Debit card checks also pinpointed him in the London area at the time and date in question. Therefore, Marcus is in the all-clear and there had been no one else on board.

Phone records showed that Alastair had rung the harbourmaster on Sunday 21st August at 3.25pm to ask about extending his trip from 22nd August until 24th August. This was granted. He then sent a message to three numbers registered to Hayleigh, Lavinia and Mindi to say that he had decided to extend his trip until 24th. Triangulation pinpointed the last known whereabouts as being a mile from the harbour. The harbourmaster confirmed seeing Alastair on Saturday 13th August when he first rented the boat, he saw him once more, which was the last time, on Tuesday 16th August when Marcus joined him. The harbourmaster then confirmed seeing Marcus leave on Sunday 21st August at about 2pm.

DCI Jerome Blackburn signed off with, *'Tragic but very much an accidental death.'*

CHAPTER 57

"Tom has received an email from the SIO on Alastair's case and they have ruled his death as accidental and will close the case. Tom, would you go over to Lavinia's and inform her."

"I think yourself or Morgan should go."

"Everything ok?"

"Yes, I just think it would be better if she had a different familiar face this time."

"All right," Morgan agreed.

"Tom, can I see you in my office for a minute please?" Wilson asked as they both went into his office. Wilson barely closed the door before he asked, "What's going on?"

"I'm not sure I follow."

"I thought the news would be better coming from you considering your friendship and partnership with Lavinia, but you didn't sound so sure. I just want to make sure everything's all right?"

"I think it would do her good to have a visit from a female friend, that's all."

"Are you sure?"

Wilson's eyes felt like they were boring into Tom's soul and he felt he was a naughty school boy getting caught telling lies by the headmaster. "I think she's a little sensitive about seeing me right now," Tom admitted.

"What did you do?"

"Why do you assume I had anything to do with it? Never mind. I went over a couple of nights ago and she showed me this whiteboard of a theory she had been working on. She was basically making the facts fit that Marcus killed Alastair and he created himself an alibi."

"I see."

"Now we know the pathologist considered it an accident, and that's North Yorkshire's Police investigation, not ours, and if you listened to her you would've said the same thing. She had no evidence. I just think she's looking for answers that aren't there and she's trying to conjure something that fits and points the finger to blame someone for her father's death. I get why she's doing it, but she can't go round accusing someone of murder, especially not now. There's no one accountable for his death."

"No, but does her theory have valid points that may be worth looking into?"

"What? No. I think she needed to do something to keep her mind occupied and I think that's all it was."

"Thank you for telling me. I'll keep an eye on her."

"I think that would be best. I need to give her time and space."

CHAPTER 58

Two weeks later

September rolled around quickly.
The investigation had no new leads, all previous investigative leads led to a dead end, they had no suspects and no one had recently died.

The killer had gone radio silent.

No one knew if that was a good thing or not but it could go one of two ways.

Either he had got bored and had had enough, the thrill was no longer there as the investigation seemed to come to a natural stop and the chasing and excitement had ended, or, he was momentarily laying off and something big and unexpected would happen any day.

The latter was the most likely possibility, but they had hoped for a miracle.

The case was at a current close, with the remit to open again if new evidence came to light that required investigating.

It was frustrating for everyone involved, after the time and the amount of investigating they had put into the case, it consumed their lives but they were also aware that it can happen from time to time and they just had to accept the fact. They were more concerned for the families of the victims and the lack of answers and justice they had received.

In the weeks that followed, the families publicised their disappointment and outrage on the local news and in the local papers. There had been groups of protestors outside the police station demanding more to be done and crying at the empty promises the team had made. Wilson could not blame them, and he wished there was something more he could do for them. He had tried, but for once, he had failed. And he was living with that every day.

And he had lost a dear friend and partner in the process.

The team carried on with their job, as they had to, as stabbings and murders did not stop. It was almost like normal service had resumed.

Almost.

No one would ever forget the case, there was still an emptiness that was felt within the murder team. An emptiness that affected the dynamic,s but everyone was still professional and did their job, an emptiness that would shadow the team for a long time.

With Alastair's death, Harris became promoted to Detective Inspector full-time. Wilson had said it was fully deserved with the work he had done on the case, but Harris still did not feel as worthy of the promotion as he thought he would, given the circumstances. But he wasn't the one to turn it down and accepted with great honour and pride.

* * *

This was the day Lavinia had been dreading the most.

Alastair's funeral.

The early morning brought radiant sun and azure blue skies. Not any consolation to the day ahead but was preferrable over grey, wet and windy weather.

The three of them pottered about in silence. Lavinia stared into her wardrobe, hands hugging a mug of steaming tea, as her eyes just stared at the black dress she would soon be wearing. Mindi was downstairs grabbing a shower and Hayleigh was hoovering the lounge. The waiting was the worst part and Lavinia didn't blame Hayleigh for doing anything to keep her mind occupied and the less she thought about the day ahead, the better.

CHAPTER 58

Alastair had been a serving police officer when he died; however, both Alastair and the family expressed their wishes to have a private funeral with close friends, family and colleagues of Alastair's, past and present only, and then an official service memorial was to be held for those who wished to attend in the months following the funeral.

Lavinia's phone kept buzzing with notifications so she turned it off completely, not wanting to read all the sympathy messages. It was lovely of people to think of them and send a message which she appreciated, but now, today, she just did not want to hear them.

Her grandparents shortly arrived at the house – they had travelled from Telford specifically for the funeral – to find Hayleigh frantically cleaning, so they made a fuss and eventually got her to stop which she was silently grateful for. Instead, she made Jen and Geoff a cup of tea. Even though Jen and Geoff and Alastair had not been family by blood, they were family by marriage, and when Maire passed, they had maintained a great relationship. Geoff really cared for Alastair and admired his love for his children and respected his job. They were as distraught as the rest of them when they heard the news and their hearts ached for Mindi and Lavinia.

Lavinia came downstairs to greet her grandparents with a hug. She welcomed their warmth, their love and their familiar scent, which was comforting. The only two people she loved more than her dad and her sister, were her grandparents, and despite the circumstances, she was happy to see them and they immediately calmed her nerves and apprehension. Geoff never failed to make them laugh and since it had been a very bleak time for them all recently, Lavinia welcomed the light and the laughter, which her nan always said was the best medicine. She was looking forward to spending a few days with them.

They just had to get this day over with first.

Reluctantly, Hayleigh, Mindi and Lavinia got ready when it was time.

Neighbours stood outside on their driveways as a mark of respect as the hearse passed the main road before stopping outside the house.

Tears already making an appearance and tissues in hand, Mindi, Lavinia, Hayleigh, Jen and Geoff greeted the hearse as it pulled up, the limousine never too far behind. The polished mahogany coffin shined through the window, flowers spelt out 'Dad,' on one side and 'Alastair' on the other side. The funeral directors exited their vehicle and approached them to offer condolences and offer support for the day ahead.

When they were ready, they climbed into the limousine, while the driver of the hearse took his seat behind the wheel, and the funeral director remained standing and took his place in front of the hearse.

The procession began and they crawled their way from the house to St Peter's Church in the Village.

Even though the funeral had been for close friends, colleagues and family only, Lavinia was still surprised to see the amount of people who had turned up and were waiting outside the church for the service to start as the hearse and the limousine arrived. When Lavinia got out of the limousine, she scanned the faces in the crowd and only recognised a handful, most of them were strangers and she felt uncomfortable at sharing such an intimate service with them. She knew, and Hayleigh had explained, that they had worked with Alastair over the years on various teams and kept in contact with him. A couple were childhood friends Lavinia had met on a few occasions, mainly during large gatherings like summer BBQs or Alastair's big birthday parties.

Lavinia saw Wilson, his wife Denise, and the team, and nodded at them in acknowledgement and appreciation. There was, however, one person she didn't see. Marcus. He never showed. Was that a sign of guilt?

CHAPTER 58

The crowd dispersed into the church to take their seats on the pews as the pallbearers were poised to walk the coffin down the aisle. Mindi and Lavinia both had wanted to carry the coffin, and they had asked Wilson also, which he was very honoured to do and stayed outside while the rest of the team went inside. Hayleigh, Jen and Geoff walked slowly behind the coffin.

Alastair had always joked that the song he would have for his funeral was ironically *'Every Breath You Take'* by The Police, and while it was only a joke between him and his children, they felt it was only right to play it. At hearing the song, tears streamed down their faces, but they had to remain composed with the coffin balanced on their shoulders.

The walk down the aisle felt like an eternity and Lavinia could not look at anyone as she passed and kept her eyes focused firmly at the front.

Once they gradually and gently laid the coffin down, Mindi and Lavinia took their place at the front to join Hayleigh, Jen and Geoff, while Wilson joined Denise and his team a couple of rows behind.

The song came to an end.

The Priest, wearing white robes with a purple stole, expertly read passages about life, death and afterlife from the Bible before breaking into a hymn, starting with 'Abide With Me'. Lavinia hated the hymns as they made her cry even more. She could barely speak, let alone sing, and so she just listened and concentrated on something else other than reading the lyrics. It wasn't just the lyrics or the hymn that made her emotional, it was knowing that afterwards, she and Mindi would read a eulogy, which was the hardest thing she had ever had to do in her life. There was so much she could say about her father, and all of it deserved to be mentioned; however, she didn't know what to say at the same time.

When the song eventually finished, Lavinia's heart rate increased at speed and she took a deep breath to steady her nerves and wash down any tears that immediately threatened to spill. Mindi took hold of Lavinia's hand as they walked together in unison to the pulpit to conduct their speech.

With Mindi and Lavinia still firmly holding onto each other for support, Lavinia cleared her throat and began with a shaky voice.

"Our dad, Alastair, was a ray of sunshine never too far away on a cloudy day." She paused as she took a deep breath, unsure she would get through her speech with dry eyes. "He lit up any room with his presence, from his laughter to his terrible jokes. When our mum died, he took over the role as both parents and we have so much to thank him for. We wouldn't be stood here today without him. I was a daddy's girl growing up and that hasn't changed. He always used to tell us that Maire took Mindi to the allotment with her, while Alastair took me to Speedway with him. He always knew the right thing to say, and he was such an inspirational person, so much so, that I wanted to follow in his footsteps. He touched the hearts of everyone he met and now my heart aches. If I grow to be half the person that he was, then I will be grateful." Another pause. Mindi squeezed her hand. "I...I can't even begin to imagine a future where he isn't present, but I will do everything I can to make him proud. He filled our lives with so much wisdom, support and love..." she looked up from the piece of paper to the audience, "and why is life so unfair? I just want him to be here, I miss him so much." Lavinia was now crying as she said the last part off script. Mindi was now crying as well and they hugged each other. Everyone watched on, hearts breaking as no one knew what they could do. They couldn't do anything, unless they could raise him from the dead, but that was impossible.

Mindi finished off the speech, reciting how much of a positive impact Alastair had on their lives, the childhood memories, and the holidays. Throughout her speech, Lavinia looked towards the stained glass windows which adorned both sides of the church, light filtering through them from

CHAPTER 58

the outside, emitting them in vibrant colours and highlighting the biblical stories. She looked anywhere, not wanting to meet anyone's eye.

As people watched on, Hayleigh, Jen, Wilson, Denise and Tom especially, cried along with them. They all hated to see Mindi and Lavinia like this, but felt everything they said in their speeches.

As they left the pulpit, Hayleigh went to meet them halfway and enveloped them both in a hug, whispering to them that they meant to world to Alastair. Hayleigh was due to say a speech next, with Wilson last in the pecking order, but Hayleigh signalled to Wilson that he should go next as she needed a moment.

With shaking hands, he unfolded the piece of paper and looked up to his wife in the crowd, she gave him an encouraging smile and he began. "I remember the first time I met him as his mentor in the police, being a freshly faced, naïve, eager young lad wanting to prove himself, just like everyone else. But little did I know, just what an impact he would make. I knew he would be someone special and that he was; I was always in awe of him. Everyone who ever worked with him knows exactly what I am talking about. He had a way with people, he was made to be a detective and he was a very proud man. I am honoured to not only call him a colleague, but a dear friend who taught me so much. I am grateful for the countless pints in the pub after a long day at work, for all the dinner parties, BBQs, gatherings and time I spent with him and his family. This is one of the hardest things I have ever had to do, but I promise to look out for Mindi, Lavinia, and Hayleigh. But now he is reunited with his dear Maire. It's not a goodbye but a see you later." Wilson was used to speaking in front of a crowd during difficult times, but nothing had prepared him for speaking a eulogy at Alastair's funeral. He rushed through his speech to reach the end before he teared up and looked to Denise when he needed a boost to carry on.

Wilson vacated the pulpit and headed back to his seat, nodding at Hayleigh in support and encouragement as he went. The sooner it was over with the better.

Originally, Hayleigh wasn't going to speak but she felt she needed to say a little something. She knew she would struggle to get through even a few lines, but with Mindi and Lavinia being her support bubble, she would be able to get through it and keep going. After her emotions had settled down, she started. "Those who knew Alastair and I, know we have a long and complicated history. There's so many things we didn't say to each other because we didn't need to, we both knew how we felt, only now do I wish I had just told him I loved him one more time. Just to hold him one more time. All I can say is it was always you, Alastair." Her voice was faltering as the emotions crept back to the surface, but thankfully she came to the end of her speech before she became too overwhelmed.

After the speeches, the Priest closed the funeral service with a few more words and the pallbearers came to carry the coffin to the graveside. Just as they had done at the beginning of the service, Mindi, Lavinia and Wilson carried the coffin back down the aisle to the song, 'You Raise Me Up'. As if the service hadn't been emotional enough, this song meant so much.

Mindi and Lavinia believed the song was perfect for their father as it was inspirational, just like he was. The song's main themes were about love, hope and faith and when things got tough, there was always someone there to guide you through the darkness with support and encouragement which made you stronger. Exactly what Alastair had done for his children. And for Hayleigh. The love of another person brought out the best in people.

A hole in the ground had already been dug up. The crowd from the church gathered around the side of the grave and watched as it got slowly lowered, inching its way into the grave.

CHAPTER 58

The Priest conducted yet another speech, and when he got to the well-rehearsed, 'earth to earth, dust to dust, ashes to ashes' line, Mindi, Lavinia, Hayleigh and Wilson took it in turns to grab a handful of earth and let it go with a quiet thud on the coffin lid.

There was a moment of silence to signal the end of the service and people filtered away, leaving Mindi, Lavinia and Hayleigh stood looking down at the coffin, tears in their eyes, holding on to each other.

* * * *

Wilson often visited Alastair's grave to discuss new cases or life in general with him. He usually took a bottle of beer or a flask of whisky with him to toast to Alastair. He always spotted neatly arranged flowers or sentimental things that had belonged to either Alastair himself, Hayleigh or the girls on his grave, for example, pictures the girls drew in primary school that was addressed to their dad or a personal message they would write to him and leave in an envelope. They would often all be at the grave at the same time, coincidentally, since they went that often.

They would take picnics and sit around the grave for hours chatting to Alastair as if he was there with them on a family outing. Lavinia wouldn't say much unless she was on her own.

She had closed off and shut people out, hiding her emotions to everyone, even to Mindi, but she could never do that with Alastair. That would be her time to grieve. She found herself wandering to his side in the middle of the night when restlessness became too much and she needed some fresh air to talk. It was her way of coping.

She did not have much contact with the murder team, again withdrawing herself. She occasionally spoke to Morgan and they recently met up in the town centre for a coffee, but they would always ask how she was doing and she never knew how to respond to that. They also reminded her of the case and she wanted to have as little to do with that as possible.

Tom tried calling and texting multiple times but when Lavinia did not respond, he stopped. Not because he wanted to, but because he didn't want to appear desperate and knew Lavinia would speak to him when she was ready, now only hearing the sporadic update from Morgan.

September also meant that Lavinia was due to return to Staffordshire University to complete her second year. One of the main reasons she did not want to go back was because she wouldn't be able to visit his grave when she needed, and that was currently at least twice a day.

In the end, it was her grandfather, Geoff, that convinced Lavinia to go back to university and finish her studies.

He caught her by Alastair's grave, not wanting to interrupt, but also not meaning to overhear her conundrum.

He approached carefully, not wanting to scare Lavinia and think he was purposefully overhearing, so he tried to walk as loudly as he could on the gravel leading up to his grave. That had worked because as soon as she heard someone in the distance, she whipped her head around and softened when she saw it was her grandfather approaching.

"We must stop meeting like this. You know there's a lovely local pub that's more sociable," he joked, trying to make the atmosphere light.

She just smiled in response; it was a smile that acknowledged you but it never met her eyes.

"Do you mind if I join you? I can go while you finish, I don't want to interrupt," Geoff said sincerely, hoping she would let him stay and talk to her.

"I would like you to stay." They both headed for the nearest bench and sat down in silence. She rested her head on his shoulder and breathed in his familiar scent. She guessed that Hayleigh had dropped him off at the entrance as he couldn't walk far without the aid of a walking stick.

CHAPTER 58

"Do you want to talk about your dilemma?" he eventually asked. Lavinia was aware of what dilemma he was referring to.

"There really isn't much of a dilemma. If there's one thing I've learnt is that family is the most important thing to me right now and I want to be where my family is. That's not Staffordshire, it's here."

"If there's one thing I've learnt in all my seventy-six years it's to take up these opportunities, take that path as it'll lead to somewhere you've not yet been and to never look back. You will always have a home, a family to go to afterwards. When I was your age, we didn't have these opportunities. We were in work as soon as we left school, your nan and I were married and had a child by your age. That was how it was in those days. There's so much you can do now, so many options, so many prospects."

"It doesn't feel right to leave, I can't, not right now. I can do Open University or go to Lincoln, somewhere more local or go back in a few years. There's many options."

"It may not feel right, but it will. Those options are to please everyone else and not yourself. They want what's best for you, always have and always will. Besides, what would you do?"

Lavinia shrugged in response.

"Your dad wouldn't have wanted you to mope around, he'd be telling you to go and then make a joke that he'll have some peace and quiet."

Lavinia's eyes filled with tears and she used her hand to wipe them away before chuckling to herself at how accurate Geoff's statement had been and she could picture Alastair joking about that. Geoff looked at his granddaughter and he saw for the first time since Alastair passed, her smile reaching her eyes.

"You know what you want to do, perhaps it just takes someone old and wise to voice them to you."

Lavinia looked at her granddad and realised how lucky she was to have the family she had. As long as she had them, she would be all right.

So she decided she would return in the end, not only for herself, but for Alastair. He would have encouraged her to continue and it's the best thing she thought she could do to honour him.

The weeks leading up to Lavinia leaving were busy, to say the least. Her time was occupied by packing up her belongings to take back to university with her, catching up with friends, and grieving. Hayleigh, Mindi and Lavinia eventually went through Alastair's belongings, when they could face it. All of his personal effects, including his wallet that was inscribed with a personal message from Mindi and Lavinia, and his watch collection were kept, one very special watch with a personal message inscribed on the inside of the face from Maire, along with all the speedway programmes he had kept since he started going forty-five years ago, his LP collection and record player, and of course his life in photographs. All his clothes, apart from his best shirts which Hayleigh kept, were donated to charity.

****

The day that Lavinia left for university arrived quicker than anyone would have liked. They started early, packing all the last-minute bits, before getting ready and packing up the car.

The last bag was put into the boot as Tom's car pulled up outside the house.

Lavinia was surprised to see him, and as he got out of the car, she realised just how much time had passed without them seeing or speaking to each other.

"I told him you were leaving," Hayleigh whispered. Hayleigh and Mindi took their seats in the car and waited for Lavinia as she slowly walked towards Tom.

Neither of them knew how to open the conversation until Tom finally said, "Hayleigh told me you're heading back to uni."

"Yeah, I think it's something I need to do."

CHAPTER 58

"Good luck, but remember to have fun too. The university years are supposedly the best years of your life."

"I will, thank you." Lavinia smiled at the comment. He was useless at making small talk. "Well I had better go. Long drive ahead for Hayleigh."

"Yeah of course. Well it was good to see you."

"You too." Lavinia gave him a smile before turning to walk away. She heard the jingle of keys in his hand as he took them out of his jeans pocket and opened the car door. "Tom."

He looked up at the sound of his name and was surprised when Lavinia walked towards him and hugged him. He immediately reciprocated the hug and smiled into Lavinia's hair. It wasn't a long hug, but it was enough and it was a start.

He watched her walk away. She gave him a wave goodbye before she got into the front passenger seat and drove away.

CHAPTER 59

Five Weeks later

Settling back into university life had been fun at first, with many distracting events occurring on campus, such as Welcome Week, in the lead up to the start of term. In her first year Lavinia was attending these events as a fresher; this year, she was attending these events knowing exactly what to expect. She walked around campus with a sense of familiarity and ease, not being the nervous first year student trying to impress and find their feet, eagerly putting their name down for every sport or society try out, thinking it was cool. During Fresher's Fair, she helped to recruit new members for her sport, Women's Lacrosse, and held give-it-a-go sessions on the Astro field behind the Sports Centre.

The hardest part had been moving into her accommodation and seeing all the framed family pictures and those of Alastair that she had taken with her in first year.

She lived in a terraced house only a five-minute walk to the university and shared with three others she had met in halls in her first year. One of those, Sarah, from Runcorn was also studying the same course, Lucy from Leeds was studying Policing and Criminal Investigation, and the third housemate, Beth, from Manchester, was studying Early Childhood Studies.

They had started the term which meant lectures, tutorials, practical lab and crime scene house sessions, library sessions and essays galore.

On top of that, Lacrosse training sessions and matches.

CHAPTER 59

Lavinia didn't have time to reflect on the events of summer and in all honesty did not want to. She had to keep looking forward if she was to carry on. While it was extremely hard, university kept her busy and that meant less time to be swallowed into a deep dark hole of depression thinking about Alastair. She realised it probably wasn't the healthiest way to deal with the loss and grief, but it was her way and it had somehow worked so she was going to carry on.

Everything had its purpose and she was managing to cope, her mind sharp and focused.

That was until a bright, breezy, above average temperature Wednesday afternoon in early November.

Lavinia was warming up to play a Lacrosse match on her home turf against Leicester. The team had completed a lap around the pitch, done the all-important stretches and were working in pairs to pass and throw the ball between them before moving onto a well-practised warm up drill, known as the 'Star Drill'.

The visitors were also adopting the same pre-game regime.

The supporters donned layers and warm clothing with drinks in their hand to watch the match and support the team.

When there were a few minutes until the start of the match, the Staffordshire Sirens huddled together in a circle, last minute game plan actions and team talk. A whistle blown by the referee signalled that it was time for the game to begin, and so they put their sticks in the centre while they shouted, "3,2,1, Sirens," and flicked their sticks upwards before moving to take their places on the field.

Once the players had settled into their starting positions, a second whistle announced the start of the game and the draw took place in the centre.

The ball immediately headed towards Lavinia, who was poised on the outside of the centre circle; she caught the ball in her net and turned behind her to sprint towards the goal, cradling her stick as she went. The girl who was defending her, was trailing behind, whilst others tried to check Lavinia's stick to get the ball out of the net and to add pressure whilst defending so she would panic and drop the ball, but all without success. Lavinia was within shooting distance and followed the left side line of the fan to attack goal. With one strong and confident flick of her stick, the ball left her net and it struck the top right hand corner of the goal, despite every effort from the goalie to stop the ball.

Both the Staffordshire Sirens and the home supporters cheered and clapped at the goal, knocking their sticks with each other in praise while returning to their starting positions.

After that early goal, Staffordshire scored three more goals while Leicester retaliated to score three goals themselves, making the scores 4-3 at half time. Leicester's defence had responded to the strong start of their opponents, with Staffordshire unable to make many far advances towards the goal before the ball got back into Leicester's possession. Leicester had made more goal attempts, but Staffordshire's goalie, Natalie, proved to be the player of the match with her magnificent reactions to catching the ball and preventing Leicester from scoring too many points. Both Staffordshire and Leicester were an equal team in terms of ability, making it an exciting match to watch.

Maegan, the mid-defence player, caught the ball just beyond halfway, thrown by the goalie after she saved it, and advanced towards the goal. She dodged her defender and had thrown it to Izzy, a free player who was running alongside Maegan, who then passed it back to Maegan when the defenders came towards her. Maegan was a fast sprinter, and made it all the way to the goal, but unfortunately her aim was slightly off as the ball had narrowly missed the net and swished past the goal to roll into the stream that ran along the back of the field.

CHAPTER 59

Paige, one of the attackers, who was close to the goal when the ball missed, ran to retrieve it from the stream. However, before she could look for the ball, a piercing scream filled the air and she was paralysed with shock.

The referee, the coach and the few players who were stood around the goal, including Lavinia, ran to see what the commotion was. The referee and Lavinia had both reached Paige at the same time. The referee understood Paige's reaction, blew the whistle and called an end to the game and shouted for someone to call the police. He tried to steer Lavinia away but she could not tear her eyes from the body lying in the stream. Just as Paige had been, she too, was paralysed with fear. Lavinia's eyes met Paige's. Paige's initial feeling of shock had switched to interest, but Lavinia's heart picked up speed and she turned white with fear.

Not because she was looking at a dead body, which most people would be repulsed by, but because the body was female, naked, one eye had been ripped out, no fingers and no toes and Lavinia could guess that there would be a tattoo on the back of her neck symbolising one of the remaining three deadly sins, as that was the killer's MO. The killer's MO she knew all too well. The killer's MO which had filled her summer with pain.

After the shock had presided, she walked over towards her sports bag on the side line and dialled Wilson's number.

CHAPTER 60

Staffordshire Police had cordoned off the field, with crime scene tape, two police cars and a crime scene investigation van.

Everyone was told to evacuate the field altogether while Paige, Lavinia and the referee were informed they were to give a brief statement to the police.

After Lavinia had described the events in detail to a PC, she calculated that it would take Wilson just under two hours to reach the university and those two hours were the prime time to collect as much evidence as possible, including witness statements and photographs in situ.

She turned her head to look back at the crime scene officers in their white SOCO suits, clicking away on the camera which reminded her too much of Marcus, retrieving equipment from their vans and entering the shallow water of the stream to recover the body, a scene that had become all too familiar for Lavinia that summer.

She should be the other side of that tape, with the crime scene officers, but here, at the university, now, she was merely a witness.

She didn't tell Staffordshire Police what she suspected and what she already knew, and Lavinia didn't know why. It didn't feel right without Wilson being there and so she decided to wait.

Until then, she joined her teammates in the on-campus bar/restaurant for a drink and to gossip away just like everyone else.

Lavinia barely said two words though, and blamed it on the shock when people asked if she was all right. She was physically present but mentally, she was elsewhere.

CHAPTER 60

What did it mean? Was the killer stalking her, letting her know he was here? Did he watch the match? Did he want to kill Lavinia and this was a warning?

So many thoughts whirled around in her mind.

News travelled fast around a small campus, as it was buzzing with different versions of the same story, like Chinese whispers. Only Lavinia knew the full story which she kept to herself.

The two hours Lavinia waited for Wilson to arrive, seemed like forever. Until she finally got a call to say he had parked up on campus.

Lavinia went to greet Wilson, only to find that he had brought the team with him, and even though Lavinia had expected that, she was still surprised to see them all. And sure enough, they were all stood in front of her: Wilson, Harris, Morgan, Norton and Tom.

"It's good to see you again," Morgan said as she hugged Lavinia, "just wish it were under different circumstances."

"What have you informed the FIs at Staffs Police?" Wilson asked, getting straight to it.

"I haven't told them anything yet. I thought that would be better coming from you," Lavinia admitted.

"Yes, you did the right thing. We'll go to the station and speak with them. I have boxes of files in the boot to show them everything we have on the case, and with their help, this time we may just strike lucky," Wilson said with hope in his voice that he didn't even believe.

"Are you coming?" Tom asked Lavinia as the others proceeded to get back in the car.

Lavinia's questionable face encouraged Tom to add, "You are one of us, you've been on this case from the very start, just as we have."

"Count me in then."

The nearest police station, home to the crime scene unit, was in Hanley, a short drive away. Lavinia and Tom got an Uber and so they met the others at the entrance to the station. The unit was housed in an unorthodox building, one you would not associate with being used by the police. The building itself was very distinct, being green, red, orange, blue and white colourful Lego-like design pattern. It was a modern five storey glass building, home to meeting rooms, private office spaces and used as a mixed-use centre owned by the Council.

The crime scene unit was on the third floor. With boxes in their hands, they used the lift to the third floor and knocked on the glass door that evidently belonged to the forensic unit of the Staffordshire Police.

From the glass door, they could see an office space with four rows of wooden desks, each row split into two different desk spaces, two computers side by side on each desk. Three Forensic Investigators (Fis)in navy uniform were sat logging evidence onto the computer. To the right was clearly the room for CCTV and technology, as that room was full of TVs, computers and hard drives.

One FI opened the door and introduced himself as Nick. Wilson, with two boxes in his hand, showed Nick his ID badge as best he could without a spare hand and explained his reason for being there. He did clarify that he had rung beforehand and was given the ok.

Then an older man, with thin greying hair and a protruding belly, wearing grey trousers, a white shirt with a navy tie, introduced himself as Barry, the Crime Scene Manager. He ushered them in and showed them into a conference room further down the hall.

They placed the boxes on top of the table and in turn, introduced themselves. When Lavinia introduced herself, Barry looked at her questioningly as she was not dressed in the typical uniform he would have expected to see on a professional forensic investigator but in her lacrosse gear. She read the apprehension in his eyes and proceeded to explain.

"I undertook work experience with the team during the summer. I am a student at the university. Apologies I am

CHAPTER 60

not dressed more appropriately, I was in the middle of a lacrosse game when the body was found in the stream, I rang Wilson straight away and have not had the chance to change," Lavinia said diplomatically.

"She's part of the team, we have all been on this case together and that's no different now," Wilson added, which Lavinia really appreciated.

Lavinia had always felt like an outsider, she was an outsider in theory as she wasn't officially a detective, but the team made a habit of making her feel like she was one of them, so much so, that at times she had actually forgotten she wasn't. Morgan had always said from the start she was one of them and to them, it didn't matter about the small detail of not having the badge to prove it, they were a close-knit community and Lavinia had proved herself on more than one occasion that she was a detective. Forget about the paperwork, that only said so much.

That justification seemed to have satisfied Barry as he evidently relaxed more, smiled at his guests and offered refreshments which were gladly accepted by everyone.

"Over the phone, you said that the MO of the body found at Staffordshire University appeared similar to that of five bodies you investigated in Lincolnshire only very recently?"

"That's correct, yes. We don't know what this means, whether it is the killer we have been searching for or whether it is a copycat. If it is the former then it seems Lavinia may be in danger as he has followed her whereabouts across country from Lincolnshire to Staffordshire. If it is the latter then it is a very excellent copycat killing, but I feel there are too many coincidences for it to be that."

"Right, and you think my team can help you?"

"Technically he has now killed in your jurisdiction so there is nothing we can do to investigate this murder other than provide you with all the material we have collected over the past few months and tell you everything we know from previous murders. We need to work together if we stand any chance of catching him this time round."

"Not that I'm questioning your own or your team's ability, but why haven't you caught him yet?"

"Good question. He is very cunning and he is very much in control. He is forensically aware as he only leaves what he wants to leave behind, which we have learnt is generic, and not identifiable, such as the size and make of his footwear or the fibre type of clothing worn. He dumps his victims in the early hours of the morning, in the dark and when no one is around to reduce the chances of him being seen. He is invisible but at the same time he is very much omnipresent. We have been unable to identify a location he keeps his victims, but from the amount of torture he inflicts whilst they are still alive, we can hazard a guess that he keeps them in a basement where no one can hear them or will risk finding them. He administers a muscle blocking drug that kills them in the end of asphyxiation. Witness statements and house-to-house enquiries are at a dead end. No one hears or sees anything. He knows the system and the way we work."

"So you think it could be an inside job? And you keep saying he? How do you know this is a man and not a woman? Or that there's not more than one person involved?"

"Our forensic criminologist has done us a killer profile based on the killings themselves and the evidence," Morgan piped up, responding to Barry's question.

"Everything you need to know is in these boxes." Wilson indicated towards the five boxes laid on the table. One for each victim.

"In summary, before we go through everything, what does your criminologist theorise?"

"The killer is male, aged between 30 and 45, physically fit, lives alone, has a job in either the public health or criminal sector working full-time with weekends off. Has a specific hatred towards women. Also has an unhealthy obsession for

CHAPTER 60

crime and is forensically aware. Maybe even going as far as to say he had a troubled, abusive and neglected childhood."

"It's not identifiable, this profile. That could be anyone walking these streets."

"I think Daniel has helped sharpen our focus as to who we are actually dealing with," Lavinia jumped in, feeling the need to defend Daniel's reputation to Barry who seemed to undermine his expertise.

The clock slowly ticked by as they all went through the case files.

Seconds turned to minutes and minutes turned to hours.

Every now and then, someone spoke to discuss a piece of information or to read aloud what they had just seen, but the room remained in silence most of the time, even if someone stood up and excused themselves to use the bathroom or to refill their cup of coffee or just to stretch their legs and do a lap around the room, just to sit down again and carry on with their mundane but necessary task.

Lavinia was by the refreshment station, filling her cup with strong black coffee to help her stay focused, when Tom approached her to do the same thing.

"You ok?" Tom whispered, as he waited for Lavinia to finish pouring her coffee into her cup from the cafeteria, not wanting to disturb the focused silence.

"As ok as the rest of us." She noticed that Tom did not seem satisfied with that answer and added, "Oh you mean with the fact that the killer is potentially wanting to kill me?" She said it with a sarcastic tone that made Tom shudder at the thought.

"You know none of us would let that happen right?"

"You can't protect me forever."

"We can try."

"I'm fine."

She left it at that. He felt there was still some hostility between them but didn't want to push her too far too soon, and so he left it at that too and returned to his seat to hear

Barry talking, "When you're in this job for as long as I have been, and Wilson will understand this, you quickly realise the world is not all sunshine and daisies as some people believe. If it's not murder, it's war, it's a cost-of-living crisis, it's homelessness, it's strikes, it's terrorism. Everywhere you look there's tragedy. Last week, we had a seventeen-year-old boy who went to Stoke College pass away from multiple stab wounds because he stood up for himself against a gang of teenage boys his age, who were in his classes. The week before that, a two-year-old died in car accident and the mother is still in a coma after being hit by a reckless driver who was high on weed because he got into a fight with his girlfriend. We had someone with mental health issues committing suicide because they had a bad day."

"This job isn't for the faint hearted that's for sure," Wilson agreed.

"So this killer of yours only seems to kill over a weekend. Why is that? You said that Daniel believed he had a full-time job during the week? This timeline is significant. The victim disappears on a Friday evening, they then get tortured and killed over the weekend and then disposed of late Sunday evening into early Monday morning. Only to be found a few hours later."

"It would seem so, lives as normal as any Tom, Dick or Harry would. You know the kind of person that could change a flat tyre or help to jump start a car or help an elderly woman take in her shopping. I agree that the timeline is significant, it's a pattern."

"He removes the left ear and the left eye. Why specifically the left?"

"Maybe he's left-ist," Norton suggests.

"It seems to have a deeper meaning than that. This whole case seems to be based on religion so I wouldn't be surprised if there's a teaching in the Bible that speaks negatively of it," Lavinia suggested.

CHAPTER 60

"You would be screwed then, being left handed," Tom joked directing his comment toward Lavinia, aiming it to be light hearted but it went down like a lead balloon.

After a few clicks on her computer Morgan brought up information from a website. "Right, I have something here," she started to say as her eyes skim read the page on the screen. "Well, Wilson, you are correct. Basically, on judgement day, those who have been sentenced to punishment, i.e. death, go to the left of Christ and salvation is on the right."

"So the killer is sentencing them to death?" Barry asked.

"He does that as soon as he picks the chosen one, they are a dead woman walking."

"Do we have any idea why he's killing these specific people? Is it a random attack, does he stalk them before abducting them?"

"We believe they committed a sin but other than that, we have no idea why. These victims have nothing else in common with each other aside from the fact that they are all female."

"Doesn't mean there isn't a more definitive link. There must be," Barry said. "Why female? Has he had a bad upbringing by a female relative? Did his mum, or aunt abuse him as a child? Did they neglect him?"

"Daniel definitely thinks he struggled with female relationships growing up, so that's perhaps why he doesn't have any particular attachment to them other than the stalking, but he can get rid of them just as easily."

"Let's go with the theory that he's stalking them before he abducts them. Walk in his shoes. How would you pick your victims?"

"Something that would make me notice them would be if there was something different about them, something that made them stand out from the crowd. Like bold fashion sense, or if someone was acting strange, that kind of thing."

"Somewhere he could hide in plain sight," Lavinia added. "Maybe he visited his victims at their place of work. Take

Tracey Evans, for example, she was a social worker. What if the killer created a false story so he would become Tracey's client to get close to her and spend time with her."

"That's dedication to the cause."

"That's the killer all over."

"That's a good point. But he would have to have spotted them before that to know where they worked and how to manipulate them."

"Ok, so he sees them somehow before, decides that that person could be a potential victim and goes undercover at their workplace before abducting them."

"It's like Daniel said, he can live amongst us as an ordinary person, you wouldn't know he was a killer if you were talking to him or bumped into him on the street. There's nothing about him that stands out. So that's his way in."

"Take it from the top, see if this theory has stance. Isla Armstrong worked…" Barry consulted the case notes. "On the Disney Ward at Scunthorpe General Hospital. Ain't that a kids' ward? How would he have access to that ward if he's not a parent? He abducts women not children."

"He could've got access to uniform and worked in a different department that had connections to the Disney ward. A role that isn't important, not like a Doctor or a Nurse, as someone would know he wouldn't work there."

"Someone like a cleaner or a supplies specialist."

"Shit! That could have been how he got access to Succinylcholine."

"That's the muscle blocking drug, isn't it?" Barry asked, locating the postmortem report.

"Yes, his signature. He gave minute doses at a time to each of the victims which over time would have been enough to eventually shut their bodies down."

"Jesus."

"We followed up on the supplies to find if there had been any drugs missing in large quantities, but it is commonly used

CHAPTER 60

as anaesthesia and gets stocked up regularly so there weren't any suspicions."

"You would come across a number of women working in the hospital in different positions so that's maybe why he thought he would try there. Saw Isla and that was that."

"Ok, Madison McKinley?" Barry asked.

"She attended the annual Parker, Prescott and Skinner event at the City Hall in Sheffield. It's widely publicised so it wouldn't have been difficult to find out about it. Similar to the hospital, he probably thought he had a wide choice of women to choose from, attended as a lawyer who worked at one of their firms or as a candidate and spotted Madison there, and again made up his mind and she became a dead woman walking as Norton has phrased previously."

"Possible."

"All of this is hearsay."

"But you can't argue with the logic."

"Who was after Isla?" Barry asked.

"Anna Shaw. The case file that says three on it."

Barry nodded as he located the file. "So what about Anna Shaw?"

"She was an Estate Agent, originally from Bristol but moved to Scunthorpe five months before she was murdered."

"The killer posed as a potential buyer?"

"It would have been easy to abduct her if they were viewing a house on their own."

"A bogus viewing."

"He's a busy man! If he works full-time how come he can find time to execute these plans?"

"Days off, lunch breaks, after work. He found time."

"Lavinia already mentioned that the killer could have posed as a client before abducting Tracey Evans."

Ruth Damson was victim number five. "Ruth was a schoolteacher at Scotter Primary. On Friday 12th August, her husband went away for the weekend on a school trip, came back Monday 15th August to find the house empty and no sign of Ruth. She was a few weeks pregnant. Found that Monday morning."

"So somehow the killer got to her whilst Ruth was at home on her own?"

"We can only presume that was what happened. The midwife, Katy, says she didn't receive any calls from her over the weekend."

"How did he abduct her then?"

"We don't know."

Victim number six. Unknown.

"What's interesting about the latest victim is, not only the change in location, but the killer waited an unusual period of time before he killed again."

"You're thinking you got too close to identifying him and he cooled off for a while, putting some distance between himself and the killings?"

"That would make sense. But it's all wrong. The victims are found on a Monday morning, but this one was found Wednesday afternoon some weeks after the last one."

"If we think he's after Lavinia, then it could be that he waited for her to go back to university."

"And now he's nearly finished," Morgan voiced what the others were thinking but no one wanted to say it aloud.

"These crosswords, do they point to any clues?"

"They highlight the religiousness of the murders, and that reminds me, has anyone got this morning's paper?"

Barry left the room and barked at the remaining staff whether they had a copy of the day's paper somewhere. One FI had left a folded copy on his desk and Barry grabbed it before returning. He passed it to Wilson who unfolded The Sentinel. He started at the back and made his way forward to the page he was looking for. He stared at the mini crossword and passed it around the table.

"Yep, that's the one. Seven clues all to do with the killings. Gerald Fischer, the puzzle page publisher for Scunthorpe Telegraph, was given an anonymous crossword and money in

CHAPTER 60

cash in an envelope. The crossword appeared on the morning that the victims were found, which seems to be the same for this one. We would need to speak with the puzzle publisher of The Sentinel to confirm it's the same story we all know so well by now."

"Who is the puzzle guru?"

Wilson looked for a name. "Chris Lansbury."

"I'll get Nick to contact this Lansbury person," Barry said and Wilson nodded his thanks. "So nothing you can deduce from these crosswords?"

"There's copies of the previous five in each of the case files. We believe the clues point to the murders as a whole as opposed to that specific victim, supporting the theory that these victims are random. If it was personal I believe the crosswords would be personal too and more directed to each victim individually."

The clues in The Sentinel were as follows:

Across
   3.Last But One (11)
   4.Lapse (7)
   5.Parts of a Play (4)
   6.Redemption (9)
   7.Worker's Respite

Down
   1.Relation, or Link (10)
   2. Epilogue (6)

No one spoke while Barry looked at the newspaper in disbelief.

"Just another way to toy with us, to play games with us," Wilson said.

"And they're all similar?" Barry asked, looking up from the newspaper and directing his question towards Wilson.

"Yes, all seem to be clues in one way or another."

"So, what are we saying for these clues?"

The absence of sound occurred once again while they all pondered over the clues and possible answers in hushed tones.

After a moment of deliberation, the team discussed their findings, and concluded:

Penultimate, failure, acts, salvation, weekend, connection and finale.

"Well he's coming to the end of his show."

"I'm sure you have gone through the inference but now that we have six in total, what can we infer across all six crosswords as a whole?"

"He's communicating to us through these crosswords, it's all an act, all for show, a game and even the crosswords are a game in itself." Morgan referred to the cat and mouse clue from the earlier crossword and the two references of game from the second and fifth crosswords. "Additionally, game and referring to the clue, slaughtered meat, from the second crossword, he sees the victims as prey, the centre of his play, and us, the detectives are the audience."

"I don't think they really add that much to the investigation. It just adds to the speculation and we can infer all we want to but it doesn't get us anywhere. We could deduce all of this just from the state the victims are found in and from Daniel's expert opinion. It's clear these crosswords are just a diversion tactic, something else we have to think about. We're thinking too much into what these crosswords symbolise that we aren't investigating the killer or the crimes because we think these will help us to get there but they don't. They ask more questions than they give us answers," Tom speculated.

"That's a different approach. But actually I can see why you would say that. Anyone else got something to add?" Barry asked.

"As we've already established, he has a very strong dislike for women, he thinks of his victims as weak, sinful

CHAPTER 60

and in need of redemption from the religious references and teachings," Norton added.

"So all in all, he is targeting women who have done bad in one way or another and believes he is doing good by torturing them for justice and therefore feels he is redeeming them and himself," Barry concluded sceptically.

"Yep, I think that pretty much sums it up," Norton replied.

"What a load of bollocks."

CHAPTER 61

Lavinia could not wait to take a shower and change out of her Lacrosse uniform. She was exhausted from the match and her eyes only grew more tired with each piece of paper she read in the case files. It had been a long day and an even longer evening.

When Lavinia had left campus to head to the forensic unit of Staffordshire Police in Hanley, it had been light. Upon her return, the streetlamps bathed the road in an orange glow, spotlighting the way for pedestrians and drivers alike in the dark.

Tom had returned with the others, finding a hotel nearby for the night. There had been so much to go through and investigate. It wasn't over yet.

The Uber stopped outside the black door to her student accommodation on Ashford Street; the place Lavinia had called home away from home, although home back in Lincolnshire would no longer be home without Alastair. This was the closest thing she had now.

She thanked the driver and shut the rear passenger door. She saw him drive off and stood on the pavement for a second, looking around at her surroundings. She saw rows of terraced houses along the street, a sandwich shop at the end of her road had been boarded up for the night until it opened at 8am in the morning. Several lights were on in the houses, and she wondered whether the people occupying those houses, students or residents alike felt safe. Or even if they thought about safety. She knew the houses occupied along her street were mainly student accommodation and the only thing they would probably have to worry about

CHAPTER 61

was making the next assignment deadline or how expensive bread and cheese was.

She enjoyed the fresh air on her face and took a deep breath.

As she turned to put the key in the lock, her eyes picked up a sound. She could her the thumping of bass music meaning someone nearby was having a party. She realised it was Wednesday night after all and that meant the majority of the students would be out tonight at the on-campus club, LRV. The music most likely meant a pre going out party.

Normally, she would be one of those students, donning on a fancy dress costume and having a few drinks with her Lacrosse team, playing lethal party games before making her way to the LRV where nothing but cheesy hits played until 3am.

But not tonight.

As she opened the door, she was immediately met by the familiar sight and warmth of her home. Sarah was sat on the sofa, ready to go out with her football team, wearing black jeans and a mesh top, when she looked into the hallway to see Lavinia entering.

"Where did you get to?" she asked concernedly, her Cheshire accent coming through a notch when she was worried.

As Lavinia made her way into the living room and sat down on the sofa, she replied, "Oh, just been with the team in Verve for a while then we went to Holly's halls." Sarah was one of her closest friends, but Lavinia couldn't even tell her anything. She hated lying but found herself to be quite natural at doing so and the lies just flowed from her mouth. Not a good thing, she noted to herself.

"Just seen on the news what happened."

"I know, it's awful."

"Did you finish your match or was it cut short because of what happened?"

"Cut short."

"I wonder what happened?"

"No idea. Didn't see the body, just heard from Paige and even that sounded horrible."

"Did Paige see the body?"

"Yeah she did. Even with Paige on our course and studying forensics, she was shaken up a bit."

"I guess it's the shock of seeing the body. Not something you expect during a match."

"Nope. But how did you get on with your match today?"

"Won 5-3."

"Well done you."

"Thank you. Means we're second in the league now."

"You could do it again this year." Staffordshire Women's Football team won their league last year and were working towards becoming reigning Champions. They have even been given another weekly training slot by the Sports Centre staff as support.

"Hoping so, but there's still a long way to go. You going out tonight?"

"Nope. Got a date with a nice long hot bath and an early night."

"Sounds better to be honest."

"I think so. Anyway, enjoy your night celebrating the win and I'll see you tomorrow." Lavinia got up and headed into her room, which was the only downstairs bedroom in the house, just left off the front door.

"Night."

CHAPTER 62

He was watching at a distance.
He was lurking in the shadows.

He was waiting for his moment.

He saw the Uber stop in the middle of the road. It wasn't clear which house the driver had stopped at, as it could have been any house in the row.

He saw her emerge from the car and she waited.

He held his breath, even though she could not see him and he had no chance of being spotted.

He did not know why she was waiting outside. Was she waiting for someone? Was she waiting for something to happen?

He watched on, never taking his eyes off her.

He thought that he had been stupid, committing crimes in this county. The amount of evidence to link the two crimes was overwhelming and he might have even got away with it all, but his plan was not over yet.

He could not rest until he had fulfilled his final act. The finale.

He saw movement and she had gone inside her house, confirming he had identified the correct house earlier.

He may never have been a student himself, but he knew they liked to party and drink and would not give up an excuse to do just that.

He knew the house was occupied by three other people.

He knew one of those would go out celebrating a home win from her earlier match.

He knew the other two would go out together.

He also knew Lavinia.

He would wait until the house was empty. Well empty enough so that only one occupant remained.

He would wait until then.

CHAPTER 63

Tom had a gut feeling that something was wrong. He couldn't explain what or why, it was just pure instinct, and he did not like that feeling one bit. Especially since the killer was roaming in the area. And seeking out his next target.

Lavinia.

He knew Lavinia was safe in her house, as long as her housemates were there; however, he knew that they would all be going out that evening, leaving Lavinia alone.

And alone in a house with no one to hear you would be prime time for the killer to strike.

He didn't want to be overprotective of her, or overstep the mark, knowing that she could handle herself in any situation.

But when it's someone who wants to kill you, that situation differs slightly and he couldn't help but fear for her life.

He sat on the edge of his bed in the hotel room. It was a standard room, with an en-suite, a desk, tea and coffee making facilities and a wardrobe that opened up to an ironing board and a hair dryer.

He sat for a while contemplating whether to conduct a covert surveillance operation overnight to make sure no one entered the house, or to stay on her sofa in case of any unwanted intruders, or whether a simple phone call would suffice.

He reached for the phone, subconsciously deciding on the latter option. He would opt for the other options if it was deemed necessary.

CHAPTER 63

He dialled her mobile number and the phone started ringing.

After three rings, it was picked up. "Hey," the voice on the other end of the line said.

"Hey," he responded letting out a breath he did not know he was holding in. Tom had thought of the actions he would take if Lavinia had not answered the phone but failed to think what he would say if she did answer, like now. So he quickly added the reason for calling, "Just thought I'd check in."

"You know you don't have to do that. I did refuse any security so you don't have to take up that role. Sarah has left to go to a pre drinks party and Lucy and Beth won't leave until a bit later so you don't have to worry or keep checking in after they've gone."

"Sorry, it's habit I suppose. Just make sure you lock all windows and doors and don't answer the door to anyone but Sarah, Beth and Lucy."

"Roger that. I have a bath running so gotta go."

And with that she hung up.

Tom should have been satisfied that she was all right, and he did feel somewhat more relaxed after doing so, but he could not shift that niggling feeling.

The only way he would be able to sleep every night was if he were to guard Lavinia's front door from a distance and that is exactly what he decided to do as he grabbed his keys, his wallet and phone from the desk and exited his room.

CHAPTER 64

Lavinia was singing away to a Natasha Bedingfield song, submerged in lavender bubble bath, that she barely heard a knock on the bathroom door. She scrambled to turn the music down so she could hear Lucy's Yorkshire accent penetrating through the door, telling her that they were leaving. They exchanged goodbyes and Lavinia waited until she heard the front door slam shut to turn the music back up.

She turned the music up a little louder this time, so she did not hear the unlocking of the gate in the back yard. Normally the security light would come on, illuminating the trespasser in a spotlight that would give him away; however, the light was broken and had been for several days. He, of course, knew this from surveying the property.

He crept slowly down the concreted yard towards the back door which would hopefully be his entry point. As a test, during the majority of his previous attempts, the back door had been left unlocked, so he was hoping luck would be on his side again tonight, otherwise his plans were disrupted.

He saw a light on in the bathroom and could hear music playing, which was an added bonus, thinking it would make his work a lot easier. There was also a light on in the kitchen and a light on in the living room. Making sure no one could see him, he grabbed the handle with one hand and slowly pulled it down and with the other hand on the door he gradually pushed it open, trying to be as quiet as he could.

The door was ajar, just enough so he could slither through the gap. He placed his right foot just inside the hallway that separated the kitchen to the main bathroom, never taking his eye off the target, and made sure it was safe to proceed.

CHAPTER 64

Putting all his weight on his right foot, he lifted the other one and slipped inside. He was as careful to close the door as he was to open it.

The door made a slight noise as it closed, but with the music playing at the volume it was, he went undetected.

He glided through the kitchen with triumph and took a seat on the sofa, feeling smug with himself. He flicked through the channels on the TV and even took a tour of the house, all the while Lavinia was blissfully unaware. He finished in the downstairs bedroom, which he knew to be Lavinia's room, and stared at the photos of Alastair.

What was he feeling? Guilt? Remorse? Sadness?

He was trying to feel something but couldn't.

He then spotted Lavinia's purple lacrosse stick in the corner of the room, propped up against the wall, with a yellow ball in the net. He picked up the stick, threw the ball into the air and caught it in the net. He attempted this a second time but missed the net and the ball fell to the floor with a loud thud. He remained quiet, thinking he had disturbed Lavinia, but as he listened closely he could hear the beat of music.

He breathed out.

He was getting too cocky and decided to stop messing around and wait.

And that's exactly what he did.

He vacated the room, switching the light off as he went.

CHAPTER 65

Tom pulled up in a bay across the street, killed the headlights, turned off the engine and sat back, looking out of the windscreen. He was close enough that he could view the front door and the downstairs window, which he knew was the window to Lavinia's room, but not too close that she would spot his car if she looked out.

He had done stakeouts before when waiting for a suspect to make a move or to protect a witness or a potential victim, so he was prepared for the long night. He brought snacks and a flask of coffee with him. And he set his watch to buzz every half hour, in hope that if he did accidentally fall asleep, his watch would wake him up.

From his point he could see Lucy was putting on make-up whilst sat at her desk staring into a light up mirror. Her curtains were fully open, her bedroom window looking out over the street.

Every now and then, Lucy would turn her head and speak to someone at her bedroom door or take a sip of whatever drink was in her glass.

After the first half hour, followed by the first watch buzz, Lucy had finished putting her make-up on and had disappeared out of view to come back into view ten minutes later to grab her bag.

No movement from Lavinia's room, even with the curtains shut and the light switched on.

A few minutes later, Beth and Lucy emerged from the front door, the cool evening air notably caught them unawares as they both shivered. Beth locked up and tried the handle to confirm it was locked before she put the keys in her

CHAPTER 65

bag. Alcohol in hand, they hastily walked down the street, heading away from the house and disappeared out of sight.

Still no movement from Lavinia.

He wrote a thorough description of what he saw and at what time to help with the timeline, just in case anything were to happen.

He noted that the light in Lavinia's room was on.

Moments later, the light was switched off.

CHAPTER 66

Lavinia had turned down the music as she was getting out of the bath and put her teal towel poncho over her head. It looked like an oversized hoodie but was made with microfibre. She felt the lavender had done its job as she was very relaxed and couldn't wait to make a cup of tea, pig out on some snacks and select an easy watching film on Netflix to fall asleep to. God, she really needed it after today's excitement.

She drained the water in the bath, picked up her speaker and exited the bathroom.

As she walked through the kitchen and into the lounge, she felt a slight chill. The house wasn't particularly cold; in fact, it was sweltering most of the time, but the temperature right now was comfortable.

She looked around and noticed that the main light in the lounge had been switched off and was replaced by a dimly lit light emitting from a small lamp on the TV stand. She guessed that Lucy or Beth sorted the lights out just before they left, but then again, Lavinia thought they would have just left the lights on in the lounge as they were. But she didn't question it further.

Then she thought to herself that the chill must have been because she had moved from a small enclosed room that kept warm, to open areas of the kitchen and lounge where the heat had more space to circulate.

She turned the music off, and thought she was just being stupid and overly cautious, which she couldn't blame herself after today.

But then she smelt something.

CHAPTER 66

Or she thought she did.

It was only a very subtle whiff, but when she sniffed again, it was definitely there.

A woody, cedar smell.

Cologne perhaps?

She thought she was going mad.

Where had that come from?

She recognised the smell but couldn't place where she had smelt it before.

It could've easily have come from Sarah herself as she used it sporadically, but she tended to stick to Vera Wang's Princess perfume, or any of Sarah's friends from the football team as a lot of them used masculine scents and a couple of them were here earlier, or, it could've come from Beth's boyfriend, the latter being the most obvious choice. There were reasonable explanations.

She proceeded to her room which was right off the wooden hallway. The hallway was submerged in darkness, which again she thought was strange as she could've sworn she kept the lights on in her room which would have illuminated the hallway for her. She could've just turned them off subconsciously.

Her mind was doing a lot of thinking tonight, her brain making her think things that were suspicious but were actually very plausible and reasonable, and she needed to switch off before she went to sleep.

Shaking her head, she reached out for the light switch, but before she could flick it on, her world went as black as the hallway.

CHAPTER 67

He exited the same way he came in, through the back yard, where the gate led out into an alleyway. From the gate he would turn right and arrive at his car which was parked at the end of the alleyway for a quick escape. It was completely dead and deserted at that time of night.

Perfect.

Only this time, he had the dead weight of an unconscious Lavinia flung over his shoulder, which slowed his pace ever so slightly.

But he was making good progress nonetheless.

The gate was on the latch, and so he only had to lift the latch to exit. The alleyway was a black hole, nothing but darkness, save for the light at either end of the tunnel. During the day, the alleyway was strewn with litter and people fly tipping, old sofas discarded, electrical equipment abandoned and even heaps of black rubbish bins dumped, an invite for rodents to gnaw through. No wonder rats were an issue for many.

He turned right and his car boot was visible and exactly where he had left it.

Reaching the end of the alleyway, he carefully took Lavinia off his shoulder and put his arm around her back as if to support her walking. If anyone even looked in his direction, he would explain he was taking a drunk friend home. A believable story and very admirable of himself, he thought. If only that were the truth. It was just a precaution, but he needn't have bothered as there was not one person in sight that would question his actions.

CHAPTER 67

Taking a swift look left and right to make sure he was all alone, he lifted the boot of the car and placed Lavinia into it, morphing her body to lie on her side in the foetal position. He then very quietly and very carefully closed the boot before resuming his seat behind the wheel. The turn of the keys in the ignition roared the car into life. Shifting into first gear, he accelerated away and headed in the direction of a place he knew that he could not be found and would not be disturbed to carry out his finale.

He beamed at the ease of it all. Lavinia had played right into the palm of his hand and it was all going to plan.

CHAPTER 68

By early morning, Tom was satisfied with his watch. Apart from Sarah returning at a reasonable hour, and Lucy and Beth stumbling back at 4.30am, with a takeaway box in hand, laughing to each other whilst fumbling with the key, there had been no activity.

Lavinia's curtains were still closed, but Tom did not expect her to be awake and up at 6.30am.

Yawning and stretching the best he could whilst sat in the car, he decided it was time to end the covert surveillance and head back in time for breakfast at the hotel.

When Tom arrived back at the hotel a short while later, he nipped upstairs to his room to freshen up. After showering and changing clothes, he was ready for the day ahead.

But first coffee, he thought, making a beeline straight for the coffee machine and opted for a double espresso, for which he received strange looks from the woman stood in line behind him, as he downed it in one and then selected hot water for an English Breakfast tea.

He had spotted Wilson and the team already sat at a table, all digging into their different breakfast items; Wilson had a mega English breakfast, doubling up on everything, which Tom knew he was taking full advantage of as his wife, Denise, would absolutely murder him if she found out he was eating a heart attack on a plate, while Harris and Norton were tucking into an English breakfast butty with a pastry on the side and Morgan had a bowl of granola, fruit and yoghurt. Tom went to take the remaining seat at the table.

CHAPTER 68

An echo of "morning" was exchanged between them all as Tom sat down.

Morgan studied him for a moment. "Not to sound rude but you look like shit."

"Always the brutally honest one," Norton chirped back.

"I was keeping an eye on Lavinia and her housemates all night."

"You do realise she objected to any kind of security or surveillance, don't you?"

"I do, but I wouldn't have slept anyway. I'm sure she was more relaxed knowing we weren't there officially."

"Anything of interest to report back?"

"Nope, apart from her housemates, no one was seen entering or leaving the property the whole time."

"Well, you'd better ring her after breakfast then and get her to meet us back at the forensic unit in Hanley 10am." The time was just before 7.30.

Tom nodded and the rest of breakfast went by with ease and small talk.

It was 8am before they got back to their rooms, to get ready for the day of assisting Staffordshire Police with their murder inquiry and another ruthless day searching through previous victims' case files to see if they could decipher any more links between the cases, between the victims themselves, and between the victim and the killer.

Tom dialled Lavinia's number only to realise it had been switched off.

How odd, he thought.

The same thing happened five minutes later when he tried again.

He tried once more before leaving his room and could still not get through.

Wilson and the team met downstairs in the reception area where Tom informed him that he hadn't been able to reach Lavinia.

"I'll go over there now before heading to the forensics unit."

"We can walk from here, you take the car and keep us updated," Wilson instructed, and with that Tom was quickly on his way.

CHAPTER 69

Lavinia's eyes opened slowly, starting with a blur and with every blink that felt like a difficult task her eyes began to focus.

Her body was aching all over. She hadn't gone out last night so she shouldn't be feeling as if she had the worst hangover in the world.

But she did.

Her neck was aching, she must have slept in a weird position. Her head felt heavy and tender, like the remnants of a migraine, and she felt nauseous and weak.

With all her might, she slowly lifted her head and was confused by her surroundings.

Unbeknown to Lavina, it was daylight outside, but to her, it could have been the middle of the night, as a couple of gas lanterns were the only warm natural glow to emit any source of light.

Despite that, she couldn't make out her surroundings that well. After looking properly, she noticed that the light was more focused on her than to help see anything else in the room, swallowing her up in a spotlight. She could make out the chair she was sat on, hard and uncomfortable. She looked strangely at the clothing she was wearing and didn't know she owned a pair of grey tracksuit bottoms and an oversized t shirt. Her arms felt overstretched and were getting sore at the shoulders, and she was going to give then a good stretch, until she realised they were tied behind the chair back and she couldn't move. She could hear an echo, like someone was moving around in a hollow space. She could smell mustiness, like it was a place that wasn't frequently met with fresh air or used that often. A strange metallic taste entered her mouth every now and then but she didn't know the source of the taste.

Is this what the other victims woke up to? Is this what they thought when they came-to?

Despite having investigated five murders, not being able to comprehend how much pain they would have been in, how much fear they would have felt, she was now living their nightmare.

She let out a groan when she tried to speak, everything suddenly felt hard to do, alerting her captor that she was now awake.

He came and perched on a stool in front of her, using a finger under her chin to pull her head up so she could meet his eyes.

Her eyes widened in disbelief and recognition and then to fear and confusion.

"You."

CHAPTER 70

When Tom arrived back at Lavinia's, he tried her mobile once more, but with the same outcome as before.

He got out of the car, sauntered over to the front door and banged on it with a closed fist which had worked as Lucy screamed out of the second-floor window.

Tom looked up to the sound of the voice and identified himself. "I've been trying to contact Lavinia all morning but she's not answering. Is it possible to be let in?"

Lucy looked annoyed at having been woken up, but obliged, shutting the window, and going downstairs.

Not understanding Tom's urgency, she opened the door to him as you would a friend. He responded by pushing himself inside and immediately entered Lavinia's bedroom. He saw the bed had already been made up. Either that or it had never been slept in. He glanced in Lucy's direction.

"Where could she be?"

Lucy shrugged her shoulders.

"When was the last time you saw Lavinia?"

"Last night before we left, she was in the bath."

"Any idea where she could have gone?"

"No idea."

A frustrated Tom pushed past Lucy and almost ran up the stairs, storming into Sarah's room.

The noise had immediately woken Sarah up. Still groggy from sleep she found her glasses which were sat on the desk at the end of the bed and asked, "What's going on?"

"Does Lavinia have any classes, lectures, lab sessions, gym sessions, work? Anything going on this morning?" Tom half asked, half demanded, earning a confused look from Sarah.

Wracking her brain to look at an imaginary timetable inside her head, she slowly shook her head. "No, she doesn't have anything on today as far as I'm aware. No lectures or lab sessions anyway."

"Do you know if she went out anywhere last night?" he asked with a softer tone. Lucy was stood in the doorway and so Tom directed his question to them both.

Even though Tom had watched the front door all night, there was always the possibility that Lavinia could have spotted him and decided to sneak out the back. He didn't understand why she would do that but couldn't rule that option out.

Lucy responded to Tom's question with, "she told us she was staying in all night. I assumed she had a bath and went to bed".

"None of you checked her room when you got in last night?"

"We had no reason to and tried to be as quiet as we could so we wouldn't disturb her," Sarah admitted.

"Beth and I may have been a bit loud, but I never saw her," Lucy added.

Tom wracked his brain, thinking of various scenarios and explanations. Then it hit him.

Shit.

In that moment, everything suddenly dawned on him, explaining so much, and he realised he had been dupped.

Immediately reaching for his phone, he dialled Wilson's number as he evacuated Sarah's room, almost slid down the stairs and ran to the back door. Trying the handle, his suspicions were confirmed.

Even though his phone call was answered after two rings, it felt like an eternity.

"He's taken her."

CHAPTER 71

Those three words did not register with Wilson to begin with, he was confused with what, or rather who, Tom was talking about.

"What?"

"Our killer, he must have entered through the back door and taken Lavinia," Tom barely breathed the words out as he paced the living room.

Wilson now understood what Tom was talking about and his face paled. He had one duty to Lavinia, one duty to Alastair to keep her safe, and he had failed. Again.

Wilson felt that he had only led the killer to Lavinia.

Sarah and Lucy joined Tom in the living room, overhearing his conversation with Wilson.

"She was fine when we left," Lucy pleaded, as if trying to clear herself of any suspicions.

"Was the back door unlocked when you left?"

"Not that I know of. I always lock it afterwards. The lock can be tough, so I always try the handle to make sure it's locked," Sarah explained.

"I didn't use the back door yesterday at all."

Tom then realised he was only speaking to two out of three of Lavinia's housemates and asked if Beth was upstairs. Lucy went to wake her.

It took a few minutes, but when Beth entered the living room, Tom explained the situation and asked her about the back door.

Wracking her brain back to yesterday, which after a few drinks last night, seemed a bit fuzzy to her and she took a moment until she answered casually. "I took the rubbish out yesterday." Then she looked horrified at the seriousness of her actions. "And I don't remember locking the door."

CHAPTER 72

His smile was menacing, there was no warmth behind it, it was chilling and made his eyes ice over with coldness.

Her heart sunk with the realisation that she had been right all along. She hadn't wanted to have been, but being trapped here with him and facing him now, confirmed her worst nightmare.

In that moment he had replaced his usual amiability, politeness and professionalism with a certain sinisterism that made Lavinia's blood curdle.

Her arms felt numb and when she looked to her left, realised why. He had attached a drip to her arm that she knew contained the muscle blocking drug, succinylcholine, one of his signature torture techniques to weaken his victims. However, her brain working behind time, then questioned why she got special treatment. He normally administered the drug via a drink. She could only guess that he was in more control with a drip as he could administer as much as he liked in one go or that he wanted to administer a lethal dose quickly in a short amount of time as it would go directly to her veins and then circulate around her body quicker than through his usual route.

She realised that with his earlier victims, he had wanted to keep them alive, to be a spectator to their own death by prolonging maximum pain, to see themselves slowly die, to realise the inevitable was coming and no one was there to save them.

But this time was different.

He didn't want to take his time to weaken, to torture his victim.

He just wanted to kill her.

CHAPTER 73

"What do we know so far?" Wilson asked. The team were situated in the incident room of the forensic unit in Hanley. They had met to investigate the latest murder of the body found in the stream at the end of the field pitch at Staffordshire University when Wilson got the dreaded call from Tom.

All efforts were put to finding Lavinia. If they found Lavinia, then she would lead them to their killer.

But if they took too long, they knew what they would find and every endeavour would be taken to ensure it did not happen.

"Lavinia was last seen just before 9pm last night, her last known whereabouts were at her home address on Ashford Street, Shelton, Stoke on Trent. Her housemates can confirm that she was in the bath when they went out for the evening, but Lucy and Beth were the last to leave and spoke to her through the bathroom door. As far as they were aware she wasn't going out and remained at home all evening. From my covert surveillance on the house from 8pm to 6.30am, and confirmed by their own testimony, Sarah returned at the home address shortly after 1.30am and Beth and Lucy at around 4.30am. Upon checking the back door to find it unlocked we can assume that this was the killer's entry and exit point. From the back door there is a gate, which leads out onto an alleyway. He had to have had his car on standby at the nearest exit/entrance of the alleyway. The house is closer to the east exit as opposed to the west exit. The east exit opens out onto Watford Street," Tom briefed, indicating on the print out map hung on the board with pins that located Lavinia's home address and the name of the streets Tom mentioned in his statement.

"Why was the back door unlocked?"

"Beth accidentally left it unlocked after she had taken the rubbish out yesterday afternoon."

"How would he have known that the back door was open? What happened if it was locked? His plan would have been ruined. He couldn't have risked being seen abducting someone using the front door."

"What we know about this person from earlier murders, is that he meticulously plans, he meets his victims, he checks out his chosen places. He may have sneaked into the back on several previous occasions to plan his route in and out. Sarah, Lucy and Beth have admitted at some point that they have all left the door unlocked. He must have thought that that was his best chance, especially when the others were out. Again, he had to have studied this to know she would be home alone."

"The neighbours' upstairs bedroom window overlooks out onto their yard, we need to check with them in case they have seen unusual activity in recent weeks like someone sneaking in and out," Tom suggested thinking aloud.

"On it," Morgan immediately packed away her pen and notebook into her handbag and stood up exiting the room. Time was of the essence and they didn't have time to sit around and discuss a plan of action, they needed to act fast.

"It would be a good idea to check CCTV in the area and see if we can pick something up. And anything that looks remotely suspicious, investigate."

"Where could he have taken her? This isn't his area of killing so he wouldn't have access to his usual killing room."

"Good point. Conduct the same lines of enquiry as we did back home with looking for remote abandoned warehouses and the like, possibly even go as far to extend that to storage units within a ten-mile radius."

****

CHAPTER 73

Morgan knocked on the front door of Lavinia's neighbours and was greeted by a male of similar age to Lavinia, whom she guessed was also a student at the university.

Morgan introduced herself, presenting her ID badge to a very confused looking man, who introduced himself as Joe. She explained the reason for her visit and asked if she could access the property to look at the viewpoint over Lavinia's back yard.

Joe obliged, opening the door wider for Morgan to enter and instructed her where to go. She hesitated in the lounge to ask him a few questions before making her way to the upstairs back bedroom.

"Were you in last night?"

"All of us were out for the evening until early this morning."

"Us?"

"Myself and my three other housemates," clarified Joe.

"Where did you all go last night?"

"We all went out to pre drinks at one of the halls on campus and then made our way to the on-campus bar and club."

"At what time did you all leave for pre drinks?"

"Pre drinks started around 8.30 but we didn't leave here until just after 9."

"You didn't hear or see anyone around that time?"

"We saw quite a few people around. At that time on a Wednesday evening, the campus and areas in the vicinity of the university are buzzing with people heading to pre drinks or heading to the on-campus club or into Hanley for a night out, so it wasn't unusual to see people."

"Did you go out the back or the front when you left?"

"We always go out the back when we're all out for the evening. If one of us stays in, then we go out the front. We only bolt the top of the gate but it's easy to reach over and unbolt the top and we leave the back door unlocked."

Morgan gave him a sceptical look, like a mother giving a 'I'm not angry just disappointed' look to a son, so he carried on. "A bit dodgy, especially in this area I know, but we lost the key to the house once and the landlord charged us stupid money to have it replaced so we've done that ever since," he explained.

"Upstairs on the left did you say?" she indicated to the room above them, as this was the reason for her visit. Joe nodded his head and Morgan proceeded upstairs. The stairs were like climbing Helvellyn, they were that steep, she thought. Once in the bedroom, which she learned from Joe, it belonged to another housemate of his, Scott, she took a quick scan around. It was relatively tidy, and with the Xbox, football paraphernalia and musty smell, it was definitely a masculine room.

She crossed over to the window which looked out onto the yard of their property. Weeds were growing in the cracks of the concrete but there were four desk chairs laid out and a BBQ that was currently covered up. To her right, she saw into Lavinia's yard. The same weeds seemed to be growing in their yard too, Morgan thought. She concentrated on the alleyway as someone walked past, and she noticed you could just about make out head and shoulders.

"And throughout the evening was Scott in his room or was he in the communal areas like the living room, for example?"

"When we got back, we showered, changed and then started drinking in the living room and ordered takeaway so we were all together most of the evening."

"Back from where?"

"Rugby, we had a match."

"And when did you get back from playing rugby?"

"Sixish, I think. We finished, watched the lacrosse game for bit and then the rugby team headed to Verve for a couple of drinks and then we came here. I didn't check the time, sorry."

CHAPTER 73

"That's all right." Morgan worked out that six o'clock was probably too early for the killer anyway. She expected he was nearby, maybe even watching from a distance, counting down the hours, minutes, seconds, feeling very calm and excited as the time ticked nearer. Even if he had been around at that time, he would have just blended in with the crowd, just another person walking in the street on a fine autumn afternoon. "The gate leads out onto the alleyway, where did you go after you bolted the gate?"

"We headed right onto Watford Street." Joe pointed out his route from the window. They couldn't see Watford Street from their viewpoint, but Morgan got the general direction of travel.

"And you didn't come across anyone hanging around in the alleyway or looking suspicious by your next-door neighbours?"

"No one, as I said, we saw loads of people, but didn't take any notice of anyone in particular."

"Did you see anyone *in* the alleyway at the time you left?" Morgan asked again, emphasising her question, getting the feeling that Joe hadn't quite understood her previous question.

A moment of silence passed between them as Joe was thinking back. "Err, there was a couple, two girls I think, at the end of the alleyway approaching Guilford Street." Joe pointed this out from the window showing Morgan the direction of travel, which was in the opposite direction to Watford Street. "And then a man walked past us as we were heading towards Watford Street."

"Can you describe this man? Was he tall, short? Was his face covered? Hair colour, length, style? Can you describe the clothing he wore?"

"Sorry, I can't. None of us paid any attention to anyone else. The four of us had been drinking here before we left, we were in our own bubble, drinks in hand, talking. We didn't bother anyone else and no one bothered us."

"Do you know your neighbours well?"

"I'd say fairly well, and I'd say out of the four of us, I probably know them slightly better. I take a similar course to Sarah, Lucy and Lavinia, so some of our modules have crossed over. I also play a sport as does Sarah and Lavinia, so our paths have crossed there as well."

"I assume you have heard about the body found during Lavinia's lacrosse match yesterday?"

"I have, yes. It's all over campus."

"Did you witness the incident?"

"Fortunately, no, I didn't. We'd not long finished our rugby match before they started, so we watched the first fifteen or twenty minutes and then we left."

Morgan thanked him for his time, handed him her business card and evacuated the house.

She closed the door behind her, stepped away from the house and looked out at nothing in particular. She took a deep breath, inhaling the fresh air and whispered to herself, "Come on, Lavinia, where are you?"

CHAPTER 74

There was a different sense of urgency as everyone gathered in the incident room to try and save the life of one of their own.

And time was running out.

Norton had the mundane task of going through the CCTV that was picked up by a camera located on the corner of Ashford Street, where Lavinia lived. He would be able to see cars entering and exiting the street only. But they had to start somewhere and it was as good of a place as any. The killer would have no doubt driven to her street by car, transported Lavinia by car and driven to the place he had taken her using the same car, so if Norton could cross reference the CCTV footage to pick up the car at multiple points from multiple cameras en route, he would be able to follow the killer's path and that ultimately would lead to Lavinia.

Once he spotted a car turning into Ashford Street, he looked up the number plate on the ANPR system to see if there was anything worth investigating further, for example, if the car had been reported stolen recently, he would look at other cameras to see if he could follow the car's journey; however, if the records checked out, which was 98% of the cars he had already investigated, he could swiftly move on.

He was getting frustrated because this process seemed to be taking too long and nothing of interest seemed to crop up. Car after car was legitimate, and he was sure he was wasting valuable time.

Harris was sat opposite Norton, conducting the same line of enquiry, only Harris was looking at the CCTV footage from another viewpoint. You could also get to Ashford Street via College Road. Whichever direction you entered Ashford Street, it was off a main road and so the killer would have had to use a main road to get to wherever he was based now. There was the possibility that the killer would not take the most straightforward and obvious route to get to Lavinia's house, of course, but there was no other way to get around it, it was inevitable that the cameras would pick him up at some point en route.

Just like Norton, Harris checked the number plates of every car that passed into view.

Norton's interest piped up as the records for the next car he saw was interesting. Norton noted the reg in his notebook and disturbed Harris.

"Harris, check if a Silver Ford Focus with the reg November Uniform six three Golf Victor November is seen from your camera viewpoint." Norton read the registration plate from his notebook and shifted around the desk to join Harris as they both looked intensely at his computer screen.

"Wind the footage to 22.12."

"What's so interesting about this car?"

"It was reported stolen a couple of days ago." Norton did not need to explain the importance of that piece of information.

"Shit," was all Harris said in response as he knew the significance of that statement.

They watched on for a few seconds, Norton's stomach twisting with nerves as they waited to see if the car would appear on Harris's screen.

"There!" Norton shouted and pointed to the screen as the car in question came into view. The car sped down Ashford Street from College Road, slowing right down as it approached the row of houses where Lavinia's was situated and turned left into Watford Street.

"Well doesn't that look as suspicious as hell?" Harris asked the rhetorical question. Harris jumped the footage on,

CHAPTER 74

only finding the car leaving Watford Street, and heading for the main road, two and a half hours after they had spotted the car arriving.

"We have to look at the cameras on the main road, see if it can be picked up."

After speaking to Traffic Control, Harris and Norton were able to search for, locate and cross reference the CCTV footage of the car, a Silver Ford Focus with the registration plate, NU63 GVN, from multiple cameras and followed his route from Ashford Street to where the car ended its journey at a storage unit.

Norton and Harris immediately informed Wilson of this update and they raced out of the building and headed in two cars to the storage unit, contacting back up, speeding along the main road with the car sirens wailing.

This was their chance.

CHAPTER 75

Lavinia knew that crying showed weakness and she didn't want to show him that satisfaction. So she tried to continue talking to put her mind elsewhere, and to distract him.

"Okay, so I want to know why," Lavinia said weakly. "Why you killed, why these victims?"

"They're not as innocent as you would believe." Marcus was sat on a chair opposite Lavinia.

"And you are?"

"I did what was needed. Ridding the world of sin."

"And you don't think killing people is a sin?"

"Not if it's for the greater good. God is my salvation, he guided me towards those who needed saving because I am the Master of Death."

Lavinia thought that was complete and utter bullshit but didn't voice her opinion, opting to tread carefully. "And so you killed them to save them?"

Marcus's face lit up as if Lavinia had just understood him. "They would have continued to lie, to cheat, people are fuelled by hatred and jealousy and would do anything for money, people are just lazy and greedy. Humanity was collapsing and I restored it. I was saving them from themselves."

Lavinia was dumbstruck, she didn't know what to say. Marcus seemed so professional and had a good work ethic, he was helpful, polite and was a friendly face in the team. She couldn't believe what she was hearing. She couldn't follow his reasonings. It was as if he was bipolar because the Marucs she knew and this person whom she was talking

CHAPTER 75

to now were different people, complete opposites. But that was your classic psychopath. No emotion, no attachment issues to their victims, no resentment. Able to live among others as an ordinary being and come across as normal, but it's like a light switch that can go off in their head and if the switch has been flicked, they turned.

But something made her pause.

What was it that Marcus had said earlier? She knew she had heard the phrase before as she recognised it. She kept racking her brain for an answer but her mind was blank.

"Why that specific MO? You know, the cutting off body parts, eye, ear, fingers and toes?"

"What do you think?"

Lavinia was taken aback that he was asking what she thought. She took her mind back to the crossword clues that were in the newspaper on the morning that each victim was found, how there were only seven clues and all related to the murders. "An eye for an eye, hear no evil. I don't understand the fingers and toes."

Marcus was nodding like a teacher nodded encouragement at a student for being on the right track to getting a question correct. "I was cleaning them of their sins, neutralising them. I did to them what they did to others. Justice."

"You know two wrongs don't make a right."

"In this case they do."

"I don't follow."

"In the Bible, you're familiar with an eye for an eye, a tooth for a tooth, that's all anyone seems to know, well the list goes further than that to mention a hand for a hand and a foot for a foot. But it goes deeper than that. The cutting off the toes symbolise punishment. They were punished for their sins. The fingers all have their own spiritual meaning and so by cutting them symbolises the transformation between the end of something and the beginning of something new, letting go of ties with the past, letting go of whatever they were holding onto, envy, greed, lust, jealousy etcetera, so they went to God as a redeemed person. Justice and redemption. They paid the price to make things right. Psalms *'blessed are those who act justly*, Zechariah, *'administer true justice'*, Deuteronomy, *'follow justice and justice alone so that you may live and process the land the Lord your God is giving you'*."

"Bible teachings are against murder. That wasn't justice. You went against everything that is moral so I don't know how you can stand there and tell me otherwise."

"I did them justice!" Marcus turned angry, he leapt off the chair and was inches from Lavinia's face as he spat the words at her which made her jump. "I could have just let them live freely in the world amongst us but what good would that have done? I saved them and I saved us." He continued to justify his actions.

Lavinia tried to follow his logic but everything she had learnt about murder in the bible was unforgivable and sinful.

Marcus turned away, his back to her, and walked to his tool station. She couldn't see what he was doing but it didn't sound good.

He was sharpening a knife.

CHAPTER 76

The cars skidded to a halt, and Morgan was already opening the car door before it had a chance to fully come to a stop. She raced out and ran to the entrance of the storage unit to reception.

She was met with a polite middle aged woman, but Morgan didn't have time for pleasantries. She introduced herself and her team who was just entering the building and demanded to speak to the manager. The woman looked dumbstruck at the sudden intrusion and it took a moment for her brain to register what was happening, but when that finally happened, she picked up the desk phone and called through to her manager.

Even though the manager took only minutes to walk into reception, the team were on edge and impatient, making the minutes feel like hours.

"Gary Waite, how may I help?" He strode into reception with authority, the urgency of their visit lost in translation. He had greying hair and a matching grey suit, a smart Rolex watch worn on the right wrist and polished black brogues.

"Is there somewhere else we can talk more privately. This is an urgent police matter."

Just like the middle aged woman, Gary looked astonished at the request; after all, police rarely frequented the storage unit so their appearance was a complete surprise and out of character.

The team followed Gary through to his office, which was a tight squeeze in the box room. But they immediately asked him if a Silver Ford Focus with the reg NU63 GVN had ever been seen to enter the site in recent weeks.

Gary checked the records but told them that they did not keep records of makes and registration numbers of cars passing in and out. Norton then suggested CCTV, which seemed to have overlooked Gary. It took him a while to figure out how to access the footage and how to rewind to a specific time and date. All the while, Morgan was losing patience. Gary called himself a manager but he was as good as a hairdresser was at keyhole surgery.

He finally found the footage for three weeks earlier and was told to vacate his chair while they worked on moving it forward. Gary did not like that but he had no choice.

Norton took Gary's vacated seat and moved the footage swiftly forward. A frustrated Norton went back over the footage again at a slower rate but no car with that reg was seen on video.

But how? They had traced the car from Ashford Street to this storage unit. Didn't they? Did they overlook something? There was a camera at the entry and exit point so any car that entered or exited the storage unit would be seen on CCTV.

"Has the driver erased himself from the footage?" Harris asked in disbelief.

"I saw a car of the same colour and make but it had a different reg number, which is why I didn't flag it up before, but I'll go over the footage once more," Norton admitted. And indeed, the same colour and make of car was seen entering the storage three days ago. Three days later and their latest victim was found in the stream at the university. And again, the car was only seen fifteen minutes after Lavinia had been abducted. But they could not make out any specific details of the driver.

"Is there a camera inside the building, by the indoor units or outdoor units?"

"Only by reception. We had issues of them not working and we've been trying to get them all fixed but that has been slow progress."

CHAPTER 76

"So no one can be seen going to their storage unit?"

"Not at the moment, no."

"Fuck." Norton realised the seriousness of faulty CCTV cameras. Marcus could have been going around the units with a body hung over his shoulder in broad daylight without getting caught because the cameras were down when they should have been fixed.

"We're going to have to look at the reception footage and get a description of everyone who is renting a unit."

"Ok, do what you need to," Gary gave permission.

Once again, Norton was locating the camera footage for reception. Once found he went back three days, which turned out to be a busy day for the company, but they cross referenced the time that the car was seen entering the site to when another person entered reception.

The man was tall, medium build.

The average male.

Thew CCTV footage was grainy which didn't help.

"How common is it that two cars of the same make, colour and model enter the same storage unit?"

"It's not that uncommon."

"Do you have a record of that person walking in right now?"

"I believe his name is Neville from memory."

"How often does he come to the storage unit?"

"He's a fairly new customer, I try and remember people's names. He comes a couple of times a week, three max."

"Is that standard?"

"Some people come and go, some drop things off and don't return until they're ready to collect. Some are backwards and forwards multiple times, just like this guy."

"His record please?"

Gary indicated that he needed to use the computer to access customer records.

"Yes, Neville Smith. Rented unit from 04/10/23 for a month. Has unit number 72 located indoors."

"That's a week before Lavinia was abducted. Can we get a key and search unit 72?"

"Erm, I should really get the customer's permission to access or if you guys have a warrant, I'll be happy to oblige."

"There's no time for a warrant. There is a woman's life a stake, she's one of us, and she could be dead if we don't reach her in time. You must cooperate if we have any chance of finding her alive," Morgan warned.

"And you think there's something dodgy happening in one of my units?" Gary asked dumfounded.

"Yes."

After a moment's hesitation, Gary agreed and found the key for storage unit 72. The team hastily followed as they took the elevator to the first level of storage units. They got off the elevator but warned for Gary to stay back in case there was a danger to his life.

Poised with guns in their hand in case they needed to react, Morgan unlocked the unit, but did not lift it up immediately. She nodded at her colleagues to check that they were ready and Norton had her covered.

The shutters flew up.

CHAPTER 77

"Where has all of this come from?" Hayleigh asked in astonishment.

Hayleigh and Tom were speaking over Zoom. Hayleigh's office door was closed, making it clear to her colleagues that she was not to be disturbed, at the strict request of Tom as the topic was very sensitive.

"Just answer the question," Hayleigh noted the urgency and abruptness in Tom's voice and retrieved the document from her files that Tom was asking to see.

She shared the screen to enable Tom to see the document and she also sent the file across to his email address so he had a copy of it. But he wanted her to stay on the line, with the document visible on her computer too, so Tom could ask questions if needed.

He flipped open a clean page in his notebook and set about to work, comparing schedules with the dates of each victim's disappearance to see if there was a correlation.

"You can't possibly be serious that one of us has anything to do with the murders."

"I shut Lavinia down for her theories and now she's been abducted so the least I can do is follow through and see if that leads us anywhere."

"But if you didn't believe in the theories to begin with, then why are you looking at them now?"

Tom thought she had asked a valid question. "I dunno, to do something, to feel useful."

Hayleigh sighed; when had all this got so complicated? She thought to herself.

A few moments of silence passed between them as Tom concentrated at his task.

Of course, he didn't think that Hayleigh had anything to do with any of the murders, but if he was to do a job, he had to do it properly. He swiftly checked her schedule and was taken aback at how full it was, her work schedule was hectic, especially since the start of this case. She had endless meetings, endless reports to complete, one autopsy after another, other bodies outside of the case that needed attention and answers. But this case had taken up a lot of her time so her usual work had taken a back seat and suffered as a result. She was busy playing catch up over the weekends, or late into the evenings or very early in the mornings, whenever she could spare a minute. Tom knew that someone would be able to verify her working over the weekends, whether at home or in the office. She was always on call too and never failed to answer a call.

He swiftly moved on to Zoe's' schedule which was empty compared to Hayleigh's. Hayleigh informed Tom that, unlike herself, she had weekends completely off. She had a busy social life, seeing various friends over the weekends, going to concerts, going on nights out and spending the weekend recovering, going on weekend staycation trips or quick trips out of the country. It was endless. Hayleigh did not know how she had the energy to do all that over two days and come to work fresh on Monday morning like she had spent the weekend relaxing and recuperating.

"That's the youth for you," Tom replied.

"You're her age, you should feel just as youthful."

"The only time I would stay up past 9pm would be if there was a reason to," Tom joked, to which Hayleigh laughed.

"And she leaves on time in the evenings?"

"That varies depending on what's come in, what's still left to do before the end of the day and what has already

CHAPTER 77

been completed. But generally I let her go anytime between 5pm and 6pm."

"Has she stayed later recently with this case?"

"No, I don't think so, maybe once or twice. I might have a terrible switch-off mechanism but I don't want her to fall into the same habit, so whatever the circumstance, unless I desperately require her assistance, the latest I would ever send her home would be 6.30."

Marcus's schedule was the one Tom was interested in the most.

Hayleigh explained that he too had weekends off, but she didn't know what he did. "I think he rides his bike, goes on long walks, watches TV. Zoe overshadows him really, she never stops talking, and to be quite honest, she is the more interesting one. Marcus just knuckles down and gets the job done. One time, they did have an in-depth discussion about a documentary on Netflix or National Geographic, he likes that channel. I didn't really take any notice but I think that was when Marcus stopped being so reserved. He occasionally helps Zoe if she needs an extra pair of hands but there's a limit to what he can actually do, being the photographer, he doesn't deal with the nitty gritty stuff."

"So would you say that he has more freedom than the two of you?"

"For sure. Less responsibilities, less workload, has weekends completely free, doesn't seem to have a wild social life, probably has minimum friends that aren't work colleagues. It sounds sad really."

"How is he at work?"

"He's fantastic, he's a talented photographer, he knows his stuff, just puts his head down and produces exactly what I want. Always helpful, I really have no complaints."

Tom noticed he had a block of time off between Tuesday 16th and Sunday 21st August, which Hayleigh confirmed was the fishing trip.

"What dates did Alastair go on the fishing trip?"

"Erm, let me check," Hayleigh opened the calendar app on her phone and checked the dates. "Saturday 13th August to Sunday 21st August. Although he extended his trip."

"Why did Marcus go later and return earlier?"

"He was needed at work and then he returned on Sunday for a forensic conference in London on the Monday," Hayleigh explained.

Tom checked his schedule which had the whole day blocked off with 'conference' explaining his absence.

Tom's brain was working overtime as he cross-referenced the dates at which Ruth Damson was last seen and found. She was last seen on Friday 12th August and found on Monday 15th August.

"So Marcus was still around on the weekend that Ruth was last seen and only went on the fishing trip a day after she was found." He was amazed at how well the timings fitted. Hayleigh also believed that he was free on the weekends, he didn't go anywhere with anyone, he was physically fit and didn't live with anyone. He had the time, time to stalk, time to plan a meticulous murder, time to torture, time to dispose of the bodies and turn up to work Monday mornings like nothing had happened, like he had had a quiet weekend. "He was also the last one to see Alastair."

"That was deemed as an accident."

"Do you fully believe that he had a fatal accident?"

"That's what the police concluded from their investigation. But of course not, I know Alastair and I know he wouldn't be that careless."

Tom's mind was working at a million miles an hour. There was only the two of them on that boat, Alastair would have known all about the investigation from Lavinia, he was a great detective, a great Captain and a great angler. Marcus had the means, the opportunity and the motive. The motive being that Alastair was figuring it out, he was closing in on Marcus. What a great plan to make it look like an accident.

CHAPTER 77

He made his return to Scunthorpe seem legitimate with the forensic conference so he could say when he left Alastair, he was alive and well and no one would question him. The realisation suddenly dawned on him. "You know what?"

"What?"

Tom stared directly into the camera. "I believe Lavinia was right."

CHAPTER 78

The door to the storage unit revealed what it was hiding. But it was disappointing.

The storage unit was rammed from wall to wall with furniture. A three-piece sofa suite, a fridge freezer, chest of drawers, two bedside tables, endless storage boxes and cardboard boxes, a hoover, bed frames and camping equipment.

The team felt the disappointment as they looked around the storage unit in silence, not expecting to see what they were now looking at.

"Looks like someone is in mid moving house," Norton observed, looking at a cardboard box labelled 'Kitchen' and another 'Front Bedroom Right'.

When they were satisfied that this was not the unit they were looking for, Morgan stepped away and headed towards the elevator where she found Greg waiting for them where they'd left him standing. "We're going to need a list of people who rent a storage unit and a key to access them all," she simply instructed. Gary nodded his understanding.

Wilson joined them. "Has anyone rented a storage unit within the last week or two weeks?"

Again Gary nodded.

"We'll focus on those and work backwards."

The detectives worked through the list, starting with the most recent renter, Lorraine Matt. The detectives got a key from Gary and searched unit 49 outside. When they opened the shutter they were face to face with a beauty salon. Three salon swivel chairs were covered up with seat covers, two mirrors bubble wrapped and again endless boxes of make-up,

CHAPTER 78

hair styling equipment and decorations. Lorraine Matt owned a beauty salon but was refurbishing the place so she kept all the equipment in storage and was due to rent a unit for three weeks with the possibility of extending if required.

The next unit, rented by Sam Finch, took them by surprise. He had rented the unit going on two weeks and when Morgan opened the shutters, it was completely empty. According to Gary, Sam had never visited the unit in person and simply rang up requesting a specific size and a quote giving the reason that it was urgent to store work equipment and took the one they offered him based on his specifications.

Their interest piped up.

CHAPTER 79

"So did you actually kill those women because they had sinned or because their initials spelled out I am Master of Death? Of course, you thought you were the master of death by killing women who had sinned. After all you said so yourself, ridding the world of sin. We still haven't identified the last victim but I'm guessing her initials are EA. We stopped you from finishing your show." This took Marcus by surprise. He thought he had been clever, but he had really underestimated Lavinia. He should have killed her first. Lavinia had only realised that fact after she wrote the victims' initials instead of their full names during the investigation.

"I was chosen by God to be the Master of death. Isla Armstrong was greedy and stole to fund her excessive indulgence; Madison McKinley worked for the most established barristers in the country, maybe even the world, everyone who works for them only cares about themselves, no one else, they think they have it all; Anna Shaw wanted it all but couldn't have it all; Tracey Evans had an affair with one of her clients; Ruth Damson kidnapped her friend's kid, and one you failed to identify, Edith Adkins, was a therapist who failed to act after a client came to her with suicidal thoughts and the client committed suicide. She had failed to help someone in need. Sinful, selfishness, leaves people suffering."

"How could you have possibly known all that?"

"I have eyes and ears. That's what stalking is about, that was why I reinvented myself, to become an ordinary person in society."

CHAPTER 79

"I agree that the world is full of sin and violence, but also sorrow, pain and suffering and all of that is because of people like you, Aiden." Lavinia thought she may have overstepped the mark, especially after the master of death revelation, but she was on a roll and felt pleased for herself by that comment that she did not see Marcus's fist collide with her nose until she heard a crunch and felt the blinding pain.

She monetarily blacked out.

She had never broken her nose before but guessed that this was what it felt like.

Blood poured down her face and dripped into her lap. Her hands were tied behind the chair so she could not control the blood flow. The metallic taste made her queasy and she spat out on the ground next to her.

It wasn't just her nose that was in pain, she also felt it in her neck and her head, not only from the contact but also from the response when her head flung back in complete surprise at Marcus's reaction. She had no time to counteract or embrace the hit. She had tears in her eyes as he smirked at her.

Marcus continued, "What did you just call me?"

Lavinia composed herself the best she could. The shock had knocked the breath out of her and she realised she was hyperventilating slightly.

Marcus was becoming impatient waiting for her to answer him, so he shouted at her, getting in her face again, "WHAT DID YOU CALL ME?!"

Lavinia took a few more breaths to calm herself before quietly answering, "I called you Aiden. That's your birth name, isn't it?" Marcus remained silent, caught off guard, and so Lavinia continued, "Earlier you said God is my salvation. It took me a while to think where I'd heard it before, but then it came to me. That's the motto of the Grace of God boarding school where you attended."

"I went to a comprehensive school in Scunthorpe."

"Is that what you tell everyone?"

"It's the truth."

"I don't think it is."

"How would you know?"

"When you said that line, God is my salvation, it all clicked into place. We never found a record of the name Aiden after the school closed. We assumed he just disappeared with the rest of the students that lived there. But you'd be the same age and, come to think of it, you do look like him. The same mischievous smile, the same height, the same build. The murders resemble those of Nigel Atterbury and Kelvin Anderson. The only person who would know about those would be Nigel's son, Elijah, whom you happened to be friends with. You somehow came across the murder encyclopaedia Nigel and Kelvin wrote, and Elijah came to be in possession of it after Nigel gave it to him. You knew how mischievous Elijah and Benjamin were, and you knew of their plan to drink acid. You needed your hand on that murder book and that was your ticket out, so you poured a lethal dose of acid into their water bottles and killed them. The school closed. What else could have been done? That was the only way. You changed your name and your appearance slightly and went about your life as if Aiden never existed. Only now you were in possession of the one thing that tied you to the school."

"Why would I do such a thing?"

"You tell me." When Marcus did not respond, Lavinia continued, "You were left an orphan, you took the wrong path in life and the school really made you want to turn your life around, it taught you everything you know now about religion and salvation and God. Only you never really changed. The school taught you to channel your anger and hurt and disappointment at life to murder, and rather than viewing murder as a sin, it made you view it as an act of justice and just like the school gave you a second chance, you gave people a second chance to cleanse themselves of sin and regret and enter the afterlife a free spirit."

CHAPTER 79

"Don't presume to act like you know me or anything about my past."

"But that's true, isn't it? Your parents died in a car accident or was there something else to it?"

"You tell me this time? You seem to know everything about me."

"I read that the car accident was caused by faulty brakes, there were no real suspects and no one was arrested."

"Well then, tragic accident. Seems to ring a bell." Marcus' reference to Alastair's death seemed to hit a nerve with Lavinia. Oh how the tables had turned and Marcus felt himself back in control.

"I think we both know that neither was an accident."

"Oh yeah?"

"Tell me if I'm wrong but I think you were neglected as a child and you killed your own parents in retaliation. That's why you have a vendetta against women, that's why you never settled in a foster home and that's why you never got close to people. You didn't trust them and I don't blame you. You were never really friends with Elijah and Benjamin, were you? You were still an outsider, you were their side kick, the one no one really remembers."

Lavinia saw something change in Marcus, he thought he was back in control, but that had only been momentary. She saw the confidence, the cockiness, the authority dissolve with every word. He had succumbed, he dropped the weapon he had been holding and collapsed on the chair opposite Lavinia. She thought he was about to cry.

"My dad was a drunk. He abused my mum and then he turned on me. She watched him beat me, but she did nothing. She kept saying it would be all right, we would get out of there and leave. Empty promises. That's all they were. She was just as bad as he was. I thought she cared about me but she only cared about herself. I always thought it would be the two of us. We would live on a farm with chickens and cows and we would live a happy life. Together. But she just fed me lies." There was a sad bitterness to his tone and for a second Lavinia almost felt sorry for him. Almost.

"No one would blame you for killing your parents, you had to get away, escape their wrath. How did you know what to do to?" Lavinia tried to sound as understanding as she could to get him on her side.

"Easy. They didn't care what I did as long as they didn't have anything to do with me, so I quickly learned tricks of the trade for something to do, even as a young boy, and books became a comfort. The only time they needed me was when they were abusing me. When I found Benjmain's murder encyclopaedia, it was like an instruction manual. It spoke to me. God spoke to me and I knew what I had to do. It wasn't mine until I killed them and then I had it in my possession."

"Why succinylcholine?"

"Kelvin used it on his victims and I was intrigued by what I read, so I did some research of my own and tried it out on Isla. That was that. Nigel Atterbury and Kelvin Anderson taught me everything I know."

"How did you get supplies?"

"Kelvin answered that one for me too, after more research and observations, I dressed as a delivery man for the hospital. No one would even notice small stocks missing here and small stocks missing there."

"What about the tattoos?"

"What about them?"

"Why brand each victim with a tattoo? I understand the meaning of them and why each tattoo was branded on each victim, but why do tattoos in the first place?"

Marcus shrugged as if he never knew why he did it either. "It was something to do, I suppose. Kelvin arranged his victims' body parts in the symbols, so I needed to do something and that's what I came up with."

"And the crosswords?"

CHAPTER 79

"Again, it was just some fun. It was a game. I knew you'd be too busy solving the crosswords and finding links as you police people do, that you'd be distracted and your attention wouldn't be on me so I was free. Free to kill. Free to hide in plain sight."

"It's clever really, these murders, you know all about forensics, you had a legitimate access to the crime scene being the photographer, so you have a reason to revisit the scene and see your handy work all close up and personal and see the commotion it all caused."

"But no one knew it was me. That's the beauty of being ignored, of being the one no one remembers, of being in the background and just hiding in plain sight. I have always been on my own."

CHAPTER 80

"So you don't know if this Sam Finch is actually Sam Finch or someone with an alias?"

"No."

"Don't you do ID checks?" Harris asked as if it was the most obvious thing in the world.

"Yes, usually we see the person face-to-face, complete paperwork, introduce ourselves, show them around, do ID checks, that kind of thing. He said he was abroad for work but needed a unit for when he came back to the UK. He kept sending us payments in advance and as long as people keep paying, we don't have any issues. He said he would come in as soon as he was back. I had no reason to not believe him," Gary reasoned.

"Right, convenient."

"But this is just an empty unit," Gary observed.

"A decoy unit," Harris shouted out as if he was answering a question on *'Pointless'* at home.

"What?" Norton questioned.

"What if Sam Finch is an alias and this unit is acting as a decoy unit so we look at it first instead of looking where we should be. Biding time but wasting ours. Clever really."

"Shit."

"What do we do now?"

CHAPTER 81

"Eny Meeny Miny Mo," Marcus teased, counting her fingers off one by one to decide which one to cut off first, with the cold blade stroking Lavinia's fingers in turn. "Little pinkie for the slaughter."

Lavinia's heart was leaping from her chest. Marcus was positioned behind the chair as her hands were tied behind the back, so she couldn't see what he was doing. That heightened her senses. Her eyes grew wide in shock as Marcus dug the blade in enough to draw blood. But he was just playing with her emotions as he stopped what he was doing, laughed wickedly and straightened up before walking around to the front and to his tool station, his back to her once again.

A couple of tears escaped her eyes and slid down her cheeks.

She was shivering with cold fear.

She thought they had shared a moment, a moment of regret, a moment of truth, a moment of understanding, but he admitted to himself that had only shown a moment of weakness and went back to what he knew best.

Torturing and tormenting.

The whole time she had been tied down in the chair, she had been fiddling with the knot, trying to undo it, but to not much avail sadly, as it was a solid knot. She felt she had undone it marginally but not enough to let her hands escape. And now she couldn't keep trying if Marcus was going to cut her fingers off.

But every time she was aware of where he was in the room, and aware that he wouldn't catch her trying, she attempted to undo the knot.

He turned around to face her and she immediately stopped what she was doing. His eyes bore into her soul and she was scared that he had caught her trying to undo the knot. But then he sauntered over to her hands again and this time cut right through bone of the distal phalange on the pinkie finger.

A shrieking scream escaped her lips.

The pain had gone up several thousand notches.

She felt weaker and weaker by the minute.

CHAPTER 82

"I think we keep doing what we have been doing. But we need to split up, we've wasted enough time," Wilson directed.

It was surprising how many people needed storage units within the last two or three weeks. The list felt endless.

Morgan and Norton teamed up to search the units outside while Harris and Wilson searched inside. They each had a copy of the list and a copy of the keys they needed to unlock the units. Gary was told to wait in his office and they would call if they required his assistance. In other words, the matter had become more urgent and he would just get in the way and was now surplus to requirement.

Morgan sprinted from one unit to another, time running out. Her hands shook as she tried to insert the key into the lock, missing the target a couple of times. "Fuck." Norton took over.

Unit after unit seemed to be legitimately used and people stored all kind of things in them.

Morgan's phone rang, she grabbed it from her pocket and answered, putting her mobile to her ear. "Tom."

"It's Marcus!"

"What's Marcus?" Norton turned to Morgan, both looking confused at each other.

"Shhh, did you hear that?" Norton gripped Morgan by the arm to get her attention. They stood still on the spot, firstly looking at each other and then around them, but Morgan strained to hear anything. She shook her head at Norton to signal she had not heard anything and could not hear anything.

"What's happening?" Tom asked, although Morgan did not seem to hear him.

"You don't think…?" Morgan couldn't finish the sentence as her mind was catching up with Tom's outburst and before Norton had time to respond, she hung up and bellowed as loud as her voice would let her. "LAVINIA!"

CHAPTER 83

Lavinia felt her mind and body give up, they succumbed to Marcus' torture.

She was going to die.

And he was savouring every moment.

"You know, you're my favourite victim. The others just gave up but you, you have a fire in you that's still burning and I need to put it out if you are to truly die at my hand."

"Then just kill me and be done with it."

"Oh, has Lavinia gone soft on me again? Don't start with that nonsense, that's what the others kept saying like a stuck record over and over and over again. That's not you. To kill you would be the easy way out, and that's not what's going to happen. I have waited too long, planned too much to just get it over and done with. No, I'm going to have my fun at your suffering and the pied piper and his mice can find your rotten corpse."

When Marcus administered another dose of succinylcholine, she couldn't explain how, but it seemed like a bolt of electricity had just entered her system and given her a jump start, she felt her body wanting to fight back. The embers of the fire had just caught flame again and the burning desire to stay alive and fight for her life was stronger than ever.

Two could play at this game, she thought, and acted to the mood. She made a tear escape her eye, which Marcus saw. He laughed but as long as he was distracted by her emotions and kept talking, she could fiddle with the rope to try and undo it.

Marcus was saying something but Lavinia had zoned out. She was concentrating as best as she could even though her mind felt like a bunch of fluffy clouds. She allowed her fingers to travel along the rope to trace the outline of the knot. If she could imagine the knot in her mind she could work with it.

It felt thick, strong and rough to the touch. It was a twisted rope and no doubt an established knot such as overhand knot or handcuff knot, named appropriately. Marcus was into fishing, so Lavinia guessed he would know the different types of knots and how to tie them. Her hands were put through two loops, one loop for each hand, with a knot in between the wrists to tighten and excess rope hung down on either side.

She was able to view the make-up of the knot in her mind and grabbed the excess rope with her free fingers. She used her dominant left hand instead of her right, a small mercy that Marcus had cut the pinkie finger on her right hand, and she felt the rope in her fingers. She felt along the rope again and felt there was an upper hole and a lower hole. She knew she needed to thread the rope through the lower hole.

She found that easier said than done. Every time Marcus came near her, she panicked that he would find her fiddling with the rope and dropped the bit she had in her fingers, so she had to do it all over again. The knots were tied tightly so she had to try and loosen the lower knot to be able to thread it through, which seemed an impossible task. She was at an awkward angle, doing it blind and without her hands free, it was difficult to get the right grip and the right part of the rope she needed.

Not only was her pinkie finger on her right hand thumping with pain, her whole hand seemed to ache with sympathy, but she had to use both hands if she had any hope of being successful.

CHAPTER 83

Their system went out of the window, and instead, Wilson, Harris, Morgan and Norton were frantically running between units, banging on the door trying for a response and opened up every unit that was occupied.

They didn't know what else they could do, but they had to be close.

Norton could not describe the noise he had heard, but he knew that their response had to be an urgent one.

CHAPTER 84

Lavinia had the knot firmly in her hand.

Again, she was able to thread through the excess rope that was hanging down which was a start.

She had to do the same on the other side.

Her hands had morphed into unnatural positions to aid in her plan.

She felt the knot loosen in the hands, but she couldn't risk undoing it completely.

This is the position she had been in before when she aborted her mission.

While her eyes were firmly focused on Marcus's back, her mind was sharply focused on the mental image inside her mind, she slowly, carefully and as calmly as she could began to fiddle with the knot.

It came away in her hands.

Just in time to see Marcus turn around with murder burning in his eyes.

She had the element of surprise on her side.

He came towards her with a saw in his hand.

She was tense as she had one shot and only one to get this right.

If she succeeded then she was getting out of here alive.

If she failed, she would be getting out of here in a body bag.

CHAPTER 85

Marcus was too focused on his task, too invested in cutting off Lavinia's ear, that she got her own back on him.

When Marcus neared her chair, she used all the power and the strength that remained in her body to swing her legs out in front of her and they collided with his groin.

The impact caught him off guard, he dropped the saw and fell to his knees, collapsing and crying out in pain.

She was stunned herself for a moment, that her plan had worked, that her legs remained strong for her.

She was still weak and in pain and when her legs caught up with her brain, she leapt off the chair and was headed to the door. To freedom.

Once her back was turned to Marcus, she was in trouble.

Despite being in pain himself, he used all his will and clambered after her, in a semi-rugby tackle.

They fell to the floor.

Lavinia tried kicking out but Marcus continued to have a strong hold on her. Instead, she tried wriggling as far up the floor as she could to try and get to a side wall to bang and hope that someone was nearby and would hear, or to get to the table of instruments. If she could knock the table down, then she might be able to retrieve a weapon which she could use to free herself. The latter was the most viable option. Her body was tiring, but she had to keep kicking and keep dragging.

She was in touching distance.

She reached out as far as she could, her fingertips grazing the table leg.

She thought she had a good hold of the table leg but when she lifted it up, the table fell away from her.

She momentarily stopped in her tracks at the sad realisation that her time was up.

Marcus had managed to recover quicker and dragged her feet first down the cold hard floor away from the table. He was not going to take risks. He flipped her over so her back was to the floor, knelt over her body, a leg each side, to keep her in place and steady so she couldn't wriggle free. Both arms were held down by his hands on either side of her head.

They stayed there for what felt like hours, just staring at each other.

When he thought it was safe to do so, Marcus removed a hand from her arm and moved to place it around her neck, putting pressure on.

He smiled triumphantly as she accepted defeat.

She had failed.

She now knew her fate.

The only way she was going to leave was via a body bag.

CHAPTER 86

Marcus was waiting for the fire to be extinguished from Lavinia, one ember at a time. As he felt her slip away, he felt stronger.

He was so transfixed, so absorbed into the cold fear of Lavinia's eyes as they stared back at him, that he did not hear the unit door open and did not see the light as it filtered into the room, highlighting the horrors.

He did not hear Wilson, Harris, Norton and Morgan shout out.

He did not hear the bang of the gunfire and he did not feel a bullet penetrate his shoulder.

He only heard Lavinia's laboured breath before he heard it no more.

CHAPTER 86

Two days later
Scunthorpe General Hospital

When Wilson entered Scunthorpe General Hospital to the ward where Lavinia had been staying in, he located her bed in the corner with a window view over the hospital car park and houses. She was dressed in the usual white hospital gown attire that did not look flattering on anyone, covers folded just below her waist, a needle in her arm that connected to an IV drip beside the bed and a book in her hand. She looked up from the book when she spotted Wilson. She looked pale, pained and bruised. He had brought along with him a pack of grapes, a bouquet of lilies and a card signed by the team. He placed the items on the table at the end of the bed and Lavinia beamed with appreciation.

"You even got the mixed grapes," her voice was raspy.

"I didn't even know if you ate grapes, but it seems to be the thing to gift to people in hospital."

"It's the thought that counts and they're great, thank you." Lavinia made the move to sit up but winced in pain and coughed as she did so. This did not go unnoticed by Wilson.

"How are you feeling?"

"Oh you know, like I've been hit by a double decker bus and then a lorry and then ten-tonne truck. You know how it is. It probably looks worse than it is."

"Well, I didn't want to say anything."

CHAPTER 86

Even though Lavinia did look like shit, Wilson had to admit, he was pleased that she had some humour left after everything she had been through in the past few months.

"But they managed to reattach the distal phalange." She held up her pinkie to show him, which wasn't any consolation to the pain and torture she went through.

"Looks brand new."

Lavinia smiled at Wilson's comment. "Have you spoken to Tom?" She had expected Tom to have visited at least once since she knew how worried he had been.

Wilson sighed.

"Is he ok?"

"He's um...." Wilson started to say.

"What's happened?" Lavinia was slightly worried.

"Nothing has happened, he's physically fine, but erm, he just...he blames himself for what happened to you."

"What? Unless he's a psychic and predicted that this would happen, he was as clueless as the rest of you, no offence, but this had nothing to do with him or anyone else," Lavinia defended.

"Despite your rejection at having security, he conducted covert surveillance on your house the night you were abducted," Wilson informed her.

Lavinia stayed silent as she was processing what Wilson told her.

"He said nothing happened, no one, apart from your housemates entered or left the property at various times throughout the night. He didn't see anything happen. He saw your bedroom lights go on and off, to him, that was you and he reported nothing out of the ordinary."

"Everyone had left and I was in the bath. When I got out, I don't remember getting to my bedroom. It must have been him." She refused to say his name.

"He entered through the back, Tom never would have seen him from his viewpoint," Wilson pointed out.

"He had no reason to believe there was anyone else in the house as he had not seen anyone enter."

"He regrets not making better decisions and putting both the front and the back of the house under surveillance, he said it seemed obvious that if he were to abduct you, he would go round the back, not risk people seeing him by going through the front door."

"But Tom would never have known what he was thinking."

"I know. I have tried to tell him all of this but he won't listen."

"Then get him to come here and I'll tell him."

"I've told him that too. He won't come and see you lying in a hospital bed, he feels too guilty."

"I don't blame him for what happened."

"I know."

"Or you."

"I know."

"Or anyone else."

"I know, but I can understand how he is feeling and why he blames himself. I've been in the same position before. Most recently, I blamed myself for Alastair's death. I was going over and over and over in my mind that perhaps if I was there too, Marcus never would have had the opportunity to kill him. If only I had gone on that trip, Alastair would still be alive."

"You don't know that, I'm sure he would have found a way regardless. Or worse, you would've ended up dead too."

"Or instead of."

"Walter, as my temporary boss, as a family friend, as my unofficial uncle, please do not blame yourself for Dad's death. I miss him so much every day and that pain is worse than I felt when Marcus tortured me, but Dad would have died for you anyway, you meant so much to him, you were like his surrogate father. He wouldn't blame you either and I certainly don't." Both Lavinia and Wilson had tears in their

CHAPTER 86

eyes. "Promise to live on as he would've and live every day to the fullest, as he would have wanted you to, because you know if you don't he'll just come and haunt you and make sure that you do."

"I'm sure he'd do that anyway, any excuse to play tricks on me."

A moment of silence passed between them before Lavinia sighed heavily. "You know it still feels surreal, like this whole case has been an outer body experience. But then reality hits and it's a living nightmare." A few tears fell down her face.

"You know, I see so much of Alastair in you. Whatever you do and wherever you decide to go, you will thrive. You make me so proud, and more importantly you make your dad proud, both you and Mindi do."

Lavinia was full on crying, tears streaming down freely. Wilson gave her a hug and left before he could shed any tears.

* * * *

After another day in the hospital, under observation, Lavinia was signed off by the doctor and was free to go. Hayleigh and Mindi were there to take her home and enveloped her in a hug when they saw her.

But before they could take her home, she asked for a small stop to the station.

"What do you want to go there for?" Mindi asked.

"Just some unfinished business I need to take care of."

They pulled up into the station car park, Hayleigh and Mindi were taking their seat belts off but Lavinia stopped them. "It's ok, you stay here, I won't be long."

"Okay."

The automatic doors separated for her and she walked into the reception. She smiled at Dorsi who sombrely told Lavinia that she was so sorry for her loss and ordeal and hoped she got better soon. Lavinia just smiled and nodded in response, not sure how to respond but appreciated her comment nonetheless.

She took the well-walked route up to the major incident room to find everyone sat in their usual places behind their desk.

The team looked exhausted, but they had to complete final reports to officially close the case and for CPS to read over, as Wilson had a meeting with them in a couple of days' time.

Morgan looked up from her computer at the door to see who had entered and she was immediately on her feet, with the biggest smile Lavinia had ever seen her give and walked over to give her a hug. Lavinia was still unsteady on her feet and the force of Morgan's hug knocked her off balance, but she was able to save herself the embarrassment of falling over.

"You look loads better."

"Feeling loads better." She returned the hug.

The others got up from their chair and followed suit, taking it in turns to exchange a comment or two and a hug.

When it got to Tom, they didn't say anything to each other nor did they hug. They just looked at one another, and he just looked sad. The other three left the room and went down to the canteen to give them both some space to talk freely.

It was the first time they had seen each other since they found Edith Adkins and she knew how guilty he had been feeling; they all did.

"I'm sorry I didn't come to see you in hospital."

"Don't worry," Lavinia dismissed. "No one likes that place anyway," she said light-heartedly. "Wilson told me." She didn't need to expand, Tom knew exactly what she was talking about

"I hope you can forgive me in time."

"There's nothing to forgive."

"If I had just done my job prop…"

"You did," Lavinia interrupted, "you couldn't have done anything different. I became a part of his plan, supposedly

CHAPTER 86

I was his finale. Please don't beat yourself up about it, I'm here, aren't I, no harm done."

He gave a weak smile. Lavinia still didn't think she had got through to him. She could say all the right words, but it would only take Tom himself to actually believe those words.

"Tom, you are a great detective and an even greater person. You have taught me so much and I wouldn't be here right now if it hadn't've been for you. Who was there looking out for me that night? That was you and you have been there for me more than anyone, so for goodness sake please stop feeling guilty. You helped put a stop to all of this and you helped save me. Please get over this battle that you have with yourself."

"I guess I can work on that one."

"You better, because looking sad doesn't look good on you and you'll stop getting sympathy from me."

He laughed.

"Well I think that's a good start, it's nice to see you laugh."

He gave Lavinia a hug and she felt him relax. "Words cannot express how happy I am to see you up and about."

"Me too." They let go and smiled at each other again. "Is Wilson in his office?"

"He is indeed."

"Good, come with me."

He looked very confused but followed Lavinia as they entered his office.

"Ah Lavinia, I didn't expect to see you, you should be getting rest."

"I've had enough rest in the hospital. Is Marcus in custody?"

"He is."

"Good. I need to speak to him."

Tom was aghast. "What? Why? He just tried to kill you, why on earth would you want to speak to him for?"

Lavinia sighed. "Please."

Wilson may not have liked the idea but he understood her need to. He nodded.

"What, you can't let her!" Tom had messed up once and he wasn't going to put Lavinia in the firing line again, even if Marcus was in custody.

"He won't do anything, he can't do anything. And we'll be there the whole time behind the two-way mirror. Lavinia would just need to give us a look if she wants to leave." He said this more to Tom than Lavinia as he needed the reassurance.

****

"Well, if it isn't the walking wounded," Marcus said as he saw Lavinia open the door. She closed the door behind her with a quiet click and turned her attention towards Marus who was simply sat at the table of the interview room.

"I could say the same to you, how's your shoulder?" She put her finger on his shoulder and saw the petrified look on his face and begged her not to. She unwillingly stopped and he breathed out. "That is just a fraction of the pain you caused those women."

"They deserved everything they got," he replied breathlessly, his chest heaving up and down as Lavinia took a seat opposite him.

"What about Alastair?"

"What about him?"

"You never got round to saying why you killed him."

"That was an accident."

Lavinia scoffed. "Yeah right. You expect me to believe that? Like killing all those women, were they accidents too?"

"I never intended to kill Alastair, I really didn't, you have to believe me. I really liked him."

"You have a funny way of showing it."

"He just got too close to the truth. I think he suspected me without telling me outright. Everything he was saying was

CHAPTER 86

ringing true. I knew he would be watching me like a hawk, and I really didn't want to kill him, but I had no choice."

"Of course you had a choice, you always have a choice and you decided to kill a friend and save your own skin. Not only a friend may I add, but also a dad, a partner, a son, a respected and a bloody great detective. I could go on."

Silence.

"I'm sorry."

"How?"

"How what?"

"How did you kill him? It must've been a well thought out plan to make it look like a tragic accident when that was far from the truth."

"I don't want to."

"Tell me or I swear to God, I will pierce your shoulder wound open with a bullet of my own."

Marcus looked very vulnerable, weak and scared in that moment, like he had shrunk into himself as if that might protect him. It was a complete contrast to only days earlier when he was so full of himself, acting all cocky as if he would be awarded the Serial Killer of the Year Award.

"The...the..um," he stuttered, "the weather was an advantage. It was storm like, heavy rain, strong winds, rocky current. Your dad and I was sat up on the deck just drinking beers and chatting. This was before the weather turned. And it turned so quickly. The wind starting picking up first and then we felt the odd spot of rain one moment and then the other it just lashed down. Your dad had a rod in the water that was going crazy so he went to check it out and then the thought occurred to me there and then. The pole. I swung it round and it hit Alastair on the back of the head. Perfect shot really. That would've rendered him unconscious and he lost his balance and fell into the sea. That was it. Turned out that even the police believed it to be an accidental death and the suspicion was no longer on me. I had to cool down for a while, but you're just like your dad, aren't you, and you weren't too far behind."

"You made one vital mistake. I didn't believe for a second that my dad would have died from an accident. Since you were the only one with him, of course I suspected you. I had to make it fit. Everything was against me and against it being murder, but I persevered and here we are with the truth."

"You have to believe me that when your dad and I first set out on the trip, murder was never on the mind."

"You can rot in Hell, actually even Hell is too good for you," Lavinia spat in disgust and simply walked out of the interview room, closing the door firmly behind her.

She walked away.

CHAPTER 87

**THE KING
VS.
MARCUS CARVER**

TRIAL PROCEEDINGS HEARD BY
THE HONOURABLE JUSTICE SIMON ALLISON
CENTRAL CRIMINAL COURT, LONDON, UNITED
KINDGOM
ON THE 14TH DAY OF NOVEMBER 2023

APPEARANCES:
MR. T. MITCHELL KC, MR. K. HAWKINS, MS. C.
DUNCAN
Appeared on behalf of THE KING

MR. SHEPHERD KC, MR. J. SMITH
Appeared on behalf of MARCUS CARVER

Monday November 14, 2023

(PROCEEDINGS COMMENCED AT 10:03 A.M.)

HIS LORDSHIP: Good morning, Mr Mitchell

MR MITCHELL KC: Good morning, My Lord. I am pleased to announce that representation is as before.

HIS LORDSHIP: Thank you. Good morning to all present. Ladies and Gentlemen of the Jury, over the course of the last week, we have heard the evidence from defence and the prosecution in turn, from witnesses and from expert testimonials. It is your job to take into consideration all evidence and reach a unanimous decision of guilty or not guilty plea. The defence and the prosecution will sum the key points which will enable you to focus on the main facts of their case to aid in this decision.

HIS LORDSHIP: Mr Shepherd KC, you may proceed.

MR SHEPHERD KC: Thank you My Lord. I have two closing topics I wish to address you on. Topic one is the mental state of Mr Carver's mind. Marcus was abused and neglected as a young boy, his parents discarded him, did not want him, left him to fend for himself. Every form of neglect and abuse, emotional, physical, sexual, Marcus suffered and that would be enough to mentally and physically scar you for life. To have issues with relationships, friendships, work. Every aspect of his life had been affected. As a severe consequence, he would not be able to feel like a normal person, he would not be able to act like a normal person, he would not be able to think like a normal person of sound mind. As a result of this difficult upbringing it is obvious that Marcus's understanding of what, to the rest of us constitutes normal behavioural boundaries, have

CHAPTER 87

been shifted to occupy a different normal with an accompanying shift in moral understanding leading to reduced capacity to function in a way that the majority of us can understand. Which brings me to the second topic. Marcus's mental capacity. Marcus's absence of sound mind, meant he lacked capacity. He did not know what he was doing and therefore, he could not be aware of his actions and is innocent of a crime that he is not aware he committed. Let the Court protect those who are most vulnerable to society.

HIS LORDSHIP: Thank you Mr Shepherd KC. Mr Mitchell KC.

MR MITCHELL KC: Thank you My Lord. Mr Marcus Carver, the defendant, is stood before you accused of murdering six women and the attempted murder of one woman. My job is to prove to you, the Jury, the burden of Proof beyond reasonable doubt. You must be convinced that there is no doubt that the defendant is guilty, that there is no other explanation. Throughout my examination and cross examination, there hasn't been another explanation, has there? We know the defendant was fully aware of his conscious decisions to abduct, torture and kill innocent women and then dispose of their body. In the time he took to torture, he cut off several body parts, and he did so knowingly and willingly. This is when he spent time with his victims. He spoke to them, he offered them false promises, he selected each victim for a reason. That reason was branded on the back of their neck in the form of a tattoo. He attended each crime scene as an official forensic photographer under the certified Pathologist. There, the opportunity to became forensically aware was most opportune. While conducting his job, he was able to admire his handywork. He had known what scene he would be photographing because he was there in sound mind, he got first hand close up of the autopsy, he was able to remain one step ahead of the police, even going as far as to publish crosswords in the paper, on the morning that each body was found. As seen throughout this trial, the crosswords acted as a game, as clues, that the defendant created himself. The defendant then stole a car and drove that very car to transport his last victim from their university home to a storage unit in the vicinity with the intent to kill. He took each victim's belongings, mobile phone, clothes, stripped them from their individuality. The mobile phones were switched off at the last known whereabouts of the victim, every plan carefully thought out, every plan carefully executed. Every action had a reaction and every action had a consequence which he was fully aware of. He had the intention and the knowledge throughout. Therefore, he was at full capacity to be culpable for his actions. Do the right thing, Ladies and Gentlemen.

(JURY DELIBERATED — COURT ADJOURNED 11.02AM)
(JURY RETURNED — COURT RESUMED 15.30)

HIS LORDSHIP: Have you all reached a unanimous verdict?

JUROR 1: We have, My Lord.

HIS LORDSHIP: And on Count 1, do you find the defendant guilty or not guilty of six counts of murder?

JUROR 1: Guilty.

HIS LORDHIP: And on Count 2, do you find the defendant guilty or not guilty of attempted murder on one account?

JUROR 1: Guilty.

CHAPTER 87

One Year Later

CHAPTER 88

Staffordshire University Graduation Day
Trentham Gardens, Stoke-on-Trent

Having worked as a student ambassador during Graduation Week before, Lavinia knew the ropes. She knew exactly where to be, at what time and what to do, which was one thing less to stress about on such an important day.

Together, Lavinia, Mindi and Hayleigh strolled through the picturesque Italian Gardens. There were several winding gravel paths one could take to meander through the gardens, meeting vibrant flowers, trimmed hedges, a scented archway of wisteria and striking fountains. At the head of the Italian Gardens, stretched out over a mile and offering serene circular walks, was the lake where the summer sun dazzled on the water's surface, making it a popular photo opportunity. In front of the lake was a famous statue of Perseus and Medusa.

Following the path north of the gardens, they came to an impressive white marque that had been erected specifically for Graduation Week. Just inside the marquee was registration on one side and gown collection/drop off on the other side, with a walkway down the centre of the corridor. This is where Lavinia ended up first, leaving Hayleigh and Mindi to walk around the corner for the café area, selling light refreshments and offered seating areas. Opposite the café, was a ramp leading into a more relaxed space outdoors, offering deckchairs and benches for friends and family to converge after the ceremony. This is where the remaining crowd from the morning's ceremony gathered. Carrying on through the corridor from the café area was the main ceremony hall on the right, which was currently being set up for the afternoon ceremony. Next door to the hall was a large room with several high tables dotted around decorated with tablecloths and balloons, an area for lecturers and students to raise a glass of prosecco post-ceremony. The luxurious portacabins offered marbled surfaces, framed artwork on the walls, square hand wash basins and designer hand wash and hand lotion.

Along the route, Lavinia exchanged greetings and conversations with many student ambassadors she had previously worked with on various occasions. They all had an important and key role in Graduation from greeting graduates, friends and family to assisting with directions and photographs to working the ceremony hall, cleaning up and putting out programmes, with the guidance and help from Senior staff members, but they were the stars of the show. She could appreciate the hard work they had all put into the event which, for her, made the day even more special.

All gowned up, Lavinia went to find Hayleigh and Mindi in the café, where they were drinking coffee. Lavinia declined the offer of a hot drink and ordered a bottle of water instead.

If Hayleigh could freeze this moment in time, she would. She thought Lavinia looked stunning in her ruby red coloured jumpsuit, her white and black heeled shoes and the black gown and grey hood with a red lining and trim that tied it all together. Many graduates had opted for a similar colour scheme of red, white and black to represent the university colours.

When called through, Hayleigh and Mindi went to find their seats in the ceremony hall, leaving Lavinia and the other graduates to queue up alongside the side entrance to the hall in alphabetical order. They would enter the hall after the guests had taken their seats which would signal the beginning of the ceremony.

It was a nervous wait, but Lavinia found Sarah which immediately calmed her, and they spoke to many of her classmates, who were all in the same boat. They took pictures, complimented each other's outfits and discussed what was next for them.

Many had jobs already lined up. Sarah being one of them, as a digital forensic investigator. Other jobs included police investigator, entry level crime scene investigator and Prison Officer. Others would go on to complete Masters or PhDs.

Unlike Lavinia, no one had travelling on the agenda.

"What countries are you going to visit?" This question came up a lot. Mindi and Lavinia didn't really have a plan – of course there were places they both would want to visit, but neither had sat down and discussed it.

"Haven't really got a plan. I expect the usual, France, Italy, Austria, Germany, Netherlands."

"How long are you going for?"

"A month-ish. Maybe more."

A few more recommendations were made by various people before they were called in. Getting back into a single line, they were let into the hall where they were led to their seats.

To Lavinia, the stage looked menacing and never ending. Like many graduates were thinking the same, Lavinia knew it would be a miracle to walk across that stage without falling over.

The ceremony began by the staff processions and the welcome speech and introductions were made by the presiding officer.

The Law graduates went first. It was a special moment to witness the celebration by lecturers, friends and family. The hall erupted in one continuous applause as each student walked across the stage, one by one. And it was pretty spectacular, Lavinia reflected, three years of hard work, of gruelling library sessions, thousands of words and many deadlines later, to be here in this moment.

Another speech.

Now for the Forensic disciplines. Forensic Investigation was the first to be called. Lavinia and classmates made their way to the ramp by the stage where they lined up waiting for their name to be called so they could walk across the stage. Just exactly like the law students had done previously.

When both Paige's and Sarah's names were called, Lavinia cheered and clapped as they took their turn to walk across the stage, shoulders back, head held high, faces rightly beaming with pride. Lavinia had a lot to be thankful for Paige and Sarah and wouldn't be stood there today without them. Lavinia saw them shake hands with the presiding officer before disappearing down the ramp on the other side of the stage. A few other students walked across the stage in the same manner before it was Lavinia's turn.

"Lavinia Newbourne."

Cheers and claps sounded as she walked across the stage, one foot in front of the other, the final destination was to make it to the other side safely. Her face lit up as she shook hands with the presiding officer who told her congratulations, before making her way down the ramp.

She had made it!

She could finally breathe.

There were a few more students for the Forensic Investigation discipline before it moved to the Forensic Science students.

At least Lavinia could relax.

She walked across that stage for one person and one person only. Her dad. He was walking alongside her the whole time and gave an appreciated smile to no one in particular.

After the list of students had been exhausted, a guest speaker conducted a speech and then the presiding officer gave a final speech and declared the ceremony officially closed. But not before, all the graduates took off their caps and threw them into the air with one final round of applause.

A guard of honour conducted by the student ambassadors were eagerly awaiting them, clapping and cheering, as they exited the ceremony hall and entered the post-ceremony tent for a glass of bubbly with fellow peers and lecturers.

Lavinia strode over to where Hayleigh and Mindi were stood eagerly waiting for Lavinia, wearing the biggest and proudest smiles on their faces. Lavinia hugged them both in turn.

"Congratulations!" Mindi exclaimed, hugging her little sister tight. "How did you get old enough to graduate?"

"I will never know, sis, it doesn't feel like the world is ready for Lavinia."

"More importantly, is Lavinia ready for the world?"

"Adulting? Never," Lavinia joked.

"Right answer. Where can I cancel my adulting subscription?"

"All jokes aside, I have something for you." Hayleigh pulled an envelope out of her bag. Scrawled on the front was Lavinia's name. In the top right hand corner, in the same scrawly handwriting, were the words 'Graduation Day'. Lavinia looked at Hayleigh confused. "It's from Maire, she wrote several letters before she passed with strict instructions to give them to you when you have reached certain milestones in both of your lives. Starting with Graduation, first job, first house etc. She trusted me to give them to you at the right times."

Suddenly the letter had a different meaning and she looked at Hayleigh with bewilderment in her eyes and hugged her once more.

"Wilson and Tom have just arrived, I'll let you read that in your own time," Hayleigh announced, giving Wilson and Tom a wave so they could see where they were stood.

Eyes still focused on the letter in her hand, Lavinia replied, "I want to read it now, tell them I won't be long." She headed off to the park area at the bottom of the field. Two children were playing on the climbing frame and taking it in turns to go down the slide. Lavinia opted for the swing, and so she sat with her back to the park, to the children playing, to the mass of friends, family and graduates.

She studied the letter as if it was going to reveal the words to her without opening it. Lavinia noticed the handwriting was

CHAPTER 88

small, neat and cursive, a little like Mindi's, she countered. She had never really took any notice of her mum's writing until now.

With a deep breath, she opened it.

My Dearest Lavinia,

If you are reading this, then it must be your Graduation day. Either that or Alastair has left it out somewhere, we both know what he's like.

I am so sorry I cannot be there to celebrate this milestone with you and what an incredible achievement it is. You've most likely followed in your father's footsteps and got a degree in Policing or a similar discipline. Am I right?

You always were like him. Which is why I know you'll thrive in whatever you do.

And I will always be there right with you, perhaps walking a few paces behind, but omni-present nonetheless.

I am so proud of the woman you have turned out to be, so ambitious, so independent, following dreams and spreading her wings. A mother can ask for no more. Every step you take, every wish you make, every dream that comes true, I will be right here experiencing it with you.

Go and celebrate this day, have a glass (or bottle!) of Champagne on me and toast to life, toast to family, toast to the next chapter in your life. I cannot wait to read it because I know it'll be an amazing one.

The future will be bright, that I am sure on. Congratulations Sweetheart.

Now it's time to show the world what Lavinia Louise Newbourne is all about.

All my warmest love,
Mum x

CHAPTER 89

By the end Lavinia's eyes were like a leaking tap, they kept streaming down her face in an unstoppable force.

It had felt like both her mum and dad had been right there with her, walking beside her on that stage, sitting in the audience next to Mindi and Hayleigh and cheering as Lavinia's name was announced.

She stared into the bushes for a while, which were lined around the perimeter of the field, swinging ever so slightly on the swing she was sat on, when she felt a presence behind her and jumped at the feeling of being watched. She knew it was only Tom but after everything she had been through with Marcus, she was still easily spooked.

"Please stop watching me creepily from a distance," Lavinia called out to Tom, not needing to look behind her to confirm his presence.

She heard the all-familiar chuckle leave Tom's lips before he began to walk towards her. "Sorry, I didn't want to interrupt." He sat down beside her on the other swing and waited for Lavinia's lead to carry on the conversation.

"Just read a letter from my mum. Apparently, there's a few she wrote before she died to be given to us at specific times in our lives."

"How special." Lavinia just hummed in response. "So, what's next for Lavinia Newbourne, Bachelor of Science with Honours?"

Lavinia turned to look at Tom who was beaming at her. "That doesn't sound real at all."

"Well, you've earned yourself that title, so get used to it, congratulations by the way."

CHAPTER 89

"Thank you." Lavinia sighed heavily.

"I also wanted to tell you that there's a space in the office for you, if you want it."

There was comfortable silence between them as Lavinia pondered the offer. "Thanks, maybe if things were different I would've jumped at that chance, but I need to get away from here, at least for a while."

"Where will you go?"

"Mindi and I have been talking about travelling around Europe for a while, so I think it's time we went and did that."

"Not jealous at all. You will come back though, won't you?"

"Of course, we've only really talked about going for a month but who knows. Mindi's contract has finished with her current law firm, and she wants to leave to get different experience so she's looking for a new job. I'm newly graduated with nothing lined up and just need a goddam break. For the first time in my life, I feel something is going to happen at the right time."

"Well, no one deserves a break more than you, that's for sure. Go and enjoy this time with Mindi. But please stay safe and come back in one piece."

"That I can promise."

"And you better send me postcards."

"That I can promise too."

"Good, I shall look forward to reading them."

They got off the swings and hugged each other. To Tom, the hug was a goodbye hug. After all, she would be leaving for at least a month and who knows where she would end up. He was thrilled that she was doing something for herself, something that made her happy because after everything she had been through with the case, she needed some happiness in her life. She needed to feel that freedom again, to explore new places, experience different cultures, to feel that strength and desire inside her that Tom knew she had the moment he met her, but over the course of the case, it had slowly dissolved. He doubted she would be able to properly settle back in Lincolnshire again, too much blood had been shed for that, but knew that wherever life took her, he would be supporting her behind the scenes, all the way.

To Lavinia, actions spoke louder than words. It was a thank you hug, Tom had been the one constant in her life during the case, looking out for her, caring for her, she would be forever grateful to him. The ups and downs, the breakthroughs, the laughs, the blood, the sweat, the tears, they had been through it all together. Partners. And Lavinia knew their friendship would live on.

After they disengaged from the hug, they walked back to join the others, who had somehow managed to sneak a couple of bottles of prosecco from one of the tents, and toasted to Lavinia.

CHAPTER 90

St Pancras International Station, London Eurostar Terminal

Once the day's Graduation celebrations were over, Mindi and Lavinia made a loose travel plan, bought interrail passes, booked hostels, spent hours shopping for travelling necessities like microfibre towels, clothes, rucksacks, packing cubes etc.

It was a stressful and mad couple of days.

But here they find themselves all packed and ready to go travelling, waiting for their call to get on the Eurostar.

First stop: Paris!

Hayleigh was amazed they had managed to do so much preparation in such a short space of time. Seeing Mindi and Lavinia with their rucksacks that were longer than their torso and probably weighed near enough their body weight, their faces excited for the adventures ahead, she wished she and Alastair had gone on more trips and travelled further and wider around the globe, but, after witnessing the stress of Mindi and Lavinia, she was glad to stick to the small comforts.

Hayleigh had brought Mindi and Lavinia down in the car, taking some holiday time for herself. She would spend a few days visiting friends who lived near London, and was looking forward to the prospect of spending her days with people who were familiar to her.

Hayleigh did not know what was next for herself, but was excited to travel that road and see where it would take her, what destination was awaiting for her at the end.

The tannoy interrupted her thoughts and called for passengers to make their way to the Eurostar.

Helping Mindi and Lavinia with their rucksacks, Hayleigh did her best not to look sad. "I know you won't message me every day, but please let me know you are all right when you can. Have the best time, go make some memories, look after each other and I cannot wait to hear all about it when you return. Safe travels."

They joined the mass of people also travelling by Eurostar and made their way up the escalators, turning around, the best they could, to wave to Hayleigh once more before they disappeared from view.

Au revoir, UK; Bonjour, Paris.

Acknowledgments

Writing a book is never a one person job, so there are a few people to mention for their contribution.

When I was younger, I was always writing stories, plays and poems, usually at my grandparents' house during the Summer Holidays. Being a young child, I had an overactive imagination, so I would have several ideas on the go simultaneously. Therefore, I knew I had to grow as a reader and as a writer before I fully committed myself to writing a manuscript. When the time came, unfortunately my Gramps was no longer with us so I have decided to dedicate my first published book to him. While it took me a few years to actually write this from start to finish, the many times I had writer's block, or when I needed motivation or inspiration, I thought of my Gramps, who helped me through the tough times because I was writing this for him. He is the first person I want to thank and for the memories we shared, a couple of which are featured in the beginning of this book. I hope he would be proud that I achieved my dream and he helped me get there.

I want to also thank my mum, Jayne, who read through my manuscript and advised on a few changes. My mum was one of the very few who knew I was writing a book, but she allowed me to write while she tirelessly and endlessly completed the housework and gardening! I thank you for your continued support and wisdom throughout my writing process.

This book would not be what it is without the professional advice and guidance of my publishers. You have been very efficient and wonderful in getting my book to a published level. I thank you, the team, for your time and greatly appreciate your amazing work.

And last but not least, to my readers. I thank you for your support in reading my book and I hope you have thoroughly enjoyed reading it as much as I have enjoyed writing it.

Until we meet again.

Printed in Great Britain
by Amazon

47228247R00341